Mayfair

From Waverly Fitzgerald

Fiction
St. John's Wood
Chelsea
Mayfair
Grover Square

As Waverly Curtis
co-authored with Curt Colbert
Dial C for Chihuahua
Chihuahua Confidential
The Big Chihuahua
The Chihuahua Always Sniffs Twice
A Chihuahua in Every Stocking

Nonfiction
Slow Time: Recovering the Natural Rhythm of Life

Mayfair

Waverly Fitzgerald

Genesta Press

First published in hardcover in 1978
by Doubleday & Company, Inc.

This edition published in 2017 by Genesta Press

Genesta Press
1211 E Denny Way #187
Seattle WA U.S.A. 98122

FOR ALL THOSE
who offered encouragement during the writing,
especially Diane, Mrs. Wolter, Harold,
Jeanne and Andy, and Steffi.

Contents

Mayfair

ONE

The Initial Skirmish

TWILIGHT. The end of a dreary, grey day in late February. The rain had been falling since early morning on the great city of London.

A brownish mist, composed of the ever-present smoke which hung over the city and the moisture of the clouds, shrouded the streets. Dimly through this fog, one could make out the figure of a lamplighter going about his rounds, muffled in a greatcoat. The wheels of the carriages squelched as they rolled along the muddy avenues, bearing great ladies returning home from afternoon calls to prepare for an evening at the theatre or conveying portly businessmen to their residences after an arduous day in their East End offices. The lights in shop windows were extinguished and the shades drawn, while fires blazed in kitchens and were kindled in drawing rooms in preparation for the entertainment of dinner guests.

Within the Houses of Parliament, another long-winded Lord delivered a speech in favour of the troublesome Ecclesiastical Titles Bill while his fellow peers groaned and settled down a bit more comfortably into their seats. In Berkeley Square, the vivacious and quick-tempered lady of the house cursed at the dressmaker delivering a gown which had been ordered the day before for tonight's special reception, because though the seamstresses had worked round the clock without rest they had not had time to apply the gilt tasselling that had been requested. Several young swells peered out of the windows of Carltons laying bets on the frequency with which passers-by would slip and fall on the pavement; the tallest, youngest, and handsomest of the group consistently won, but spent his earnings on another round of brandy for his friends. In a dainty house in Mayfair, a beautiful, young woman laughingly dismissed the crowd of admirers who had spent the afternoon lounging in her drawing room, heedless of their protests about her cruelty in sending them out into the inclement weather. Throughout the city, the populace scurried, hurried, dashed towards shelter or scrambled into a waiting carriage as if terrified of contact with moisture, except in the crooked lanes and narrow courts of the rookeries, where the ragged urchins continued to run through the puddles barefoot for want of any other place to be.

And the great drops of rain continued to fall—on the lone pedestrian attempting to circumvent the worst of the puddles as on the shiny barouches of the leaders of fashion, on the great West End mansions as on the leaking roofs of the hovels in St. Giles and Seven Dials, on the flock of frightened sheep being driven down Park Lane on their way to market as on the steaming, exhausted pair of chestnuts drawing a ponderous and mud-spattered coach down Upper Grosvenor Street.

The coachman of this particular equipage peered out from the box and muttered to himself.

"One, two, three," he mumbled. "Aye, they said it 'ud be the third house on the left, but why be there so few lights? 'Twould be a pity if nought was ready, the young ladies havin' travelled so far an' all today."

He shook his head, commanded the horses to stop, and slowly descended from his perch on the box. The rain streamed off his greatcoat in rivers as he limped stiffly towards the strangely deserted-looking mansion and pulled at the knocker on the front door with all of his might.

He repeated this last action twice before the door swung back to reveal a very small, very timid, and very grimy maidservant clutching a candle.

The coachman harrumphed and said, "It be the Misses Merrell, come up from Sussex they have today, and sore in need of a warm welcome." Clouds of steam issued from his mouth along with these words.

"Oi'll get the missus," squeaked the little maid and scuttled off down the corridor, a corridor that presented a bleak vista to the coachman who feared for the comfort of his employer's daughters, for there was not a stick of furniture or a lamp burning in its dank, dark recesses.

Yet, he reflected, the young ladies would doubtless be eager to leave the cramped confines of the carriage, and accordingly, he retraced his steps and threw open the door of the coach. Lady Sibilla was the first to exit, leaping down gracefully and racing towards the open door of the house, followed immediately by her three pet dogs. The coachman shook his head at the sight of these beasts. Nothing but a bloody nuisance, he considered them, what with having to stop every few hours to give the dogs a chance to exercise, but then Lady Sibilla had refused to leave Partridge Park without her pets. Her stubborn insistence had encouraged Lady Sophia, who was not so scatterbrained as her older sister, and she had brought along her large, striped tabby, Marmalade. The coachman had predicted dire consequences for this melange, but Marmalade, now cuddled in his mistress's arms as she slowly descended the carriage steps, was too old and too lazy to be perturbed by the presence of any number of his arch enemies. He merely blinked his bright, yellow eyes once as Sophy paraded sedately up the walk and into the house.

The coachman feared for the safety of the last occupant of the carriage who had been locked up with this menagerie for the past day, but she scrambled to the door and sprang to the ground in a flurry of petticoats, as irrepressible as an India-rubber ball.

"Thankee, Jem," she said, kissing him lightly on the tip of his nearly frozen nose, and danced away to join the young ladies. Aye, they would miss her sorely in the servants' hall, he thought sadly, for Peggy was the darling of the Partridge Park staff with her high

3

spirits, sparkling Irish wit, and cheerful good will. He didn't doubt that the young farmer with whom she had been walking out would miss her also, but then a maidservant with Peggy's beauty and charm should certainly find a better catch in London, perhaps even a shopkeeper.

He expected that there would be some sort of reception provided for the three visitors by the time he had unloaded the many trunks and portmanteaus and deposited them in the hallway, but even the little maid with her one pitiful candle had not returned. The three dogs were not displaying their usual curiosity but were pressed in a sorry huddle on the cold marble floor, and Marmalade, still cradled by Lady Sophia, was crying, a thin, plaintive cry that echoed eerily in the barren hallway.

"Can it be that we've come to the wrong house?" asked Peggy, bending down to comfort the dogs.

"They said it 'ud be the third house from the left, and this be it," the coachman answered in a rumble, taking off his rain-soaked cap and scratching his head.

"Oh no," said Lady Sibilla, who was lost in the shadows at the end of the corridor, although her light confident step could be heard. "I remember the house from Nell's wedding. But what have they done with all the lovely furniture? You remember, Sophy, the grandfather clock, and the oak cabinet with the fancy carvings?"

"Of course," replied Lady Sophia, in her frail, baby-soft voice. "You hid there when we played hide and seek, and we could not find you, Sibil. But where is our aunt? Do you suppose she has not yet arrived?" Her uncertain words trailed away.

Sibilla returned from her exploration, her slender form emerging gradually out of the gloom.

"Why, there's a light in this room," she said, throwing open a door that was midway down the abandoned corridor, and thus she was the first to see Aunt Lucy.

It was a bizarre scene that presented itself to her eyes, and even the courageous Lady Sibilla was thrown aback. She had discovered the dining room, but it was a room as inhospitable as the entry hall. No paintings or sconces relieved the sombre oak panelling of the walls. The chandelier was muffled in swathes of holland, looking

4

like a giant cocoon attached to the ceiling. And the long oak table and its companion chairs were also shrouded in sheets. Only at the far end had a small space been cleared away, and there, with the light of the single lamp falling upon her forbidding countenance, sat Aunt Lucy, obviously interrupted in the task of consuming her solitary supper.

The flickering light distorted that lonely figure, so that Sibilla could gather only a fleeting impression of a massive black bulk, like the body of a monstrous spider, attached somehow to two short and ponderous arms that clutched a knife and fork, and the whole surmounted by a disproportionately tiny head which seemed to contain only a pair of very dark and heavy eyebrows, two hooded eyelids, and an enormous hooked nose. The small, pursed mouth was barely apparent, except when it opened, as it did now, to reveal a cavernous black hole, surrounded by long, horselike teeth.

"One of my nieces, I assume," said this mouth, as Sibilla watched aghast. "I thought I told you to wait in the drawing room." It was an ominous, booming voice that filled the empty room like a death knell.

"I'm afraid you've made a mistake," said Sibilla, stepping forward boldly, though all of her instincts told her to retreat.

Mistake was a word that Aunt Lucy had never heard applied to her own formidable personage. She frowned.

The back door which led to the kitchen flew open with a bang and the untidy little maid came pattering into the room.

"Oh missus," she said in her squeaky voice. "Cook 'as pas't out on the floor, an' oi cain't rouse her, no matter what oi do, and the young ladies 'as arrived. Oh!" she concluded as she saw the dim figure of Sibilla at the far end of the room.

"So they have," returned her mistress, removing her gaze from Sibilla and fastening it upon her plate once more. "Show them to the drawing room!"

The maid came scuttling down the length of the table and whisked past Sibilla like a small, brown mouse. With one last amazed glance at her aunt, Sibilla turned and left the room.

Frantically, the servant girl had flown across the hall and was scrambling about the opposite chamber, lighting a few oil lamps and throwing dusty holland covers from the settees and chairs they concealed. This room seemed to be the depository for all of the treasures the house had formerly contained; clumps of furniture smothered in sheets stood scattered about. Pictures and mirrors, masked by wrappings of newspaper, were stacked against the walls. From the shadows of a distant corner, Sibilla could hear the hollow tocking of the grandfather clock.

Sophia and Peggy and the coachman had followed her to the door and stood on the threshold looking about in wonder.

"So gloomy," murmured Sophy.

The dogs snuffled up to Sibilla, who patted them on their respective heads with an air of abstraction.

"Sure, and it could be a mausoleum," Peggy added, springing forward to help the maid in her task, but jumping back in mock terror as she uncovered a life-sized statue of a stern Athene brandishing a sword.

"We would like a fire, please," said. Miss Sibilla in a grim voice, addressing the maid, who bobbed a hasty curtsey and pattered out of the room.

"Are ye sure ye'll be all right?" asked the coachman, lurking still at the entrance, torn between his loyalty to the ladies and his fear that the owner of the house would discover him in the heart of the mansion, an unpardonable sin for a mere coachman.

"Oh Jem!" cried Peggy, flying down upon him with a comfortable hug. "I'll care for Miss Sibil and. Miss Sophy. Never you mind about us. We'll manage somehow, I expect."

The coachman shook his head again, donned his still-dripping hat, and backed out of the room. The snap of the door closing behind him sounded like the bang of a coffin lid.

"Oh Sibil!" Sophy sighed. "I feel faint." She loosed her grip upon Marmalade, and fell down upon a dusty couch, pressing one plump, white hand against her forehead.

"Don't be ridiculous, Sophy!" her sister retorted unsympatheticcally. "You've always been perfectly healthy, and this is not an appropriate time to indulge in hysterics!"

"As appropriate as ever will be," commented Peggy gloomily, surveying the shambles before her. "Whatever is going on here, Miss Sibil?"

"Confound it if I know," Sibilla replied. "I daresay we'll find out shortly, but let's make ourselves comfortable until then."

And so it was that when Mrs. Lucy Pleet, after devouring the last crumbs of her dinner and savouring the last drops of the port wine, condescended to cross the hall to welcome her nieces, she found a very domestic scene.

A blazing fire had been started on the hearth. Huddled about the cheerful flames, an oasis of warmth and brightness in the dreary room, were the following:

One large Irish wolfhound, Oscar, who was quite the size of a small lion, and who lifted his head and snarled as Aunt Lucy paused on the threshold.

One reddish-brown fox terrier, known as Muffin, who jumped up and quivered, all of his fur standing out on end.

A spotted retriever, called Slow, who continued to sleep with his head in the lap of a young lady, dressed unobtrusively in grey merino with a white linen collar and cuffs, but whose thick mane of curly dark hair and startling grey eyes, fringed with dark lashes, did not seem those of a servant.

There was a large, hostile cat with orange eyes, who was sheltered in the arms of another young lady, clearly a gentlewoman, who was curled up before the fire, in a delicate dress of white tulle, her blond ringlets shining like gold. She seemed much younger than her eighteen years as she lay there asleep, her rosy cheeks cushioned by her hands, her pale, pink lips parted to reveal pearl-like teeth.

And finally, there was Sibilla, whom Aunt Lucy had already seen, but not quite like this. She was watching the fire from the depths of a winged armchair, and the soft glow made her ivory skin seem translucent and illuminated her large dark eyes. Her fragile colouring and oval face were set off by the thick halo of smooth, dark tresses wound about her head, and further enhanced by the delicate lilac shade of her silk gown. In short, she was a beauty, and this was a possibility that Aunt Lucy had not anticipated.

"Come, Muffin!" Sibilla called in her low rich voice, and the high-strung little dog bounded towards her outstretched hand, inadvertently stepping upon the cat in his haste. Marmalade was aroused in a trice, which awakened Sophy, who clutched at him just as the large striped creature charged Muffin. The sight of the enraged cat struggling to reach her, terrified Muffin, who made an abrupt about-face and jumped into Peggy's lap, where Slow was sleeping. The usually placid retriever, who had been peacefully dreaming of green fields and rabbits, awoke with a shock and bit down hard on Oscar's tail which happened to be directly in front of him. Yet Oscar bade no heed to this affront to his dignity, as he continued to snarl at the intruder.

In a few moments the commotion had subsided, and Sibilla, glancing at her aunt, found her not quite so intimidating as before. In truth, she felt a twinge of pity. Mrs. Pleet was dressed in the severest mourning, from her jet earrings to the black crape ruching which finished her black wool gown, yet Sibilla knew that Mr. Pleet, whose dour face looked out at her from a brooch pinned over his widow's heart, had been dead for more than eight years. His relict, it seemed, had assuaged her grief with food and drink, for she was a massive woman with upper arms as large as hams, and a bosom that swelled forward like the prow of a battleship. As Sibilla had noticed earlier, Mrs. Pleet's head was small in comparison to this ocean of flesh, although it betrayed evidence of the same appetites; her small black eyes were almost buried in the plump doughlike expanse of her face, but the two fierce black eyebrows above them seemed to have taken upon themselves the function of expressiveness.

At the moment they were low on her forehead, and almost met at the top of the massive nose. Sibilla guessed that this grimace connoted displeasure, which suspicion was corroborated when that booming voice fell upon all of them, quelling even the dogs with its cold tones of domination.

"These creatures!" said Aunt Lucy. "Where did these creatures come from?"

For a startled moment, Sibilla thought perhaps her aunt was referring to herself and her sister, then realized she meant the pets.

The wolfhound continued to snarl, adding a tone of persistent menace to the scene.

"Quiet, Oscar!" Sibilla called to him softly, whereupon he settled back down upon the hearth, continuing to eye Aunt Lucy warily.

"Stand when in the presence of your elders!" snapped Aunt Lucy. "I see that my sister has failed, as expected, to instill any sense of good manners into her daughters!"

It still rankled Mrs. Pleet that her younger sister had married some seven years before she had finally caught the eye of Mr. Samuel Pleet, a wealthy Yorkshire mill owner. This was a marriage of desperation for the twenty-nine-year–old spinster, and she was bitterly aware that she had married beneath her class, just as she was bitterly aware that her younger sister's marriage to the present Earl of Corrough had been a love match. It was a source of immense satisfaction to her that the Earl and his Countess remained on their Sussex estate, unable to garner enough rents from their properties in England and Ireland to bear the enormous expense of a London Season for their youngest daughters, while she controlled the late Mr. Pleet's immense fortune and had condescended to invite her two nieces to stay with her in London. She preferred to forget that the house in which they were gathered was Corrough House, which the Earl had been forced to let for ten years, but which he had graciously loaned to his sister-in-law for her daughter, Lucinda's, presentation to Society. Lady Sibilla and Lady Sophia were merely ornaments which Mrs. Pleet hoped would aid Lucinda in her conquests by providing her with invitations to gatherings where plain Miss Pleet would not have been welcome on her own.

With this thought in mind, Aunt Lucy reviewed her nieces, as a captain reviews his troops. Both girls had risen awkwardly at her command and stood—or, as Aunt Lucy thought, lounged—before the fire.

Lady Sibilla was the taller of the two, with a slender, graceful figure, long white hands, on which a tiny amethyst ring glinted, and a classically beautiful face framed by her luxurious dark brown hair. Aunt Lucy noted every detail as she paced back and forth—the fiery, one might say, defiant, look in Sibilla's dark eyes, the elegant curve of the neck, the subtle colouring and flattering cut of the lilac-striped gown which gave Sibilla an air of composure and worldliness beyond her nineteen years of age.

This one would definitely be trouble, Aunt Lucy thought. "Stand up straight, miss!" was all she said, as she passed on to study Sophy, who was flushed with embarrassment at her aunt's harsh corrections. Sophy hated disapproval of any kind, and she trembled a bit under Aunt Lucy's fierce scrutiny. Much more easily managed, Aunt Lucy said to herself, noting that Sophy would not meet her gaze and that her demeanour was shrinking. And yet despite Sophy's timid posture, it was evident that this girl had the sort of beauty so in vogue in fashionable drawing rooms; her complexion was as white as Parian with a wild-rose colour in her cheeks, her eyes were large and blue, and her blond hair fell in soft ringlets about her face. Slighter than her sister, and with a pleasing roundness of form, she had a babylike quality which Aunt Lucy hoped extended to her disposition. If so, she could be easily quelled by a word or glance of authority, whereas Sibilla would require entirely different tactics. Mrs. Pleet could not yet determine what those should be, but she had never surrendered or retreated thus far in the battle for her daughter's future happiness, and she knew she would not fail now. It enraged her that her two nieces were so lovely, but although initially this seemed a problem, her calculating mind was already seeking a way to turn this to her advantage.

Having finished with the two sisters for the moment, she faced in another direction.

"What is this?" she asked in tones of distaste, glowering at Peggy who stood in the background patiently, contemplating the fire.

"Peggy Banks, ma'am," the girl replied cheerfully in her clear, rich voice.

"Curtsey when you address your superiors," Aunt Lucy said abruptly, "and always call me Mrs. Pleet."

"Yes, ma'am, Mrs. Pleet," and Peggy bobbed quickly, continuing to look directly at the older woman with her large, grey eyes and never losing her serene smile.

"Can she be—" Aunt Lucy hesitated and almost spat out the last word "—Irish?" She could not entirely be blamed for her disgust; the

Irish were the lowest race in England at the time, and advertisements for servants usually finished with the phrase, "Irish need not apply."

"Shure then, and purroud I am of it," said Peggy, thickening her natural brogue for Aunt Lucy's benefit.

"Insolent girl," hissed Mrs. Pleet, clenching her fists. "You can be dismissed tomorrow."

"I fear not," Lady Sibilla interjected in her low, expressive voice. "Peggy is part of the family. She has been my friend and companion since my father brought her to Partridge Park when we were both seven. He promised her she could come to London with me when I came out, and so she has."

"Ridiculous!" stated Aunt Lucy, "Who is she?"

"My mother was Bridget Banks. She died when I was five," Peggy recited slowly, "and then I was raised at Corroughsmere until the Earrul died. When the present Earrul came to Ireland for the funeral, he took me back with him."

"I daresay she'll be running off to Mass and all of those other heathenish Popish rituals," Aunt Lucy speculated grimly.

"Sunday's always been my day off," Peggy said quickly, bobbing and adding, "Mrs. Pleet."

"Speak when spoken to," snapped Aunt Lucy. "Absolutely preposterous! A day off every week! Unheard of! You may have every fourth Thursday afternoon. No more. And you will stay under the condition that you remain upstairs acting as lady's maid to Miss Sibilla and Miss Sophia, but you are never, I repeat, never, to be found on the drawing room floor. I have not the slightest notion why my poor sister would allow her husband to bully her into granting such privileges to a mere serving girl, but such goings-on will not occur in my household. You are dismissed, Margaret—I assume your Christian name is Margaret?" Peggy nodded warily. "You will find Lily in the kitchen, and she will show you to a room."

Having heard these edicts in grim silence, Peggy marched briskly towards the door, a set stubborn look to her mouth, and the retriever, Slow, stumbling along after her rapid feet.

"Say 'Good night, Mrs. Pleet,' when you leave the room!" commanded Aunt Lucy.

"Good night, Mrs. Pleet," mumbled Peggy, bending down and repeating more clearly, "Good night, Slow, honey." Then with a snap of her head which set all of her dark curls bouncing, she went out, slamming the door behind her, before Aunt Lucy could frame a retort.

The favouritism shown to Slow recalled to Mrs. Pleet's mind another order of business.

"These creatures!" she said distastefully. "Surely you do not propose to inflict these beasts upon my household!"

The retriever, sent away by Peggy, had returned to Sibilla's side, and she put a protective hand on his head as she responded to her aunt. "These are my pets, and I am responsible for their welfare. Let me assure you, they will give you no trouble."

"Certainly not," said Aunt Lucy briskly, "as they will be confined to the garden. Fortunately, there is a small one behind the house. I don't hold with this nonsense of letting animals have the run of a human habitation. As for that—" she pointed at Marmalade, who was sitting calmly at Sophy's side "—we may have a need for him. I would not be surprised to learn that the house was infested with mice; it seems to have gone to complete rack and ruin. But keep it out of my sight and away from visitors."

With an abrupt clap of her plump hands, Aunt Lucy finished with that subject and turned to her second objective, assuming an air of affability which startled both sisters. She flopped her great bulk down upon one of the couches, sighed deeply, and indicated with a wave of her hand that the girls were to follow suit. Sibilla settled into her previous seat, while Sophy sat rigidly at the edge of a fragile chair.

"Tell me the news," Aunt Lucy said confidingly. "I have not had the opportunity to write to Maria for such a long time. How is your dear mother's health?"

"Still poorly," Sibilla replied slowly, measuring her words. "She remains confined to her bed, as she has been for the past ten years, although the doctors can find nothing wrong. She is not in pain, but weak and tires very easily." Secretly, Sibilla had decided that her mother had given up on life after having tried for some fifteen years to provide an heir to the Earldom and succeeding only in producing seven healthy daughters, while her two sons were born sickly and died infants. But this was a theory she shared only with Peggy.

"I see," Aunt Lucy said complacently, nodding her head. "And the Earl? Still having trouble with his properties, I imagine?"

"Well, the crops have been bad lately," Sibilla responded, in the same low, careful voice, "and then what with the labourers asking for higher wages and the tenants complaining of high rents, he has a difficult time of it."

"Yes, we all know about the disgraceful complaints of the lower classes," said Aunt Lucy grimly, "who are allowed to form secret societies and run rampant about the countryside destroying other people's private property."

Sibilla opened her mouth, as if about to respond to this, and closed it again.

"And your sisters," Aunt Lucy continued her interrogation. "It seems to me the eldest married a soldier."

"Charlotte," Sibilla replied. "She married Major Dudley Garling-house of the Horse Guards during her first Season. They live in London."

"Your mother was quite distressed about that," Mrs. Pleet said with satisfaction. "Penniless, isn't he?"

"He has no immediate prospects," Sibilla admitted grudgingly.

"But he's so very handsome," Sophy interjected eagerly. "They fell in love at first sight, didn't they, Sibil?"

"Humph!" Aunt Lucy commented, and squelched Sophy's sentimental notions with one sharp glance.

"And then the next married a poor parson, did she not?" Aunt Lucy added ruthlessly.

"Oh, but Amy is so very happy," Sophy eagerly offered, forgetting momentarily her aunt's views on romance. "She met him at a missionary meeting during her first Season and our parents wouldn't hear of such a match, so he did not even declare his feelings. Imagine Amy living through a whole year without knowing that he loved her! Then, the next Season, Nell accepted Lord Cloudsleigh, and since she had made such a good match, my parents gave permission to Amy and Reverend Brittle. They live with their eight—or is it seven children,

13

Sibil?—in a poor section of London and do good deeds for their neighbours."

"Rubbish!" was Aunt Lucy's opinion. "Suffering and poverty are nature's admonitions to the undeserving. Misguided attempts at benevolence have always been more productive of evil than good."

Sophy subsided once more.

"I did hear of Nell—Eleanor's—marriage to Lord Cloudsleigh, that would be Baron Cloudsleigh, whose father is the Marquis of Merryfield with estates in Cambridgeshire." Mrs. Pleet shook her head sadly. "Why Nell—Eleanor's—husband is old enough to be her father, and his son by his first marriage must have been nearly her age when the wedding took place."

"He was twelve," Sibilla said stubbornly. "We met him at the wedding; he had been away at school for some time."

"No good can come of such a marriage," commented Aunt Lucy cheerfully. "It's no wonder that I hear Eleanor flirts shamelessly with all the young swells about town. But I do not understand why her husband permits it."

Both sisters looked at each other fiercely, but could not deny the charges their aunt had brought.

"Whatever happened to the next two?" asked Aunt Lucy blithely. "I heard nothing after Eleanor's marriage."

Sibilla and Sophy glanced at each other again.

"Effie decided to stay at home and never marry," Sibilla said cautiously. "Nell brought her out for her Season, but Effie found that the social whirl was not to her liking and returned home in the middle of it and has been there ever since." There was much more she could add: Effie's abrupt arrival in the middle of the night, her declaration that she would never return to London, her stubborn refusal to speak about Nell's house and Nell's hospitality, her denials that a specific incident might have caused her sudden flight. No one yet knew the reason for Effie's return, but Sibilla suspected an unhappy love affair, for Effie was listless and sat gazing out of windows for the first several months, until she put on her sturdy shoes and took to tramping about the countryside and attending church services regularly.

"Effie?" inquired Aunt Lucy brightly. "That would be Euphemia, the fourth. But what of the fifth girl, Catherine, or Kitty, I believe your mother called her."

"Kitty!" The very name had a peculiar and immediate effect upon the two sisters. Sophy flushed and sighed, remembering her favourite sister, indeed the favourite of the family, laughing, loving Kitty. And Sibilla stiffened. As the unofficial spokesman for the Merrell family, she found it difficult to frame her reply. At last she decided that blunt honesty was the best approach and thus, bracing herself, she said, "Kitty vanished in the middle of her first London Season!"

TWO

The Lines of the Battle Are Drawn

THIS CASUAL REMARK fell into a deep silence. Aunt Lucy bristled all over and, by the workings of her cheeks, seemed to be trying to choke out a response, but it was several minutes before she managed the strained words, "Vanished? Whatever can you mean?"

"Vanished," Sibilla repeated stubbornly. "Believe me, every effort was made to trace her, but none were successful. My mother, of course, suspected that Nell knew more about the affair than she was saying, and so that is why she cut off all communications with Nell—"

"What?" interrupted Aunt Lucy in a strangled voice. "She cut off all communications with Lady Cloudsleigh?" Despite her disapproval of Lady Cloudsleigh's morals, Mrs. Pleet was quite willing and even eager to receive invitations from her since Nell was an acknowledged leader of the *ton*.

"Yes," Sibilla said calmly. "She has not spoken to or written to or seen Nell for three years, and we are forbidden to have any contact with her while we are in London." Sibilla did not add that she, for one, refused to obey this capricious and unreasonable demand; she was enjoying her aunt's consternation.

"How did it happen?" Aunt Lucy managed to gasp, still reeling under the impact of this double assault.

"Well," Sibilla said, casting back in her memory for the details, "Kitty went down to London to stay with Nell and have her Season. Judging from her letters, she was a great success and had many offers, but she turned them all down because she was enjoying herself so much. She received quite a few invitations to stay with people, so after the Season ended she and Nell set off on a round of visits across the country. They were at Merryfield Manor in Cambridgeshire, staying with Nell's father-in-law, the Marquis, when the whole company decided to go down to London for a week. They set off but when they reached the city, it was discovered that Kitty was in none of the carriages. Of course, they raced back to Merryfield Manor, but she was not there either. All of her bags were gone and no one had seen her since that morning. We thought she had probably eloped, for Kitty was—is—impulsive, and that we would receive a note from her telling us she was married, but all of the rest of the party was accounted for, and no one has seen or heard of Kitty from that day."

There was another long silence. A tear trickled down Sophy's cheek. The only sounds were the contented snoring of Oscar upon the hearth and the crackling of the dying fire.

"I had no idea," Aunt Lucy finally managed to say. "What a ghastly scandal! That will surely affect your..." she paused thinking of her daughter "...prospects."

"Possibly," Sibilla commented wryly. "We are more concerned about Kitty's well-being than our 'prospects,' as you call them." This rebuke went unnoticed by her aunt.

"But why have I not heard of it?" Aunt Lucy demanded sharply. "Perhaps this information is not an *on dit* around town."

"Perhaps not," Sibilla said softly. "I am sure there were many inquiries about Kitty the next Season, but since we have not been in contact with Nell, I do not know how she answered them."

"Well, it is to be hoped that she thought of something discreet," snapped Mrs. Pleet, beginning to recover her composure. "I must say I should have been informed of this before I undertook the grave responsibility of presenting the pair of you. But I suppose we'll have to manage with the present situation, no matter how awkward. And now, as it is quite late, I propose that you retire. I'll send Lily in to show you to your rooms."

She rose and waddled out of the room like a grim, black beetle. As soon as the door closed behind her, Sophy glanced up at her sister, who was watching the fire once more.

"Oh Sibil!" she said, in her soft, breathy voice. "She despises us!"

Lady Sibilla shrugged her elegant shoulders. "Sophy," she said intently, although she continued to stare into the heart of the dying coals, "we must manage somehow, as she said herself. Do you realize that this may be our only chance? Do you propose to spend the rest of your days at Partridge Park? Well, perhaps you would not mind because of Leslie—"

Sophy blushed at the mention of her lover's name. Unfortunately, his offer had been rejected by her parents as he was merely the son of a local squire.

"But I," continued Sibilla, in the same intense voice, "intend to make a future for myself. We are in the centre of art and music and drama and government for the country, and we can meet the people with the power and the wealth to change their lives and the lives of those around them. I plan to become one of those people, although how—" Her voice trailed off, just as a draught swept through the room. The hall door opened and Peggy bounced into the room, a broad grin on her face.

"What a Gorgon!" she said insouciantly, as she plopped down into an empty armchair. "I've been sent to show you to your rooms; I gather that Lily has disappeared. Sure and you've been closeted with her for hours. You look as if you've been through a battle. What has she been saying?"

"Quizzing us about our family," Sibilla replied grimly.

"Oh!" Peggy's eyes grew wider. "Did she ask about Miss—"

"Kitty," finished Sophy for her, at the same time nodding solemnly.

"I should have liked to have seen her face when she learruned of that," Peggy said, but her cheerful words were undercut by the sorrow in her voice, for Peggy had idolized Kitty.

"I told her about Nell also," Sibilla added softly.

"Lor'! And I'm sure that put a dent into her plots," Peggy commented. "She's a schemer, that one—"

Her words were cut short by an icy voice at the door saying, "Good night, ladies!" All three turned just in time to see a flash of a black skirt as Aunt Lucy trundled off down the corridor.

Peggy burst out coughing, which shortly turned into a fit of the giggles, and finally with only whispered comments, she took up a candle and led the two sisters to their rooms.

It was surely the dampest, darkest, dankest house that any of them had ever seen. The noise of the rain was louder on the upper floors, and there were no fires lit in the chilly bedrooms.

Sibilla's room seemed to have been furnished with castoffs. A plain wooden bedstead, a dusty chest of drawers in mahogany, a massive oak wardrobe, and two unmatched, spindly legged chairs were the only pieces of furniture. The walls were papered in an oppressive floral design of grey and dark blue, and the solitary window was shrouded with musty blue velvet curtains. Pushing these aside, Sibilla found that a tall tree obscured any view, and it pressed so close to the side of the house that its wet leaves brushing against the pane made her sleep uneasy. Still, she was too exhausted to care overmuch about the comfortlessness of this chamber, and she snuggled quickly into the bed, grateful for the warmth of the dogs whom she had decided not to exile into the rain, resolutely refusing to think about the prospective scene with her aunt until the morrow.

Peggy woke her early, sauntering into the room with a cheerful Irish ballad on her lips and a basin of steaming hot water in her hands.

"What a household!" Peggy remarked, as she set down the basin and Sibilla lifted her dark head from the pillow while the dogs went wriggling off the bed to welcome Peggy. "The cook has already started drinking, Lily has wandered off with the butcher's boy, and your aunt—that paragon of perfection—is enthroned in the study, interviewing people for various positions. I hope that she thought to advertise for a cook or we will all be reduced to skin and bones."

Sibilla understood the reason for Peggy's bleak prophecy when she descended to the dining room with her sister to discover what one assumed to be breakfast spread upon a buffet. The dismal collation which met their eyes consisted of a dirty platter heaped with cold omelettes which were watery in texture and grey in colour, a tarnished silver tray displaying columns of rigid and greasy rashers of bacon, and a cracked china teapot which produced a lukewarm, brownish liquid which appeared to be, but did not taste like, tea. The holland cover had been removed from the table, but the surface was unvarnished and still spotted with stains.

"Who lived here before Papa loaned the house to Aunt Lucy?" asked Sophy with a frown, as they settled themselves and tried to digest their unappetising meal.

"The Marquis of Dower," Sibilla mumbled in reply, struggling to swallow a mouth full of cold eggs. She succeeded and said more clearly, "He used it for a town house, though he was often at his estates in Ireland, especially after his wife, our Aunt Flora, died twenty years past. But he died last year; I suppose the house has been shut up since that time."

"Did he die here?" asked Sophy nervously, for she read romantic novels voraciously although she was terrified of ghosts.

"No, Sophy," Sibilla returned with amusement. "He was killed in a carriage accident in Ireland."

"And Aunt Flora?" inquired Sophy uncertainly.

"You goose!" Sibilla said affectionately. "She died before we were born, in childbirth. They had only one child, our cousin, the present Marquis of Dower. The old Marquis never married again. And our family had the use of the house before the Marquis took it over. Mama presented Charlotte and Amy and Nell for their Seasons from this house. Surely you remember, Nell's Breakfast was given here."

"I was only six at the time," Sophy replied petulantly. Having found the food completely inedible, she tried a sip of tea, and then said, "Do you suppose we'll meet our cousin, the Marquis of Dower?"

"Certainly," Sibilla responded. "Kitty mentioned him in one of her letters. He must have been eighteen at the time, and she said he was a most handsome and charming young man, and very popular with the ladies—a popularity aided no doubt by the fact that he's heir to such a substantial fortune. But I must confess I am more curious about when we will finally meet Cousin Lucinda. Where can she be?"

"Having her beauty sleep, no doubt," Peggy answered briskly as she bounded into the room, grimacing expressively at the meagre breakfast. "I've been instructed not to make the slightest sound in the vicinity of her room for yet another hour. I've smuggled the dogs into the garruden, but they seem quite lost. Why don't you undertake to cheer them up? It's a lovely day today."

And it was a lovely day when Lady Sibilla and Lady Sophia decided that breakfast was a futile project and adjourned to the garden. The rain of the previous day had vanished and only a few fluffy clouds dotted the sky. There was a crisp tang in the air, a delicious scent of wet earth, and the sparkling panorama of glossy leaves and grass. The dogs came bounding to meet the two sisters, and Muffin, who had been declared untrainable because of her excitable nature, decorated their gowns with a fragile pattern of muddy footprints. Under the disapproving gaze of Aunt Lucy, who could view the proceedings through the french doors leading off the study, Sibilla chased her three pets around the trunks of the spindly elm trees, while Sophy giggled helplessly at the spectacle. Having exhausted the animals and arrayed themselves in new dresses, the two retired to the sitting room where Sibilla struggled through Ruskin's *Seven Lamps of Architecture,* and Sophy eagerly devoured *The Lady of the Lake.*

Peggy interrupted this instructive interlude to announce that Aunt Lucy and Cousin Lucinda awaited them in the drawing room.

This chamber was in the same condition as the previous night. Although the thickets of white-sheeted furniture were less ghostly in the light of day, the general decrepitude was more apparent. The hearth was blackened by smoke; the faded mustard wallpaper was peeling from the wall in strips; cobwebs festooned a bust of the young Queen Victoria.

Aunt Lucy stood before the mantel, her thumbs hooked into the gold chatelaine she wore about her waist, staring ahead with grim officiousness as if she was the chairman of the board at an important meeting. So absorbed was Sibilla by this amazing sight that she was entirely oblivious of the presence of her cousin for several minutes. And when she finally became aware of Lucinda, who was seated demurely on a stool to the right of her mother, Sibilla realized why she was so easily overlooked for Lucinda was the palest and plainest of creatures. She wore an inconspicuous gown of buff merino, her hair was a flat, undistinguished brown, and her eyes were of the same shade of brown, so that she seemed to fade into one beige blot. Furthermore, she had her mother's tendency to plumpness, her mouth was arched into a petulant downturn, and her brow was crinkled with distaste.

Here was the reason for Mrs. Pleet's harshness of the previous evening. Beside Sibilla with her dark vitality and Sophy with her blond prettiness, Lucinda would completely vanish into the background.

"My daughter, Miss Lucinda Pleet," her mother said proudly, laying one chubby hand on Lucinda's shoulder. "Lucinda, your cousins, Miss Sibilla and Miss Sophia." Perhaps Sibilla was the only one who noticed that Aunt Lucy refused to address them by the title of "Lady," which courtesy they had acquired as the daughters of an Earl.

"How do you do, Cousin Lucinda?" Sophy was saying from behind her in a soft voice. "It is a lovely day today, is it not?"

"I am sure I don't know," Lucinda replied ungraciously. "I have only this moment arisen."

"It is difficult to find an unobstructed view in this house," Sibilla offered helpfully, meanwhile wondering if her cousin was as brainless and rude as she seemed.

"Indeed!" snorted Aunt Lucy, surveying the drawing room with distaste. "I expected that a house on Upper Grosvenor Street, and so close to the Park, would be fashionable. Instead, I find this shambles. I have sent for decorators from the top London firms, and the workmen shall be in and out for days, attempting to make this ruin presentable before the rush of the Season. I have also to hire a complete staff of servants. I am shocked to discover that your father could not afford to maintain a resident staff. Meanwhile, you will all require new wardrobes." She stared pointedly at Sibilla and Sophy's morning dresses. "I have sent a note to the dressmaker, Madame Doucette, whom my friends inform me is all the rage, but you will need to purchase hats, gloves, evening slippers, and other incidentals, and I have not the time to spare to go running about London on such frivolous errands. You will need a chaperone, and therefore I propose that you write a short letter to your sister, Charlotte, asking her to accompany you on a shopping expedition. I had thought we would ask Lady Cloudsleigh, but since her acquaintance is denied to us—"

"But why, Mama?" Lucinda interrupted, twisting about to peer up at her mother. "You expressly said that knowing Lady Clouds-leigh would be one of the advantages of my being presented with my cousins."

"Her name alone and the connexion will have to suffice," Mrs. Pleet said abruptly. "An unfortunate family disagreement, the nature of which we will not discuss, has created this situation. I expect we shall see her at parties, and," she glared at Sibilla and Sophy, "I would like to know what your mother expects me to do in that awkward encounter. Especially if we cannot invite her here—"

Sibilla shrugged. "I suppose it would be only polite to be friendly when and if that does occur. I do not see how anyone will know whether or not she comes here."

"You don't see much then, do you?" countered Aunt Lucy with anger. "Everyone knows everything about everybody. That is the motto of the Season. And a motto that you would do well to remember. Not one word that you utter, not one young man whom you smile upon, not one indiscreet remark or too-prolonged conversation, will go unnoticed. And it is my determination," here she drew herself up to her full height, which was not much over five feet, four inches, though she equalled that in girth, "that there shall not be a breath of a scandal or a scrap of gossip that will reflect on my daughter's character and, by association, on yours. Your futures are at stake here and your prospects can be blighted forever by one foolish error. I trust that I make myself perfectly clear."

Sophy bobbed her head quickly up and down, while Sibilla acknowledged this sermon by inclining her head slightly.

"And now, I have work to do," Aunt Lucy said sternly. "Write the note, let me see it, and then amuse yourselves until your sister arrives."

With this abrupt dismissal ringing in their ears, Lady Sibilla and Lady Sophia adjourned to the sitting room to compose the commanded letter; Lucinda remained for a *tête-à-tête* with her mama.

"What shall I say, Sophy?" asked Sibilla, who was considered the "literary" one of the family and whose role it was always to compose such missives.

23

"Start with 'Dear Charlotte,' suggested Sophy timidly, leaning over her sister's shoulder to stare at the blank paper.

"'Dear Sister Charlotte,'" Sibilla said, reading aloud as her pen flew along the page, "'Sophy and I have just arrived in town and are staying at Corrough House on Upper Grosvenor Street with Aunt Lucy Pleet and her daughter, Lucinda. They are most anxious to make your acquaintance and requested that you visit us as soon as possible. Perhaps you could accompany us on a shopping expedition, for we need very many items of apparel, and I am sure you know the best places to shop. Looking forward to seeing you again shortly and hearing all of the news of London, we close and affectionately remain your loving sisters, Sibilla and Sophy.'"

She dashed off her signature in her bold, angular hand and passed the pen to Sophy, who signed more hesitantly, forming her rounded letters with exaggerated care.

This epistle was promptly brought to the attention of Aunt Lucy, pronounced adequate, and immediately carried off by Peggy. Sibilla's suggestion that they accompany Peggy and the letter met with cold disapproval, and so they again retreated to the sitting room where Sibilla insisted that Sophy should pose for a sketch entitled "The Lady and the Wounded Lion." Oscar was smuggled into the house to portray the lion and obediently adopted a supplicating position on the hearth. Sophy's role demanded that she lean forward with one knee slightly bent, stretching out her arms towards Oscar's supposedly injured paw. It was an awkward pose and Sophy's countenance expressed this discomfort, rather than the mingled emotions of pity and timidity which Sibilla wished to portray. Yet if Sophy was not Sibilla's best subject (at a moment's notice Peggy could become a Roman gladiator, a ferocious bandit, or a melancholy lady incarcerated in a tower), she was the most compliant.

Sophy always did as she was asked and always agreed with what anyone said. It was somewhat of a family joke that if Sophy was told it was dreadfully cold, she would wear her heaviest mantle on a sunny June day, whereas if she was told it was warm, she would venture out in her lightest summer dress in the midst of a snowstorm. Sibilla considered this complaisance Sophy's most irritating trait, although it could also be quite endearing, for Sibilla loved to draw and having surpassed the botanical sketches requested by their governess, now appointed herself the task of expressing human conflicts in figure studies. But she was always amazed, as now by Sophy's docility.

Sophy had fallen in love during the past year with Leslie Whitefoot, the eldest son of a neighbouring country squire. But when that unfortunate young man's proposal was rejected by her parents and she was told never to see him again, Sophy obeyed.

Nothing her lovesick swain attempted broke Sophy's vow of obedience. The passionate notes conveyed through Peggy were rejected unopened. He leaped over hedges and appeared before her while she was walking through the gardens and she turned silently and returned to the house. On the evening of their departure for London he stood in the rain for hours beneath her bedroom window, throwing pebbles and calling her name, and Sophy had refused to open the window.

Perhaps it was only natural that as the youngest of seven sisters, Sophy had surrendered under the pressure of the many conflicting demands upon her, and adapted like a chameleon to whatever role was required of her. Sibilla secretly envied this passivity, although she found it difficult to imitate. She was certain that Sophy would soon meet a wealthy and titled young man whose offer of marriage would be gratefully accepted by their parents, and Sophy would manage to be completely content in such an arranged marriage. Not so easy for herself, thought Sibilla, as she drew in the lines which would constitute Oscar's mane in the picture. She was not sure that marriage would satisfy her ambitions, for she longed to have some effect upon the lives of those around her, somewhat like her sister Nell, whose house was a literary and artistic center for London Society. But Lady Cloudsleigh never spoke of happiness or her husband in her letters, a high price to pay for popularity, Sibilla felt.

There was a quick patter of feet in the hallway, and Peggy burst through the door, her cheeks aglow with excitement, her grey eyes dancing.

"She'll be here in a moment," she said, gasping for breath between her words. "I ran all the way back. I do believe she was grateful for an excuse to get out of that house. And such a house!"

Sophy tumbled into a heap on the floor, rubbing her stiff joints. "Why?" she asked simply.

"That Horace!" declared Peggy. "The boy. You remember how he behaved while they were staying at Partridge Parruk. He is even worruse, if you can imagine it, when at home with his mother. I do believe she would jump from the roof if he requested it. It's 'Mama, do this,' 'Mama, I want that,' with no pause. The poor maid is as browbeaten as Mrs. Garlinghouse. Horace went into a fit of temper as soon as his mother mentioned going out, and cerrutain I am, that she willna leave till he is quiet."

"Poor Charlotte," murmured Sibilla, laying down her sketchbook and crayon. "Did you see the Major?" The entire Merrell family was agog with curiosity about Charlotte's husband, whom they had met only at the wedding. He refused to accompany his wife and children on their annual pilgrimages to Partridge Park.

"No," Peggy answered briefly. "He wasna there, but the maid mentioned a carrud parruty he was having this evening. Your sister said everything was in readiness and that she would prefer to be out when his friends arrived."

A heavy tread in the hallway announced the presence of Aunt Lucy, who filled the doorway like a dark Fury.

"I do not pay my servants to gossip with their superiors," she said severely to Peggy, and then turning to Sibilla and Sophy, "Your sister has arrived." A faint sniff at the end of this sentence conveyed the information that she was not favourably impressed with Charlotte Garlinghouse.

THREE

A Strange Sight in Berkeley Street

MRS. CHARLOTTE GARLINGHOUSE was a tall, thin, gaunt woman, looking much older than her twenty-nine years. Her dark hair, streaked with grey, was pinned back severely; her bleak, large grey eyes were rimmed with brownish circles; her thin, pale lips were set in a grim smile. She sat primly on one of the dusty couches, dressed in a faded, worn, walking costume of puce-coloured poplin. A rent in one purple flounce, a carefully mended spot evident on the shoulder, the thin tips of the fingers of her tan gloves, and the outdated satin bonnet all bespoke a genteel poverty. Charlotte was in a highly nervous state, her gold earrings quivering with anxiety, and her gloved hands clasping and unclasping in her lap.

As her sisters were shepherded into the room by Aunt Lucy, she rose in a succession of short, jerky movements, and stood solemnly; her hands clenched before her.

Sophy, with her instinctive graciousness, eased the awkward moment by flying across the room and hugging her sister affectionately. Sibilla, in turn, was gathered into Charlotte's rather cold and rigid embrace. This ceremony having been completed satisfactorily, all present found a seat, Charlotte glancing timidly at Aunt Lucy.

"So pleasant to meet you, Mrs. Garlinghouse," that awesome personage said in her most polite and chilling voice.

"Oh yes," responded Charlotte with trepidation. "One cannot imagine what a shock it is to find my little sisters so grown that they are embarking upon the grand adventure of a London Season—" Her voice trailed away at the end of this statement and her self-composure disappeared also. She lapsed into twitching silence.

"How is your husband, Major Garlinghouse?" Aunt Lucy inquired frigidly.

Mrs. Garlinghouse started and picked at the purple tassels that trimmed her jacket. "Oh, he is very well, very well, indeed," she replied uncertainly.

Sibilla thought to soothe her sister's ruffled nerves by remarking casually, "Peggy said he was hosting an intimate card party for some friends today."

Instead, Charlotte jumped. "Oh no!" she exclaimed in her frail, reedy voice. "Oh, he never plays cards. And he never gambles," she added gratuitously. "Absolutely not. Oh, he wouldn't think of it," she continued before subsiding once more.

Aunt Lucy surveyed this interchange with interest. "I think the girls mentioned how much they would enjoy going shopping with you," she said smoothly. "It is such a lovely day, and I am sure a drive would do them well."

Charlotte cleared her throat several times before saying, "Why, I came in a hackney coach. We are not able—that is to say, we do not have—rather, our carriage is undergoing repairs at the moment."

Aunt Lucy smiled a slow, malicious smile. "Of course," she said sweetly. "You shall walk. The exercise will be invigourating. I'll fetch Lucinda." She swept out of the room like a ship leaving a port.

Without the constraining presence of their aunt, Charlotte relaxed somewhat, sighing and allowing her hands to rest quietly in her lap.

"So that is our mother's eldest sister," Charlotte began cautiously. "She is certainly—"

"A Gorgon!" Sibilla suggested quickly, using Peggy's favourite epithet.

"So difficult to like," agreed Sophy.

"But so very generous in offering to bring you out," Charlotte commented.

"Quite true," Sophy said eagerly. "Most generous."

"Altogether remarkable," was Charlotte's summary, and both sisters nodded in agreement with this assessment.

The stifling pause that next occurred was broken only when Lucinda entered the room with a jolt, pushed forward by her mama. Her plain brown hair, curled into tight ringlets, bobbed around her plump face. The brilliant Prussian blue of her elaborately trimmed walking costume contrasted unpleasantly with her sallow face. Her small mouth was pursed into a pout; she did not seem anxious for her cousins' company.

"Lucinda is eager to go!" announced Aunt Lucy with artificial cheeriness. Within the subsequent frantic moments, the members of the shopping party were guided to the door and found themselves walking briskly down the street towards town.

Even in this quiet backwater of Mayfair, the streets were thronged with carriages and the pavement crowded with passersby. Sibilla, who had fallen in line with Charlotte, while Lucinda and Sophy trailed behind, looked about hungrily at the young swells dashing past on the seats of their fast phaetons, at the elegantly dressed women who descended haughtily from shiny barouches and swept up the walks towards the magnificent town houses that lined the street, at the beggar huddled against the iron fence, at the diminutive flower girl offering her wares in a thin, piteous voice, at the ballad seller hawking a lurid composition entitled "Murder in Camberwell."

Charlotte, inured to the panorama of the city scene, hurried the small company along, sweeping them across the thoroughfares whenever a swell of pedestrians dared the belligerent London traffic.

As they approached Regent Street, they slowed to gaze longingly at the windows, at the ornate parures of gems glittering in the jewellers' shops, at the ravishing bonnets displayed by milliners, and at the glimmering lengths of cloth offered by the mercers. Lucinda, who had been sullen and indifferent, came to life, her face suffused with enthusiasm as she bounded in and out of various establishments, ordering a pair of gloves here and a length of lace there. Lady Sibilla and Lady Sophia felt their enjoyment ebb as they followed her disconsolately, unable to purchase any of the delicacies which they desired for neither had any ready cash nor did Charlotte offer to provide it.

Several hours later, they bent their steps homeward, Lucinda having assigned parcels for each to carry. Suddenly, Lady Sibilla dropped hers, uttered a small shriek, and stood stock still gazing up at a house on the other side of Berkeley Street.

"Sibil, what is it?" asked Sophy anxiously, hurrying to her side. "You look as if you'd seen a ghost!"

"Kitty!" murmured Sibilla, still in her trance.

Sophy turned her head in the direction of Sibilla's look, but saw only a small, elegant, greystone mansion with a glossy green door and an empty green balcony, lined with geraniums in red pots.

There was no sign of life, except perhaps for the parrot who moved restlessly about in his cage on the deserted balcony.

Puzzled and worried, Sophy took her sister's arm and shook it saying, "Sibil, Sibil, what is it?"

"I thought I saw Kitty," Sibilla muttered tonelessly.

Charlotte came scurrying up. "What has happened?" she demanded. Lucinda bent to retrieve the package which had been kicked aside by several passers-by.

"Sibil says she saw Kitty!" Sophy exclaimed, her blue eyes wide with wonder. "Over there!" She waved her hand, indicating the other side of the street.

"Oh, no!" Charlotte said softly under her breath, as if half-believing this wild supposition. She repeated more firmly, "Oh no, Sibilla must be mistaken. You are mistaken, are you not, Sibilla?"

"I suppose," said that young lady, recovering somewhat from her daze. "I saw a young woman with two small children on that balcony, and just for a moment, she looked so like Kitty that I thought—" She looked up once more at the bleak windows, shook her head, and allowed Sophy to lead her on down the street.

Behind those silent windows, the young woman who was pressed against the curtains, felt tears come to her eyes as the small party continued its progress down the street.

"Mama!" said the small boy, who clung to her rose-coloured silk skirts. "Why did we not stay and watch the people?"

"Oh chickies!" Kitty laughed, swooping down upon Alex and his younger sister, Clarissa, in a whirl of perfume and laces and long, auburn ringlets. "You are my most precious sweethearts. I saw someone I knew a long time ago, and it startled me for a moment. But they would not want to know me now —" She glanced about the small delicate chamber in which this conversation took place, a room that was the appropriate shrine for her beauty.

Fragile mahogany chairs, the seats worked in floral designs of roses, lilacs and daffodils stood against the walls which were panelled halfway in mahogany and finished with rose watered silk. Before the small white marble hearth, three settees, one in spring-green, one in pale blue, and the third in shades of buttercup-yellow, stood on an Aubusson carpet of the same, muted tones. A portrait by Winterhalter of Kitty with her two children was hung above the mantel. She had been painted in an evening gown of the same wild rose as the walls, *décolleté* to expose her lovely white shoulders and fine, long neck, and falling into a frou-frou of soft flounces at the bottom. Her auburn hair was dressed high on her head, spilling into a soft cluster of curls over one shoulder. Her wide mouth curved in a mischievous smile but her green eyes looked down fondly at the two children portrayed on either side, Clarissa in white muslin with a green sash, and Alex standing proudly in a blue suit.

To one side of the room stood a baby grand piano, the gleam of its rosewood surface reflecting a vase of roses, which were slowly dropping their shell-pink petals, adding an indescribably sweet smell to the fragrance of potpourri, which already lingered in the room. Against the other wall stood a rosewood cabinet, displaying gaily painted pieces of Copeland ware, and beside it were several cages of canaries whose chirps and flutterings filled the air.

It was a lovely room, and Kitty gazed at it longingly as if the reappearance of her sisters had somehow the power to wrest these material possessions from her grasp, but the determination, which was evident in that stubborn square chin and those ambitious green eyes, was twice as strong when she turned her head to watch the two children. Baby Clarissa, adorable in pink muslin, her large, dark eyes alert with interest from her throne in a great, green armchair, and little Alex, standing manlike by her side, his dark eyes clouded with worry and his hands clenched in small fists, because for the first time he saw his beloved mother troubled by a situation he could not understand and, therefore, not alter in her behalf.

"Oh!" said Kitty softly, dropping to her knees and hugging him firmly. "Not to worry, my sweeting. We three are together, and soon Mr. Cloudsleigh will come to visit. Would you like that?"

"Oh yeth!" lisped Clarissa. "I love Mither Cloudthlee."

Alex kissed his mother solemnly on the cheek and said, "Yes, Mama. He will tell me another story about the horses, won't he?"

"Of course, my darling," Kitty murmured, pressing his dark head more closely to her shoulder as if she would never let him go.

FOUR

Callers at Cloudsleigh House

SIBILLA CONTINUED TO PUZZLE about her strange apparition for several moments, but her mind had cleared enough by the time the shopping expedition passed through Berkeley Square so that she noted carefully which of the imposing mansions must be the house where Nell resided with Lord Cloudsleigh. She intended to visit her elder sister at the earliest opportunity, but it would be a tricky business, what with Aunt Lucy's constant surveillance, the necessity of providing an adequate excuse for her absence, and her own uncertainty about traversing London alone. Peggy must accompany her, she decided, and was content for the remainder of the journey back to Upper Grosvenor Street to envision all of the fascinating and influential people she would meet at one of Nell's parties.

Her opportunity arrived much sooner than she thought for when they reached Corrough House they found that Aunt Lucy was busy supervising the workmen, Sophy and Lucinda both declared themselves in need of a nap, and Charlotte with a faint air of disappointment bade them a formal good-by.

Sibilla was dismayed by the lack of closeness she felt for Charlotte, but it was not a surprising phenomenon for Sibilla had been only seven when Charlotte was married, and despite her autumnal

33

visits to Partridge Park, the disparity in their ages made communication difficult.

She shook this disturbing problem from her mind and went in search of Peggy, whom she finally ran to ground, chatting with one of the newly hired grooms in the stableyard. The young man was quite clearly not pleased by Sibilla's interruption; he lounged away, his dark, handsome face sulky, and kicked a nearby pebble viciously. But Peggy was enthused by the plot as Sibilla described it.

"How very thrilling!" she exclaimed happily, as they set off again in the direction of the heart of Mayfair. "Roscoe—that is the groom's name," she confided with a blush, "was telling me of all the sights of town. Madame Tussaud's Waxworks on Baker Street—they say she first set up in business by displaying the decapitated heads of the noble folk who were guillotined in France—and the Pantechtiton, and Diorama in Leicester Square, and the Zoological Gardens, and then the Great Exhibition opening in three months. We shall not have a moment free." As she continued to recite a catalogue of all the delights in store for them, Sibilla relentlessly set her course towards Cloudsleigh House. A short time later they were standing on the front steps, staring at the impressive, black-painted door and its elaborate gold knocker.

"Oh, Sibil!" Peggy said suddenly. "I do declare I am frightened!"

"Nonsense!" Sibilla replied sternly; she could be as dictatorial as Aunt Lucy at her best. She pulled on the heavy knocker, and the door swung open swiftly to reveal a frowning butler whose set chin protruded forward at an angle above their heads.

"The tradesman's entrance is around the side," he said with chilly hauteur, and was about to slam the door when Sibilla said quite as icily,

"Please be so good as to inform Lady Cloudsleigh that her sister, Lady Sibilla Merrell, has called to see her."

The butler started and unbent a little to peer carefully at Sibilla as she tapped her foot impatiently on the doorstep.

"May I see your card, ma'am?" he asked dubiously.

"I have just arrived in town," she snapped, "and my cards with my London address have not yet been printed. If you do not intend to admit me, kindly say so, and I will be glad to inform Lady Cloudsleigh of the—"

The butler made his decision in a moment, though he did not seem altogether certain that it was the right one.

"To be sure," he muttered, opening the door a little wider. "Please step this way."

Sibilla and Peggy followed him through the vast, black-and-white tiled entrance hall into a magnificent drawing room, panelled in ivory silk, furnished with exquisite French furniture, and hung with lavish paintings of country scenes and lovely women. Above the mantel hung a picture of Lady Cloudsleigh, which Sibilla studied carefully.

Nell had never been a beauty, but she presented herself with drama. In this portrait, she was dressed in an Eastern costume of glistening gold. Her dark hair was concealed beneath a turban of shimmering cloth, but her large, luminous eyes shone and her sensuous red lips were parted slightly in an amused smile.

Sibilla's mother, Lady Corrough, had always claimed that her daughters fell into two distinct groups. One included Charlotte, Nell, and Sibilla, all possessed of dark colouring, clever minds, and slender figures; those in the second group, Amy, Effie, and Sophy, had lighter hair colour, blue eyes, and a tendency towards plumpness. Kitty, auburn-haired and green-eyed, of course was excluded, for Kitty was the miracle of the family, the shining goddess among a group of extraordinarily talented and beautiful women.

Sibilla had never appreciated the comparison with Charlotte, who, although she must once have been beautiful because of her striking colouring, seemed to Sibilla a prematurely aged and embittered woman, but Sibilla had always wished to emulate Nell, who was not only lovely, but quick-witted, ambitious, and magnetic. And yet she had not seen this much-admired sister for several years, and her nervousness increased as Lady Cloudsleigh did not appear.

"Don't furret yourself, Sibil, dear," Peggy crooned soothingly. "She must be very busy; she will be down as soon as she can."

"Of course," Sibilla murmured in a low voice. She began to roam about the room, picking up small silver ornaments, or touching the cream-coloured French brocade which covered the couches. Peggy watched helplessly as Sibilla wandered aimlessly about and was re-lieved when the double doors were thrown open and Lady Cloudsleigh flew across the room to embrace Sibilla.

Nell was not quite as tall as her younger sister, and managed to convey an air of bright alertness and vivacity by rapid movements and her impetuous gestures. Having kissed Sibilla quickly on both cheeks, and having held her back at arm's length to take in her becoming pale yellow afternoon dress, Nell graciously turned her attention to Peggy, who was shrinking back, aware of the ambiguity in this situation, for a servant would not accompany her mistress on a call.

"Why, it's Peggy!" Nell exclaimed, in her bright, eager voice, her dark eyes surveying Peggy, her head tilted to one side, like a sharp little bird.

She was dressed almost mannishly, thought Sibilla, though she acknowledged the total effect was breathtaking. A tight dark jacket, devoid of any ornamentation, over a plain linen front, accentuated the womanly curves of Nell's figure, while the width of her dark skirt, which was trimmed merely with a thin, red braid, dramatized her tiny waist and the fluidity of her quick steps. Her dark hair was drawn back in a severe chignon, suiting her attire and complement-ing favourably the paleness of her complexion and the liveliness of her dark eyes. Diamond earrings quivered in her ears and flashed as she walked, and another large diamond glinted on one of her long, elegant fingers.

"I'm so pleased you came today," Nell said breathlessly, as she turned back to Sibilla. "I'm entertaining a select company, and you must meet them. The Marquis of Dower, Ashford Cloudsleigh, the well-known Member of Parliament, Mr. Lanning Tombs, a poet, and Bruno Rushforth, a painter—he did my portrait—"

"I am afraid," Sibilla interrupted in a quiet voice, "that it would be disastrous for me to meet anyone here—at Cloudsleigh House. You see, our mother—"

"Oh, I know!" Nell remarked with a flash in her dark eyes and a toss of her head. "That stupid ban of silence because of Kitty. I declare that girl has caused me more turmoil since the day I offered to present her—"

36

"Do you know where Miss Kitty is now?" asked Peggy eagerly, forgetting her previous timidity.

Nell turned on her in an instant. "I am sure I do not," she said quickly, "and I would not want to know." She spoke convincingly, but Peggy thought the strange glint in her eyes and the nervous gesture she described with her hand concealed some knowledge. "I do know that she is quite happy and well cared for. She sent me a letter several months after her disappearance, but then," she appealed to Sibilla, "that was after Mama had washed her hands of me, and frankly, Kitty was quite adamant that she wanted to be entirely anonymous in her new life. But that is not to the point. You must come and meet my guests. You can be assured that they will not mention seeing you here, dearest Sibilla. Do come."

"But my dress," Sibilla began, smoothing her skirts nervously.

"It's lovely, my dear," Lady Cloudsleigh said appraisingly. "You do have the best taste. It's quite amazing, or should I say, appalling." She giggled slightly but her bright eyes studied Sibilla critically.

"Come!" said Nell firmly, holding out her hand, and reluctantly Sibilla came to her side. "And Peggy also!" Nell declared.

"Oh no, ma'am!" cried Peggy, shrinking back into her corner. "I cannot, ma'am! Oh, no, I couldn't!"

"Of course, you can," Nell said abruptly. "You are not some shy little maidservant, who cannot read or write. And these are people who appreciate good conversationalists and lovely young women, and are not afraid of unconventionality. You will join us!"

And even Peggy fell under Nell's commanding spell and followed meekly to another drawing room, the opposite of the first in which they had waited, for this one contained a fireplace of black marble, oriental rugs of maroons, dark blues, and deep greens, couches of burgundy and black, and walls panelled in black silk relieved by white woodwork. In this sombre setting, Nell was at an advantage, her severe costume seeming both appropriate and attractive, while Sibilla felt ill-at-ease since the brightness of her yellow dress was a shocking splash of colour in the room. Peggy, in her usual black silk gown, blended into the shadows, which was precisely where she wished to be.

37

The occupants of the chamber rose as the three women entered, and Sibilla thought it odd that they were all gentlemen. Nell in a laughing, gay voice introduced them one by one, but Sibilla murmured only conventional greetings and could not sort them out until the presentations were over and she could sink back into a dark armchair near the fire. She supposed that the fire was lit only for the effect of the bright flames against the ebony marble, for the room was suffocatingly warm and the black velvet drapes at the other end were closed. Bizarre curios lay scattered about on the mosaic-topped tables—brass sculptures from India, carved bits of lava—and most strange of all, a brightly plumaged macaw in a gilt cage, who interrupted the conversation periodically with loud obscenities. Sibilla winced at these, while Peggy laughed delightedly.

Once accustomed to these unusual accoutrements, Sibilla was able to attend to the company. The Marquis of Dower, she decided, must be the handsome, young man, sitting on a low stool alongside Peggy. He had dark, curly hair, striking blue eyes, and broad shoulders which strained against the velvet material of his elegant, tight-fitting coat. Peggy seemed alternately enchanted and disturbed by what he was saying, for she would listen with absorption for a few minutes, then start back and shake her head at him with a wide grin on her face, only to succumb to his next whispered inquiry.

Nell sat on a sofa between two men, with whom she alternately flirted. One was very thin and very tall; his dark, lank hair fell in strands on his collar; his face was that of a spectre or a saint, extremely pale, with gaunt cheeks and abnormally large, dark eyes which gleamed with fervour; his quick, white hands flailed the air frantically as he spoke. Nell's usual air of intensity paled in comparison to this gentleman's frenetic activity. The man at Nell's other side lounged against the back of the settee with an air of indifference. His attire was spectacular: green trousers, a canary waistcoat, a vivid orange stock, and a velvet jacket of a plum colour. Thick side whiskers concealed most of his face, he smoked a meerschaum pipe, and his light brown hair was tousled.

Sibilla remembered that one of these was a poet and the other a painter; she guessed, quite correctly, that the consumptive-looking person was the poet, one Mr. Lanning Tombs, and the gentleman in the creative colour combination was Bruno Rushforth, the painter.

Which left two men unaccounted for, thought Sibilla. They were deep in conversation to her left and she was able to study them for several minutes. The older man, who was somewhat over thirty, was one of the handsomest men Sibilla had ever seen; she admired his ascetic face, his bold black eyes, his well-trimmed dark moustache almost concealing his sensuous firm lips, and his striking costume — dark trousers striped with cherry, complementing his cherry-coloured jacket and his pale pink waistcoat. A coral pin thrust into his white stock was the only ornamentation.

The younger man was almost as handsome as his companion. They were related, Sibilla assumed, for they had the same waving dark hair and black eyes, although the younger had a darker, saturnine complexion which contrasted with his flashing white teeth. He sported a dandy's costume of a low-cut ivory satin waistcoat, a black silk cravat held by a gold-and-diamond pin, dark, very tight trousers which revealed the leanness of his thigh muscles, and yellow silk gloves.

Watching them, Sibilla was certain that she had seen both before. At last she recalled that Nell had presented them as Cloudsleighs; the elder must be Ashford Cloudsleigh, who was the half brother of Nell's husband, and the younger could only be Nell's stepson, Valerian. Calculating rapidly, she realized that both had been at Nell's wedding. Valerian, only twelve years of age, had been a handsome youth, slim and elegant, and Sibilla, four years his junior, had fallen madly in love.

She blushed as she recalled that the dream lover whose countenance and actions filled the pages of her journal had been modelled after this man, and at that very moment, he turned away from his conversation with his uncle and addressed her.

"I say, you are most quiet for a female," Valerian remarked with arrogant coolness.

Sibilla felt a vast confusion, followed by quick anger. "How absurd," she said smoothly, in her low, melodic voice. "I am sure that your discussion with your uncle concerns topics of national interest, while, as everyone acknowledges, women can speak only on matters of dress, household furnishings, and the disgraceful conduct of servants nowadays."

Ashford laughed at this biting criticism, but Valerian, more vulnerable because of his years, responded bitterly.

"What think you then of the Ecclesiastical Titles Bill? That was our immediate concern."

"Leave be," interjected Ashford, in the deep, rich tones which had brought him fame as an orator in Parliament. "She is just up from the country and cares little for our trivial London problems."

"To the contrary," Sibilla said coolly, her mind struggling to assimilate the information which she had garnered from her reading of the newspapers. "I am dismayed that so many learned men would waste such a prodigious amount of time on such an insignificant matter."

"Bravo!" murmured Ashford, while Valerian said with sarcasm, "Pray tell us what is insignificant about a question which has been debated by Parliament for several months now."

"It is quite obvious," Sibilla replied with a shake of her head. "If the Roman Catholic bishops in England are given territorial titles, as they are in every other country, and if that is illegal, then the matter should be dealt with in the courts. And if it is not illegal, I do not understand why Parliament would be so up in arms about titles, names, mere words on scraps of paper. All of this furor about Papal aggression is absurd. No matter what name he bears, no bishop will be able to raise an army within the country, and as to interference from other nations, what difference is it to them whether the bishops have titles or not. I consider the whole thing a senseless diversion from more important considerations, such as relief for the landowners and the agricultural labourers who are unable to make a profit out of farming because of the strict impositions and the colossal taxes levied upon them."

"'Pon my word, she's remarkable! Astounding! What a clear analysis!" commented Ashford, pulling at his moustache. "I've been trying to convince Valerian of these very points for some time now, but the boy is as obstinate as a block of marble." Valerian, at these words, signed his uncle to be silent.

"You are quite wrong, you know," he said, addressing Sibilla earnestly. "Why the Ecclesiastical Titles Bill—"

"The deuce take it!" exclaimed the macaw stridently, and Sibilla lapsed into helpless giggles at this well-timed remark.

"You see," Valerian said, swiveling towards his uncle, "a woman can never be serious when it's most important. They are only good for—"

"Really, my good chap," Ashford interrupted firmly. Valerian scowled, but Ashford said, with a half-bow towards Sibilla, "You are sure to take in all of the fashionable drawing rooms, having both intelligence and beauty, and a certain *je ne sais quoi*—"

"Beware of Uncle Ashford!" Valerian interjected rudely. "He is well-known as a lady-killer, an unprincipled libertine, a connoisseur of feminine beauty in all of its various forms—"

"Why, really!" cried Lady Cloudsleigh, springing from her seat and standing before the petulant young man, tapping her fan against one hand. "You do your uncle too much justice. Surely you should know there is nothing a woman adores so much as a challenge, and the confirmed bachelor is sure to be the focus of her most ardent attentions, though your uncle is not to be included in that category, since he is such a happily married man." Her voice dripped with sarcasm, and she cast an arch look at Ashford as she said these words. "Now the Marquis of Dower is the prime catch of this Season, and has been for many before it, I wager."

She glanced in his direction, and he looked up startled, from what appeared to be an engrossing conversation with Peggy.

"I thank you for recalling me to the present, Your Ladyship," he said smoothly, rising as he spoke, "for this young Irish temptress," Peggy turned a bright pink, "has so far beguiled me that I have overlooked an important engagement. If you will please excuse me," he bent to kiss Peggy's hand, "I must take my leave of this charming company." He bowed politely to Sibilla and succumbed gracefully to Lady Cloudsleigh's fragrant embrace. "Good day." And with another quick bow on the threshold, he was gone.

"Oh dear," Sibilla said, jumping up from her seat. "I too have lost count of the time. Peggy and I must be going immediately. I have enjoyed myself immensely." She gave Ashford Cloudsleigh her most attractive smile, and nodded faintly to Valerian.

"You must come again, my dear little sister," Nell said fondly, rushing to hug her. "I am at home every Wednesday, and Friday evenings there is always a petit diner after the Opera."

"We shall certainly try to be present," murmured Sibilla conventionally, doubting very much that this would ever be possible.

She and Peggy bid the other gentlemen farewell and exited rapidly. The sun was already setting, and its reddish glow painted the roofs of the houses and shone against the windows so that they seemed to be afire. There was a hustle and bustle in the streets of Londoners hurrying home to dinner, but Sibilla far exceeded their pace in her haste to get back to Corrough House before Aunt Lucy would notice their absence. Although she was breathless from trying to match Sibilla's rapid steps, Peggy endeavoured to discuss Lady Cloudsleigh's guests.

"What think you of the Marquis of Dower?" she gasped, ducking around a lamppost to avoid a collision with a portly gentleman in a bowler hat.

"He's quite handsome, and excessively charming," Sibilla replied, looking back over her shoulder.

"Aye, a very Devil, he is," Peggy sighed. "He talks with the true blarney of the Irish. Oh Sibil, he has promised to take me to the Great Exhibition," she continued, entirely forgetting Roscoe, the groom.

Despite her desperate haste, Sibilla was taken aback by this statement and hesitated a moment. Although Peggy was not quite a servant, neither was she one of the upper classes, and there could be only one role such a girl could play in an aristocrat's life.

"Peggy!" Sibilla exclaimed, her eyes dark with concern. "You must be very careful!"

"Oh, indeed, I shall," Peggy answered insouciantly, her grey eyes dreamy. "You need not worry about me. I can care for myself, I can. It is the Marquis who you should worry about."

Sibilla, paused to answer this flippant remark, thought better of it and continued her progress down the crowded sidewalks.

"What of Mr. Valerian Cloudsleigh?" Peggy called out, running several lengths behind Sibilla.

"Pshaw!" Sibilla replied, not deigning to look back. "He is an arrogant young dandy, spoiled and rude. His uncle is the gentleman of the family."

"Yes, but he must be having an affair," Peggy said wide-eyed, catching up with Sibilla at last, "for did you notice how Lady Cloudsleigh teased him about being a happily married man? Perhaps she is his lover. Lord Cloudsleigh was nowhere in evidence."

"Doubtless he does not enjoy socializing," Sibilla said thoughtfully. "I believe he is a scholar of some sort and works on a book."

"But why were there no other ladies present?" Peggy persisted. "Surely Lady Cloudsleigh has female friends."

"It seemed an informal sort of gathering," said Sibilla, tiring of the subject. "I am sure the gentlemen came to call upon Nell, and as fortune would have it, no women visited her today. Come along, Peggy, Aunt Lucy will be livid if she finds us missing."

FIVE

A Domestic Scene

UNABLE TO AFFORD THE LUXURY of a hackney cab to carry her home, Charlotte Garlinghouse had walked the weary distance back towards her lodgings near Vincent Square. When she passed the gates leading to the dingy courts where the London poor lived, she winced and strode more briskly, which made her the natural target for the cheeky street urchins, who followed her, begging for coppers and taunting her for her air of gentility.

By the time she reached the corner of her street, Charlotte's nerves were sorely frayed and she pondered ruefully the choices that had brought her to her present sorry state. If only, she thought, she had not been so beguiled by the handsome Major Garlinghouse. She recalled poignantly their first meeting at a ball at Holland House. Although much in demand for dances because of her striking looks, her partners always found her singularly lacking in conversation for Charlotte imposed severe standards upon herself and seldom could think of anything to say which met her own strict expectations. She could not respond easily to flattery but always assumed a more serious tone than was required, and knowing nothing of politics or sports, she was completely silent when confronted with these topics.

But Major Garlinghouse, who had been a lieutenant when she met him, was easier to talk to than any man she had ever met. He had whisked her away for a dance, and when she responded with her usual blank stare to his polite flatteries, he had convinced her during a moonlit stroll through the gardens that his compliments were sincere, but that he could understand why a woman with her charm and beauty would be tired of such idle pleasantries. Then he proceeded to tell her of his life and upbringing, as the youngest child of a large Warwickshire family. His older brothers had gone into the church, the diplomatic service and politics, leaving him only the arena of the military where he intended to make his name famous. Charlotte was enthused at the opportunity to encourage an ambitious young man who seemed to need a good woman to stand by his side and encourage him to realize his goals. To all of the other men she had met, she seemed a mere ornament, a useless appendage, but here was a man who needed her, in whose life she could take an active part. She allowed him to kiss her on that moonlit night, near the gently plashing fountain, and henceforward his handsome face and fine figure filled her dreams, both sleeping and waking.

Dudley Garlinghouse pursued her with all of the ardour of a young man in love, appearing the next morning with roses, and squiring her at every ball and soiree throughout the Season. Charlotte's mother was aghast, for Charlotte's most persistent suitor, though good looking, was penniless and had no expectations, but in the face of Charlotte's impassioned pleas and Lieutenant Garlinghouse's earnest protestations of undying devotion, she finally consented and their marriage was celebrated at the end of the Season.

It was perhaps then, faced with the spectacle of Charlotte's six younger sisters occupying the front pew of the church, that Dudley Garlinghouse realized that his wife, though she was the oldest daughter of John Merrell, next in line to the title of Earl of Corrough, would never have any substantial fortune of her own. At any rate, their honeymoon at Bath was miserable.

Charlotte, totally unprepared for her husband's demands, thought him a raving beast, and he, in turn, treated her brutally because of his anger and disappointment. Still, Charlotte was determined to be a good wife and mother and dutifully presented him with young Charlotte, known as Lottie, the first year, and Horace, who would be the Earl of Corrough after her father's death, the following year. But the children drove them farther apart; Lottie was her father's darling, and he spoiled and petted her, ignoring his wife, and she focused all of her pent-up affections upon Horace, who promptly grew into a temperamental brat.

They had not shared the same bed for many years, though Charlotte speculated with hostility that her husband had no difficulty finding others to fill that particular need, for he was still a handsome man, although his blue eyes were often bleary with alcohol and his once trim figure was now showing the signs of excess.

If only that tiresome Captain Wheedle had not appeared on the scene, thought Charlotte with a sigh. He had become close friends with the Major shortly after their marriage, and whenever the Captain called, her husband always left for a night of debauchery that would see him returning home in the wee hours of the morning, singing obscene ditties at the top of his lungs, and rattling the doorknob to Charlotte's room, which was now kept firmly locked.

As she went up the steps to the front door of the house of which they occupied the upper floor, she shuddered, for she heard the raucous shouts and profanities which always accompanied her husband's "discreet card parties." Charlotte turned the key and tiptoed past the door of Mrs. Pritchard, the dour landlady, whom she was certain would turn them out upon the streets in the immediate future.

Lottie, an unusually thin, leggy child with stringy dark hair and pale, grey eyes, was hunched in a bundle at the top of the stairs.

"What are you doing here? Where is your brother?" snapped Mrs. Garlinghouse, who had never forgiven her first-born child for alienating her husband's already wandering affections.

"I do not know, Mama," said Lottie dutifully, rising with awkwardness and hugging her frail body with her thin, brown arms. "I think he is with Papa."

"How dare he!" shrieked Charlotte. "He knows I will not permit that!" She pushed past her daughter, flung open the door which led into the drab, little parlour, and attempted to enter the dining room where the party was taking place but the door was locked.

"Let me in!" Charlotte shouted, pounding on the door with all of her might. "Major Garlinghouse, I insist that you open this door this minute!"

The commotion within subsided for a moment and she heard her husband respond in his slow, drawling voice, "Now you know damn well, Charlotte, that we don't want females bothering us when we're engaged in serious business." She could tell from the slight slur of his words that he had been drinking heavily.

"My son is in there. Send him out!" Charlotte pleaded, continuing to hammer at the door.

"Now, now, Mrs. Garlinghouse. The boy will come to no harm," said an oily voice which Charlotte recognized as that of Captain Wheedle. "It is time for him to learn to be a man instead of a puling sissy." He laughed unpleasantly.

There was a scuffle in the room. Charlotte fancied that she heard a squeak of protest from Horace, and a rumble of several masculine voices. Terrified for her son's safety, Charlotte realized that the other entrance to the dining parlour would not be locked and scrambled through the dark hall, into the small, dirty kitchen, crashing through the swinging service door in a whirlwind of petticoats, tassels, and flounces.

It seemed a scene straight from Hell to Mrs. Garlinghouse's horrified eyes. The tiny room, which was painted a brown colour and windowless, was filled with choking clouds of tobacco smoke, which drifted listlessly beneath the harsh light of the gas lamp. Playing cards, empty glasses, pound notes, and gold guineas lay scattered across the wine-stained linen cloth which covered the square table. Two of the men, who sat opposite each other, Charlotte had never seen before with her husband; the older one, a very unprepossessing man with shocking, bright red hair and a prominent Adam's apple, spoke comfortingly to the younger one, an undersized youth, who rested his head on his hand and stared at the pieces of paper in front of him with dismay. To his right, Captain Wheedle, a ferretlike man with deep-set, hooded eyes, poured the frightened boy another glass of wine and tossed the empty bottle into a pile of discarded bottles on the floor. But Charlotte was most concerned about her son, who sat on his father's lap across from Captain Wheedle, his round face flushed with excitement, his pale eyes watering from the smoke, and his chubby fist clutching a pair of dice which he let slip onto the table as his mother stormed towards him.

"Mama!" he squealed in his high voice. "Papa is teaching me how to play cards." Major Garlinghouse glanced sideways at his wife, amusement in his blue eyes, and a contemptuous smile twisting his mouth.

"How dare you, you Monster!" Charlotte shrieked, snatching at Horace, who in his attempt to avoid her grasp, fell upon the floor and began to wail loudly. She darted around her husband, who laughed and remained seated, but the red-haired man reached Horace first, whisked him from the floor, tossed him into the air a few times until his sobs were stopped by his astonishment, and then handed the boy to his mother.

"Quite sorry to distress you, ma'am," he said in a rough, uncultured voice. "I would not have permitted your son to be present if I had realized it was against your express wishes." He looked down with disgust at his host, who was still chuckling and reaching for another bottle of port. "Mr. Sylver and I will take our leave and," he glanced at both Major Garlinghouse and Captain Wheedle, "settle our financial matters with you gentlemen later."

Charlotte gasped at the name "Sylver" and almost dropped Horace. As she stared with shame and fear, the inebriated youth lifted his head, and she saw that he was indeed one of her cousins. He stared back at her with bleary, blood-shot eyes and nodded wearily.

"I am sh–shorry to meet you in sush an unap–unap–unappealing condishun, Cousin Charlotte," he said with great deliberation.

It had been many years since the Sylver cousins had visited Partridge Park, and this boy had been a mere child at the time of her wedding, but yet she recognized the typical characteristics of the Sylvers—the stocky build, the sandy-coloured hair, the wide mouth and freckled countenance.

She tilted her head to one side studying him. "You must be Randall Sylver," she said slowly.

"Yessh," he replied, looking sadly at the floor and trying to stop the spinning of his head by holding it firmly in both hands. His red-haired companion helped him gently to his feet, placed his coat over his shoulders, and guided him towards the door.

As soon as the door closed behind them, Charlotte turned on her husband, her eyes flashing. "What is the meaning of this outrage?"

she cried. "Have you sunk so low that you lure my cousins to this den of yours and fleece them of their money in my very house? How can I hold up my head in Society after this? What if Uncle Sylvester learns about your little swindle?"

"You are a shrew, Charlotte, my dear," said her husband good-naturedly, draining his glass.

"Not to worry, Mrs. Garlinghouse," Captain Wheedle said in his unctuous voice. "Your uncle, the Earl, will never learn of this particular episode. Young Randall is afraid to let him know the extent of his debts, and I have no doubt that, as always, his good-natured friend, Mr. Dabney Griggs, will foot the bills. He was the mouse which we hoped to catch in our trap today, but he's a cool one, he is. The wealthiest young man in London," he leaned back in his chair and lit a cigar, "and not accepted anywhere because of his antecedents. His father made a fortune speculating in the railroads, but his praiseworthy son has not given away a penny of it to this day. A shame when you consider how well it could be put to use in other places."

Her anger subsiding, Charlotte found herself fighting back tears. "Indeed, I imagine you consider taverns and barmaids more appropriate recipients—" Recalling the presence of her son, she stopped abruptly, and pushing Horace before her, ran from the room. The slam of a door and the clicking of a lock announced that she had once again barricaded herself in her room.

Captain Wheedle looked at his friend with ill-concealed disgust. "You must have been in your cups, Dudley, when you married that skirt," he said coolly.

"Do not torment me, Wheedle," Major Garlinghouse said hoarsely, looking up from an intense contemplation of his empty glass. "I have tried, I swear it, to get rid of her, but no matter whether I beat her or her precious son, refuse to give her housekeeping money or flaunt my other women in her face, she continues to play the role of the martyred wife. I think she is afraid to run back to her stuffy parents and admit that she married a no-good rotter, after having cajoled them to accept me as a son-in-law." He sighed heavily. "And no dowry, to speak of. And no prospects. That whining brat will someday be the Earl of Corrough, and I will have nothing. Nothing!"

He tossed the glass at the wall and watched it splinter upon the floor.

This startling noise brought Lottie, who had been crouched outside the door, running into the room.

"Papa!" she said, throwing her arms around him, and burying her dark head in his lap. "Are you all right, darling Papa?"

The Major, who loved this child with a love that he felt for no other person, became immediately benevolent. For Lottie, he could metamorphose from drunken oblivion to sobriety, from anger to cheerful optimism, from selfish petulance to selfless devotion.

"My angel!" he said softly, caressing her wispy hair. "You must be a brave girl and watch over the house and Mama and Horace, for the Captain and I have business to conduct tonight." Lottie looked up and nodded her head solemnly. "But I promise that when I return I shall have a present for you, my sweet. Would you like that?"

"Oh yes, Papa," said Lottie clearly, "but not so much as I would like to have you at home—and happy."

Captain Wheedle sneered at this innocent sentiment, but Major Garlinghouse, for the first time in his life, felt deeply ashamed.

SIX

The Presentation of Miss Fleet to the Polite World

LADY SIBILLA WAS DEPRESSED. In fact, she was upset. Indeed, she was angry. Yet she stood smiling, her mouth set in a polite imitation of enjoyment, her head nodding stiffly towards the guests as they paraded past into the drawing room.

The occasion was the evening reception at which Miss Lucinda Pleet was presented to Society. The locale was the newly decorated interior of Corrough House, and the characters were the hostess, Mrs. Pleet, her debutante daughter, Lucinda, and the two maidens chosen to be assistants to her debut, the Ladies Sibilla and Sophia Merrell.

Aunt Lucy headed the reception committee, dressed in an evening gown of black velvet, which clung much too tightly to her massive proportions and was much too warm for the unseasonably hot weather. Her fleshy countenance glistened with perspiration, and she tried to relieve her discomfort by waving a large fan of black ostrich feathers, but to no avail.

To her left, stood Lucinda, in the usual white muslin. She was as pale as her gown, and because of the heat her carefully curled coiffure had fallen into lank strands about her plump face. Despite Lucinda's discomfiture, Sibilla had to admire her resolution, for she was polite and even gracious to all of the relatives, young gentlemen, and matrons who expressed their delight at being presented to Miss Pleet.

Sibilla herself twitched with displeasure. Her gown of pale pink, a colour which she detested, was too tight, a problem which Madame Doucette, the dressmaker, had not been able to correct before the reception. Of course, it nicely displayed her tiny waist, but the scanty coverage of her bosom made Sibilla uncomfortable. Aunt Lucy had insisted that Sibilla should pin a lace fichu to the top of the dress, a solution which Sibilla would have eagerly applied if it had been her own idea, but instead she stubbornly refused to do so and accordingly winced under the lecherous gazes of the young swells and dandies.

The natural antagonism between the young girl and Aunt Lucy had only increased with time. The evening upon which Sibilla and Peggy had arrived home late from their clandestine visit to Lady Cloudsleigh had been the opening of the hostilities. Sibilla had been sent to bed without her supper, a method of punishment which extended throughout an entire week, and Peggy had been denied her afternoons off for the duration of their stay in London. Of course, Peggy had paid no heed to these restrictions, and escaped with Roscoe, the groom, to view Madame Tussaud's Waxworks the very next day. Surprisingly, Roscoe was not chastised, but Peggy was threatened with immediate dismissal and subsequently confined to her room. However, Peggy was incorrigible; she should have been upstairs, but Sibilla could see her now, whenever the door to the dining room swung open to admit another guest, demurely pouring glasses of champagne.

Peggy's conduct had not been the only problem of the preceding sennight. Muffin, the nervous fox terrier, had invaded the house one afternoon and bit Mrs. Pleet on the ankle. Sibilla's protests had been so vociferous that Aunt Lucy had not shipped the dogs immediately to Partridge Park as she had planned, but she contrived to have the servants open the garden gate several times a day, in hopes that the creatures would run away. Fortunately, Sibilla's pets were well-trained and remained on the grounds.

Last, but certainly not the least pressing of Sibilla's worries at the moment, was the question of Madame Doucette's bill. The dressmaker had blithely suggested, created, and delivered several elaborate gowns for both Sibilla and Sophy, but her charges were exorbitant, though she seemed content to wait for her payment. Aunt Lucy made no offer to relieve her nieces of this financial obligation, and in desperation, the two sisters had sent a letter to their parents begging for a supplement to the small allowance they had been given on the eve of their departure for London. As yet, there had been no reply.

Despite these catastrophes, Sophy was as cheerful as always. She wore a simple dress of *ciel bleu* which matched her eyes, and she seemed to be enjoying the occasion immensely, fluttering her eyelashes at the older men and giggling delightedly at the compliments of the younger men, in such an ingenuous manner that their wives and mothers were charmed rather than distressed.

Very few of the invited guests had arrived, for an evening reception was not quite so attractive a prospect as the opportunity to feast at a large dinner party or to waltz through one of the glittering ballrooms of a prominent London hostess. It was even rumoured, Peggy had confided earlier to Sibilla, that Lady Cloudsleigh had deliberately chosen to host a spectacular soiree on this particular evening. It seemed, as Aunt Lucy had predicted, that all of London knew of the breach between Lady Cloudsleigh and her family. Sibilla could not decide whether to be angry with her older sister for depriving her of the opportunity to meet such notables as Lord and Lady Palmerston and the Prime Minister, Lord John Russell, or whether to be pleased that Aunt Lucy's ambitious attempt to launch her daughter would be dimmed by the absence of several influential luminosities.

The groups of people drifting in and out of the opulently furnished drawing room were entirely unknown to Lady Sibilla. Dumpy matrons, friends of Mrs. Pleet from her adolescence, greeted her with shrieks of excitement, exclaimed over Lucinda, nodded politely to Sibilla and Sophy, and then headed towards the buffet laid out in the dining room, their gangly, uncomfortable sons and portly husbands trailing behind them. Although the three girls had been standing for several hours, they could not leave their posts, and Sibilla felt as if she would faint from the oppressive heat, the boredom, and the fatigue of being polite to so many uninteresting people. This was not the glamour of the Season which she had envisioned.

Just as she felt that she must excuse herself and go in search of fresh air, a familiar name was pronounced by the small, grey man whom Aunt Lucy had hired as the butler.

"Major and Mrs. Dudley Garlinghouse," the butler said nervously in a high-pitched voice, "and Captain Jared Wheedle."

Sophy's constant smile melted a little, and her blue eyes widened with admiration, as she stared unabashedly at Charlotte's husband, for the Major was in fine form for the occasion, his blond hair falling in graceful, natural waves, his side whiskers and moustache luxuriant, and his eyes, glinting with deviltry and amusement, were complemented precisely by the elegant blue-grey material of his form-fitting coat, which was paired with a rich orange satin waistcoat and tight grey trousers. He greeted Mrs. Pleet warmly, expressing his extreme disappointment that she had not been able to grace the London scene more often, enthused over Lucinda, who he declared would be the Belle of the Season, and turned to Sibilla with an interested gleam in his eye.

"Ah, my adorable younger sister," he said, bending over her proffered hand. Sibilla shivered a little, for he unexpectedly turned her hand over and pressed his lips against her wrist, nicking the flesh slightly with his teeth. This sensuous gesture, which Sibilla reluctantly admitted was highly effective, was certainly not the proper way for a married man to greet his sister-in-law. Watching him perform the same obeisance for Sophy, Sibilla shuddered and was almost unable to meet Charlotte's pathetic grey eyes. In comparison to her richly attired husband, Charlotte seemed a plain brown wren in an old-fashioned gown of a faded maroon colour.

And then there was Captain Wheedle, an odious little man, thought Sibilla. He fussed over Lucinda, who blushed beet-red in response to his extravagant compliments and stuttered as she tried to frame a reply. To Sibilla's great delight, Captain Wheedle stared at her coldly and uttered only the most noncommittal of greetings; she hoped that this change of behaviour was due to his realization that she was not a mere schoolroom miss who would succumb to idle flattery. She failed to understand exactly the distinction which Captain Wheedle drew between her and her cousin; it was a simple criterion—money. Lucinda had it aplenty and he knew the Merrell sisters had none, which was the reason for his equally cool acknowledgment of Lady Sophia.

Charlotte wished to linger talking to her sisters, but her husband took her firmly by the hand and led her towards the dining room, Captain Wheedle following more slowly.

Sibilla, resigned to another endless hour of greeting fat, faceless dowagers, found to her surprise that the next guests, as announced by the spirited butler, were,

"Sylvester, Baron Champford, and Randall Sylver."

She and Sophy both watched eagerly as their cousins greeted Mrs. and Miss Pleet, for they had not seen the two young men for several years, all visits to Partridge Park, with the exception of Charlotte's, having been curtailed after their mother became an invalid.

"Sylvester!" Sibilla called out excitedly, as he turned to her, and she embraced him with more vigour than was suitable according to Aunt Lucy's reproving glance. "I declare you look exactly the same."

"As a boy of twelve, I daresay. You are highly uncomplimentary, dear cousin," replied Sylvester, Baron Champford, holding a monocle to his eye. Despite the severity of his tone, Sibilla recognized the twinkle in his merry, brown eyes.

"Oh, I doubt not that you have acquired additional breadth," Sibilla replied mockingly, surveying his plump figure squeezed into a lemon-yellow coat, plaid trousers, and a brown silk vest, although she knew the apparent heaviness of his form masked formidable strength for her cousin was ranked highly among amateur fighters. "But as for height," she continued, with a mischievous gleam in her dark eyes, "why you are precisely the same."

"Not pretty at all, cousin," Baron Champford responded sorrowfully. "If you do not exhibit a bit more discretion and decorum, you shall return to Sussex a maiden aunt for, I assure you, I am a man of influence about town. If my many followers learn that the latest Beauty of the Season is equipped with a malicious tongue, it shall go badly for you. I warn you."

"Oh, pooh!" Sibilla remarked lightly without a sign of fear. "Your many followers include only your poor brother, Randall, doomed always to lurk in your shadow. Randall, how very wonderful to see you again!"

Randall, a scrawnier, more effete version of his brother, noted more for his skill in scholastics than in pugilistics, turned gratefully toward Sibilla's smiling face, after stumbling over his introduction to Miss Pleet.

"L–l–lord, Sibil, it is good to s–see you again," he said earnestly, with only a trace of the slight stutter which he usually displayed in company. "You have become a raving beauty."

"Nonsense, Randall," Sibilla said fondly, "though I must confess I seem to have little competition tonight." She glanced about contemptuously at the few pink-and-white misses who wandered through the drawing room, usually by the side of their mamas.

"Don't be puffing yourself up, Sibilla, my dear," Baron Champford drawled slowly, turning from his intense scrutiny of Sophy, who was blushing prettily. "Of course there is no one of any consequence here," he went on, despite Aunt Lucy's warning glare in his direction, "not when Lady Cloudsleigh is hosting the most important gathering of the year. You must know, my dear cousin, that Lord John Russell's government is in serious trouble, and all of the Ministers are expected to be there, as well as the more influential Members of Parliament, not to mention their interfering wives. Why women should be allowed to meddle in serious matters such as politics is more than I can understand—" He broke off, discomfited by Sibilla's fierce frown.

"Damn it all, Sibil," he said earnestly, "you must admit you are the weaker sex!"

"The weaker sex!" retorted Sibilla scornfully. "Pshaw! When we bear the children, run the households, educate the future generations of British citizens, while men lounge about occupying their time with going to clubs, hunting, gaming, and an occasional jaunt down to the office or to Parliament to greet old friends."

"Enough said!" Baron Champford answered turning his head to one side as if totally disinterested. "As my friend Valerian has often said, a woman's strength lies in the manipulation and deception of a man, while a man stands on his own merits."

"Valerian!" Sibilla snapped, her eyes flashing. "Mr. Cloudsleigh! That puppy! What does he know of women?"

"Puppy! Really, cousin," Sylvester responded, his fashionably bored air disintegrating beneath her ferocity. "He is the same age as I and, therefore, at least four years your senior. And as for women, I'll wager he has had more in his twenty-two years than either his Uncle Ashford or his father, Lord Cloudsleigh, combined."

Sophy gasped at the impropriety of this remark. Sylvester's brother, Randall, pulled at his arm, saying, "Not at all the thing, to speak like that in front of females, you know."

But Sibilla, undaunted, had just opened her mouth to deliver a scathing reply, when the butler shouted in his squeaky voice:

"Mr. and Mrs. Ashford Cloudsleigh and Mr. Valerian Cloudsleigh."

SEVEN

Lady Sibilla Meets Her Match

As IF HE KNEW INSTINCTIVELY that he had been the topic of discussion, Valerian glanced up at the conversationalists while handing his cane and top hat to the butler. Sophy blushed deeply and turned her head away, but Sibilla met his gaze with determination, her head held high so that she looked down upon him.

"By Jove, she's lovely tonight," said Ashford, nudging his nephew in the ribs. "You must try to be more agreeable to her."

"Who is lovely?" Valerian inquired peevishly, but his uncle was unable to reply, for they had reached the head of the reception line and Aunt Lucy's broad countenance beamed with delight when she saw the influential Member of Parliament and his frail, aristocratic wife.

"Ah, Mrs. Cloudsleigh," said Aunt Lucy, after greeting Ashford profusely, "how very pleasant to see you here. One hears that you have been ill."

"The doctors are of no use whatsoever these days," complained Mrs. Cloudsleigh in her petulant, little-girl voice. "I have been confined to bed for several months at a time, and still they cannot tell me what is wrong." She was a short, frail woman, dressed in a youthful pink tulle gown, swagged with roses and covered with pink net frills. Her silver-blond hair, curled in a profusion of ringlets, her large, opaque, grey eyes, her small, rosebud mouth, and her slight, underdeveloped figure all seemed those of a young girl, but the bitterness in her eyes, the haggard lines in her cheeks, the perpetual pout of that pretty mouth, all betrayed what she was, in truth, a frustrated woman who had retreated into hysteria and invalidism when she discovered that her childhood ideals were illusions.

And her ideal had clearly been Ashford, for her eyes watched him warily as he engaged in polite banter with Sibilla. Ashford was the most handsome of the Cloudsleighs, a handsome family.

Even Lord Cloudsleigh, Nell's husband, who was now nearly fifty, was a distinguished-looking man, with grey streaking his black locks and his dark eyes more compelling than ever because they had sunken slightly. Valerian, with the same combination of dark, curly hair and liquid, dark eyes cut quite a figure about town, reducing the young Society misses to quivering adoration and the young milliners and housemaids to adoring acquiescence if he glanced in their direction. But Ashford, with his air of arrogance and command, in addition to the same dark colouring combined with a more delicate and spiritual face, was clearly the cream of the crop.

Young Caroline Wellton, the only daughter of the much-admired Baron Wellton, a prominent politician, had been secretly in love with him for several years before he arrived one afternoon, hat in hand, to ask her father for her hand in marriage. She was shocked, thinking he had never noticed her, and in truth, he had not, until he realized that he was twenty-eight, that it was high time he found a wife, and that such an alliance would further his blossoming political career. Baron Wellton had gratefully condoned the match, and retired from the political scene, advising his friends and former constituents to apply to Ashford for any favours or advice.

Caroline, trained to be a hostess for her father, was most efficient in organizing gatherings for Ashford, and despite the fact that his wife continuously compared him unfavourably to his father-in-law, Ashford found these parties immensely rewarding. This happy state of affairs did not last more than a year. Gradually, as Caroline discovered that all of the pretty pouting ways and foot-stamping fits of temper that had charmed her father into doing as she pleased served only to irritate rather than charm her husband, she withdrew into perpetual illness. The parties ceased, the honeymoon was over, and Ashford had not entered her bedchamber for several years.

Caroline liked Valerian, who was following her through the reception line, even less. Ashford had been only twelve years old when his nephew was born, and he had watched over the motherless boy carefully, providing him with the companionship and advice his father would not provide, and helping him through the subsequent upheaval when Lord Cloudsleigh remarried Eleanor Merrell. Ashford had always been closer to his nephew than his wife, and it was no secret that Valerian had opposed the marriage to Caroline; he thought she was too weak and conventional a woman for his admirable uncle.

Yet it was Valerian who took her arm comfortingly as they approached Lady Sibilla who was still chatting pleasantly with Ashford.

Mr. Cloudsleigh glanced around, as if lost, and said abruptly, "Oh Lady Sibilla, I should like to present you to my wife, Mrs. Cloudsleigh, and of course my nephew, Valerian, whom you have already met."

Caroline nodded slightly, her curls bobbing, and said sharply, "How can she have met him already? She is just being presented tonight!"

Sibilla looked appealingly at Ashford who responded smoothly, "A chance encounter on Oxford Street. Come along, Caroline, and meet the other Merrell sister, Lady Sophia, I believe."

Sophy curtseyed and smiled demurely as Valerian came up to Sibilla.

"Good evening, Lady Sibilla," he said coolly. Although his voice remained noncommittal, she saw his glance fall towards her bosom and remain there as he said, "It is rather warm in here, is it not?"

"Quite," she said shortly, turning sideways to interrupt his fixed gaze. "I don't believe you have met my sister, Sophia. Sophy, this is Mr. Valerian Cloudsleigh, the son of Lord Cloudsleigh, Nell's husband, you know."

Sophy, who succumbed easily to handsome men, had barely recovered from the shock of meeting Ashford, when she saw Valerian, dressed in a tight-fitting buff jacket with deep brown velvet lapels, and dark mole-coloured trousers.

"Oh!" she gasped, in her soft, breathy voice. "How pleased I am to meet you, Mr. — Mr. Cloudsleigh."

"Ah, fair damsel," responded Valerian, bowing low and pressing a kiss upon her proffered plump, white hand. "You should call me Valerian, for we can be considered related, as your sister is my stepmother."

"Laying it on a bit too thick, old man," commented Baron Champford wryly. He had been standing by during the introductions and now stepped forward to greet his. friend.

"Sylvester!" exclaimed Valerian, welcoming his friend with a firm handclasp. "I thought you would have been at Cloudsleigh House!"

"Going there immediately," Baron Champford responded shortly, "but had to drop by and see how my cousins took on their first night out. Besides, Randall insisted he had to meet someone here on a matter of business." He looked about for his younger brother, whom he finally spotted in a heated discussion with Major Garlinghouse and Captain Wheedle at the end of the room. "Must go and help him out. Doesn't know quite how to handle these characters," he said, thumping Valerian so vigourously on the back before he moved off, that Valerian almost fell upon Sibilla.

The altercation between their cousin Randall and Major Garlinghouse and Captain Wheedle was nearing the point of violence when Baron Champford approached the group, and within a few moments he had extricated the angry, red-faced young man from the argument, which seemed to be one of a financial nature, and ushered him towards the door.

"Why, you have only just arrived!" exclaimed Mrs. Pleet harshly, stepping forward as if to prevent their exit, and waving her black ostrich feathers in an agitated manner.

"So sorry, Aunt Lucy!" Sylvester called out blithely, maintaining the firm grip under which his younger brother squirmed, "but we have other engagements. We will be calling on you shortly." And with a quick bow, the two brothers had vanished into the night.

In the following minutes no other guests arrived and the assembled company seemed restless, so Mrs. Pleet allowed the three girls to circulate, warning them that they must return if there was an onrush of late arrivals.

Lucinda was at a loss when so abruptly severed from the protective custody of her mother, but sympathetic Sophy took her in tow and led her about the room, greeting people here and there. Sibilla paused on the threshold for a moment and studied the new decorations, not quite certain whether they were as ostentatious as she suspected or just not to her taste. Crystal chandeliers and sconces and vases glittered everywhere, casting fitful, bright beams of light which made Sibilla wish to shield her eyes from the brilliance. Mrs. Pleet had chosen a deep plum for the heavy, velvet draperies which were caught back with gold ropes and finished at the top with a pelmet of cherry-coloured velvet. The elaborately carved settees, pushed back against the walls to allow room for the guests, were reupholstered in combinations of lilac, orange, and white, and glass jars containing floral arrangements of the same colours were dotted about upon heavy gilt side tables. An enormous gilded and garlanded mirror hung over the mantel and reflected the kaleidoscope of vibrantly dressed people, riotous colours, and dazzling lights.

Sibilla did not have long to reflect upon these changes however before two young men, Mr. Treswick and Mr. Crampton-Manners, one a barrister and the other an attaché at the embassy, pounced upon her. There was no dancing, for Corrough House did not contain a ballroom, but Sibilla accompanied them on a tour to the sitting room where the dowagers and middle-aged gentlemen sat engrossed in card-playing, and to the dining room where her escorts vied at plying her with cold ham and roast, various jellies, and, especially, champagne.

Peggy chatted eagerly with Sibilla's two companions, although the servants were expected to confine themselves to uttering only the few words necessary to determine whether or not the ladies and gentlemen required more of any of the dishes or beverages. While they stood talking, Sibilla consumed several glasses of champagne and decided that Mr. Treswick looked just like a horse while Mr. Crampton-Manners resembled an owl. She became bored with the conversation, which fluctuated between the problem of properly breaking in a pair of greys which Mr. Crampton-Manners had just purchased and the exploits of Chicken Horton in a boxing match which Mr. Treswick had recently witnessed, and wandered off towards the drawing room.

"That's her, that's the one!" hissed a plump, turbanned matron as Lady Sibilla passed her and her companion, another dowager, in the hall.

Sibilla continued her stroll nonchalantly, although she listened eagerly for the next words.

"You mean she is one of the Merrell sisters?" asked the second woman, the feathers in her coiffure waving in agitation and horror in her voice.

"Indeed she is," confided the first speaker; her fan which concealed her mouth did not hide the excited glitter in her beady eyes. "Her sister, Lady Kitty, vanished—or so they say. I have it on reliable authority, that she is—" Her voice evaporated into a whisper, and though Sibilla strained to hear more she could not distinguish a single, intelligible word.

"Think of that!" declared the second matron, when her friend had finished. "Absolutely shocking! You would not expect a well-bred young girl to descend so low!"

Sibilla stopped with a gasp, and both women glanced at her and then retreated behind their fans. Determined for a moment to run back towards them and shake them firmly until they confessed to whatever they knew about Kitty, Sibilla at length regained her shattered composure and continued on her way, her head held high, but her cheeks flaming red.

She thought to find her sister Sophy and relieve her troubled mind by sharing the disturbing information. But Sophy was unavailable for confidences. She sat on a white brocade sofa in one corner of the drawing room, her gay blue skirts spread around her, the gold bangle on her plump, white wrist glittering as she laughed merrily at a comment made by one of the young men in the group around her. Beside her, Lucinda, her pallor and the colour of her dress matching the white covering of the sofa, sat stiffly, her mouth tensed in a tentative smile, although her brown eyes displayed a spark of animation.

"Oh Sibil, there you are!" exclaimed Sophy earnestly. "You must join us. We are discussing Mr. Ruskin's latest work. This is Mr. Cloudsleigh, as you must remember," Sibilla glanced at Valerian who stood attentively beside her sister, "and his friend, Mr. Griggs." Sophy indicated a tall, awkward, red-haired man. "He has promised to take Lucinda and me for a ride in the Park in his curricle."

"And you shall come also, Lady Sibilla," said Mr. Griggs quickly, in his rough voice, which rang true with tones of sincerity and friendliness.

Sibilla, who felt a pang of annoyance at being included so late in this expedition, was grateful for this conciliatory remark, and flashed her most gracious smile at the young man.

"We were agreeing with Mr. Ruskin that it is the spirit and the nobility of the artist which produces great art," Sophy was saying eagerly, as if reciting a lesson. "For example, the creators of the great Gothic cathedrals who were moved by a yearning towards God."

Sibilla lifted her eyebrows slightly. Sophy had thrown down the copy of Ruskin's work which her older sister was reading, declaring it too stuffy and philosophical for her taste. Valerian misinterpreted her hesitation.

"Obviously, your sister does not feel the same," he said mockingly to Sophia.

"And you are quite right," snapped Sibilla, although previously she had been a devout disciple of the great art critic. "How do intention and morality affect results? A man with every honourable motive may paint a picture designed to elevate the viewer's sense of piety and compassion, and yet if his execution is bad and his subject poorly chosen, it will accomplish nothing, while I am sure, an artist who spends most of his hours pursuing every vice in London, could dash off a painting which, because of its harmony and design, would have an immediately beneficial effect upon whoever saw it." She paused, amazed at this reversal of her former opinions. Why did this odious man always goad her into an argument? She sighed wearily, deciding that she was upset because of the gossip she overheard and was slightly put out at finding Sophy the center of attention.

"Well put, Lady Sibilla," said Mr. Griggs softly. "Not only is that an interesting point, but I think it could be easily proven by a careful study of the lives of the men who we now acknowledge as geniuses."

"Indeed," Sophy added, her blue eyes wide with interest. "I am certain you are right, Mr. Griggs, but pray, give us your examples."

Valerian scowled a little as the red-haired man began his discourse. Sibilla noticing this, realized that he now felt as abandoned as she had.

"I do enjoy reading Mr. Ruskin," she said softly to him as Sophy and Lucinda listened raptly to Mr. Griggs.

"By Jove," Valerian replied with an accent of condescension in his voice, "a female who reads something more than sentimental novels."

"You are the rudest man I have ever met," Sibilla retorted childishly, and stalked out of the room.

The study seemed the only safe retreat, and she was scuttling down the hall towards that haven when the other Mr. Cloudsleigh, Ashford, spotted her, knew that she was in acute distress, and stopped her.

"Lady Sibilla," he said in his rich, well-modulated voice, "what is wrong? Please let me be of assistance. Has someone offended you?"

"Oh, your horrid nephew," Sibilla replied, allowing him to lead her to a bench in the dining room.

"You must make allowances for Valerian," Ashford began. "His mother died shortly after he was born, and he still has not learned how to appreciate women—"

"Oh no," Sibilla interjected. "He doesn't disturb me. It was just that shortly before I heard the most awful gossip—" She paused, and Ashford could see that she was close to tears.

"Gossip, what gossip?" he inquired gently.

"Oh, it is too dreadful," Sibilla said, her words coming in choppy phrases rather than her usual fluent sentences. "These two, fat, old women—and I could not hear what they said—how unfair for them to judge me by something I did not do—or to judge Kitty for that matter—and why won't anyone tell me?—what can Kitty have done that would be so dreadful—and everyone knows, even Nell, and—just everyone—my sister—and I cannot find her."

She bent her head and stared at the pink skirt of her gown, struggling to maintain some composure.

"I am sorry, I could not hear all of what you said," Ashford was saying, his voice coming to her from a long distance. "Who is it that you cannot find?"

"Kitty, my sister," Sibilla said simply, raising her eyes to meet his, teardrops sparkling in her long lashes.

Ashford started back for a moment, and his eyes became wary and opaque as he replied in a strained voice, "Ah yes, I remember your sister, Kitty. She was the Belle of the Season several years past."

"You did not hear that she vanished mysteriously?" Sibilla questioned him. "For it seems all of London knows, and furthermore they know where she is or what she is now."

It was several minutes before Ashford could reply, but at last he said stiffly, "No, I had not heard. But I swear to you, Lady Sibilla, by all that is dear to me, that I will find your sister for you."

There was a sudden scream from the living room, followed by several shrieks, the splatter of broken glass, and the thud of overturned furniture. No sooner had Sibilla jumped to her feet than she was promptly knocked down again by Oscar, her pet wolfhound, who bounded into the room and threw himself upon her lovingly, followed closely by Muffin and Slow.

"Oh dear," said Sibilla weakly, and her amused look slowly widened into an irresistible grin. "Oh dear," she said again, as Aunt Lucy's forbidding black bulk filled the doorway to the dining room, while the heads of the other startled guests appeared over those massive shoulders. Slow, the retriever, settled himself at Sibilla's feet, but Oscar, irrepressible Oscar, had strolled over towards the sideboard and was gulping down several cutlets.

"Remove those beasts from my house!" Aunt Lucy said in a voice as cold and strong as steel. Sibilla, trying to drag Oscar away from his unexpected banquet, found that she was being helped by Valerian, who was able to control the massive animal, while Sibilla rounded up the skittish Muffin and the obedient Slow.

"I don't know how they got in," apologized Sibilla, as they led the dogs down a hallway lined with staring guests, towards the back of the house. "They did not come through the kitchen, for I was in the dining room, and they would have had to pass me. But there is a door to the garden off the study, which was not supposed to be open tonight."

Valerian nodded, struggling with Oscar, who was angry at having been disturbed at his meal and then being mishandled by a total stranger. "Whose dogs are these?" he asked, as Sibilla passed through the door to the study.

"Mine," she responded quickly, noticing with perplexity that the french windows at the far end of the room stood open.

"I had no idea you liked animals," Valerian was saying, struggling to form his words while he tugged at Oscar, who had braced his legs against the threshold to the garden. "Why, I have a menagerie you should meet: two parrots, three macaws, a clutter of guinea pigs, two foxes, a few pheasants—" He broke off abruptly as Oscar changed his mind and went racing into the garden. Sibilla who had preceded him and was stooping to scold Muffin and Slow, looked up to see Oscar speed by her.

With a gasp, Sibilla realized why the dogs had been able to enter the house, for on a garden bench, in full view by the light spilling from the study, was Peggy, still in her dark silk dress and stiffly starched apron, but her frilly cap had come loose and her rich, dark curls spilled over her shoulders and hid the man who held her in a passionate embrace. As Oscar, with a gruff bark, bounced upon the couple, the man looked up and Sibilla recognized him as the Marquis of Dower.

"Confound it, Val," said the Marquis to his friend. "Can't you see when you are not wanted."

Valerian chuckled, and drew Sibilla back into the study, closing the french windows behind them. She was flushed, partially worried about Peggy, and embarrassed at having witnessed such an intimate scene in the company of a strange man. Valerian stopped her as she headed quickly for the door by stepping into her path so that she collided fully into him. When she tried to move to one side, he held her by the wrist with one hand and used the other to tilt her face up to his, noting the rosy flush in her cheeks and the depth of expression in her liquid, dark eyes.

"They set a very good example, don't you think?" he asked softly, and before Sibilla could reply, bent his lips to hers, gradually drawing her into a full embrace, to which, to her horror, she responded. Because her knees became weak and her legs began to tremble, she put her arms about his shoulders to prevent herself from falling, and then discovered that his kisses, which were interrupted by throaty mutters about her beauty and her softness, were so sweet she pressed against him, begging for more.

At this moment, Aunt Lucy flung open the partially closed door to the study.

EIGHT

At a Soiree in Berkeley Square

EVERYONE WAS THERE. A long line of carriages impeded traffic for several blocks as they waited to turn into the gravel drive before Cloudsleigh House, emitting their perfumed, polished and bejewelled occupants before the broad stone steps. An attendant in Lord Cloudsleigh's livery of black and coral helped the ladies down from the carriage steps and escorted them up the black carpet which led to the open ebony-coloured door.

"A black carpet!" shrieked one lady guest. "How clever! How daring! How like Nell!"

Within, the crystal chandeliers glittered upon the black-and-white marble tile. A little black page in a coral uniform flashed his white teeth as he scampered back and forth to a cloakroom carrying the coats, capes, canes, mantles, and hats divested from the guests by a pretty housemaid in a black silk dress. Several rooms had been thrown open for the large party: the formal ivory salon; and the darker, exotic drawing room; along with the austere library where Lord Cloudsleigh spent most of his days; the conservatory, warm and humid with the odours and atmosphere of hundreds of tropical plants, especially ferns; a smoking room and a card-playing room had been set aside; and all the doors were open from the conservatory onto the marble terrace, lit by torches, which led down into the fragrant gardens.

The most important and influential people in London were all present. The Prime Minister, Lord John Russell, Lord Palmerston, and other Cabinet members, as well as many of the significant Whig politicians, were in conference in the smoking room, for the Government was in danger of defeat as a result of the furor over the Budget and a low vote in their favour on the County Franchise Bill. Lady Palmerston had rallied a group of women in the salon and was leading a spirited discussion of the same problems, for while women were forced to remain inactive because of their gender, well-informed ladies managed to expend considerable amounts of energy and exert considerable influence upon the men in their lives by their passionate involvement in politics and philanthropy. Wherever the government and social conditions were not being discussed, the topic of conversation was likely to be art, music, or literature, for Lady Cloudsleigh did not like simpering debutantes and their meddling mothers but preferred to invite an older crowd of people and introduce them to the latest rage in poetry or portraiture.

Tonight, she was championing Mr. Lanning Tombs, the poet, whom she led through the rooms with one small hand tightly grasping his bony wrist. He looked appropriately decadent and romantic in a black velvet jacket and trousers, which illuminated the deathly pallor of his skin and heightened the eerie effect of the glitter in his sunken, dark eyes. And he spoke like a poet also, in quick, staccato bursts of words, tripping on his own phrases in his haste to express his unconventional ideas.

Some of the ladies present were terrified of him and the sharp judgment in those flaming eyes; others felt faint in the presence of so much intensity and envied Lady Cloudsleigh's proprietary hold on this alien and exciting individual; while a third group speculated cynically on whether or not Nell's husband knew that he was being cuckolded.

Lord Cloudsleigh spent most of the evening in the library, where he felt most comfortable, surrounded by the walls of books which nourished him throughout the lonely days. A few old friends and young scholars who knew him by reputation sought him out and engaged in heated discussions of the baron's classification system for Filicineae. Few women glanced at him, although he was a distinguished man, with the waves of white in his thick, dark hair, and his alert, black eyes, but the Baron Cloudsleigh was used to this phenomenon.

One of the women who did seek him out, Caroline Wellton Cloudsleigh, the wife of his younger brother, was welcomed warmly, for she was always gentle and considerate of Lord Cloudsleigh. He did not know that her concern was motivated by her dislike of his second wife, and that during the time she spent inquiring about the progress of his latest essay or the book that had been twenty years in the writing, she was actually aching to inform him of his wife's latest infidelity.

While she chatted brightly with the Baron, her husband, Ashford, joined the group of solemn men in the smoking room and did not re-emerge for some time. Caroline, having finished with being gracious to Lord Cloudsleigh, looked about for an escort; she felt incapable of meeting the beautiful and ambitious women of the soiree without her hand on the arm of a strong, capable man. She guessed that Ashford was closeted with the politicians and searched instead for Valerian, whom she finally located in the bizarre little drawing room which Caroline considered disgusting, if not because of the appalling colours and odd curios, then for the obscenities of the macaw that was one of the conversation pieces of Lady Cloudsleigh's parties.

To Caroline's dismay, Valerian was engrossed in conversation with an incredibly lovely young woman with striking auburn hair and wide, green eyes, dressed in a simple yet dramatic gown of mint-green and wearing an exquisite necklace of emeralds which gleamed against the ivory of her skin. Mrs. Cloudsleigh squinted her eyes and stared at her; there was something familiar about this woman, but she could not place her, and hesitantly approached Valerian.

"Valerian!" she called out in her childlike voice as she neared him. "Ashford has abandoned me, and I feel so all alone."

Valerian turned, started, turned back to his companion and whispered a few words, and then met Caroline with his arm extended for her small, greedy hand.

"Mrs. Cloudsleigh," he said formally. "I would like to present to you Mrs. Meadows."

The beautiful young woman inclined her lovely head and said in a passionate, bell-like voice, "I am delighted to meet you, Mrs. Cloudsleigh. I have heard so much good of your husband, and of your father, Baron Wellton." There was an undercurrent in her voice; Caroline could not decide if it was mockery or amusement. Valerian and Mrs. Meadows exchanged quick glances, which made Caroline feel as if she was left out of a private joke.

"I am equally pleased," she said uncertainly. "Valerian, I am dying of thirst. Pray accompany me to the dining room to procure some refreshments?"

"Of course," Valerian said smoothly, turning to Mrs. Meadows, whom Caroline was staunchly ignoring and inquiring if she would like something.

"How thoughtful!" replied the young lady, her large green eyes dancing with delight. "If you could find a glass of sherry for me, Mr. Cloudsleigh." She underscored the last two words dramatically. Caroline wondered if this woman was one of Valerian's lights-of-love, for she spoke as if she was well-acquainted with him.

"Certainly, Mrs. Meadows," he replied, with the same peculiar emphasis, and walked off with Caroline clinging to his arm.

"Who is she, Valerian?" she asked petulantly, as they entered the dining room, a vibrant chamber with its cherry-red striped paper and portraits of Cloudsleighs past and present hung upon the walls.

"Oh, a young widow," her nephew replied lightly, handing her a glass of lemonade, for Caroline was a teetotaler declaring that alcohol hastened old age. "Can you imagine, she is only twenty-one and has to support herself and two small children?" He asked one of the many attendants to bring him two glasses of sherry.

"How dreadful," said Mrs. Cloudsleigh vaguely, staring into her glass. "How does she manage?"

No sooner were these words past her lips than Caroline wished to have them back, for although Valerian answered calmly that Mrs.

Meadows gave singing lessons and taught piano, the gleam in his eyes betrayed that this woman was one of the notorious London courtesans. So she was one of Valerian's amours, she thought rapidly, and then, how shocking that Lady Cloudsleigh would permit such a woman at one of her exclusive gatherings, although it was quite like Lady Cloudsleigh to encourage unconventionality.

"I feel faint, Valerian," she declared suddenly. "I believe I will find the dressing room and lie down for a few minutes."

"An excellent idea," her nephew agreed glibly as a waiter approached with the two crystal glasses of sherry. He quickly reentered the drawing room, only to find his fair companion was deep in a laughing conversation with his friend, the Marquis of Dower.

"Oh Valerian!" she exclaimed, as he drew near. "You have brought me the sherry." She extended a long, delicate hand for the glass and sipped at it while Valerian glowered at Edward.

"Ned," he said brusquely. "I thought you were well-occupied."

"I was well-occupied!" laughed the Marquis of Dower, shaking his dark, curly hair out of his eyes. "My good fellow, you were doing as well as I. You must remember that the lights were on in the study and the windows uncurtained. We had a fine view."

Valerian scowled at this, and refused to explain when Mrs. Meadows teasingly tried to draw him out. The Marquis of Dower eagerly launched into an explanation, but Valerian cut him short, warning him that his own conduct was as open to reproach.

In the midst of this agreeable disagreement, Baron Champford and Randall Sylver appeared.

"Why, I believe I've seen you recently!" Baron Champford exclaimed, holding his monocle to his eye and examining Valerian. Valerian frowned and downed his sherry with one gulp.

"We stopped by Corrough House to meet the latest heiress to be placed upon the London marriage market," he explained to Mrs. Meadows apologetically. She looked puzzled and inclined her head to one side so that her auburn ringlets fell upon one creamy white shoulder. "I refer to Miss Lucinda Pleet," Valerian continued, "a singularly unprepossessing young woman, although with her fortune she should not have to worry about receiving a suitable offer, despite the dragon of a mother who guards her."

"If the mother comes with the daughter," Baron Champford offered jestingly, "the price might have to be much higher before any man of sound mind would venture into that arena."

"I need more sherry," said Valerian abruptly, and left as quickly. He encountered his uncle in his journey back to the dining room, and said urgently, "Caroline is lying down in the dressing room, and she is in the dark drawing room."

Ashford nodded, patted Valerian on the back, and was about to continue down the hall, when he turned back, pulling Valerian by his coattails.

"What was that altercation in the study?" he inquired with an amused glint in his dark eyes.

"Oh that!" muttered Valerian. "I merely helped Lady Sibilla take her dogs back into the garden, and her aunt burst in upon us and declared that I was molesting her niece."

"The point is, were you or were you not?" asked Ashford. "I tell you, she's a deuced fine girl, almost as fine as my lady, and if you do not take advantage of that situation, you are not a Cloudsleigh."

"I suppose by her aunt's standards, I was out of line," Valerian remarked offhandedly. "I merely kissed the girl. And she seemed to like it. But I know not why you try to push her upon me. She's a little spitfire; for a country wench in London for the first time, she pretends to know a lot, but her opinions are—"

"Surprisingly well-informed," laughed Ashford, shaking his head. "I suppose she is a bit too clever for you. You prefer the meek, agreeable ones."

"Uncle Ashford—" began Valerian, but Ashford cut him off, smiling and waving his hand to indicate that he wanted to be on his way, a way that led him down the hall to the curious drawing room where he found Mrs. Meadows still surrounded by the Marquis of Dower and the two Sylver brothers. But as soon as he entered the room, she looked up, sensing his presence, and her face glowed with radiance as she extended her hand to him. Ashford crossed the room rapidly, and kissed her palm softly, before saying in a low voice, "Mrs. Meadows, how beautiful you are tonight!"

"Why, Mr. Cloudsleigh, how kind of you to say so," she replied in her sensuously warm voice. The attraction between the two was so palpable that the younger men retreated unconsciously and finally turned and fled with polite bows and murmured good-bys.

"It is very warm in here, is it not?" remarked Mrs. Meadows pleasantly, smiling up at Ashford with undisguised affection. The fire in the black marble fireplace was lit as usual, and the room was suffocatingly close from the throngs of people which filled it.

"I agree. A walk in the gardens is prescribed," replied Ashford, but the usual smoothness of his voice was tempered with a hoarse urgency, and he could not resist putting his hand upon her slender waist as they passed through the guests on their way to the coolness of the gardens.

Much later when they returned and stood on the terrace, uncertain whether to separate or enter the drawing room together, Lady Cloudsleigh, in a white satin gown liberally sewn with pearls, her poet trailing behind her, found them and exclaimed, "Good Lord, Ashford! I thought you of all men would have better sense. Your wife has been wandering about asking everyone if they have seen you." She paused dramatically, then beckoned to Ashford with a hand sparkling with diamond rings. "Come with me, and I will tell Caroline that I extricated you with difficulty from a political discussion, and you—" she said turning to the lovely woman, whose green eyes had grown sad, "wait here for Valerian. Lanning, find him for me, please, my sweet, the young man in the buff jacket who is flirting with Lady Calverley's daughter, and bring him out here for—Mrs. Meadows."

With a quick kiss upon her slender, cool hand, Ashford was gone, and the young woman leaned against the cold marble of the terrace balcony and stared off into the dimness of the gardens from which came the suppressed giggles and low whispers of other revellers.

"Gracious lady," said a low, male voice at her shoulder, and she whirled about, only to laugh at the sight of Valerian.

"How you frightened me!" she exclaimed with feigned displeasure, but her rueful smile belied her words.

"Beautiful one, you torment me!" Valerian responded, and there was more than the conventional tones of flattery in his voice.

"How can it be otherwise?" she said simply, and allowed him to lead her into the conservatory and thence into the salon, where Mr.

Ashford Cloudsleigh and his wife were conversing politely with an aged, gouty landowner and peer. She did not even permit herself to look in his direction, but clutching Valerian's arm more firmly, took up the flippant tone she always used with him. "Flirting with Lady Calverley's daughter? Really, Valerian. You know that silly girl thinks every compliment is a declaration. You shall be married off before you know it."

NINE

Mrs. Pleet's Strategy

THE RECEPTION WAS OVER. The last guest had departed hours ago, promising to call within a sennight.

The overworked household staff laboured to collect all of the soiled dishes and retrieve the pieces of broken crystal scattered about the rooms. The energetic butler consumed glass after glass of port in the kitchen while the cook joined him in both his consumption and commiseration about the overbearing strictness of their mistress.

Lucinda, glowing with a sort of triumph, had been ushered upstairs and undressed by her newly acquired personal maid, Susan, and had fallen immediately into a deep sleep. Sophy, also flushed with the excitement of the evening, had been led to her room by a slightly intoxicated Peggy and had drifted off rapturously into slumber, Marmalade clasped in her arms. The renegade, Sibilla, had been permitted to finish off the evening after her unfortunate, nay, unforgivable lapse, and yet despite this horrendous faux pas, she too slept soundly, perhaps because of the quantities of champagne which she had consumed.

But Aunt Lucy, sitting bolt upright in her favourite armchair in the study, remained awake and alert, sipping at her usual nightly glass of sherry and reviewing the evening's skirmishes with ponderous deliberation. Although there were certain facts she refused to face, notably the insurmountable barrier between the mercantile and aristocratic classes, she did not avoid the unpleasant thought that her precious daughter, Lucinda, was not such a valuable commodity upon the marriage market as her penniless cousins. Mrs. Pleet had already acted to correct this deficiency in interest by spreading the word that Lucinda was heiress to a substantial fortune through several channels which she knew would disperse that information in a highly efficient and effective manner. But that might mean that only fortune hunters would pursue her daughter, while the desirable young men would continue to congregate about Ladies Sibilla and Sophia, attracted by their superior personal charms. Something must be done, and Aunt Lucy envisioned a future in which both sisters were either married or securely engaged.

She carefully surveyed the gentlemen who had been present at the reception. Captain Wheedle, who had paid Lucinda an inordinate amount of attention, was an adventurer, she decided, although she had put out subtle inquiries as to his financial situation which she hoped would bear fruit in the near future.

Mr. Dabney Griggs, that red-haired interloper, who had not been invited but had come along with the Marquis of Dower, was a wealthy man, she knew, but clearly not the one for her daughter, for he had no breeding, which his speech, his dress, and his manner revealed — and worse, no title. However, he remained an excellent prospect for either Sibilla or Sophia. He seemed a forthright, earnest young man, and she was certain that he would offer for a girl who had been placed in a compromising situation with him. This could be arranged.

But for Lucinda, neither Baron Champford nor his brother would do, for they were first cousins, although they might be able to introduce Lucinda to someone suitable. She had heard, however, that they belonged to a select circle which included Mr. Valerian Cloudsleigh and the Marquis of Dower. And, a small smile of satisfaction came to her face, either of these would do.

Valerian Cloudsleigh, after the death of his grandfather would be Baron Cloudsleigh, and after the death of his father, the Marquis of Merryfield. But the Marquis of Dower was an even more delightful prospect, known as the handsomest man in London, already the possessor of his late father's enormous Irish estates and equally ample income, and the most sought after bachelor for the last several Seasons. Yes, these were the two men she would consider for Lucinda, and if they did not consider Lucinda, she would have to insure that some event occurred that would force them to that consideration.

Having settled this problem, her restless mind returned to Sibilla and Sophia. How she wished she had not offered to present them along with her daughter, but there was no use in regretting an action already taken, especially an action which had given them the prestigious Upper Grosvenor Street address.

Sibilla, after her shocking display of insubordinacy this evening, must be the first to be married. Since Dabney Griggs was clearly available, he would have to offer for Sibilla. Sophia was much more manageable, and Aunt Lucy was certain that she could keep a careful eye on her, once Sibilla was safely taken out of her hands, although she would have to restrict her contact with Valerian Cloudsleigh, for Sophia had flirted with him shamelessly—before he had been discovered kissing her sister.

Luckily, no one knew of this episode, except perhaps his uncle, Ashford Cloudsleigh, who had ventured into the study while Mrs. Pleet was castigating the guilty parties. But Aunt Lucy counted upon the well-known politician to be discreet, for he had removed his nephew from the reception with promptitude. Unfortunately, this had meant that he and his lovely wife, Caroline, had also departed, and they had been Mrs. Pleet's most noteworthy guests.

With perhaps the exception of the Marquis of Dower. He had arrived shortly after the girls had been relieved of their receiving duties, a circumstance which Aunt Lucy now bitterly regretted, had made the round of the drawing room dazzling the greedy matrons and their eager daughters, had stepped into the dining room for a glass of champagne, and then disappeared. Lucinda had been commanded to stand by her mother's side and was there when he reappeared, but unfortunately he did not even glance in her direction as he made his farewells to the hostess. Ah well, thought Aunt Lucy, if the two Sylver brothers and Valerian Cloudsleigh could be encouraged to call, perhaps they would bring the Marquis of Dower along with them.

Aunt Lucy smiled again, a tight, smug smile of satisfaction, and poured herself another glass of sherry. Then her eyebrows knitted together as she recalled the other major catastrophe of the evening. The Merrell family would be the death of her, she declared silently. For Major Garlinghouse had been discovered by his own wife, of all people, fondling the eldest of the Holly girls on the sofa in the back sitting room. Charlotte had gone into hysterics, which Sibilla had calmed, and Lavinia Holly, that sly, sour-faced minx, had claimed that Major Garlinghouse told her that he was a surgeon and could advise her about the pain she had been experiencing in her legs if he examined her, whereupon they had retired to the privacy of the back room. She had been hurried from the reception by her mother, Lady Holly, along with her two equally unattractive younger sisters. But the ploy was a good one. If the major had been anything but a married man, Lady Holly could doubtlessly have convinced him to offer for Lavinia under such provocation. Perhaps something similar could occur to Sibilla and Dabney Griggs.

As for herself—Mrs. Pleet smiled again, finishing off the sherry, a smile barely recognizable as such in the bulk of her face. The Retired Admiral, George Crank, had paid her much attention, trotting back and forth obediently with glasses of champagne. Of course, he had an only child, Mary, whom he must present since her mother had died many years before, and Mary would benefit by association with Lucinda, for she was an incredibly plain and awkward girl. But if Admiral Crank had other ideas, Mrs. Pleet chuckled to herself, he might as well forget them—although it would be pleasant to have him standing attendance upon her at parties—for she had vowed never to marry again, not after suffering the indignities which Mr. Pleet had pressed upon her in order to produce Lucinda, the one and only heir to his flesh and fortune.

Thinking of this, Aunt Lucy's mind turned again to the scene which she had interrupted in the library. Sibilla had actually seemed to be enjoying Valerian's advances. Hot-blooded wanton.

No doubt this was the way her mother had ensnared the Earl of Corrough. But such a strategy would do Sibilla little good with such a man as Valerian Cloudsleigh. Mrs. Pleet had heard that although he was only twenty-two he had already acquired and discarded a string of mistresses. No, Sibilla would have to look back at that little escapade with either regret or nostalgia after she became Mrs. Dabney Griggs.

Aunt Lucy brought her sturdy fist down upon the surface of the mahogany desk before her, and the resounding thump which bounced back from the walls of the chamber reassured her. She was still in control. She lifted herself ponderously and prepared to retire for the night.

TEN

The Little Brittles at Home

LADY SIBILLA PACED about the confines of her dim, blue bedroom. She had pulled aside the heavy velvet draperies earlier in the day, but it was raining and only a grim, grey light penetrated through the small casement. The fact that Oscar, who had been smuggled upstairs by Peggy, matched her step by step, only irritated her today, and she pushed him aside roughly and bade him to sit down while she tried to compose herself.

Six days had passed since the reception, and many of the guests had called, among them Sylvester and Randall Sylver, the Marquis of Dower, Mr. Valerian Cloudsleigh, Mr. Dabney Griggs, Major Garlinghouse and Captain Wheedle, Mr. Treswick and Mr. Crampton-Manners, Mrs. Ashford Cloudsleigh, Lady Holly and her daughters, Miss Mary Crank, and a score of others. Throughout this social onslaught Lady Sibilla remained confined to her quarters.

Sophy rushed up after each of these visitors had departed and shared all of her observations with her sister — how dashing Valerian looked in a grey jacket with black lapels; how the Marquis of Dower thought she looked "exquisite" in her new morning dress; how Dabney Griggs repeated his offer to take her and Lucinda for a ride in his curricle on the first fine day; how Mr. Treswick had spilled tea all over his new blue satin vest; how Major Garlinghouse had called at the same time as the Hollys, and Lady Holly had hurried Lavinia out of the drawing room with a most peculiar expression on her face. But none of these anecdotes seemed to comfort Sibilla in her enforced exile. She longed to interrupt Sophy's facile flow of conversation to discover if any of the callers had inquired after her, but Sophy rattled on and on about the bouquet of violets which Captain Wheedle had brought Lucinda, and the lovely bottle-green walking costume which Mrs. Cloudsleigh had worn.

It was now four in the afternoon of the sixth day and Sibilla pictured the scene in the drawing room: Aunt Lucy in one of her splendid black silk mourning costumes, presiding over the silver tea service, and taking in every nuance of expression and undertone of conversation; Lucinda, sitting stiffly on a sofa beside her mother, in another of her plain, pale dresses, with a timid smile set on her lips; and Sophy, the spark of warmth in the picture, with her gaily coloured gowns and her amiable manners.

The missing element, Sibilla, glared at the walls which confined her, frowned at her journal which bulged with the confidences she had added since the reception, scowled at her sketches which lay scattered upon the faded counterpane, and then leaned her head against the cool glass of the window.

What could she do? While she remained under Aunt Lucy's roof she was bound to obey the rules of the house, rules which would always force her and Sophy into the background as the poor relations, the same rules which had dictated that the reception was to be considered the presentation of Miss Pleet to Society, while Sibilla and Sophia were introduced as her friends. They were subtle distinctions, Lucinda's white gown contrasted with the pastel dresses of her two cousins, but clear enough to the circles in which Aunt Lucy moved. The majority of the guests had been cordial to the two Merrell sisters and effusive about Lucinda.

Sibilla reflected with despair upon the years she had spent at Partridge Park, filling the idle hours reading aloud to her mama or designing a new embroidery pattern for Sophy or riding in the woods with Oscar loping behind her. A visit from a neighbour, a letter from Charlotte or Amy, a new book borrowed from a friend, these had been the bright points in a succession of slow, placid days. And yet, here she was in London, the starting point of all her dreams, and she was imprisoned in this dreary house, guarded by her odiously vulgar aunt, and unable to venture out into the exciting world beyond the doorstep. That one brief foray to Cloudsleigh House had been sufficient illustration of what she was missing: the startling, lovely rooms filled with works of art, the company of cultured people, and the stimulating conversation.

She stalked around the room once more, considering her alternatives. She could flee to Nell's house, but this transgression would be promptly reported to her parents and she knew they would descend upon London immediately and carry her back home. From Peggy's description of the Garlinghouses' abode and judging by Charlotte's strange behaviour, she could find no refuge there. This left Amy. Sibilla knew that Amy's husband was a minister, that he considered his mission to be among the poor, and she realized that Amy never mentioned parties or guests in her letters. Still, it might be possible for Sibilla to lodge with them for a while until she hit upon a more likely scheme which would enable her to live the life she desired.

Without a moment's hesitation, Sibilla threw open the door to her room, asked the maid dusting the tables in the hall to summon Peggy, and dressed herself for a walk. To her dismay, Peggy did not approve of this notion and told her so soundly.

"Sure, and you cannot go there," she said flatly. "Why, faith! and they live right in the heart of the Holy Land. No gently burred female would venture near there, not even in the brightness of day, not even if accompanied by three gentlemen."

"It cannot be that dangerous," Sibilla replied with a tone of uncertainty in her soft voice. "And what do you mean by the Holy Land?"

"Dangerous and disreputable," responded Peggy with her hands on her hips. "It's a breeding ground for curriminals and a lurruking place for every thief and pickpocket in the city, a section of little hovels, on narrow, darruk streets—"

"How do you know this?" Sibilla interrupted curtly.

"I visited Amy several days past, I did," Peggy said in a prim tight voice, unlike her usual cheerful tones. "I wished to see how she was."

Sibilla was abashed. She had been in town for nearly a fortnight and she had not even sent a note to her elder sister.

"And how was she?" she inquired softly.

"I would think overworked," replied Peggy, with the same curiously restrained expression, "except she seems so utterly happy."

Sibilla smoothed down the flounces on her pale blue walking costume thoughtfully, finally looking up at Peggy with solemnity. "I should dearly love to visit her," she said. "Don't you think we can find a man to accompany us?"

As Peggy considered this suggestion, a few dimples appeared beside her pretty mouth, and she offered meekly, "Perhaps Roscoe might do."

"Roscoe?"

"Yes, the groom," Peggy laughed lightly. "He has been upset with me of late, but I think he cannot turn down this errand. I'll be back in a moment." And with a quick rustle of silk skirts, she was gone.

Roscoe's answer was affirmative, although Sibilla sensed that there was a marked constraint between him and Peggy as they proceeded through the deserted streets. The rain had stopped for a short time, but few of the city dwellers had ventured out, and the skies above, swollen with dark clouds, threatened another downpour. The trio passed through Mayfair rapidly, and were soon in an area of small, dingy houses set on narrow, dirty streets, in which every now and then, the dark opening of a small courtyard appeared. Peggy headed through one of these apertures suddenly, and Sibilla and Roscoe, endeavouring to overtake her, found it difficult to make their way through the twisted labyrinth of small, dark passages.

The houses were old, seeming as if they would crumble at the slightest touch, and in pitiful condition. Doors were falling from their hinges, door posts were worm eaten, and broken windows were stuffed with straw and old hats to keep the little precious warmth inside. Women, with bloated faces and haggard eyes, loitered in the doorways, while ragged children played among the heaps of garbage and the stagnant water in the gutters. A few seedy-looking men, one with a florid complexion and a patched coat, studied her insolently, and she tried to hurry along, but her steps were slow in her effort to keep her skirts out of the mud and filth.

The sight of Peggy's dark, curly head, peeking out from the dimness of a small, ramshackle dwelling, was a cheerful promise that their pilgrimage had come to an end, and Sibilla and Roscoe scurried through the door with relief.

But the interior was a shock to Sibilla and she stopped on the threshold, trying to hide the telltale signs of horror and amazement which she knew must show on her countenance.

Amy and her family lived in the most abject poverty, or so it seemed to Sibilla's eyes. She did not realize that few of the dwellings she had just passed could boast such comforts as clean, white-washed walls, a few scraps of worn Turkey carpet on the floor, and the small, bright fire which burned in the grate. The dim room was thronged with people, most of them children. Sibilla had time to observe a dark-haired girl dandling a baby boy; another girl, slightly younger, industriously polishing the one wooden table; a fair-haired infant lying on a mattress, watched over by a decrepit crone; and a group of five children huddled about another old hag who was reading aloud from a Bible, before her older sister, her stomach swollen with yet another addition to the already overpopulated Brittle family, scurried out of the rear doorway and swooped down upon her.

"Sibilla, my angel," Amy cried out soothingly as she gathered Sibilla into her arms. Caught in that loving embrace, Sibilla remembered the days of her early childhood, when Amy cared for her and Sophy as tenderly as any mother. Tears came to her eyes and she found herself saying, "Oh Amy, what a lovely family!"

Amy did not find anything remarkable in this comment. She beamed upon Sibilla and then commanding the attention of the occupants of the room, rattled off their names. Beside the little Brittles, Rebecca, Rachel, Jacob, Susannah, Joshua, and Job, Amy introduced the other individuals as if they were relatives, Mrs. Elkins, Mrs. Prattle, and a hulking, vacant-eyed girl whose name was Bessie. Peggy had followed Amy from the back room, bearing the littlest Brittle, baby Esther.

"Pleased to meet you," Sibilla said, with a swift curtsey, and felt like an idiot, for they had all turned back to their appointed tasks, with the exception of Mrs. Prattle, who said with delight,

"Lor', I nivir thought I'd see the day when a pretty young lady 'ud curtsey to me, an' sez she was pleased to meet me," the woman chuckled to herself. "Oh Lor', what a day! What a day!" She wiped tears from her eyes as she laughed and rocked herself back and forth.

Stricken, Sibilla looked at Amy, who soothed her with the words, "Never you mind Mrs. Prattle. She's led a hard life and nearly everything amazes her these days." Taking the baby from Peggy and bestowing it upon Sibilla, who clutched it fast and stared at it with some dismay, Amy led the way into the back room, a dark tiny chamber filled with straw mattresses, and one wooden bedstead.

"We can talk more privately here," she said, as she settled down, plumping the thin counterpane beside her. Sibilla awkwardly lowered herself to the seat, fearful that at any minute she would drop the baby.

"Rebecca, put the water on for tea!" called out Amy, and the older girl scrambled for a brass teapot which they could see her hanging above the fire.

"Who are those people?" Sibilla asked, trying to speak in casual tones though she thought her voice probably revealed her disapproval.

"Mrs. Prattle, and Bessie, and the others?" Amy asked as if confused by the question. "Oh, we have an extra room and they had no place to stay."

Sibilla was afraid that her mouth dropped open for she had seen the "extra room" as they passed through the rear door, another tiny, dark chamber smaller than the one they were in.

"Mrs. Elkins is a widow who supports herself by selling stationary and writing letters for those who cannot write, and Mrs. Prattle was married to a sailor who deserted her. She buys pieces of lace and material and sells them. But business is never good on a rainy day—too few people on the streets—so they both stayed in. And Bessie, Bessie was a flower girl, but she is not clever enough to know right from wrong and Reverend Brittle thought she would fall unknowingly into the evil ways of other flower girls, so we took her in. She watches over the children if I have to go out on an errand. And you, Sibil, what are you doing? You must be enjoying the Season." Her voice became wistful.

"Oh Amy," cried Sibil, breaking down at last. "How can you live so?"

"Why, Sibil, whatever is wrong?" Amy asked simply, putting an arm about her sister. "I know," she guessed at last, "you think I miss all of the delights of the Season. No, I had two weary years of that.

I would never wish for it again. Not that it was not fun, until I met Reverend Brittle. But he made me see that all of the frivolities I longed for and the attention I craved, were leading me into the errors of vanity and pride, and worse, inconsiderateness, for these people who he cares for can barely scrape together enough for bread and tea every evening for supper, perhaps once a week a herring or a meat pie if they are lucky. What I spent on gloves in one year would have supported a family of four!"

"But to live like them, when you have come from—" Sibilla bit her lips but the hasty words had been spoken.

"It is not entirely of choice," admitted Amy brightly. "Reverend Brittle places God and his mission as founder of the Society to Redeem the London Poor, above his family, as he should. I knew his views when I married him, and I am proud to have a husband who follows his convictions."

"Mama and Papa could give you money," Sibilla suggested eagerly.

"And it would go straight to the Society to Redeem the London Poor," Amy explained ruefully. "Which is exactly where it should go," she added in firmer tones.

Rebecca brought in two cups of weak tea, and Sibilla sipped hers gratefully for the back room, removed from the fire, was terribly cold.

"What is that noise in the front room?" Amy asked her daughter quietly.

"Peggy and Roscoe are playing bears, and Jacob and Susannah are riding on their backs," Rebecca explained dutifully.

"I do not think your father would like to see such a spectacle when he comes home, do you, Rebecca?" Amy asked gently.

"No, he would not." Rebecca hung her head. "I will tell them to stop."

She departed and within a few minutes, the riotous grunts and shouts stopped.

Sibilla sighed and shook her head.

"How could you marry such a man, Amy?" she asked in desperation.

Amy mistook her question. "Ah, how could I marry such a man, indeed," she said musingly. "He is far too good for me, so far above me in his thoughts, and beliefs, and the straightforward manner in which he carries them out. I was very lucky, I suppose. And you, Sibil, have you met the man you want to marry yet?"

"Oh no!" Sibilla's response was quick. "I should not even know what to look for."

"I guess you have not met him yet," said Amy with genuine sorrow, "for you would have known as soon as you saw him that he was the man you must marry, just as I knew when I saw Reverend Brittle. There is nothing to look for, you simply know. It's a beautiful feeling; I hope that with God's grace, you shall experience it soon."

"I hope so too," mumbled Sibilla, and putting down her teacup, began playing with the baby to hide her distress.

The peacefulness of the moment was shattered by the loud wailing of a girl, reeling with gin, who burst into the room shrieking, "Oh Mrs. Brittle, they have taken my Jimmy to Newgate!" The sight of "one of the toffs in Reverend Brittle's house" nearly made her turn and run, but Amy gradually calmed her and elicited the story. It seemed that Jimmy was a pickpocket and had been spotted by two policemen while plying his craft that morning. The girl, who was now sixteen and had been living with him since she was fourteen, had been comforted with gin by her neighbours, and this had only intensified her grief, so that she was sobbing about killing herself as Amy held her soothingly and promised to make inquiries about Jimmy's fate on the next day.

Once the girl had cried herself to sleep in the adjoining room, preparations began for a meagre dinner, and Sibilla was amazed by Amy's good humour as she directed her children at their various tasks and welcomed several odd-looking individuals who arrived to share in this meal. Unwilling to stretch the frugal portions any further than necessary, the visitors excused themselves and set out for Upper Grosvenor Street in a heavy downpour.

The weather suited Sibilla's dreary mood, and she made no effort to keep the rain from soaking into her silk dress, while Peggy and Roscoe shared an umbrella behind her.

Had she been wrong to want to live like Nell, she wondered, for now the afternoon spent at Cloudsleigh House seemed shallow and superficial, lacking the vitality that flooded the tiny premises which Amy and her family occupied? And yet, the Brittles were engaged in a constant battle for survival. She doubted that the children knew the name of the Prime Minister or that they would ever see a painting or hear a concert. Sibilla could not agree with the harsh declarations that Reverend Brittle seemed fond of making, nor with his overriding concern with religion and the saving of souls, and yet Amy had chattered on about these subjects which had never been mentioned throughout her girlhood, with complete seriousness and devotion, never questioning her husband's ideas. If this was a foolishness engendered by love, and Sibilla did not doubt that it was foolishness, it was still strengthening, for she herself felt revived, and she noticed the difference between the sturdiness of the little Brittles and the slyness and malice in the eyes of the ragged urchins outside.

Sibilla sighed, as she studied herself in the mirror, having entered Corrough House secretly by the back entrance and divested herself of her sodden garments. She knew that Sophy too could find this complacent joy, for Sophy would adopt her husband's views and adapt to his style of life, as Amy had. Sophy and Amy were both alike in this, both waiting to be parts of larger units, both eager to find a niche in which their roles were defined and their path outlined for them.

But Sibilla, although she could not have described it, knew that she had her own individual path, and reviewing Charlotte's unhappy marriage and Nell's loveless one, Amy's content domesticity and Effie's devotion to spinsterhood and good works, she doubted that any of these were appropriate for her. She dried her wet hair carefully with a towel.

Her alternatives had narrowed, her future was uncertain, and she was sure to come down with a cold.

ELEVEN

A Most Awkward Situation

THE NIGHT WAS CRISP AND CLEAR. The horses stood impatiently stamping their hooves on the cobblestones and shaking their heads, while their breath rose in clouds of steam. Warm yellow pools of light from the carriage lanterns illuminated the scene.

Sibilla was the first to enter the vehicle, helped by Roscoe who gave her a conspiratorial wink. She settled down on the front bench, smoothing the lace flounce of her cherry-red dress, and arranging her matching velvet cloak about her bare shoulders. Sophy, in a similar gown of blue, joined her, followed by Lucinda, in bright yellow which drained all the colour from her face, and Aunt Lucy in the same black velvet costume she had worn for the reception. Several minutes of rearranging and adjusting did not ease the cramped quarters, for all four ladies wore enormous crinolines, and the slow drive to Trendle House was rendered even more painful by Aunt Lucy's recitation of the rules of etiquette for balls.

"Never dance with the same man more than twice. Ignoring the dancing and sitting with a man in obscure corners is both ill-mannered and indiscreet. You must remain seated beside me until asked to dance and return promptly when the dance has ended. Your partner will escort you to my side." Aunt Lucy cleared her throat and continued, "You must always accept an invitation to dance from any of the host's sons—"

"Of course we will," interjected Sibilla indignantly. "They are our cousins." Thinking of Baron Champford and Randall and remembering their conviviality at the reception she wondered if they had persuaded their mother to send an invitation to Corrough House, for the Countess of Trendle had never condescended to visit her sister-in-law.

"Never dance with one man after you've refused another," went on Mrs. Pleet, ignoring the intrusion. "If you do not have an escort for supper, you will go in with me. Never help yourself at the supper table but allow your escort to provide you with what you need."

As she droned on and on Sibilla began to get nervous, and her fears were not allayed by the interminable delay as their carriage joined a long line of others conveying guests to the ball or by the formal and glittering expanse of the entryway, paved in frosty-white marble and blazing with the light reflected from three large crystal chandeliers.

Sibilla's suspicions about Lady Trendle were soon confirmed for she saw the Countess flinch as the butler called out in ringing tones, "Mrs. Samuel Pleet, Miss Pleet, Lady Sibilla Merrell, Lady Sophia Merrell."

The Countess, a stern and haughty woman whose self-importance was based on her own impeccable family background, her select circle of titled friends, and her ability to explain to anyone who cared to listen exactly who had married whom and who had inherited which estate back to the time of the Conquest, had been determined to overlook the existence of her sister-in-law who had married a mill owner, and the Merrell girls, whose sister had vanished several years past. But she had one soft spot, her second son, Randall, and when he had joined his older brother, Sylvester, in urging her to invite their friendless cousins, she had reluctantly sent an invitation. But this was worse than she had ever imagined it could be, she thought, bracing herself as the huge black bulk of Mrs. Pleet came closer into view and she saw the portrait brooch of Mr. Pleet pinned at the low point of the décolletage, like the figurehead on the prow of a ship.

"Good evening, Mrs. Pleet," she said in her coldest voice. "I am so glad you could attend tonight." She shuddered again as Lucinda curtseyed politely before her. Why would anyone dress such a terribly plain daughter in such a bright and vulgar dress, Lady Trendle wondered, noting with relief that the Merrell girls were quite charming. It was too bad a family scandal had preceded their debut, for they looked nice enough to be married off quite satisfactorily if their market value had not been damaged by the foolish behaviour of their sister, who was still an occasional topic of conversation. Only the other day, one of Lady Trendle's closest friends had sworn that she saw Kitty with an Italian at one of the gaming tables in Baden last autumn.

As the party passed her and entered the ballroom, she reminded herself to have a quiet talk with her sons. They must understand that she could not afford to invite such people to her parties, despite the relationship. She was certain that Lady Muftow would not speak to her for a fortnight. It was quite enough that they insisted on bringing their friend, Mr. Griggs, whose father had made his fortune in railroad speculation. At least Mr. Griggs remained in the background, while her social instinct allowed her to guess that Mrs. Pleet would push herself and her dowdy daughter forward.

However, Aunt Lucy showed no signs of doing so immediately. She led the three girls to the ballroom and seated herself ponderously on a fragile chair which seemed as if it would crumble under her weight, signing them to take their places on either side of her. And so they sat for some time, watching the dancers, the elegantly dressed women with their sparkling jewels and elaborate costumes, and the gentlemen in tight-fitting jackets and bright waistcoats.

Unfortunately, the first person who Sibilla recognized was her sister, Lady Cloudsleigh. At the same moment Sophy saw her too.

"Look, Sibil," she whispered, "isn't that Nell, in the red dress, dancing with the thin gentleman?"

Sibilla nodded warily, hoping that Nell would not notice their presence and wondering what they should do, but it was too late for Nell swept triumphantly off the dance floor and placed herself directly in front of Mrs. Pleet.

"Mrs. Pleet, I believe," she said haughtily, inclining her head slightly, "and this must be your too, too charming daughter, Lucinda. I have heard such utterly delightful stories about her. And my precious sisters, Sibilla and Sophia."

She unbent a little to embrace them quickly, and then putting her hand firmly on the arm of her escort, who Sibilla knew was Mr. Lanning Tombs, addressed Mrs. Pleet again.

"I was so sorry," she said, in a voice just loud enough to carry to the on-lookers who were listening eagerly, "to miss your reception the other night. I have been told it was simply devastating." The ruby earrings in her ears flashed as she flung her head back and the ruby necklace around her throat glittered in the candlelight. She was a beautiful and angry woman as she stood there defiantly, in a red gown that was a little too low at the neck and a little too tight through the bodice. Lanning Tombs shifted uncomfortably beside her, though he watched Aunt Lucy with a glint in his eyes which seemed to reveal his pleasure at seeing her in this awkward situation.

Having commanded the attention of all in the immediate vicinity, Nell delivered her last scathing remark to her humiliated aunt. "I shall certainly be at your next social occasion. I would not want to be deprived of the pleasure of my sisters' company. Pray, tell me, when shall it be?"

Aunt Lucy, flushing and staring straight through Lady Cloudsleigh, refused to answer. Several minutes passed as Sibilla wished she could vanish instantaneously.

Finally seeing that she would receive no response, Nell flung herself away from them with a low chuckle, and Sibilla began to breathe again.

"Why was she so peculiar, Sibil?" asked Sophy anxiously, but she did not have time to hear her sister's reply for Baron Champford approached them with his brother, Randall, and Dabney Griggs.

"My little cousins," he said, pulling out his monocle and pretending to inspect them. "Much too pretty to be wallflowers. Some brave young man would have ventured along shortly to request the hand of the fair Unknowns in a dance." He sighed with mock seriousness. "Alas, if I were young again, I would ask myself," he paused and contemplated the ceiling sadly, "that is if I could dance."

"Pray don't be ridiculous, Sylvester," said Sibilla crossly, for while Baron Champford was delivering these flowery sentiments, Mr. Griggs had solicited Lucinda for a dance and Sophy was upon the floor with Randall. "I am sure you can dance perfectly well."

"Not true," replied Baron Champford, shaking his head solemnly. "Ah, such a shame that you will have to forego the pleasure and remain a spectator."

"Sylvester—" began Sibilla warningly.

"Very well then," he suddenly conceded, "if you wish to punish yourself, you shall be permitted to do so." And he swaggered onto the floor with Sibilla.

The musicians were performing a lively polka, and Sibilla soon discovered that all of her cousin's grim predictions were true. He never kept time with the music, he trod upon her feet repeatedly, and perspired profusely, stopping every now and then to wipe his face with a large green handkerchief.

She was grateful when the ordeal had ended and could not even bring herself to conceal her reactions.

"Lord, I pity the young ladies present here tonight," she said frankly, as he led her to her seat, "for Aunt Lucy assured us that they cannot refuse the host's son if he asks for a dance."

"Ah, but I never ask anyone to dance. Much the safer way," gasped Baron Champford, breathless from the energetic manner in which he executed the polka. "My pleasure, cuz!" And with a bob of his head, he was gone to seek revival from the punch bowl.

The combined attentions of Lady Cloudsleigh and Baron Champford and his brother brought sudden fame to the three girls, and they were besieged with partners.

Sibilla danced with Randall, a stiff and awkward partner though immeasurably more successful than his brother; with Dabney Griggs, whom she found remarkably easy to talk to because of his lack of pretension; with the Marquis of Dower, who was an excellent dancer and who flirted with her shamelessly, requesting that she cede him one of the red roses she wore in her hair as a token of favour, which he swore he would treasure forever. She danced with Lady Muftow's gangly son, James; with a handsome captain from the Horse Guards; with Mr. Crampton-Manners, who bored her with the details of his personal training regime for his newly bought pair; with her uncle, the Earl of Trendle, who was exceedingly spry for his age and who confided that her mother had always been his favourite sister.

When she was not dancing, she exchanged confidences with Sophy, who was bright with enthusiasm and enjoying the attentions she received everywhere. The three girls were so popular that Lady Holly decided on the spot to invite them to represent three of the "Months" at her quadrille ball; Aunt Lucy thought the notion of a quadrille ball at which twelve maidens would represent the twelve months of the year, all in appropriate costumes, was delightful and she accepted with alacrity. The matrons gossiped about the Talbot scandal (for it was rumoured that Lady Augusta Talbot's relatives had conspired to immure her in a convent in order to gain control of her fortune, while others insisted that the girl had a genuine vocation), and the young ladies gossiped about the young men.

It was all in all very pleasant and though Sibilla worried about why Valerian Cloudsleigh, who danced twice with Sophy, was avoiding her, she did not give it much thought.

As luck would have it, Sibilla was drooping against the wall, fanning herself after a romping schottische, when Baron Champford passed by and would not believe her excuses that she, did not wish to dance, for both her sister and cousin were on the floor.

"You know I will not dance with you again, dearest cuz!" drawled Sibilla, imitating his affected tones.

"To be sure! 'Tis understood," he replied smoothly, "but I shall not see my cousin become the subject of rumour. I can hear the dowagers now, 'Did you notice Lady Sibilla Merrell did not dance one dance!' No, I would sooner sacrifice myself once more upon yonder field of battle," he motioned at the dance floor, "than allow my cousin to fall under such a criticism. But I think I see my way clear to a solution," and with that he was gone.

Sibilla continued to fan herself and to watch Sophy and Lucinda as they whirled about the room, when she heard a commotion to her left, and the muttered words, "Oh, I daresay, not the Merrell!" Baron Champford came into view propelling a very unwilling Valerian Cloudsleigh in her direction.

She flushed with anger and embarrassment, and determined to refuse the dance, but afraid of the scene it would create when Mr. Cloudsleigh at last stood over her and asked stiffly for the pleasure of her company, she agreed with a cool nod of her head. They did not speak to each other further, but once upon the floor, Sibilla found that he was an excellent dancer, and abandoned herself to the pleasure of waltzing. The dance did not seem long enough, and she was still floating on air, refreshed and excited by the exercise, when he bowed, mumbled a thank you, and walked off, leaving her alone in the middle of the floor.

Humiliated by this lack of courtesy, Sibilla stalked back to her seat, head held high and cheeks flaming, only to discover that it had been the last dance before supper and that the guests were making a rush for the supper room. She waited anxiously for her cousin, Randall, whose offer she had accepted early in the evening, brooding upon her grievance against Mr. Cloudsleigh, a grievance that became magnified as she saw him lead Sophy towards the supper room, one of his long, elegant, white hands resting upon Sophy's plump one, which was nestled confidently in the crook of his elbow. Lucinda went in with Mr. Dabney Griggs, and Sibilla, looking around wildly for Randall, certain that everyone had witnessed her humiliation on the dance floor and now her lack of an escort for supper, saw Aunt Lucy approaching.

"Go fetch my cloak from the upper floor, second door on the right, and be quick about it," her aunt hissed. "I should think you would be grateful to escape from observation for a moment as I am sure everyone saw your paramour abandon you on the dance floor, evidently considering that a girl who would allow herself to be kissed by a gentleman she had just met, was worthy of no consideration or civility. Now your sister, Sophia, is a lady, and I am sure he appreciates the difference. And don't open your mouth to talk back to me, Miss Impertinence, but go get my cloak before someone suspects the truth about you."

Sibilla was so dazed by this scathing condemnation, which echoed her own fears, that she rose like an automaton and obediently scurried towards the stairs, never stopping to wonder how Aunt Lucy knew of the whereabouts of her cloak, which had been left with the maid when they first entered, or why she needed it now.

She was surprised to hear a soft laugh and the rustle of a silk gown in the hall as she reached the top of the stairs, but it was too late to turn back. She recognized the couple, who were locked in a passionate embrace in the shadows of the hallway; it was her sister, Lady Cloudsleigh and Mr. Lanning Tombs. But they did not even pause or look up, though they must have heard someone pass by, and she scuttled for the shelter of the bedroom.

The second door on the right was slightly ajar, and Sibilla slipped into a dim, deserted room, containing a lovely rosewood bedstead and a matching armoire and dressing table, but no evidence of any cloak whatsoever. Sibilla could hear the chatter of the people below, and the whispers of Nell and Mr. Tombs in the hall; she remembered the sight of Valerian leading her sister in to supper, and relived again that moment of humiliation and Aunt Lucy's ringing denouncement. The tears of anger and frustration which she had been holding back began to fall, and grateful for the isolation of the darkness, Sibilla flung herself upon the bed and began to cry wholeheartedly.

The couple beyond the door moved away, the diners in the supper room chattered in loud voices, but she heard none of it, immersed in her own private world of misery.

This was how Dabney Griggs, who had been wrested away from Lucinda and sent upstairs to fetch a vinaigrette, found her.

"Excuse me, miss," he said about to close the door and retreat, when Sibilla lifted her tear-streaked face and he recognized her by the light from the hall.

"Why, Lady Sibilla," he said softly. "May I be of assistance?"

"Oh, everything is wrong," sobbed Sibilla, unnerved by his tenderness. "I just cannot—" She laid her head back down on the pillow and covered her head with her arms, ashamed that he would find her in a moment of such weakness.

But Dabney Griggs, touched by her vulnerability, came up to her with caution, put one arm about her gingerly, and said, "Lady Sibilla. Pray do not cry. Tell me what is troubling you, and I will endeavour to right the problem."

"But you cannot help me," wailed Sibilla, turning to look at him, "I—"

She stopped aghast and stared at the open door. Outlined against the light from the hallway was the frail figure of Lady Muftow.

"Wait, you don't realize!" cried Sibilla, leaping up from the bed and away from the shelter of Mr. Griggs's comforting hold. Lady Muftow only sniffed and stalked off down the corridor.

TWELVE

The Courting of Sibilla

"AND SO, LADY SIBILLA, with full knowledge that my birth and breeding are such that they might not be acceptable to your parents, and yet with a sincere desire to right the wrong that I have done to you, and with the firm belief that an extended acquaintance would enable me to proffer you the love and devotion which I am sure every young girl expects from a bridegroom, I humbly request the honour of your hand in marriage."

This was the close of a long speech by Mr. Dabney Griggs, who was alone with Sibilla in the drawing room at Corrough House, and who nervously turned his flat-brimmed beaver hat about in his rough hands as he spoke. The object of this speech had jumped up at the start of the discourse and wandered over to the hearth, where she stood looking down upon the fire. With his last words, she whirled about and said impatiently, "Mr. Griggs, I cannot accept your offer. Why, I hardly know you, sir."

"I am entirely sensible of that fact, Lady Sibilla," replied her suitor. "But the nature of the situation is such—"

"It does not require such drastic action," snapped Sibilla, turning about to gaze upon the fire and shaking her head.

"On the contrary," Mr. Griggs said calmly, although the incessant motion of his hands belied this tone. "I think you do not perceive the jeopardy in which I have placed you. Lady Muftow is one of the best-known hostesses—"

"Gossips!" interjected Sibilla, with her back turned.

"Very well then, gossips," repeated Mr. Griggs earnestly. "Whatever the word, all of London has heard that you were found in my embrace in a dark bedroom at—"

"I was not in your embrace," said Sibilla with precision.

Mr. Griggs made a sound dangerously close to a snort and threw his hat down upon a sofa.

"Lady Sibilla," he said seriously, "I understand your repugnance at contracting such a mésalliance, but it is your reputation and honour that I wish to defend. I do not cherish any hope that you are attracted to me personally, but I urge you to consider the precarious position in which you will be placed socially if you do not consider such a solution as the one I offer you."

"Mr. Griggs," pleaded Sibilla, turning to look at him desperately, "I do not find you repugnant. I do not consider marriage with you to be a *mésalliance*. And I do not feel that my parents would find you unacceptable! But—" she waved her hand to stifle his eager outburst "—I will not marry you, no matter what the consequences."

"There is someone else," he said tonelessly.

"No, there is not!" retorted Sibilla with anger. "In truth, I think I shall never marry."

Dabney Griggs studied her with his direct gaze. "Pray, what did you hope to accomplish in London?" he inquired candidly.

Sibilla flinched. "It's very well for you to think that way," she said hotly. "You've never been shut up in the country for years, without any friends or contact with your neighbours because no one is suitable for you to—"

"Marry?" commented Mr. Griggs dryly.

Sibilla hesitated, at the fine edge between anger and amusement. "Quite true," she laughed, but she saddened as she added more slowly, "I seem to have no other function in life—for sale to the highest bidder."

"What else can you long for?" asked Mr. Griggs. "To be a good wife and mother," the two words were synonymous, "is a noble endeavour. Do you wish to be a seamstress, a milliner, a cook, a governess, a housemaid?"

"Sometimes," Sibilla admitted ruefully, sighing. But when Dabney opened his mouth to contest this desire, she added quickly, "But then I would be in someone's employ and even more subject to their domination. I suppose it would not suit."

"Lady Sibilla," said Mr. Griggs fervently, "as my wife, I would allow you the utmost freedom. You need not fear my domination."

"Mr. Griggs," replied Sibilla primly, "I will not be your wife, much though I appreciate your magnanimity in offering for me."

Dabney cursed under his breath, and ran his hand through his fiery red locks. "Why then, what can be done to rectify this situation?" he asked, accepting her answer at last.

"If only Aunt Lucy had not interfered," said Sibilla, pacing about the room, "and if only I knew why?"

"What? Mrs. Pleet?" expostulated Mr. Griggs. "What had she to do with this tragedy?"

"I should think melodrama more to the point than tragedy," snapped Sibilla. She brought one small white fist down on the mantel. "Why did you come to that room at that time?"

Mr. Griggs rubbed one hand over his eyes. "Miss Pleet," he answered finally, looking up cautiously at Sibilla, "she needed her vinaigrette."

"So Lucinda is in this plot also!" said Sibilla, her dark eyes blazing. "That meddling little nobody!"

"I beg your pardon, Lady Sibilla," Mr. Griggs said officiously, crossing his arms over his chest and attempting to look imposing. "Miss Pleet, I am certain, was not a party to any scheme." He toyed nervously with his gold watch chain. "As I recall, her mother approached her and spoke to her for several minutes before she asked me to fetch something for her. But what has that to do with your accusations?"

"Only that my aunt," replied Sibilla with scorn, "sent me upstairs to search for a nonexistent cloak!"

Mr. Griggs took this in solemnly. "But how can she have known how long it would take you to find the object?" he inquired, "or that you would still be there when I came up? Or that—" he coughed discreetly " —I could be counted upon to—place you in that—compromising position?"

"Oh, she knew that I was discouraged and depressed, and she said some harsh things that I am sure she knew would upset me," Sibilla said, hastily dismissing his questions, "but you have given me the clue to this entire puzzle. Compromising!"

"Compromising?" repeated Dabney uncertainly.

"She wished to place me in a compromising situation!" Sibilla announced with a light of triumph in her eyes.

"Nonsense!" was Mr. Griggs opinion. "I have met Mrs. Pleet only upon two occasions, but I know that she is a respectable woman who would not wish to put herself or any of her nieces under the harsh light of public scrutiny and disapprobation. Such a notion is preposterous. What could she hope to gain from such an action other than scandal and diminished expectations?"

"Scandal for me! Diminished expectations for me!" explained Sibilla almost gleefully. "Then there would be a wider field for Lucinda, whom she cannot hope to marry well while Sophy and I capture the greater attention!"

"Why, I do not follow you at all, Lady Sibilla," Mr. Griggs complained.

"Lucinda is plain and unattractive, she cannot hold a decent conversation, and she dresses like a child," Sibilla pointed out amiably. "Aunt Lucy hoped to bring her off, using our influence, but she did not bargain for Sophy and me. And she will find that she cannot manipulate me the way she does her daughter!"

"I do not understand your vehemence," Mr. Griggs said reprovingly. "Lucinda—Miss Pleet—is a very pretty young lady and has much to say for herself." Sibilla seemed interested by this new revelation about her cousin's character. "Furthermore," continued Mr. Griggs, "without any undue—"

But his speech was cut short by the entrance of Sophy and Lucinda, who burst into the room, arms locked, cheeks flushed.

"Congratulations, Sibil!" cried Sophy, throwing herself into her sister's arms. "Aunt Lucy told us that you are betrothed to Mr. Griggs!"

Lucinda stood a little bit apart, her brown eyes fixed upon Mr. Griggs, who fidgeted and crossed and recrossed his arms.

"I am not engaged," Sibilla said shortly, disentangling herself from Sophy. "And neither is Mr. Griggs. There must have been a misunderstanding."

"Is that true, Mr. Griggs?" asked Lucinda quietly in her small voice.

"I offered for Lady Sibilla and was refused," Mr. Griggs said curtly. "And since this is the case, I feel my presence here might be irritating, and I will withdraw." With these words, he bowed quickly and stalked from the room.

"What can be wrong with him?" asked Sophy, glancing back and forth from her sister, who seemed angry, to Lucinda, who was flushed.

"He's annoyed with me," admitted Sibilla. "He wanted to save my honour," she glanced at Lucinda who was listening avidly, "at the cost of his happiness. I wouldn't allow him to do so."

"Your honour?" questioned Sophy. She and Lucinda had been hurried from the ball shortly after Sibilla's transgression but had never been informed of the details.

And they would not learn them now, for the energetic butler stuck his head into the room, piped out, "Mr. Valerian Cloudsleigh" and withdrew, as Valerian strolled into the room, a bandbox punched with ragged holes under his right arm.

"Good morning, ladies," said Mr. Cloudsleigh, brandishing his hat in his left hand and making an exaggeratedly low bow.

Lucinda adopted her usual shrinking behaviour, Sophy brightened and came towards him with a sweet smile, while Sibilla, confused and dismayed, observed him hesitantly.

"What do you have for us, Mr. Cloudsleigh?" Sophy quizzed him.

"It is for Lady Sibilla," said Valerian, with a trace of embarrassment and less suavity than usual.

Sibilla continued to study him thoughtfully. Valerian, noticing the constraint and tension in the room, acted impulsively, whisking the bandbox from under his arm and releasing its contents upon the floor. A small brown rodent went scrambling under the nearest settee, followed by a black-and-white ball of fur which hid under Sibilla's skirts.

Lucinda screamed, and Sophy jumped back, holding up her gown to reveal neat ankles. But Valerian did not even notice these for he was watching Sibilla, who bent to retrieve the animal which had escaped to the dimness beneath the furniture.

"How adorable they are," she said softly, as she cradled them in her arms. "What are they—Mr. Cloudsleigh?"

"Guinea pigs," he said, with a delighted grin on his face. "Come from South America somewhere. That's a mating pair. You'll soon have hundreds of them about. They breed like rabbits."

"Goodness gracious," said Lucinda, profoundly shocked by the turn of the conversation.

"They look like mice," said Sophy petulantly.

"Oh no, they're not at all alike," commented Sibilla, her face radiant. "Come and look, Sophy. They are so precious."

Sophy approached cautiously, and, putting out one timid finger to touch the pigs, was bitten. She yelled and leaped backward, sucking her injured finger and pouting.

"All animals bite if they feel threatened, Lady Sophia," said Valerian, as she scowled at him.

"Indeed!" Sophy replied quickly. "I am sure I can understand. Marmalade—"

"Oh, the cat!" exclaimed Sibilla. Her dark eyes clouded with anxiety. "How can I protect them from Marmalade?"

"I keep mine in bird cages," said Valerian smoothly, settling himself in an armchair, although the ladies remained standing, and setting his hat down upon a side table. "Have you no empty cages in the house?"

"I believe there were," Sibilla said thoughtfully. "Sophy, go fetch Peggy and ask her if she knows whether or not they were discarded in the housecleaning."

Ever-obedient, Sophy immediately trotted off on her errand, and Sibilla asked the guest if he would care to take tea with them. Upon his cheerful acquiescence, Lucinda departed to order the tea, and thus Aunt Lucy found Valerian and Sibilla alone together, seated on the carpet, playing with the guinea pigs and laughing merrily as the little animals went squeaking in and out of the folds in Sibilla's frou-frou of silk skirts.

"Sibilla!" hissed Aunt Lucy. "Mr. Cloudsleigh!" She advanced into the chamber and jerked Sibilla to her feet with one strong arm.

Valerian scrambled after the pigs who headed for shelter. "What are those rodents doing in my house?" asked Mrs. Pleet sternly.

"Gifts for Lady Sibilla," said Mr. Cloudsleigh, calmly, balancing them, one in each hand, "to atone for my thoughtless behaviour at the ball." He turned to Sibilla apologetically. "I had just witnessed a most unpleasant event." Sibilla flushed and wondered if he too had seen Nell and Lanning Tombs.

At this moment, Peggy's smiling face appeared at the open door, her arms enfolded around a giant gilt bird cage. Espying the glowering look of Mrs. Pleet's eyebrows, she set the cage down and pattered off down the hall. Valerian strolled across the room and inserted the two animals into their new home.

"Where is Mr. Griggs?" asked Aunt Lucy sharply, her fingers digging into Sibilla's flesh like claws.

"Yes, what is wrong with Griggs?" added Valerian jovially, "I saw him leaving. He seemed deuced perturbed but wouldn't tell me why. He's a queer fellow on occasion."

"You are addressing the future Mrs. Griggs," Aunt Lucy rebuked him. Valerian suddenly dropped his devil-may-care attitude and fixed his attention upon Sibilla who squirmed trying to break loose from her aunt's grasp.

"Certainly not!" Sibilla retorted, throwing back her head so sharply that her loosely bound hair came undone and tumbled down her back.

She looked like a young animal caught in a trap, thought Valerian, with her eyes glittering and her cheeks flushed.

"I refused Mr. Griggs's offer, Aunt Lucy," Sibilla flung at Mrs. Pleet, who let her go so abruptly that Sibilla stumbled and fell down upon a nearby footstool.

"Refused! You little fool!" cried Mrs. Pleet. "How can you ever lift up your head in Society again?"

"Very well," responded Sibilla, "if you will cease your infernal meddling in my affairs."

"Here now, not at all the thing," interjected Valerian feebly.

"Certainly not. She is a willful, stubborn, disobedient child," said Mrs. Pleet, goaded beyond endurance. "And you, Mr. Cloudsleigh," she turned on him, "what are you doing here?"

Startled, Valerian replied quickly, "I came to invite you, all of you, to the Opera tonight. My father and stepmother won't be using their box, and neither will my Uncle Ashford, and I thought perhaps the young ladies would like a chance to see the Opera from a private box."

"Oh, how wonderful!" exclaimed Sophy, her eyes glowing as she entered the drawing room. She and Lucinda had been cowering outside, afraid to face the tempest which buffeted Sibilla. Lucinda followed her, gingerly balancing an enormous silver tea service.

Aunt Lucy studied the young man cautiously, seemed to rummage through the tangle of ideas and schemes in her mind, and accepted the invitation. While the tea was being poured, Sibilla excused herself meekly and left the room. She did not reappear downstairs throughout the course of the day, but was waiting, ready, in the hall with Sophy and Lucinda when Valerian returned to escort them to the Opera.

THIRTEEN

Flirtations at the Opera

HER MAJESTY'S WAS PACKED when they took their seats during the second act. Sibilla eagerly scanned the theatre, enthralled by the sight of all of the boxes filled with the best-dressed women in London.

Valerian, who had seated himself behind her, leaned over and whispered, "See the third box from the centre. That is the Trendle's box. I believe your cousins are present." He lifted his lorgnon to inspect the grand tier more closely, and passed it to Sibilla who eagerly identified Baron Champford, Randall, and their mother, Lady Trendle. But as she began to make a sweep of the grand tier from loge to loge with the powerful glasses, Valerian snatched them away from her without a word, and shortly rose, without explanation, and left the box.

Trying to ignore this inexplicable behaviour, Sibilla listened raptly to the opera, the first she had ever heard. She was annoyed that the singing was in Italian and worried about the story line, for she could not unravel the plot since they had arrived late. But she found herself more and more moved by the beauty and the richness of the singing, though she had little time to fret over her inability to comprehend the actions of the performers, for the box was besieged by gentlemen visitors. Dabney Griggs avoided Sibilla's eyes but talked politely with Sophy and Lucinda. Mr. Treswick presented Sibilla with a sweet-smelling gardenia, which she tucked into her hair. Several strangers came by, perhaps expecting to find Lady Cloudsleigh, the usual occupant of the box. Most were "heavy swells," overdressed, overperfumed, overly polite, and seemingly reluctant to quit the premises despite the intimidating glares of Aunt Lucy. However, when they were not introduced to the young ladies, they merely bowed and withdrew.

Throughout this socializing, the opera went on, but when the curtain fell, the murmur of conversation and the rustling in the audience swelled to a crescendo. The Cloudsleigh box was flooded with callers and Sibilla greeted Sylvester and Randall Sylver with delight.

"I daresay you are enjoying the evening's entertainment," drawled Baron Champford, as he sauntered into the box and took the seat vacated by Valerian behind Sibilla.

"Oh, it's lovely!" she sighed eagerly. "I've never heard such lovely singing. Did Valerian—Mr. Cloudsleigh—tell you we were here?"

"Valerian?" her cousin jumped. "Is he here, confound it?"

"Yes, he escorted us," said Sibilla with a little frown. "You mean, he did not—"

"What the devil?" murmured Baron Champford to himself, and then more distinctly, "Damn it, cousin, I have eyes. I could see you for myself. The most radiantly beautiful woman here tonight."

"Don't be ridiculous!" commented Sibilla, shaking her head. "I am your cousin. You do not have to ply me with idle flatteries. Save that for a young lady you are going to marry."

"Marry!" exclaimed Baron Champford, shuddering as if someone had poured cold water upon him. "Marry! Lor', cousin, don't bandy that word about in front of me. I hear it often enough from my mother. Marry!" he shuddered again.

"Well, then, where can Valerian be?" mused Sibilla to herself. "He disappeared shortly after we arrived."

"Deuce take it, he's probably with Mrs. Meadows again," her cousin replied, suddenly hesitating and adding, "that is to say, he's probably calling upon the ladies."

"Who is Mrs. Meadows?" Sibilla inquired breathlessly, but seeing the set and stubborn look on Sylvester's face, she desisted in this line of questioning and instead indulged in a frivolous conversation with him and Randall, cautiously begging for Baron Champford's lorgnon during a lull. With this instrument in hand, she began to survey the audience and presently sighted Valerian, alone in a box with a beautiful, young, auburn-haired woman. Sibilla dropped the glasses with dismay; she felt tears spring to her eyes. What a provoking man, inviting them to the Opera and then running off to carry on a clandestine flirtation! When she had regained some of her composure, she eagerly lifted the lorgnon again and studied Mr. Cloudsleigh and his fair companion. The woman kept her head bent, and Sibilla could see only the auburn curls spilling across her white shoulders, the exquisite emerald necklace which glittered in the lights (a gift from Mr. Cloudsleigh, no doubt, decided Sibilla), and the fluttering, provocative manner in which she wielded her lace fan. Valerian was bending close to her ear to speak to her, and suddenly, the woman lifted her countenance to his with a breathtaking smile, a smile which pierced Sibilla's heart. She dropped the lorgnon and stared off into the blur of lights and colours that composed the floor of the theatre.

But there was something familiar about Valerian's choice of female company, and she lifted the glasses again to scrutinize the couple when Baron Champford, realizing the motive behind his cousin's abdication of the conversation and her absorption in the opera panorama, calmly removed his lorgnon from her grasp and treated her pleas for its return as attempts at humour.

Confronted by frustration everywhere she turned, Sibilla abandoned herself to the music when the curtain lifted again and ignored the frivolous conversation behind her. She was thrilled by the ballet, which consisted more of gymnastics and spectacle than any serious dancing. However, Sibilla, who adored dancing of any variety, was rapt in admiration of the ballet dancers, despite the caustic comments of Sylvester who had remained in the box with them.

"You're watching Eulalie, the third from the left," he whispered to his brother. "She looks innocent as a dove, but she costs more than a phaeton and pair, and is as avaricious as a moneylender."

Sibilla quickly located the object of this speech, and saw a baby-faced blond girl, who performed with extraordinary verve and a catlike grace. She wrinkled her nose at Sylvester's insinuations, assuming his sarcasms were a necessary part of his pose as man of the world, though when the ballet dancers were treated to an ovation, she noticed the repeated shouts for "Eulalie!" and saw that the bouquets thrown towards that demoiselle were studded with bracelets.

Valerian returned during the last act, displacing Sylvester, who protested so loudly that Sibilla worried that the singer, who was in the midst of a melancholy aria, would notice and falter. Indeed, it seemed that the Opera was merely a backdrop for the social dramas being played in the boxes and the stalls.

Passing through the crush-room after the performance, Valerian was continuously stopped by his acquaintances: handsome, young men who had been at Cambridge with him; matrons desperate to thrust their young daughters beneath his eyes; older men who seemed to know him because of his friendship with Ashford Cloudsleigh. Sibilla, continually buffeted by the crowds, felt suddenly like a young girl recently up from the country. She caught only occasional glimpses of people she knew: the Countess of Trendle deliberately ignoring their party, Mr. Crampton-Manners deep in conversation with a shrinking debutante, and Lady Holly shepherding her flock of unmarried daughters.

When Valerian completely vanished in the shifting throng, Mrs. Pleet decided that they should nevertheless call for the carriage and trust that he would rejoin them before it was brought round to the door. As they waited, Sibilla, who had been instructed to watch for Mr. Cloudsleigh while Mrs. Pleet maneuvered Lucinda in the direction of the Marquis of Dower, caught sight of her quarry escorting the lovely red-haired woman towards her waiting barouche. Sibilla, both fascinated and horrified, could not wrench her gaze from the couple, the lady beautiful in a velvet cloak of deep bottle-green, laughing and leaning on Valerian's arm for support as she stepped into the vehicle, and her companion, his eyes never leaving her face, his whole manner attentive and adoring, his kiss tender and prolonged as he bent over her proffered hand.

He remained a few minutes gazing after the departing conveyance before he sauntered towards Mrs. Pleet's party, and Sibilla, turned away, confused by the intimacy she had witnessed, only to fall into the willing clutches of the Marquis of Dower, who had been struggling through a tedious conversation with Lucinda.

"Ah, Lady Sibilla!" breathed the Marquis, taking hold of her arm and drawing her close to him. "You are the moon among a galaxy of stars, lighting up this dim night."

"The stars are suns when seen in their own sphere," replied Sibilla disconcertedly, aware of Valerian's presence behind her and trying to remove her hand from her admirer's firm grasp.

"Ah, but we are earthbound, dear Lady Sibilla," the Marquis whispered in low tones, "and to us poor mortals, the moon is the ruler of the night, the goddess of love and romance, Artemis—ah, you would be a fair Artemis!"

"Artemis was not the goddess of love and romance, good fellow," said Valerian calmly stepping between the two. "It's a wonder Oxford ever gave you a degree. Aphrodite is the goddess of love and romance. That is not to say that your comment is off the mark; Sibilla should be Artemis, the virgin goddess whose heart could never be touched by love, but for the love of whom men died."

Sibilla was inarticulate after this exchange of compliments, but fortunately the two men were locked in a battle of stares, which concluded with the Marquis stalking off into the night. Not quite knowing what was happening, Sibilla allowed herself to be drawn into an alcove, where Valerian, taking possession of both of her hands and kissing them alternately, whispered, "But you are not Artemis. You are Sibilla, the Sibil, the wise one who knows the future. What does the future hold in store for us, my little prophetess?"

"I—ah—I'm sure I don't know!" exclaimed Sibilla, put off balance by his intensity and fearful of immediate interruption by Aunt Lucy.

Valerian chuckled, a low throaty sound, and said more distinctly, "No, the Sibil could never foresee her own future, no more than Cassandra. But what of others? Your sister, Sophy?"

"Oh, Sophy," said Sibilla, glancing around fretfully. "She will be married before the year is out and have lots of children and be so happy being a wife and mother that she will never wonder whether or not she is really happy."

Valerian laughed again. "And your cousin, Miss Pleet?"

Sibilla paused and replied more thoughtfully. "Why, I think she will surprise us all, and her mother most of all, but I cannot predict exactly the manner in which it will all come to pass."

"And that leaves Artemis, the virgin goddess, alone on the battle-field of London Society," teased Valerian, but his bantering tone faltered as he saw the flush come to her cheeks and her eyes fill with tears that glittered in the fitful gas light.

"I daresay, it will be so," Sibilla murmured brokenly, and was relieved to hear the shout for her carriage.

FOURTEEN

Flirtations in the Park

AUNT LUCY HAD ACCOMPLISHED one of her schemes without spending a precious penny; it was imperative that her daughter be seen at the Opera, and through the graciousness of Mr. Cloudsleigh, this had taken place. Now it was necessary that they appear for the daily parade of fashion in the Park, but a phaeton was regrettably too dear in addition to the hire of the carriage, and the heavy carriage was too ponderous a vehicle to show the young ladies off to their best advantage.

Fortunately, Mr. Griggs had offered to take the girls for a ride in his curricle before the contretemps with Sibilla (Mrs. Pleet had totally forgotten her own crucial role in this affair), and being a man of honour, he appeared to repeat his offer.

Aunt Lucy insisted that he wait in the drawing room for an hour while Lucinda submitted to having her hair crimped, and Sibilla and Sophy were attired in fresh frocks after a morning spent romping with the dogs. For Sibilla, Aunt Lucy chose a plain brown dress which she hoped would subdue the fatal effect her niece seemed to have upon men (she had not missed the rendezvous with Valerian after the Opera) while she allowed Sophy to wear a dainty, becoming gown of soft blue, for Sophy's admirers could easily be transferred later to Lucinda's camp.

The three young women were, of necessity, cramped in the curricle, which should comfortably transport two, but they were delighted by the cool breeze and the bright sunshine.

Although the curricle was a vehicle designed for swiftness, it could not be shown to this advantage in the crowded London streets or in the teeming drives of the Park. However, because it was open, it displayed its occupants to the curious eyes of the fashionable world, which assembled in the Park every afternoon between three and five, and so they paraded up and down the Ring, Sibilla feeling like a brown wren between Sophy in her pretty blue gown and Lucinda in a dress of rich magenta.

Major Garlinghouse and Captain Wheedle, mounted on horses, accosted them, one riding on each side of the open carriage, and Sibilla wondered if they ever reported for duty since she had never seen them in uniform and they seemed to have their days and nights completely at their own disposal. She had ample time to wonder for Captain Wheedle was occupied with Lucinda, while Major Garling-house traded pleasantries with Sophy.

Sibilla, in the midst of this verbal activity watched the passersby, spotting her sister Nell in a phaeton with a handsome young man, and Lady Holly with her daughters clustered around her in another carriage. Suddenly she noticed Valerian Cloudsleigh, dressed all in black and mounted on a huge black stallion, wending his way through the crowds. She was about to call out to him, when he whirled his restive steed about and pursued a rose-coloured phaeton passing in the other direction.

Sibilla's heart sunk as she saw that the occupant of this conveyance was the auburn-haired woman, who had been beleaguered with suitors until Valerian cut a swath in their midst.

Having learned a bitter lesson at the Opera, Sibilla faced front and concentrated her diminished attention upon the gentlemen who thronged her own carriage once the Captain and the Major were dis-placed, among them Mr. Treswick, Mr. Crampton-Manners, Lord Muftow, and the incorrigible Marquis of Dower, who introduced his friend, an older man by the name of Lawrence Lanston. Sophy and Lucinda were not interested in this latecomer, for he seemed to be an old roué with his hooded eyes and the bluish circles beneath them, but Sibilla found the world-weariness in his dark eyes attractive, and enjoyed the wit in his repartee about the pitfalls of a London Season, a topic which he discussed in mingled tones of sarcasm and compassion.

She was not unaware that the Marquis of Dower was plying Sophy with compliments about her likeness to a cultured rose (distinct from a wild rose, as he pointed out, with cynical amusement), and wondered why Peggy had succumbed to the attentions of such a heartless flirt.

As they made the turn at the Achilles Statue and started back in the opposite direction, they encountered the rose-coloured phaeton, traveling towards theirs, Valerian on his black mount still a willing satellite. The young lady was laughing once more (she's always laughing, thought Sibilla, obviously the giddy type) when she suddenly lifted her head and for a moment, looked straight at the occupants of the curricle.

"Kitty!" breathed Sibilla, and then the woman bent her head so that only her auburn curls and the creamy line of her neck were visible above her rose-coloured gown.

Just the colour of Kitty's hair, thought Sibilla in a daze, chastened by Kitty's desire for anonymity, for her long-lost sister had buried her head against Valerian's shoulder, and he had placed a protective arm about her, darting a glance at Sibilla that could only mean he wished her not to interfere or comment on what she had seen.

Yet Sibilla could not resist her impulse to watch the pair, and so she saw Kitty order her tiger to whip up the horses, watched helplessly as the phaeton pulled out of the line of vehicles rambling across the Park, and as Valerian spurred his horse to a trot to match the pace of the carriage.

Sibilla read voraciously, had five older sisters, and enjoyed the candid confidences of Peggy. It took her but a few minutes to put together the pieces of this puzzle. A beautiful young woman, always dressed in exquisite taste, and wearing costly jewels. Seen about town alone in luxurious and smart equipages. Always accompanied by one young well-to-do gentleman and surrounded by a throng of male admirers. Unwilling to let her family know of her whereabouts and ashamed to meet her sister in public.

Despite intricate mental convolutions, Sibilla could reach only one inescapable conclusion: her sister, Kitty, was a Cyprian.

FIFTEEN

Lady Cloudsleigh's Transgression

SIBILLA DISCLOSED HER AMAZING information only to Peggy, and to her dismay, that usually practical and realistic young woman stoutly refused to believe a word against her adored Kitty.

"Sure then, Miss Sibilla, and you don't believe such a thing about your own sister?" she protested, her eyes burning with indignation. "If it was Miss Kitty you saw, and mind you, I have my doubts it was, for there must be ever so many women in London with red hair and gurren eyes—"

"Peggy!" Sibilla exclaimed. "I can recognize my own sister, I should hope!"

"Well, then, she is keeping to herself for some purpose," Peggy continued adamantly, "and all will be revealed to us in time." She shook her head at Sibilla. "And doubting your own young man, you are. It's a shame, Miss Sibilla. Faith, it's a shame!"

"He's not my young man!" protested Sibilla.

"And now you think to convince me that you would kiss a gentleman, as you did Mr. Valerian, without intending to wed him," Peggy said reproachfully.

"Certainly not! That is to say—I did not—I would not, but—" her mumbled excuses ceased as a new problem distracted her from the old. "Peggy!" she gasped, "you have no hopes that the Marquis of Dower will marry you?"

Peggy smiled, an expression passing over her face which Sibilla had never seen before, for her gaze was averted and her lips twisted a little at the corners as a blush stained her cheeks and her eyes dimmed.

"Lord, no," she replied softly. "I've kissed enough young men without any hopes for marriage. You must understand, Miss Sibilla, that my ways and means are different from yours, because of our different stations in life, though our futures may be equally happy, God willing."

"And what precisely is the difference in our stations in life?" asked Sibilla quickly, perplexed as always by the discrepancy between Peggy's nominal position and the unusual privileges granted to her.

"Ah," said Peggy, with a breathtaking smile. "We all have need of our secrets, Miss Sibilla. Miss Kitty is no exception. Sometimes secrets are the foundations for happy futures." She turned as if to leave the room, but Sibilla stopped her with another warning.

"Peggy," she called out, "the difference in rank between you and I, no matter what your secret, is not half so grand as that difference between you and the Marquis of Dower."

Peggy paused, and faced Sibilla with the same unquenchable smile upon her face. "Take heed, Miss Sibilla, that you do not become like your aunt. I declare, you have many of her concerruns and attitudes; that remarruk might well have been hers. Titles, wealth, marriages, nothing can stand in the way of two people who belong together. Why the Marquis of Merryfield, your young man's grandfather, married his housekeeper."

"Valerian Cloudsleigh is not my young man, I am not like Aunt Lucy," sputtered Sibilla, "and the Marquis married his housekeeper only after his first wife's death, and she is not yet accepted in Society."

"Aunt Lucy again," commented Peggy wryly. "I doubt that either of them is the least concerned with the stamp of approval granted by the haut ton. Not if they are content with each other. Ned and I should be quite pleased to spend the rest of our days in Ireland, far from the disapproving eyes of the London hostesses."

"Ned?" questioned Sibilla aghast.

"Ned?" retorted Peggy, with a mocking curtsey. "You know him as the Marquis of Dower." Peggy had a natural gift for mimicry and she pronounced these last four words in the same tones as Mrs. Pleet, at the same time sweeping her silk skirts to the ground with the haughtiness and grace of a grand lady, and stalking from the room with her head held high.

Sibilla had little time to ruminate upon Peggy's disclosures, for Sophy came bustling into the room, full of chatter about callers, dresses, and brandishing a bouquet of golden roses which Captain Wheedle had sent to her.

"Oh, and, Sibil, Madame Doucette is here to take our orders for our dresses as the 'Months' in the quadrille ball given by Lady Holly," Sophy concluded her rapid summary of the latest gossip. "She has the most exquisite ideas for our dresses. Lucinda, as January, is to have a white tulle dress, puffed to the waist, and trimmed with sprigs of holly. As April, I am going to wear a gown of *ciel-bleu* satin, with ruches and revers of lavender satin, and embroidery of forget-me-nots and pansies."

"What of my costume?" demanded Sibilla, forgetting the weighty problems of marriage and the future in the excitement of discussing toilettes.

She was led down to the sitting room by her younger sister, and after an enjoyable afternoon spent poring over engravings of the latest Paris fashions and samples of fabric, chose a currant-red faille dress with a deep flounce and an overskirt of black lace, which Sibilla considered would create an interesting Latin effect, appropriate to her intended depiction of the month of July.

Lucinda, Sophy, and Mrs. Pleet departed on a round of calls, but Sibilla cried off and closeted herself in the study to indulge herself in worrying about their financial situation.

The wherewithal to pay the dressmaker's mounting bill was still a problem, for the Countess of Corrough had responded to her daughters' desperate pleas with a polite letter detailing the vagaries of her health, revealing the interest of a neighbouring clergyman in Effie, an interest which was seemingly not returned by their sister, and describing an afternoon musicale held by the Whitefoots (she had felt well enough to attend, but the exertion had sent her to bed for the subsequent fortnight).

The second vexation on Sibilla's list was her lack of jewellery. Lucinda had modelled a splendid suite of diamonds which she would wear on the evening of the quadrille ball. Sibilla and Sophy had only strings of pearls and gold lockets—as the youngest daughters in the family, they had been at the tail end of the distribution of family treasures.

Sophy could probably manage to be presentable with the demure amethyst necklace and earrings which had been Sibilla's christening gift from an eccentric aunt who lived alone in Cornwall and was a Greek scholar and a poetess.

But as for Sibilla, her thoughts kept returning to the ruby necklace which Lady Cloudsleigh had sported at the Trendle ball. Despite her reluctance to visit her sister after the intimate scene she had witnessed on the same occasion, the glitter of the gems and the thought of a chat about Kitty were more compelling. Besides, it was unlikely that Nell had ever been aware of Sibilla's presence, so absorbed had she been in her poet. Contenting herself with the thought that many women conducted mild flirtations for amusement, Sibilla hurried upstairs and dressed herself in a walking costume of pearl-grey.

Peggy did not answer the bellpull, and finally, after struggling to fix all of the buttons with the help of a buttonhook, Sibilla went in search of her. She did not find the object of her search, but she discovered the reason for Peggy's absence when she descended to the kitchen where the housemaid, Lily, the cook, the butler, and Roscoe, the stable groom, were grouped around the trestle table, imbibing freely from a bottle of port.

"Coo, and he was a gentleman, he was," Lily was squeaking in an excited voice when Sibilla approached. "A crest on the door and everything."

"Ah, she has been putting on the grand airs long enough," predicted the cook, in a rumbling, hoarse voice. "She will end where many a loose skirt has ended before—in the streets." She took another long swig from her glass, wiped her mouth thoroughly with her apron, and said reprovingly, "I hope you take a lesson from this yourself, Lily."

"Oh! I'm as good as engaged to George," responded Lily rapidly. "The butcher's boy," she explained with a sideways remark to the butler. "You can be sure I would not dream of behaving as Peggy does. Why, she was not in her room three nights this past week!" Her voice rose to a fever pitch as she triumphantly revealed this last tidbit of gossip. "You were courtin' her, weren't you, Roscoe?" she questioned the groom who had been staring into his glass gloomily. "What do you think of her now?"

But Roscoe did not satisfy Lily's curiosity upon this point, for he noticed Sibilla as he raised his head to reply, and stood abruptly, pulling at the forelock of his hair in deference. The cook, following the line of his gaze, quickly scrambled the bottle of port beneath her apron, and the others rose, Lily with rounded eyes and an open mouth.

"We do not pay the servants to gossip," Sibilla said severely, forgetting she had last heard these words from Aunt Lucy's lips and applied to Peggy herself. "I am looking for my personal maid, Peggy Banks. Is she here?"

"Oh no, miss, she is out," replied Lily quickly, bobbing up and down several times.

Sibilla, though expecting this statement, frowned. "And I suppose that my aunt took the carriage?" she said looking towards Roscoe.

"Indeed she did, miss," he replied. Sibilla shook her head and was about to turn away when he added, "but there are two saddle-horses free and I should be glad to accompany you upon an errand, if that was your wish."

"Why, that is very thoughtful of you, Ros—ah, very thoughtful," she replied. "It is necessary for me to visit my sister, Lady Cloudsleigh, in Berkeley Square. I will meet you at the front of the house."

As Roscoe left to ready the horses, Sibilla nodded to the timid housemaid. "Lily, I will require your aid in helping me into my riding habit."

"Oh yes, miss," responded that young woman, scurrying away from the table and pattering up the stairs after Sibilla.

Lily was unnaturally silent while helping Sibilla remove the walking costume and don the riding habit instead. This was a mannishly cut garment with a tight basque and a slim, black skirt, worn with a white front and a small black hat. Pulling on her soft leather gloves, Sibilla pronounced herself finished with Lily's services, and the trembling maid hurried off to join her comrades in the kitchen.

Fortunately, it was a lovely day for a ride, and Roscoe, sensitive to the need to protect Sibilla's reputation from the consequences of being seen without a chaperone, led them down a maze of secondary streets and mews, finally emerging in an alley which ran alongside the stables of Cloudsleigh House. Sibilla sensed that he was deeply disturbed by the kitchen gossip, for he was utterly silent and his handsome lips were curved in a sullen downturn. She guessed that he was unused to finding his affections spurned, and knew that Peggy, with her bright, charming character and her pretty, flirting ways, was irresistible to many men. Yet though she longed to advise him about Peggy and her seeming fickleness, Sibilla was unable to murmur more than a polite "thank you" as she slid down from her mount, for the gap in their social stations forbade any intimate exchange.

Gathering the trailing skirts of her riding habit, Sibilla ran lightly up the front steps and pulled upon the brass knocker of the front door, waiting impatiently for some response, for any of the occupants of the carriages or the passers-by who thronged Berkeley Square could see her, recognize her, and spread a report which would eventually reach Aunt Lucy's ears.

Therefore, she was grateful when the well-trained butler opened the door and ushered her inside, though she was dismayed to hear that her sister was "not at home."

Knowing that this was often a polite excuse made when the lady of the house did not wish to see callers, Sibilla pleaded desperately, "Are you certain she is not at home, not even to her sister on a matter of urgency?"

"She is not at home, ma'am," replied the butler officiously, refusing to acknowledge Sibilla's unspoken suggestion.

At this moment, a figure passing through the upper hallway paused and came towards the unexpected caller.

"Why, it is Lady Sibilla, is it not?" inquired this personage, who Sibilla, after a few minutes' study, recognized as Baron Cloudsleigh, Nell's husband.

"Indeed it is, Lord Cloudsleigh," she replied, curtseying gracefully. "I am very pleased to see you again, sir."

"And I am equally pleased to renew my acquaintance with you, my dear," the scholar responded. "Come and have a few words with me. It has been such a long time since I was privileged to visit with my wife's family."

As he led her down the hall towards his library, Sibilla was favourably impressed by both his manners and his countenance. Though nearly fifty, he yet retained the handsomeness characteristic of all the Cloudsleigh men. Only the rounding of his shoulders and the sadness in his dark eyes betrayed his age.

Sibilla settled herself into a well-cushioned armchair across from his imposing mahogany desk and admired the shelves of books which covered the walls from floor to ceiling.

"You must do an excessive amount of reading," she said hesitantly.

"Ah, well," laughed the Baron, "I enjoy it. What of you? How do you occupy your time?"

"Oh, returning calls, going for drives in the Park, parties, balls," said Sibilla. And then realizing how purely frivolous this seemed, added, "Occasionally I do sketches or write in my journal." Her voice trailed off uncertainly.

Here was a man who was spending his life immersed in scholarship, striving, as she had learned from Nell, to write a comprehensive book upon his specialty within the field of botany, and she could only prattle about the typical pastimes of a young woman engaged in the pursuit of a husband.

But Baron Cloudsleigh did not seem to notice what Sibilla considered the insignificance of her achievements.

"You sound like an industrious young woman," he said genially. "The amount of time the social life requires of its followers staggers the imagination of those like me who are used to the more solitary and sedentary life of a scholar. And what of your sisters? I understand you came to London with one of them."

"Yes, my sister, Sophia," Sibilla answered politely. "She is the youngest of the family. Once she and I are married, we will all have flown the nest."

"But you have an unmarried older sister, I thought?" inquired Lord Cloudsleigh, nervously toying with his spectacles which sat on a pile of papers before him. Sibilla shuddered awaiting the sound of the fatal name, Kitty. "I believe her name is Euphemia — Effie — she spent some time with us."

Sibilla brightened, although she wondered briefly how he could have forgotten so completely the magnetic presence of Kitty. "Oh yes, Effie," she said quickly. "Effie came back to Partridge Park — our family's country house — and goes about the estate on nature walks and participates in all the services at the village church — "

Nell's husband, who had been listening to this information intensely, frowned. "But is she happy?" he asked gruffly.

"Oh!" said Sibilla startled. She had never worried about Effie's peace of mind, for Effie had always been the loner in the family. "Why, I suppose she is." Seeing the concern upon Lord Cloudsleigh's face, she added hastily, "She seemed very low when she returned from London, but she declared that she would never return to the metropolis, and then threw herself into all sorts of local charities, and seems to be quite content with that."

"Ah," said the Baron. "Quite typical!" He stared at his papers for a few minutes, then shook himself and said more distinctly, "She's quite an unusual young lady." He looked at Sibilla with his dark, unfathomable eyes. "Perhaps you do not realize what a remarkable group of women you have for sisters."

Sibilla reflected briefly on the families she had known in London, especially Lady Holly and her daughters, and nodded quickly.

"Ah well," said Lord Cloudsleigh. "I overheard your discussion with Mills. You are quite right. Lady Cloudsleigh is at home. I believe you will find her in the exotic drawing room." He thrust his spectacles upon his head and began to fumble with the papers before him. Taking this as her dismissal, Sibilla arose, curtseyed politely, and left with a conventional farewell. Having an excellent head for directions and locales, she remembered which was the exotic drawing room and entered it unannounced.

She regretted this action as soon as she had turned the knob and thrust open the door, for her sister, Nell, seated upon the bench before an ebony piano, was once more in the embrace of her poet,

Mr. Lanning Tombs. Tempted to turn and run, Sibilla found that the noise of her entrance had alerted the pair, for Nell freed herself from Mr. Tombs' encircling arms, and turned a flushed face towards her younger sister.

"Sibilla!" she exclaimed breathlessly. "What a surprise! How lovely to see you!"

Privately doubting this sentiment, Sibilla dutifully advanced and was greeted by a rather agitated Mr. Tombs, who left the room with temerity.

Nell seemed unusually restless for she arose from the piano as soon as Mr. Tombs quitted the room, and roamed about, wringing her hands and darting quick, speculative glances at Sibilla. Finally, her composure departed, and she crossed the chamber rapidly, took Sibilla's hands in her own, and said beseechingly, "Sibil, you must try to understand. I love that man."

SIXTEEN

Lady Cloudsleigh's Strange Philosophy

SIBILLA, PREPARED FOR ANY confession but this, took her hands back and stared at Nell with horror.

"Sibil!" cried Lady Cloudsleigh, retreating to stare at the fire in the ebony hearth. "You must understand me, for no one else does, especially not my scholarly husband, the botanical genius!" Her voice vibrated with despair.

"But, Nell," exclaimed Sibilla, driven by desperation to honesty, "you are a married woman! A flirtation is fine—but love?"

"I do declare to you, Sibilla," said Nell, whirling about and holding out her arms in supplication, "I love that man. I never loved Arthur. He was the best of the lot when I came out. He was—is— kind, gentle, handsome, intelligent—and he offered the sort of life I wished. Entertaining, meeting important people, having a lovely house like this to decorate and invite people to," she waved her hands desperately. "But excitement, Sibilla! Adventure and intensity and passion! They were all lacking. Arthur is boring! Boring, completely, utterly, without redemption, boring! He thinks of nothing but his comfort and his ferns! I'm a young woman still. I have more to live

125

for than a group of sickly ferns that require names. Say you understand, dear sister, please tell me you understand my anguish—"

Sibilla, while privately considering that Nell was indulging in her usual dramatics, approached her sister and embraced her. "Poor Nell!" she said softly.

"You do understand," murmured Nell brokenly, clinging to her younger sister desperately.

"But, Nell," said Sibilla in the same quiet voice, holding Lady Cloudsleigh at arm's length, "you do realize that as a wife your duty is to your husband."

Nell stiffened and backed away from Sibilla. "I thought you were sympathetic," she declared indignantly. "But you've been trained to mouth all those same platitudes I learned as a girl. I warn you, Sibil, that they will not make you happy!"

"Sometimes the happiness of others is at your mercy," replied Sibilla meekly.

"Oh no!" cried Nell, fixing her sister with her intense dark eyes. "If I am not happy, I cannot make Arthur happy! You must think of yourself first, Sibilla!"

"But that is selfish!" declared her younger sister, aghast.

"Selfish!" mocked Nell. "Lanning would tell you that selfishness is our best quality as human beings."

"He is certainly selfish, willing to alienate you from your husband's affections," accused Sibilla.

"Nonsense," answered Nell. "My husband's affections were never with me, rather with his ferns and his own comfort."

"Nell, that's not true!" Sibilla said indignantly, remembering the adoring looks the Baron had spread upon his intended bride before the wedding.

Nell grudgingly admitted the point in contention. "At first, he was very solicitous," she confessed, "but he never knew me, he never understood what sort of person I am and what I require for happiness. He needed a wife, and I seemed to be eligible for that position."

"What else?" asked Sibilla. "You came to London for your Season, you flirted with the available men, and you accepted his proposal." Her voice became hesitant at the end for she reflected upon her present position and Dabney Griggs's recent proposal.

"Ah! You wonder what you are doing here yourself!" declared Nell, immediately aware of Sibilla's confusion. "We are raised for nothing else but to be wives! But do they ever teach us how to be a wife? Look at our mother! An invalid, retreating from all of the demands made upon her! If it wasn't so ludicrous, I should do the same myself. I am nearly thirty, and it has required all of those years for me to discover what I need in a man—excitement, a mind, a man who thinks and feels and expresses his feelings! A man who is not afraid of the judgments of Society or the conventions of the haut *ton*! A man who is not so afraid of his own shadow that he retreats to his library and lives between the pages of his books!"

"Quite true, Lady Cloudsleigh!" said a rough voice from the threshold. "I do prefer the serenity of the scientific world."

Both sisters were appalled by the sudden apparition of Baron Cloudsleigh, but Nell did not rush to her husband's side as Sibilla would have wished. She remained before the fire, contemplating her bejewelled white hands.

"Arthur prefers a minimum of fuss, in all areas of endeavour," she said bitterly, casting scornful eyes at her husband.

"I am sure Lady Sibilla is not interested in our domestic disputes," Lord Cloudsleigh said chidingly. "She must have come on an urgent errand, and you have not offered her any opportunity to reveal it."

With a contemptuous toss of her head, Nell turned towards her caller. "Sibilla?" she questioned.

"I am invited to participate in a quadrille ball," Sibilla said hastily, "and I wanted to borrow a necklace to match my gown."

"What colour is it?" asked Nell stiffly, pointedly ignoring Lord Cloudsleigh, who departed as quietly as he had come.

"Currant-red," mumbled Sibilla, "with a black lace overskirt."

"I have just the thing," her sister replied. "Wait here a moment."

Left alone in the middle of a tempest of emotions, no less intense for the civility which overlaid their expression, Sibilla strove to regroup her thoughts. The pleasant facade of Nell's marriage had at last shattered, revealing a contract constructed from loneliness and desperation, yet bringing comfort and satisfaction to neither of the partners. In an effort to recover her equilibrium, Sibilla tried to assign blame—Lord Cloudsleigh, for allowing his wife to use their marriage towards her own ends without ever offering her a chance to share in his concerns; Nell for accepting her husband's title and wealth but refusing to grant him her affections; Mr. Tombs for seducing a man's wife in his own home. And yet all three were equally guiltless. Sibilla perceived that Baron Cloudsleigh was the sort of man who would never demand attention but wait patiently in the hope that it would be freely given. Nell, beautiful and intelligent, eager to enjoy the glittering life of the London *ton*, finding that the prizes she had won were not enough. And Lanning Tombs, encouraged by a charming and passionate woman and ignored by her elderly and reclusive husband.

"Here you are, Sibil, my dear," proclaimed Nell in deliberately carefree tones, as she swept back into the room, a glittering strand of jewels dangling from her hand.

"Oh no, Nell, I couldn't wear those!" Sibilla said in horror, as she stared at the ruby necklace and the companion pendant earrings, the same her sister had worn at the Trendle ball. "What if I should lose them?"

"They will not unclasp of their own accord," commented Nell dryly, fastening the necklace about Sibilla's neck and helping her don the earrings.

Studying herself in the large mirror over the mantel, Sibilla was almost hypnotized by the gleam of the red fire encircling her neck. Nell looked on with an indifference that at first amazed Sibilla and then brought to mind the previous conversation. "You are not considering giving all of this up?" she said accusingly.

"I consider it," Nell replied calmly, "but you are quite right, it would be most difficult to renounce." She studied the rings on her fingers casually, and glanced about the room with apathy. "And yet—I should give Arthur a chance to be content again without me."

"Fulfill your promises as his wife," pleaded Sibilla. "What can Mr. Tombs offer you?"

"Ah, I know quite well, quite well, what Mr. Tombs can offer me," responded her sister with an absent-minded look in her eyes, toying with a curio taken from a nearby table. Shaking herself out of this seeming trance, she turned to Sibilla and said, "The necklace and earrings are yours. They were a gift from my husband and mine to dispose of as I please."

Torn between a desire to protest and a surge of greed which commanded her to be silent, Sibilla could only stammer her thanks and a farewell. Too late, she remembered that she had never questioned Nell about Kitty. So troubled did she appear on the journey home, that it was Roscoe who wished that he could offer her advice and consolation.

SEVENTEEN

A Young Lady of Fashion Entertains

"DEVIL!" CRIED KITTY, tossing her auburn curls at the Marquis of Dower, who sprawled upon the pale blue sofa in her sitting room while she performed upon the rosewood piano. "I declare you make such statements just to torment me, you monster!"

"Ah, the divine Lady Kitty!" drawled the Marquis. "I assure you that I am quite serious. She will make an excellent mistress for my household, having the appropriate background—"

"What is this?" inquired Valerian, who was handing his cloak and cane to the maid as he entered the room.

"Oh Val, darling!" cried Kitty, rising gracefully to welcome him. "Ned is regaling me with the most ridiculous story about marrying a little housemaid he has been flirting with," she said as he bent to kiss her outstretched hands. "He does it only to tease me, you know, for he has been swearing that I am the only woman for him these past four years. I should hope I could not be so easily supplanted."

"Certainly not in my affections, Lady Kitty," Valerian said smoothly, with an askance frown at the Marquis. He seated himself upon the rose-coloured sofa and added, "You know Ned as well as

I do, Lady Kitty, and you know well that Ned could never do something that would be such horrid bad *ton*. Such a marriage is well enough for the railroad barons and elderly Irish peers—" Ned coughed politely, and Valerian cast him a reproving look "—but not for the Prince of the Dandies."

"Ah!" said Kitty, clapping her hands and laughing delightedly. "I knew you would take my side! You must listen to him, Ned."

"Have I ever failed to support your wishes, Lady Kitty?" inquired Valerian in a bantering voice, but with an undertone of sorrow.

"No, indeed you have not," responded Kitty, her playfulness blending into sincerity and deep compassion. "You have been my truest friend in London, Mr. Cloudsleigh!"

"No!" declared the Marquis, rising. "I will not have you fawning upon young Cloudsleigh there! I demand another duet, Lady Kitty."

"*Bien súr,*" replied the lady, seating herself again at the piano. Her lovely contralto voice and his deep bass were merged in the strains of a popular ballad when the door to the sitting room opened again, and Dabney Griggs appeared. He seated himself alongside Valerian and listened politely to the melancholy conclusion of the song, applauding vigorously when it was finished.

"Mr. Griggs!" exclaimed Kitty. "How pleasant to see you again! May I offer you some sherry?"

"It would be my pleasure, Mrs. Meadows," responded that earnest young man, who preferred to address her by the name she used in Society, despite the familiarity evinced by his friends' usage of "Lady Kitty."

Kitty, dressed today in a simple house dress of pale yellow foulard, sprigged with blue and rose floral patterns and trimmed with ruches of the same colours, rang for the maid who brought in a cut-glass goblet of sherry for the new arrival.

As Valerian and Dabney exchanged the latest news, Kitty seated herself beside the Marquis and tried to elicit more information about his latest light-of-love. She was interrupted in this pleasant task by the announcement of two other visitors, Baron Champford and Randall.

"The loveliest lady in London," remarked the eldest of the Sylver brothers laconically, settling down upon the only unoccupied sofa in such a proprietary manner that his younger sibling was required to take up his position upon the piano bench, a bit removed from the rest of the company.

"Do tell us the latest *on dits*, Sylvester!" requested Valerian mockingly; as Kitty called for two more glasses of sherry.

"And she serves the finest sherry in town," commented Baron Champford, eyeing his glass speculatively. "Won't you tell us, dearest cousin, what it is?"

"Of course not," replied Kitty, with a gentle smile. "Women have need of their secrets. Some time I may be down at my heels in Calais, and you will visit me only to sample my sherry."

Baron Champford took another sip, raised his eyes to heaven in a grimace of appreciation, and proceeded to regale the company with stories gathered from his acquaintances at the clubs and his visit to Tattersalls.

"It is rumoured," he reported with an assumed ennui, "that Lady Muftow's eldest son, James, is head over heels for Eulalie, the ballet dancer, and she is threatening to publish some very incriminating letters if she is not given a handsome annuity. Doubtless, Lady Muftow is livid with rage, but there is little she can do. It seems the young fool was careless enough to suggest marriage in several of his missives."

"Never mention marriage," murmured Valerian lazily. "Cardinal rule."

"You should know, old man," commented the Marquis of Dower, chucking a pillow at his friend.

"Lord Cheeseborough put his greys up for sale," continued Sylvester, unperturbed by the commotion. "It's said that he invested unwisely in land speculation and will soon be retiring for the Continent. And Mrs. Cloudsleigh is also departing, to Italy, I believe, in search of a cure in the sun."

Kitty started. "Mrs. Cloudsleigh?" she said in uncharacteristically hoarse tones.

"Not your sister, my dear, Lady Kitty," Baron Champford added smoothly. "The wife of the estimable Member of Parliament, Mrs. Ashford Cloudsleigh."

Valerian studied Kitty anxiously as she turned to him.

"Is this true, Val?" she asked breathlessly.

"Confound it if I know," the young man replied carelessly. "Caroline is always taking some bird-brained notion into her head. I would not be surprised to learn of such a scheme. You must inquire from Ashford directly."

"What's that?" said a rich, deep voice at the sitting-room door, and the topic of the conversation entered. "Did I hear my name taken in vain?"

"Oh, it was a mere nothing," answered Kitty in a playful voice, rising quickly to link her arm in his. "Move, Ned, now that the guest of honour has arrived, we must provide him with a suitable throne."

"I am not obtuse," the Marquis replied, unfolding himself lazily from his seat. "I can determine when my presence is no longer required. But I claim a private audience with you, my lady Kitty, tomorrow in the afternoon." He bent to kiss his hostess's proffered hand and then lounged casually out of the room.

A short time later, the other visitors made their excuses and withdrew, Dabney Griggs volunteering to accompany Sylvester and Randall Sylver to a popular boxing establishment to watch Baron Champford defend his title against an upstart challenger, leaving only the younger and elder Cloudsleighs with Kitty.

"Thought you'd be at the Commons," Valerian said quickly to his uncle when the door closed behind the others. "Interesting debate scheduled for today."

"No, confound it," Ashford replied with irritation, "I've been cooped up all day helping Caroline with her packing."

There was a flash of tension in the room.

"Then she is leaving?" Valerian inquired in a strained voice. "Sylvester was just reporting her plans when you came in."

"'Pon my word," his uncle responded, shaking his head with annoyance, "that young man seems to absorb gossip by osmosis; sometimes he knows even before the event occurs." He sighed wearily. "Yes, it's quite true. Her good friend, Lady Firbush, has convinced her that only Italy's sunny climate can relieve her nervous condition. And yet for some godforsaken reason they intend to journey up to Chester first. Caroline wants to see her father, and he has a horse entered in the Chester races. They'll leave directly after

Easter, return to London for the opening of the Great Exhibition, and depart for the Continent immediately afterwards."

Kitty edged nervously towards the door to the hallway as Ashford rambled on about his wife's itinerary.

"Celia, send in the children!" she called out at the end of his speech, and with the fury of an unleashed volcano, little Alex and Clarissa scrambled into the sitting room and threw themselves upon Ashford and Valerian, thereby preventing any further discussion of the topic of Mrs. Cloudsleigh.

EIGHTEEN

The Hazards of Gaming

VALERIAN EMERGED from Kitty's house deep in thought, and made his way down Bruton Street east, so absorbed in his worries that he actually collided with Randall Sylver, who was preoccupied with his own problems.

"'Scuse me, Val," muttered the younger man, trying to edge off into the crowd.

"Hold on a moment," said Valerian, insuring compliance with this request by taking hold of Randall's coattails. "Thought you were watching your brother go at it with Chicken Horton?"

"Was," mumbled Randall, keeping his head down. "But I had an appointment to keep."

"An appointment, eh?" Valerian nudged his companion and winked conspiratorially. "Mind if I walk with you? What direction are you heading?"

"Foley Street," Randall answered desperately, setting off at a rapid pace. Valerian was hard put to keep up with him, and it was not for several minutes that he realized this was not an amatory expedition upon which Randall was embarked. His companion was so pale that his freckles stood out like blots of ink upon his face, and his fists alternately clenched and unclenched at his sides.

Therefore, when Randall tried to shrug him off when they reached Foley Street, Valerian first jokingly offered to accompany Randall upon his errand, and when this assistance was curtly refused, insisted on being admitted to his confidence.

"It's a mere nothing, of no consequence," Randall repeated nervously, but Valerian, noting his furtive glances towards a certain door on the far side of the street, guessed the nature of his secret.

"You've been playing deep and are dipped in the pocket, I daresay," he ventured.

Randall started, and then wearily nodded his head. "I have an engagement to play to recoup certain losses," he confessed.

"Not a good practice," Valerian reprimanded him. "And neither is that the establishment in which you would find an advantage," he added, waving his hand towards the gaming hell across the street.

"Can't help it," Randall muttered. "Have promised to meet someone there."

"Then let me come with you," Valerian suggested, putting his arm beneath Randall's elbow and guiding him towards the building. "What's your game today?"

"Hazard," said Randall curtly. Valerian whistled and shook his head but was silent as they passed over the threshold, after having been inspected by a stout and beery individual whose bulbous nose approximated the shape of a potato more than a human nose. To Valerian's dismay, this unsavoury person seemed familiar with young Randall, whom he waved by peremptorily, subjecting Mr. Cloudsleigh to a painstaking scrutiny before grunting his approval.

Randall had quickly disappeared through the crowd of rough characters seated in a haze of tobacco smoke in the tap room, and Valerian quickly jostled his way through this throng, at last gaining entrance to a smaller and more private room, where Randall was already seated at a table, his hands clutching the dice and his eyes feverish in anticipation of the game. Seated across from him were Major Garlinghouse and Captain Wheedle.

"Why, see who's come to join us!" exclaimed the captain, rising and coming over to shake Valerian's hand.

"Delighted to see you, Val!" called out Dudley Garlinghouse. "Come to join us at hazard, have you?"

"Whist is more to my liking," Valerian replied coolly, regretting that he had ever offered to accompany Randall Sylver. If Randall was in the clutches of this avaricious pair, he was truly in need of assistance, yet Valerian had been struggling to acknowledge Major Garlinghouse as merely an acquaintance, a difficult task for the other man was determined to use his relationship by marriage to gain the favour of the Cloudsleighs.

At Valerian's request, despite some petulance on Randall's part, the dice were put away and the cards brought out. Valerian, an accomplished player, had expected to be able to help Randall make up his losses. It was, therefore, extremely disturbing to discover that his young partner relied on luck rather than strategy, and preferred to wager heavily upon great risks which would have paid off handsomely had they ever turned in his favour, which they never did. Rather than bettering Randall's precarious financial situation, Valerian found that he went down heavily to the tune of nearly fifty pounds, a sum which he paid promptly and gently steered the younger man out of the gaming hell.

Randall was sulky and agitated rather than grateful for Valerian's well-timed assistance.

"We should have played another rubber," he protested bitterly. "I could feel my luck turning."

"Whist is not a game of luck," Valerian chided him softly. "A good player can win with a bad set of cards."

"Well, hazard's my game anyway," muttered Randall, kicking a stone in his path, which scudded upwards and nicked a spirited chestnut full in the side, causing that beast to try vigourously for several minutes to unseat his rider.

Valerian, about to read the younger man a lecture on the dangers of gaming, sighed and passed it off as a thankless task. "Do you play with those two often?" he asked gently.

"Dudley and the Captain? I should say so," Randall answered quickly. "They took me around and taught me the different games, and then they often loan me some of the ready when I'm doing paricularly well."

"Do you owe them now?" Valerian continued his interrogation in the same soft tones.

"Several hundred," Randall replied, his face reddening and his voice becoming hoarse.

Valerian stared at his companion aghast. "You'll never get free of a debt like that if you try to win it back on the gaming tables," he said bluntly. "Why don't you ask your father for the money?"

"Oh, the governor has told me he won't give me another penny, and he threatens to cut me out altogether if I continue 'throwing it away,' as he terms it," Randall responded with carefree desperation. "My mother can give me a bit, but she has only pin money. She gave me most of her trust fund long ago. I know I should be able to come right again in time. I've gained as much as I owe now in one night of play."

"Not recently, I wager," said Valerian with sarcasm.

Randall shook his head slowly.

"Listen," Valerian stopped him. "You must believe me that your best course is to borrow that money from your father, or some other member of your family, pay off all of your debts, and never deal with those two again." Seeing the cloud pass over Randall's face, he added in a lighter tone, "Now let us leave these unpleasant topics behind. I shall not bother you with them again. Come along to my lodgings; I have some good Havannah and some splendid Glenlivet."

NINETEEN

An Auction at Lady Holly's House

THE DRESSING ROOM PROVIDED for the female guests at Lady Holly's quadrille ball was in a state of pandemonium. Each mirror was thronged with a host of young ladies, all attempting to compare themselves with their neighbours and put the finishing touches to their coiffures. In the centre of the room several of the "Months" were having bows tied and buttons hooked, and all were chattering away about dressmakers, trimmings, and jewellery.

Sibilla's ruby necklace was a cynosure of attention. Still disturbed by the circumstances in which she had acquired it, Sibilla responded to the many compliments with the curt reply that it was a family heirloom, which was the same answer she had given Mrs. Pleet. She was well satisfied with her coiffure, an arrangement of thick braids of her glossy dark hair, ornamented by a single red rose, and her simple yet striking costume, bereft of the passementerie, tassels, bows, and lace ruffles common to the evening dresses of the other "Months," required no last minute adjustments. She spent the time discussing the latest variations of the quadrille with September, a quiet girl attired in a buff-coloured silk dress trimmed with zinnias, who had an extraordinary command of the patterns involved in each figure.

"The opposite lady and gentleman advance and retire, the rest do the same," said September in her soft, breathy voice. "Then the ladies advance and a gentleman passes between them, and this is repeated till all of the gentlemen have done the same, whereupon everyone returns to their places and turns."

"I learned La Wellington; it was the only figure that my sister and cousin could remember. Is it much danced at this time?" Sibilla inquired anxiously.

"Indeed, it will doubtless be called," September responded, eager to soothe Sibilla's fears. "But you need have no fear. Any lady who can dance, glide, tread the polka, and knows how to go through the lancers, can take part. Just rely on the leader's instructions and watch your companions if you are in doubt."

"Who is the leader?" cried May, a giddy girl in a flounced dress of pink-coral grosgrain, the gauze overskirt looped up with bunches of pink roses. "Lavinia tells me it's a secret. Only Lady Holly knows, and she won't tell who she asked to be the leader!"

"And no one will know, until the dance begins," said Lavinia in tones of hauteur and with raised eyebrows. She was portraying December in a cherry-red velvet gown trimmed with white ermine. Sibilla, who disliked the older girl, secretly hoped she would be too warm in the velvet.

"But who is invited to participate?" asked May with a giggle.

"I believe the Marquis of Dower is coming," said Lavinia, with an air of superiority. The other girls squealed. "Baron Champford." There was another outburst of feminine approval. "His brother, Randall, Dabney Griggs, Arthur Crampton-Manners, Charles Treswick, James and Simon Muftow, Embury Clarke, Edgar and Edwin Calverley."

"Eleven," mused September thoughtfully.

"Yes, eleven," piped Mary Holly, dressed in a *lilas-ancien* silk gown as February. "Mama will not confess who she has asked to be the leader."

"But we have a nice guess, don't we, little sister?" said Lavinia smugly.

"Oh yes, indeed we do," chorused Mary.

"Tell, tell!" begged the other girls, but Lavinia quelled their excitement with the imperious statement, "That is our conjecture, one which will be confirmed only by the vision of the leader himself." And so saying, she swept from the room with an arrogant twitch of her velvet skirts.

Taking this as a signal, the other "Months" put an end to their primping and descended sedately to the small ballroom, transformed into a bower of greenery for the event, where they were shown to their assigned seats. Several of the gentlemen who had already arrived were milling about under an arbour at the other side of the floor, clutching small pieces of paper in their fists. These papers were inscribed with such cryptic words as "March," "June," and "October," and thus indicated the identities of their partners. Once the young ladies were seated — a veritable rainbow of colours and costumes — their escorts set off across the floor, trying to guess the month which each female sought to portray and thereby locate their partner for the quadrille.

This occasioned quite a bit of merriment and not a few tempers were roused when November was asked if she was June, and May was mistaken for September. Since the young men continued to arrive and choose the names of their designated partners out of a basket held by Lady Holly, this turmoil continued until ten o'clock when the quadrille was scheduled to begin.

To Sibilla's disappointment, Arthur Crampton-Manners had chosen her as his partner. She tried to nod politely to his incessant chatterings about how well his chestnuts did the distance on a race to Richmond, and looking about the room wondered with some malice if Lady Holly had arranged the couplings for Lavinia Holly was matched with the Marquis of Dower, while Mary Holly was seated alongside Baron Champford at whom she cast great sheep's eyes. However, Aunt Lucy, glowering from the dowager's side of the ballroom did not seem well pleased with Lucinda's partner, the correct and formal Mr. Dabney Griggs.

In short, all the men had arrived, but the mysterious "leader" and Sophy's partner. Sibilla tried to cast consoling looks at her younger sister, who sat bright and flushed with anticipation beside an empty gilt chair, endeavouring to appear totally at ease despite the absence of her escort.

The musicians, on a dais at the far end of the hall, had finished tuning up, and now motioned to Lady Holly wondering whether or not to begin the quadrille. She argued with them angrily for several minutes, turned away, motioning them to be silent, turned back and commanded them to begin, and while she was so engaged, a lone male figure entered the room. Valerian Cloudsleigh, in a nicely fitting coat of black superfine with a pale blue satin waistcoat, heavily embroidered, matched with grey trousers, bearing in his hand an ivory nosegay holder full of forget-me-nots, cornflowers, and gentians which he presented to Sophy. As Mr. Crampton-Manners whispered in Sibilla's ear about how she should go for a ride in the Park with him on the morrow, she once more cursed Lady Holly for having so obviously assigned partners, for how else would Valerian have known what colours Sophy would be wearing?

This entrance had created quite a stir among the assembled company, and Lady Holly, whirling about from her quarrel with the musicians, spotted Valerian and came swooping across the room.

"Ah, Mr. Cloudsleigh!" she enunciated so clearly that all of the chaperones and lookers-on could hear every syllable. "We have been waiting for you to begin the dance. Pray, take up your position as leader!"

Valerian bowed slightly to this suggestion, proffered his hand to Sophy, who was trembling with excitement and fear at being the partner of the leader, and led the other couples out upon the floor.

Sibilla found that once the dance began she did not mind the escort of Mr. Crampton-Manners, who was so absorbed in his contemplation of his feet and who mumbled to himself over and over again the instructions for each figure ("Then the gentlemen advance, then the gentlemen advance, then the gentlemen advance," he would say desperately while advancing), that Sibilla was free of his attentions and could watch the other dancers. Baron Champford was a comic spectacle, always heading in the wrong direction at the wrong time, and repeatedly calling out to his partner for advice on what to do next. Sophy was performing prettily, following gracefully Valerian's lead and they made a charming couple in the first set.

Sibilla was breathless from the exercise when the musicians stopped, and the gentlemen went off to fetch refreshments for their wilting partners, who sat fanning themselves upon their chairs and accepting the compliments of the mothers, chaperones, and younger sisters who composed the audience. Sibilla, alone, dreading the return of Arthur Crampton-Manners, was startled by the sudden apparition of Valerian Cloudsleigh who held out a small package wrapped in tissue and tied with a red bow.

"A favour for July," he said with an engaging smile and a slight bow.

Speechless from surprise, Sibilla only nodded faintly and bent to undo the parcel, which contained a splendid French black lace fan with gilded mother-of-pearl ribs.

"Oh, it's exquisite, Mr. Cloudsleigh," she said softly, with an uncustomary shyness.

"Your appreciation was my desire and is my pleasure," replied Valerian swiftly.

"What's that?" snapped Aunt Lucy, waddling over and glaring at the delicate frivolity which Sibilla was slowly folding and unfolding.

"A fan, a gift from Mr. Cloudsleigh," said Sibilla uncertainly.

"Humph!" snorted Aunt Lucy. One of her heavy eyebrows raised itself while its companion bent towards the bridge of her nose, indicating extreme disapproval and an offended moral sensibility. Sibilla suspected that this was too dear of a present for a young lady to receive from a mere acquaintance. But the sensuous beauty of the fan was compelling, and she raised it defiantly and fanned herself coolly.

"Your servant, Lady Sibilla," said Mr. Cloudsleigh, with a smile of approval, and withdrew.

Sibilla's suspicions were soon corroborated.

"You must return that piece of frippery," Aunt Lucy commanded with anger. To Sibilla's calm request for a reason, Mrs. Pleet had two. "First, it is too costly a gift for a lady," Aunt Lucy laid heavy emphasis on the latter word, as she appropriated the fan and studied it appraisingly, "to receive from a gentleman who is not her intended spouse."

"Perhaps we are secretly betrothed," suggested Sibilla pertly, attempting to repossess her present.

Aunt Lucy rapped her over the knuckles with it instead. "Don't be preposterous, miss!" she snapped. "You cannot marry your own sister's stepson. Only think what people would say! Very bad *ton!*" She returned to her earlier line of argument. "In the second place, it was ill-advised of Mr. Cloudsleigh to single you out from all of the other guests to be the recipient of his attentions. You will be noticed and talked about. I believe Lady Muftow witnessed the entire thing and after your little episode with Mr. Griggs—"

"Why, I am not paying Mr. Griggs the slightest mind tonight," Sibilla pointed out sweetly, glancing over at the tall, red-haired man who was bending to whisper in Lucinda's ear. Lucinda responded with a becoming blush and an enchanted smile. Suddenly, with pink in her cheeks and a sparkle in her eyes, she was a very pretty woman.

Aunt Lucy, spotting the battle being lost in another part of the field, hurried away, still clutching Sibilla's fan, to skirmish with Mr. Griggs. Apparently she was successful in routing that enemy, for when the musicians began the next set, during which the young ladies were required to choose their new partners, Lucinda reluctantly approached the Marquis of Dower. Sophy comforted the rejected Mr. Griggs by soliciting his hand. Sibilla, casting about for a partner, saw her cousin winking at her wildly with a desperate look upon his face as the bouncy May bore down upon him.

"Deuced glad you rescued me, cuz," Baron Champford said, wiping his brow with a green silk handkerchief which he removed from the pocket of his flaming orange waistcoat, as he led Sibilla towards the dance floor. "Lord, I hate these functions. Never come to them. Avoid them. Wouldn't have shown tonight, but Val insisted on it. Said he needed the support of his friends. Don't know why he came."

"He's the leader," suggested Sibilla helpfully.

"Humbug!" her cousin replied. "You don't think that is a distinction, do you? Having bloodthirsty females swarming all over one like a flock of hornets! No, Valerian must have some dark purpose which he refuses to reveal. To endure this sort of torture without a murmur!"

"Really, cousin," said Sibilla reprovingly.

"This is no more than an auction," responded Baron Cloudsleigh, launching into his oration with renewed enthusiasm. "That avaricious harpy, Lady Holly, trying to convince contented bachelors to enter into the bonds of—"

"Sylvester!" exclaimed Sibilla, upset.

"'Tis true, cuz!" Baron Champford replied. "The Season is no more or less than an enormous Tattersalls for young fillies, some sure money-makers, some with fancy pedigrees, others with good form, a never-ending procession of roans, chestnuts —"

"I declare I will not listen to another word!" protested Sibilla and her threat was quickly transformed into reality when the musicians began and the lively strains of the music drowned Sylvester's next phrases. But for Sibilla, though she continued to advance and retire, turn, chassé and chain, her innocent enjoyment of this party was gone. The colourful dresses, the sparkling jewellery, the quaint notion of the twelve months, the wilting greenery festooned upon the walls, all seemed pathetically like trimmings in a shop window. Even the hilarious contortions of Baron Champford failed to raise her spirits.

The mamas and chaperones sat on the sidelines anxiously, noting every tenderly bestowed smile or whispered word, hoping without hope that her daughter or charge would be the one to capture the elusive prey, but willing from desperation to accept any honourable offer.

For very few of these young men were thinking even remotely of marriage. The Marquis of Dower had been the catch of the Season for too long, without showing the slightest predisposition to matrimony or yet attractions to any maidens of marriageable age, for the matchmakers to place any hope upon his conquest. When a man had everything — good looks, wealth, charm, a title — when he spent the winter in Paris and was found on the moors in autumn, when he was invited everywhere, hunting with the Melton men, yachting with the R.V.Y. club, and jockeying his own steeplechaser to victory at the National, what need had he for the burden of a wife and family? He carried on love affairs with elegant Duchesses and found excitement in evading their husbands, while companionship and pleasure were provided by a string of mistresses, each replaced by another young and eager beauty when the former had lost her novelty and appeal. Too clever to be manipulated into marriage, too unprincipled to be concerned with reputations he ruined by his exploits, and yet too attractive to be forgotten, the Marquis of Dower was the lodestar of the London Marriage Mart, appearing in the daydreams and haunting the night-dreams of every unmarried young woman and her mother.

Valerian Cloudsleigh, without having shattered so many hopes or broken so many hearts as his bosom companion, was not yet the focus of so many dreams, for he was younger, had not the personal fortune, nor the immediate prospect of a title, and the tales of his ballet dancers enshrined in villas in St. John's Wood and young widows provided with lodgings on Berkeley Street, were legion. "Still sowing his wild oats," was the opinion of the matrons.

Baron Champford should have been a likely candidate, but he was terrified by the very word "marriage" and his younger brother, Randall, was deplorably too shy. Dabney Griggs was, unfortunately, the son of a man who had started his life as a porter in a railway terminus, but his fortune was promising if his appearance was not. And so it was towards him and Mr. Treswick (good family, slight prospects), Mr. Crampton-Manners (possibility of working his way up at the embassy because of his charm, his only redeeming virtue), and Mr. Embury Clarke (handsome, ambitious) that the mamas directed their effort.

Sibilla, without being in possession of all the gossip and stories which the chaperones traded at every social occasion, guessed these same facts, as she danced woodenly through the remainder of the evening. "A bird in a gilded cage," she thought, her smile frozen on her face, and yet the only escape was into another cage.

TWENTY

Put Through Their Paces

EASTER FOLLOWED HARD UPON the quadrille ball, and the three girls, dressed in their best, attended services with Aunt Lucy at fashionable St. George's in Hanover Square. Suffocated by the heat and closeness of the church, oppressed by the crowding, and dispirited by the sight of the women, luxuriously clad, bejewelled, feathered and furred, Sibilla, in her new role as cynical spectator, derived no pleasure from the message of resurrection and new life, though Easter had always been her favourite religious holiday.

In truth, she paid little heed to the sermon, her thoughts wandering instead to Amy and the Reverend Brittle and wondering how Easter was being celebrated in that small congregation. Amy, surrounded by new life which she herself had created, must be far happier, and yet she had come to that role in life by enduring the same trials Sibilla was now experiencing.

With a quick glance to the left, Sibilla could see the small, elegant form of her sister, Lady Cloudsleigh, resplendent in a heavily trimmed gown of *lilas-ancien* silk, and displaying an enormous amethyst necklace and pendant earrings, her head, topped with a frivolous lavender bonnet, was bowed deferentially, and one small gloved hand rested intimately on the arm of Baron Cloudsleigh. Sibilla knew that the apparent felicity of this couple was a fraud, and it troubled her deeply.

As they left the church, Sibilla was further disturbed by a glimpse of the auburn-haired young woman who she was certain was Kitty, accompanied by two small children and escorted by Valerian Cloudsleigh. What path had Kitty chosen? Were those her children, and Valerian her lover? Did her situation bring her happiness, and was it worth the price of losing her family and her good name in the world?

Sibilla tried to discuss these topics with Sophy, but her younger sister could only prattle of the Great Exhibition and the Royal Academy show, both of which would open the following week, and a planned luncheon at Richmond. That marriage was inevitable, and that bliss was equivalent with wedlock, were indestructible axioms in her mind; she thought Sibilla's fears were preposterous.

"Why, only look at our sisters!" she said when confronted by Sibilla. "Charlotte and Major Garlinghouse—"

"I do not think she is happy," Sibilla said mildly. "She seems so nervous and timid, and he flirts so."

"Doubtless that is why she seems high-strung," Sophy replied innocently. "Her husband is so very handsome and attractive to the ladies, but she is his wife. He may tease a little. I imagine many foolish young girls throw themselves at his feet, but he returns to Charlotte. You recall how she talks about him, as if he were a God, an Adonis among men."

"She might be in love, but still be unhappy," Sibilla pointed out calmly.

"Oh yes!" agreed Sophy. "But not when you are married to the man you love. And think of Nell—"

"I was thinking of Nell," Sibilla said brusquely, unwilling to divulge all of her thoughts about her sister. "She is married, but unhappy."

"Why, how could she be unhappy?" Sophy asked indignantly. "You saw her at the church today. Baron Cloudsleigh was most attentive to her, she had that lovely purple gown and that stunning hat, she has an elegant town house and a country estate, she gives parties that are the talk of the town—"

"Perhaps—" began Sibilla, but Sophy would not hear of it.

"Humbug!" she retorted. "He may be an older man, but he is yet handsome and patient and generous. Nell never talked about romance and flowers. She wanted a title and wealth and an influential position in Society, and she has all of that, while her husband seems pleased to have such a beautiful and popular wife."

"That might be only external appearance," ventured Sibilla carefully.

"Marriages can be made," Sophy retorted quickly. "I believe that any man and woman can fall in love and create a good marriage as long as they wish to do so. I certainly intend to do so."

"And have you found the man who wishes to do so yet?" asked her sister chidingly.

Sophy blushed and giggled. "Why, you know," she said softly, "the men in London are nice enough, but Leslie, despite his lack of polish and knowledge of the world, is still much closer to my ideal." She sighed softly, and added, "The men here know how to make compliments and dance and say pretty things and speak of the latest books and paintings and plays, but I do not quite believe that they care about any of those things, whereas with Leslie, we only talked of simple topics — the neighbours, the crops, the weather, the amusing people we both knew — but it meant more to me than what I discuss now."

"You should have insisted on marrying him!" Sibilla exclaimed, touched by this confession. "Despite what Mama said!"

"Oh no!" Sophy was genuinely shocked. "If Mama and Papa thought he was not the man for me, I could not go against their wishes. Why they might have refused to come and see me. Can you imagine being married without Mama and Papa there? I would not feel married. Or living alongside Partridge Park and not being able to ride over to inquire about the news? And my children, the poor babes, would have grown up without knowing their grandparents? That would not be a marriage to me!"

"Nell is not in contact with them," Sibilla pointed out dryly. "Nor Kitty."

"And I am sure they suffer for it," Sophy answered hotly. "It is Nell's own fault. She never bothered to explain to Mama what had caused Effie to return home or what she knew of Kitty's disappearance. She cut herself off. And I will wager that when she has children she will regret her contempt for their approval."

"And I would wager that Nell will never care," Sibilla argued earnestly. "Sophy, when you become a wife, your husband should be more important to you than your family. If you cannot give him your complete love and devotion and attention, then what hope does your marriage have?"

Sophy shook her head wisely. "Ah," she said, "but if my family does not approve of the man I intend to marry, then he must not be the right one for me, because I intend to give my husband all the love and — all those other things you spoke of — but I also intend to enjoy the continued respect of Mama and Papa, and therefore I must find a man they will approve."

"And have you found such a perfect being?" inquired Sibilla with some sarcasm.

Sophy flushed again. "Why, I am certain they would like Mr. Cloudsleigh—" Sibilla looked at her strangely, and Sophy said quickly, "Well, he did spend a great deal of time with me at Lady Holly's ball. Or perhaps Mr. Griggs."

"Mr. Griggs!" remarked Sibilla, provoked beyond measure.

"You rejected his suit, Sibilla, you know you did," said Sophy, stung by her sister's scorn, "so I know you are not interested in him, and he is most polite and thoughtful."

"But you cannot even choose between him and Mr. Cloudsleigh," Sibilla said spitefully.

Sophy put her head up proudly. "Neither of them has declared any interest," she replied primly. "But either of them might, you know." When this sally did not improve her older sister's disposition, she added rapidly, "Just think, we are to have new dresses for the luncheon at Richmond. I should like lilac foulard and a scarf mantilla of the same, what do you think?"

Sibilla, put out of countenance by what she considered to be her younger sister's obstinacy, only grunted in reply, and it required all of Sophy's pretty manners and cajoling ways to draw her out into a discussion of the relative merits of mantillas and paletots, foulards and silk, lilac and lavender and grey.

When Madame Doucette appeared the following day, Sibilla had decided on a dress of pale green wih a lace paletot with long sleeves, while Sophy was promised lilac foulard with a scarf mantilla and Lucinda would appear in an underskirt of red-and-white striped foulard with an overskirt and lace fichu of figured alpaca.

The dressmaker took Lady Sibilla aside on this occasion, and inquired, a little more sharply than previously, about the payment of her bill. Sibilla assured her that the promised sum was being sent by her parents and would be paid in the immediate future. After the woman had left, Sibilla dashed off another dunning letter to Partridge Park, but with little hope of a positive response.

Meanwhile, their time was filled with countless calls, parties, balls, teas, routs, and rides in the Park. Sibilla, still discomposed by Baron Champford's remarks, was unable to enter into these activities with the same relish as Lucinda and Sophy, and eventually her attitude was noticed by the young men whom they encountered daily. Even the Marquis of Dower, who usually paid Sibilla only the most superficial of attention and plied her with compliments as extravagant as they were silly, dropped his bantering tone one afternoon in the Park and asked with genuine concern why she seemed so dispirited.

"Oh, one cannot enjoy the Season forever," said Sibilla with an attempt at lightheartedness. "One grows tired of pleasure if it is never-ending."

"True enough," responded the Marquis. "Yet you seem to be experiencing despondency more than ennui."

"Surely, you are more apt to feel that way," Sibilla answered quickly, trying to turn the topic of conversation from herself.

"Despondency!" laughed the Marquis, trying to hold in his high-spirited chestnut. "Ennui, perhaps, but only when socially acceptable! At one of Lady Cloudsleigh's parties, for instance, where your importance is measured in terms of your boredom. But no, I am never enervated by Society, no matter how fashionable it is to pretend otherwise. There is always a new wine to be tasted, a new tobacco to be smoked, a new horse to be tamed, or a new young lady to be—" He laughed again, throwing back his head in surrender to his delight. "Almost committed a horrendous *faux pas*," he said to Sibilla, when he had finished with his merriment. "Never you worry your pretty head about such matters. You'll be married off before the end of the Season."

"Precisely the problem," murmured Sibilla, repeating her comment when the Marquis stooped to hear it.

"Why a problem, Lady Sibilla?" he inquired with his boyishly engaging smile. "'Tis the dream of every young woman who comes to London!"

"But a marriage that is happy—" began Sibilla.

"Oh, if you want a marriage that is happy," the Marquis said lightly, "then you do indeed have reason to be despondent. Marriage is not an institution that was created to bring happiness. Some people speak of how your joys are shared in a marriage. It's possible, but then your sorrows are doubled, or quadrupled, I have no doubt. Never look to marriage for redemption from suffering. If you wish to be unhappy, be alone and unhappy. Then at least you have the pleasure of indulging in your own misery, knowing that it is your own creation. And if you do marry, never marry for love. Marriage would not be so bad if it were not contaminated by the notion of love. The ecstasies of love seem so desirable only in comparison to the pits of despair and darkness into which love also plunges the lover." And with these reassuring words, he spurred his impatient horse, which carried him off among the throngs of Parkgoers.

Sibilla caught a glimpse of the rose-coloured phaeton with its auburn-haired occupant once more at the far end of the Park. Valerian Cloudsleigh, on his coal-black steed, was escorting the vehicle as it roamed the drives, but upon this occasion Sibilla was never near enough to say she had identified her sister.

She wondered why Valerian plied her with gifts, the charming guinea pigs, who lived squeaking in their bird cage in a corner of her bedroom, and the exquisite French fan, which had been confiscated by Aunt Lucy. It was possible these were attempts to assuage a conscience filled with guilt for having transformed a respectable young woman from a noble family into his paramour, who lived her life in fear of being recognized by members of that same family. And yet it did not make sense. Would Valerian have kissed her as he did that evening in the library if Kitty was his mistress? Or was he perhaps that unscrupulous? She had no doubt that the Marquis of

Dower was such a man, considering his attentions to Peggy and his denunciations of marriage and love.

Sibilla sighed and, perceiving Mr. Treswick approaching on a roan stallion, waved to him so appealingly that he immediately attached himself to her. Deciding to limit herself to these more conventional and safe individuals, Sibilla mistakenly exerted too much of her natural charm and wit upon Mr. Treswick, who was so overwhelmed that he appeared the next morning at Corrough House to ask for her hand in marriage.

He was not surprised when Sibilla politely declined his offer, for he thought her a goddess among women and thus too far above him, and told her so. But Aunt Lucy was appalled. Sibilla had now been the recipient of two proposals, both from eminently respectable and acceptable young men. Both she had rejected. Mrs. Pleet owed a letter to her sister, the Countess of Corrough, and decided to elaborate upon these events in the hope that the Countess would chastise her wayward daughter. Sophy, too, had received an offer, from an infatuated young Cornet in the Guards, a marriage unacceptable to both Sophy herself and Mrs. Pleet, but Lucinda had, unfortunately, received none. Thus, when Mrs. Pleet called the two sisters into the study for lectures upon their behaviour, she was understandably incensed. Sophy emerged crying from her interview while Sibilla, after a stormy interlude, returned to her room white-faced and trembling.

She was not in a receptive mood for the vision of Peggy, pink-cheeked, dreamy-eyed, crooning an Irish lullaby and bringing in a steaming basin of hot water.

"Stop making so much noise!" Sibilla snapped. "I don't see what you have to be so happy about!"

"Why, Miss Sibil," replied Peggy soothingly. "The night is clear, all of the stars are out, it's been a lovely day today, and you are going to Richmond for a picnic luncheon tomorrow."

"And what are you doing tomorrow?" continued Sibilla, unaffected by Peggy's optimism. "I trust you are not indulging in a foolish affair with the Marquis of Dower, who is not the slightest bit interested in marriage, or love, for that matter."

"You're upset by something, Miss Sibil," said Peggy with sorrowful eyes, "or you would not be carrying on this way. Your aunt has been scolding you, or something else has gone wrong."

"I am not upset, I am not carrying on, and I am not worried," said Sibilla, extremely upset by Peggy's insights, "except by your extraordinary thick-headedness in refusing to see that the Marquis of Dower does not have any honourable intentions towards you."

Peggy laughed, her low, sensuous chuckle. "Of course he does not, Sibil, my dear," she said with delight. "I am well aware of his intentions. But women have ever been the clever sex. Ned does not know what he wants. I do." And she began singing her lullaby again.

"Stop that!" cried Sibilla, unaccountably annoyed. "You will make a fool out of yourself, you will be ruined, and you will have no reason to run about singing silly songs at the top of your lungs."

Peggy slammed down the basin of water which overflowed and trickled down the bureau. "I have told you before and I will tell you again, Miss Sibil," she said, her hands on her hips, "that you are likely to turn into another Mrs. Pleet. You both follow your own strict codes of morality and behaviour, never looking outside your limits to understand that every rule has an exception, every law a loophole, every perruson a weakness. You may never be married, and you may never be in love, but only because of your own intolerance. I shall be both!" and she stormed out of the room, slamming the door behind her and leaving Sibilla in a flood of tears.

TWENTY-ONE

An Unsatisfactory Expedition to Richmond

THIS FIT OF WEEPING left Sibilla with red eyes and swollen lids on the morning of the planned luncheon at Richmond. She bathed her face in water at least a dozen times before she felt capable of descending to breakfast. Inexplicably, Aunt Lucy had never dismissed the cook, although a caterer had been hired for the reception, and Sibilla was confronted with the same unappetizing spectacle of luke-warm eggs, weak tea, and cold bacon which had been the staple fare since the first morning at Corrough House. She and Sophy had accustomed themselves to supping on toast and coffee, which was kept warm in a silver urn with a candle beneath it, but their boycott had done nothing to prevent the prodigious quantities of inedible food which were produced by the kitchen daily.

Peggy could not be found to dress either Merrell sister, and Sibilla, planning to apologize for her hastily spoken words of the previous evening, suffered through the inept ministrations of Lily instead as she donned the new promenade outfit consisting of a green silk gown and an ecru lace *paletot*, matched with a becoming straw hat.

Indeed, Lily was so clumsy that Sophy and Sibilla had to dress each other's hair, for Lily's attempts had produced unacceptable coiffures. Sophy recrimped her hair and wore it looped up and pinned underneath a lilac bonnet, while Sibilla braided her thick locks and pinned them to the back.

Lucinda, under Sophy's influence, had become more sensitive to good taste in clothing and coiffures, and for the outing she wore her hair fastened in two braids on either side of her face while the rose colour of her plain alpaca waist and her fetching bonnet brought a tint of colour to her normally pale complexion.

The trio waited nervously in the sitting room under the reproving eye of Aunt Lucy for the gentlemen; Dabney Griggs was the first to arrive. Perhaps he had inquired of Aunt Lucy, or perhaps he had a secret source of information within the household, but he presented each of the ladies with a nosegay that suited their attire. After tucking one bloom into the front of their dresses, Sophy and Lucinda arranged their bouquets of lilacs and roses in crystal vases in the sitting room; Sibilla immediately placed one of the gardenias from her fragrant bouquet into the ribbon of her hat before asking that the rest be sent up to Peggy's room.

Shortly after the arrival of Mr. Griggs, who sat awkwardly upon a chair and inquired repeatedly about their health, Mr. Cloudsleigh appeared, dressed in a striking costume of pearl-grey, with a black stock for the only contrast, and he had not even been seated before Mary Crank was brought in by her father. Following hard on her heels were the two Sylver brothers, who burst into the room crying that the horses were fresh and they must depart immediately.

Because the party was so large, it had been decided to take two vehicles: the Trendle barouche and Mr. Cloudsleigh's phaeton. For propriety's sake, Aunt Lucy declared that Sibilla could ride in the phaeton if seated beside her cousin, Randall, while Valerian would command his fine matched pair; Mary, Sophy, and Lucinda would ride with Mr. Griggs in the barouche while Baron Champford tooled the ribbons.

It was a lively journey for the two young men had placed heavy bets upon which could make Richmond in record time, and they drove at such a breakneck pace that Sibilla did not have to worry about conversing with her monosyllabic cousin, Randall, for the words were snatched from her mouth as she tried to speak. She watched the scenery fly by, held firmly onto her hat, and prayed that they would not be overturned into a ditch.

Valerian achieved their destination only minutes before the Trendle barouche, and there was some discussion of whether or not a record had been broken. Once the argument was settled, the party rented boats and rowed about on the Thames. Lucinda and Sophy, eagerly pairing off with Dabney Griggs and Valerian Cloudsleigh, seemed to be having an enjoyable time for their girlish laughter could be heard pealing across the wide river. Sibilla, confined in a boat with the indolent Baron Champford, his excruciatingly reclusive brother, Randall, and the petrified and inarticulate Mary Crank, did the lion's share of the rowing and the conversing.

"Such a lovely day," she said for the fourth time.

"Indeed!" squeaked Mary for the fourth time.

Baron Champford said nothing, as usual, but continued to puff at his cheroot which surrounded the company with clouds of thick, evil-smelling smoke. Mary Crank began to choke, and though Randall signalled at his brother desperately, Sylvester did not notice, so rapt was he in the contemplation of the smoke rings he was forming. Mary fanned herself rapidly for a few moments with one small white-gloved hand, and then collapsed in the bottom of the boat in a swoon.

Baron Champford leaned back even farther and indicated with a sweeping gesture that his brother should go to the rescue of the ailing female. Sibilla, attempting to keep the boat from drifting down river, could only watch helplessly as Randall poured handfuls of the dirty Thames water over Miss Crank, irrevocably soiling her white poplin dress. Sibilla was not surprised when Mary, finally revived after suffering near-drowning, was violently ill. This catastrophe rendered the timid girl completely speechless, and brought to a quick end the boat ride.

Sibilla, being handed onto firm ground by Baron Champford, who had finally disposed of his cigar, could not say that she was ungrateful to Mary. Her hands were blistered, and her head was aching from the brightness of the sun. She aided Mary into the coolness of the inn, saw that she was provided with a quiet, dim room where she could lie with cold compresses upon her head, and descended to find Lucinda and Sophy with their companions gathered in the dining parlour.

After informing the others of Mary's condition, Sibilla joined them at a table on the balcony overlooking the river. Seated between Baron Champford and Randall, Sibilla encountered a moody silence on her one hand, and was regaled ceaselessly on the other hand with tidbits of gossip and lessons on the epicurean creed, mumbled by her cousin in between destroying the culinary masterpieces placed before them.

"Why, there is James Muftow with his—Eulalie!" he remarked, gesturing towards a very *tête-à-tête* pair at the farther end of the terrace, and while Sibilla was still craning to see the lovely young woman who was clinging tightly to the arm of her escort, Baron Champford added, "What an extraordinary sauce! No fish in all of my acquaintance has ever had the good fortune to smother in such an exquisite sea!" And Sibilla turned her attention back to her plate, only to hear, "See there, Randall! Young Embury Clarke with Jared Wheedle and a few others. They seem to think this is an impromptu Crockford's. What is it they are playing? Hazard?"

This statement roused the attention of his younger brother who had been merely toying with his food, while imbibing prodigious quantities of wine, but Sibilla, unable to appreciate the fish with the same relish as her gourmand cousin, listened in to the conversation taking place across the table between Sophy, Valerian, and Lucinda.

"I declare," Sophy was saying with bright eyes, "that the women of London do not know how to manage their servants." She put down her fork neatly as she pursued this popular topic. "Why, Sibilla and I were raised with our maid, Peggy. She was like a sister to us, and because of the personal attention she receives, she has always been a wonderful servant, attentive to all of the little details which another maid would forget, always available when she is needed because she foresees the patterns of our lives in a way which a stranger cannot." Sibilla reflected wryly that this was certainly an inappropriate time to be singing Peggy's praises, but Sophy, entirely forgetting her maid's absence that morning, went on, "If every mistress treated her household staff with consideration and thoughtfulness, being as concerned with their needs and lives and upbringing as she is with that of her children, there would be no more talk of the servant problem."

Valerian, who watched Sophy with admiration during this speech, turned his attention to Lucinda who added softly, "My mother has ever been plagued with inadequate service. But though she seems most meticulous in her hiring, she will tolerate almost any sort of behaviour afterward, and then her servants are always leaving her. I believe she has had ten lady's maids in the past two years."

"But I've seen her with her lady's maid!" Sophy exclaimed. "She's rude and impatient, she asks for one thing one minute and then the opposite the next; she treats her like an idiot—why would anyone stay in such a situation?"

"When she has the choice of such a sympathetic mistress as you," Valerian offered with a warm smile.

Sophy coloured. "I should hope I could be somewhat more understanding when—" she paused delicately.

"You have your own household," Valerian continued smoothly. "We have heard your admirable views on the care and treatment of servants. What of child raising?"

Sophy blushed again, but eagerly launched into this new topic with aplomb. "Why, I should spend much more time with my children than most mamas," she said quickly. "In many families, the children are relegated to the nursery and spend all of their waking hours with a nursery maid or nanny. My children shall see just as much of me as they do of the nursery maid," she declared hotly. "I shall take them about with me on errands, allow them to sit with me when I am sewing or entertaining close friends—"

Bored by this subject, Sibilla turned back to her plate, wondering why both Mr. Cloudsleigh and Mr. Griggs seemed so absorbed by Sophy's analysis of domestic matters. Perhaps men enjoyed this keyhole vision of the mysterious concerns and daily activities of their women; Sibilla, having heard these topics discussed endlessly by her mother, sisters, aunts, in short, every female of her acquaintance, thought there would be time enough to learn about the management of a household once she had one to manage. At the moment, she preferred to talk about things which seemed infinitely more significant, and thus she embarked upon a spirited dissertation about the

Great Exhibition, a dissertation which ended as it began, as a monologue, for though the others listened with interest no one had anything to offer.

"There we see the crucial difference between these two lovely sisters," remarked Valerian jovially, lifting his glass of wine. "Sophy will make some lucky dog an excellent wife and mother for his children, while Sibilla is ideally suited to be the perfect mistress."

Mr. Dabney Griggs looked at him reprovingly, and Valerian added quickly, "The perfect mistress of an intellectual salon."

His earlier meaning was still apparent and Lucinda seemed offended, but quickly recovered when Mr. Griggs proposed a stroll through the gardens surrounding the inn. She and Sophy, with Mr. Griggs and Mr. Cloudsleigh as escorts, departed. Sibilla, furious with Valerian for having humiliated her once more, refused to accompany them and went up instead to visit the invalid, while Baron Champford announced in no uncertain terms that a walk would spoil the digestion of his meal.

To Sibilla's dismay, Mary Crank was pale and feverish, and Sibilla realized that Miss Crank should be driven back to her home immediately, where she could slip out of the damp dress which now clung to her clammy skin.

Racing back down the stairs, Sibilla managed to rouse the lethargic Baron Champford, who wearily agreed to prepare his barouche for the return to London, and finding Lucinda and Valerian in front of the inn, informed them of the change in plans, and asked them to locate Dabney and Sophy, who had wandered farther on their walk.

But when Sibilla returned, supporting the frail and shivering form of Mary Crank, no one had been able to find the missing couple, and it was rapidly decided that Lucinda, distraught with worry over her friend, Valerian, Sibilla, and Baron Champford would depart with the invalid in the barouche, while Randall would wait for the return of Sophy and Mr. Griggs, who could be trusted to pilot Mr. Cloudsleigh's phaeton.

The journey back was as unpleasant as it was lengthy. Even the slight rolling motion of Baron Champford's well-sprung carriage was too much for Miss Crank, and when they were not stopping to allow her to relieve her continuous nausea, they were proceeding at a pace so slow that it irritated the spirited pair of matched chestnuts, who were fresh and eager to proceed at their customary headlong pace. As they approached the city, they were caught in a tangle of traffic, buffeted two or three times by herds of cattle being driven to market, and halted once because of a collision between a dray and an omnibus.

Lucinda and Sibilla were totally absorbed in trying to minister to Mary, who kept declaring in a feeble voice that she wished she could die, while Valerian offered his assistance by hanging out of the window, cursing impeccably at all of the drivers who impeded their progress.

At last, their destination was reached, Mary was carried into her father's house by Valerian, and the doctor was sent for immediately. The girls wished to stay to learn his diagnosis, but the Crank household was in an uproar, so they reluctantly returned to Corrough House.

Baron Champford departed as soon as possible, pleading an engagement, but Valerian, awaiting the return of his phaeton, remained. Aunt Lucy expressed her disapproval of the pell-mell flight from Richmond, saying that they should have waited until Sophy had been found, and declaring that Mary Crank was a pampered and silly miss whose frailty was an illusion fostered by her doting papa. She insisted that the two girls entertain Mr. Cloudsleigh during his wait, which meant that Sibilla played the piano for nearly two hours, which she did competently, while Lucinda sang, which she did poorly. Valerian, lounging back against one of the ivory settees, was at first amused, then tolerant, and inevitably bored.

Although Mrs. Pleet grudgingly invited him to dinner, he departed in a hackney coach, saying that he had a previous dinner invitation, and requesting that Mr. Griggs return the phaeton to his lodgings whenever he appeared.

The two girls went upstairs to dress for dinner and Aunt Lucy retired to her study to indulge in some furtive consolation from her bottle of sherry. Sibilla, unnerved to discover that Peggy was still missing and upset because repeated messages sent inquiring after Mary Crank's health had brought no response, was unprepared for the avalanche of Aunt Lucy's wrath which descended upon both her daughter and her niece during the evening meal.

"I am astonished that you would permit your sister, whom you know full well is giddy and flighty, to remain behind with two men," she began energetically.

"One of whom is our cousin," Sibilla pointed out dryly, putting down her fork, for the roast was stringy and tough.

"I have no doubt that she has by now eloped with Mr. Griggs," Aunt Lucy asserted, gulping down a glass of wine, and motioning for the butler to pour her another. "He is such a sympathetic and likeable—" she glowered at Sibilla "—and wealthy young man."

"Mama! Sophy would not elope with Mr. Griggs," Lucinda cried startled. "Why, she does not even like him—or well, if she does like him, she has shown no interest in him—as a husband, that is."

"Not like the interest you have shown," Mrs. Pleet snapped, pausing for several forkfuls of roast which she chewed vigorously, swallowed, and then said, "I saw the way you carried on at the quadrille ball, giggling for all the world like an ill-behaved school-girl. But he is not the man for you. Why his fortune is nothing to the jointure your father—" she hesitated a moment and raised her eyes to heaven as if the departed Mr. Pleet hovered above them "—has provided for you. You need a husband with some breeding and some taste, a man from a good family, such as Mr. Cloudsleigh."

"I don't believe Mr. Cloudsleigh is interested in me, Mama," Lucinda said primly, folding her napkin and placing it beside her place, a signal which the butler responded to by removing both.

"Of course he isn't interested," Aunt Lucy mumbled with a full mouth, "not when you caterwaul as you did this afternoon instead of sing—"

"But, Mama! I was upset about Mary and—"

"Upset by the fact that your precious Mr. Griggs was lost in the woods somewhere with your cousin, Sophia," Mrs. Pleet concluded more clearly, having washed down her meal with another glass of wine. The butler filled her glass again. "And not when your other cousin," Aunt Lucy directed this scornfully at Sibilla, "encourages his advances by her sly glances and softly spoken words, learned no doubt from her wanton 'maid' who has completely vanished!"

"Peggy is gone!" Sibilla said startled.

"Vanished, much like your sister, Kitty," said Aunt Lucy ruthlessly and smugly. "All of her personal belongings are gone, along with some of the silver and plate, I have no doubt."

"Peggy is not a thief, and not a wanton!" protested Sibilla.

"I am certain you will revise your good opinion of her," Aunt Lucy said with great satisfaction, "when you hear that she has been carrying on a clandestine affair with a spurious gentleman for some time, according to the staff, a 'gentleman,' I might add, whom they have never seen, but whose carriage she has been witnessed entering and leaving at all hours of the day and night.

It is precisely what I would have predicted would come of allowing a member of the lower classes the freedom your parents permitted her. I can say that I am not only pleased that she has removed her corrupting influence from my household, but gratified that she saw fit to steal one of those mangy beasts when she left."

"She has taken one of the dogs?" exclaimed Sibilla, and then, without waiting for an answer, sprang to her feet and raced towards the garden. Oscar and Muffin greeted her with excitement, for they had been lonely of late, but Slow, the placid retriever, always Peggy's favourite, was absent. He was too lazy and docile to have ventured out of the garden on his own; Sibilla, with her arms around Oscar's neck and tears on her cheeks, knew for a certainty that Peggy was really gone.

After indulging in her grief for a few minutes, a grief made more poignant by the memory of her unresolved quarrel with Peggy, she transformed a part of her sorrow into anger at the neglect suffered by her pets, and stormed into the kitchen, demanding a large portion of the dinner scraps for her starving animals, and insisting that if the dogs remained underfed, someone would be looking for a new situation.

The cook only shrugged her shoulders as Sibilla went back out into the night, bearing the bowl of leftovers. She knew that Mrs. Pleet was her employer and that Mrs. Pleet did not care about the welfare of the dogs. She and the butler and the scullery maid and Lily sat down for another energetic discussion of Peggy Banks' moral character, and even Jane, the prim and proper lady's maid, who refused to fraternize with the rest of the staff, paused as she brought her plate down to the kitchen and listened to the gossip eagerly.

TWENTY-TWO

Lady Sophia Accepts a Proposal of Marriage

ALTHOUGH SHE WISHED TO retire to her room to engage in a little self-pity, Sibilla was unable to do so, for Aunt Lucy accosted her as she mounted the stairs and insisted that she be present in the sitting room for the return of her erring sister.

While Lucinda sewed quietly near the fire, her face so unusually pale that Sibilla feared she had contracted the same illness which afflicted Mary Crank, and Sibilla pretended to read a novel, Aunt Lucy paced about the room, stopping every time she passed the sideboard to pour herself another glass of sherry. As the hours passed and the night deepened outside, Lucinda became more and more pale, Sibilla increasingly restless, and Mrs. Pleet exceedingly intoxicated, and yet the absent trio did not appear.

The grandfather clock had just announced eleven o'clock with its hollow chimes when there was a noise outside of a carriage arriving, the shuffling of feet in the hall, and Sophy appeared in the door of the sitting room. Her face was wreathed in smiles, but her blond locks were tumbled, her hat missing, her dress torn and covered with dust, and one hand was wrapped in a white linen handkerchief.

Sibilla, delighted beyond her own expectations to see her sister alive and well, flew to embrace her, but Lucinda retained her seat beside the fire and only looked at her erstwhile friend with woeful eyes.

"Where have you been?" thundered Aunt Lucy, just as Mr. Griggs appeared behind Sophy on the threshold. "And where is Mr. Trendle?"

"He did not come with us," Dabney Griggs answered in low tones and with downcast eyes. "He remained at Richmond. Mrs. Pleet, if I may have the privilege of speaking to you for a few moments in private?" He looked apologetically at Lucinda, who would not raise her eyes, and then followed the black bulk of Aunt Lucy as she indicated the direction of the study.

Lucinda swayed in her chair, as if about to swoon, and her sewing dropped from her hands, but Sibilla, hanging upon her younger sister, did not notice.

"Sophy, what happened?" she cried. "Why is your hand bandaged? Where is Randall?"

"He remained behind at the inn," Sophy said hesitantly, glancing at Lucinda, who appeared totally absorbed in watching the fire. "He was gaming with some friends, and refused to come back with us, despite everything Dabney—Mr. Griggs—did to persuade him. We returned to the inn, minutes after you left, according to Randall, and Dabney—Mr. Griggs—wanted to set off immediately, but then he spent a long time trying to persuade our cousin to come with us. They almost came to blows. I was so mortified." She sank down upon a chair; Lucinda did not look up or indicate in any way that she was listening to Sophy's tale. "At last, he saw it was to no avail, and we set off in the phaeton, but there was a horrid accident just outside Richmond, a large carriage collided with us, forcing us off the road. The phaeton was overturned. I was thrown clear, although Mr. Griggs was tangled up with the reins and almost kicked to death by the horses, and when we were finally righted by a farmer passing in a cart, he saw that the wheel was loose and one of the horses lamed, and nothing could be done about it. Dabney—Mr. Griggs—could not find another horse, no one could repair the wheel, and at length, we left the phaeton with an ostler at a nearby inn, and after a long wait, and being unable to find any other means of transportation back to London, he—Mr. Griggs—bought a dilapidated old cart and an old nag from a farmer who was bringing supplies to the inn, and we returned to London in that."

"But how were you hurt? Are you sure you are all right now? And Mr. Griggs?" asked Sibilla anxiously.

"Oh, I cut my hand on a rock when I was thrown from the carriage," Sophy replied with nonchalance. "It was a mere scrape. Mr. Griggs bound it for me—"

"Lady Sophia?" She was interrupted by the appearance of the butler at the door. "Your aunt, Mrs. Pleet, requires your presence in the study."

Sophy did not seem altogether surprised by this summons, for she rose quickly, squeezed Sibilla's hand with her one good hand, looked once more towards Lucinda who continued to ignore her, and hurried after the butler.

"An exciting story," said Sibilla, seating herself across from her cousin on the other side of the fire.

"If it is a true one," responded Lucinda bitterly.

"What is wrong?" asked Sibilla softly, disturbed by Lucinda's unhappiness.

But there was no response to her question. Lucinda merely compressed her lips into a thin, grim line and continued to stare at the centre of the hearth.

The answer came from another direction, for within minutes Aunt Lucy, Mr. Griggs, and Sophy had re-entered the room, and Aunt Lucy, approaching the sideboard, poured glasses of sherry for them all, before saying, in tones of expansiveness more surprising than her former wrath, "I am pleased to be able to announce that Mr. Griggs has requested the pleasure of Miss Sophia's hand in marriage," Sibilla gasped softly, and Aunt Lucy looked at her with ill-concealed triumph, "and that Miss Sophia has done him the honour of accepting his kind proposal. Let us drink to their impending nuptials."

As all raised their glasses in a toast, Sibilla in a daze, and Sophy and Dabney uncertainly, the glass slipped from Lucinda's hand and splintered upon the hearth, and she fell upon the carpet in a swoon.

The toast was never drunk. Aunt Lucy, frightened by her daughter's weakness, called for the butler, and followed him as he carried Lucinda's still-unconscious form to her room. The newly betrothed couple set down their glasses gingerly, and Sophy clung to Dabney's hand as if life depended upon it, while Sibilla watched with uneasiness as Lily tried to remove the crimson stains of the spilled sherry from the hearth rug.

TWENTY-THREE

The Great Exhibition

THE SEASON CONTINUED DESPITE the upheaval of the Corrough household. Lucinda remained in bed for several weeks, suffering from a mild case of "brain fever," the same illness that afflicted Mary Crank. Sophy, radiant and tremulous, made hundreds of calls and showed herself and her prospective bridegroom at countless soirees, receptions, déjeuners, musicales, and balls.

A letter was dispatched to Partridge Park announcing Sophy's engagement—without the usual paragraph pleading for money, for Dabney Griggs, knowing the nature of the Merrell family's finances, had generously offered to cover Sophy and Sibilla's old debts and left an advance with Mrs. Pleet for future expenditures. Sibilla, feeling fractured and often *de trop*, divided her attentions between her ailing cousin and her high-strung younger sister.

"Brain fever" was a convenient catch-all phrase applied to depressions, hysterias, and fevers. Lucinda suffered alternately from all of these ailments, but Sibilla, suspecting that her cousin was actually pained with a broken heart, thought that cheerful company would be as healing as all of the nostrums the doctor recommended, and devoted much of her time to running errands for Lucinda and reading aloud to her. Since romances worsened Lucinda's condition, they were instead making their way through a travel book, and Sibilla was touched by her cousin's gratitude for any small kindness. Sophy, formerly Lucinda's close companion, kept away from the sickroom, for her presence aggravated the invalid's suffering.

But as time went on it seemed that Sophy began ailing with an attack of "nerves," for she became fatigued and irritable and jumped at sudden noises or roughly spoken words. Her complexion, always creamy and even, became almost waxen in hue, while spots of high colour flamed in her cheeks.

Sibilla naturally attributed this change to the constant demands made upon Sophy's every waking hour. Mornings she spent penning letters in response to the congratulations that poured in from relatives and friends and shopping for items for her trousseau. In the afternoons she accepted callers at home or returned calls with Aunt Lucy beaming by her side. And since the news of her betrothal had spread, scores of invitations to dinners, receptions, and balls arrived at Corrough House.

Dabney Griggs weathered this storm with his usual reserve and formal manners. He accompanied his bride-to-be on shopping expeditions, rode with her in the Park, and was her escort to every evening function. When they were left alone in the drawing room by Aunt Lucy, there was no one to witness the sudden shyness which overcame them both and their stammering attempts at conversation. And if Sophy cried into her pillow every night, no one but Marmalade was the wiser.

Except, perhaps, for Aunt Lucy, locked in her study with the now necessary comfort of her bottle of sherry, for she alone knew that Mr. Griggs had not meant to offer for Sophy. He had explained the details of Randall's absence and the carriage accident with painstaking scrupulousness, stressing the fact that he and Sophy had never been strictly alone together and laying heavy emphasis upon the fact that they had abandoned the farm cart and hired a hackney coach as soon as they neared London and that he had ridden on the box with the cab driver rather than inside with Lady Sophia.

But when he had done with this complete elucidation and Aunt Lucy continued to fix him with her beady eyes, never murmuring a word of understanding or acknowledgment, he reluctantly stammered that he would be pleased to offer for Sophy's hand if Mrs. Pleet thought it necessary. She did.

And Sophy, in turn, when brought into the presence of her glowering aunt and informed that Mr. Griggs wished to make a respectable woman of her after her shocking conduct, could not bear the thought of offending poor Mr. Griggs, who must really care for her after all to make such an offer, or of infuriating Mrs. Pleet, who seemed to consider her a ruined woman. She turned to Mr. Griggs and, with the most beseeching look in her tear-dimmed blue eyes, told him she would consider it the greatest privilege of her life to accept his generous proposal.

If either of them regretted their impulsiveness and selflessness, Mrs. Pleet could discern no signs of it, and though she fretted about her ailing daughter, a mild case of brain fever was preferable to having Lucinda marry beneath her.

While the event of Sophy's betrothal to Dabney Griggs continued to rack the foundations of Corrough House, events of greater moment were occurring. The Queen and Prince Albert opened the Great Exhibition on May first, and the city of London, always teeming during the Season, became even more crowded, as throngs of foreigners and visitors from outlying shires descended upon the city to view the greatest achievements of mankind. And on the eve of this great triumph, an accident on the Cheshire junction railway claimed the lives of many people returning from the grand day at the Chester races, among them Mrs. Ashford Cloudsleigh, her companion, Lady Firbush, and her father, Baron Wellton.

Because of this tragic event, the tickets held by the Cloudsleigh family for the opening of the Great Exhibition devolved upon the occupants of Corrough House, and therefore Sibilla, Mrs. Pleet, Sophia, and Dabney Griggs were among the hundreds who thronged into the Crystal Palace when the doors were opened at nine o'clock. They sat gazing in wonder at the vaulted glass ceiling above their head, at the great elms which had been preserved in natural splendor under the grand transept, at the tantalizing vista of the crowded exhibits, and waited for the trumpets which would herald the Queen's arrival. The Duke of Wellington arrived (it was his eighty-second birthday) and was seen in the northeastern part of the transept, surrounded, as usual, by a group of beautiful women.

Outside, half a million people were massed in the Park, despite the cool, crisp weather, waiting for a glimpse of the Queen. A sudden shower drenched them, but they remained stolidly patient and it passed. Just as the battery across the Serpentine fired a salute and the royal carriages drew up, the sun burst through brilliantly. The "Queen's Weather" graced the Great Exhibition. Sibilla and Sophy craned for a view of the Queen as she appeared with Prince Albert, the Prince of Wales, and the Princess Royal, and settled down in a throne covered with a magnificent crimson cloth.

The Prince Regent read a report on the Commission proceedings, the Queen expressed her concern for "the welfare of the people and the common interests of the human race," and the Archbishop of Canterbury delivered a prayer.

As five organs and a vast choir delivered the "Hallelujah Chorus," the Great Exhibition was declared open, the boundary ropes were taken down, and the ticket holders scrambled to view the Crystal Fountain, the Koh-i-Noor diamond, and the Throne.

It was nearly impossible to examine the exhibits closely on opening day, for the crowd pushed and shoved as they milled about under the glittering roof of the Crystal Palace, but Sibilla returned again and again over the following weeks to study the massive sculptures, the opulent furniture, the Milanese stained-glass windows, the gleaming silks and satins from China, and, most remarkable of all, the people who filled the aisles, staring with rapt admiration at the wonders thus displayed. There were bucolic groups from remote rural areas, shepherded perhaps by an agitated clergyman; companies of workers from factories and mills; Chinamen with their long pigtails and outlandish clothes; dark-skinned, solemn Indians; Germans; French; Italians; and Americans who spoke in the rough accent which Sibilla would have expected from such a barbaric nation. The American display was the source of some embarrassment to them, for when the Exhibition opened, the extensive spaces they had requested were nearly empty, spotted with a few ship models, rocking chairs, blocks of copper ore, and a long line of barrels of fine flour. France exhibited silks, ribbons, Sèvres porcelain,

Aubusson. carpets, Beauvais tapestries, artificial flowers and piano-fortes; porcelain bowls and ivory carvings came from China; cutlery from Belgium; engraved goblets from Bohemia; massive Gothic furniture from Austria; elaborate ornamental plate and great malachite wares were sent by Russia; watches were displayed by Switzerland. And representatives of all of these nations strolled about the crowded aisles, chattering in their native languages. Several times, Sibilla saw the Duke of Wellington, who visited the Exhibition frequently; once she thought she saw Peggy on the arm of the Marquis of Dower, but when she hurried to approach them, they had disappeared. Sibilla stored up all of the knowledge she gleaned from these expeditions and hurried home to regale Lucinda with tales about the riches she was missing, a circumstance which probably contributed more than any other to Lucinda's recovery.

Sophy and Dabney Griggs accompanied Sibilla to the Crystal Palace whenever they could spare the time, but as this was seldom, she relied more often on the reluctant escort of her cousin, Baron Champford, who declared himself exhausted after perusing three exhibits and retired to the refreshment rooms. Regretfully, alcohol was not served, and he had to content himself soda water, lemon-ade, and ginger beer, and flirting with the pretty girls who staffed the concession stands, an occupation which always put him into an expansive mood by the time Sibilla had completed her survey of whatever transept she had chosen to do that day and was ready to return home.

During this period of time, Sibilla sorely missed Valerian Clouds-leigh, whom she knew had accompanied his uncle to Chester for the grim task of identifying Mrs. Cloudsleigh's body and attending the funeral. Somehow she felt that he was the only person who would laugh with her at the vulgar proportions of some of the giant statues and the overly ornate and ridiculous furnishings and decorative objects, including a commode of various woods, marquetry, carvings, painted china and gilt mouldings, or a bird cage of 2,522 pieces composed of twenty-one different kinds of wood. Doubtless he could also help her to appreciate several of the mechanical and industrial objects, which she viewed without comprehension, or point out to her the superiority in design of the elegant vehicles displayed in the transportation section.

But the Cloudsleighs remained sequestered behind the walls of the family mansion, indulging in a grief made more poignant by the knowledge that not one of the mourners had felt much affection for the dead woman.

Baron Cloudsleigh, alone in his library, recollected with moist eyes but an acutely perceptive mind, the three women who had brought joy and grace into his restricted life. His first wife, Janina, a quiet-voiced, even-tempered, young Irish beauty when he first met and courted her, had been a devoted and adoring wife, who never raised her voice or expressed an opinion and yet managed to light the fires of scholarship that had always burned within her husband so that he began the years of research which provided the foundation for his book. She had been an exquisitely beautiful mother who at last found the opportunity to express all of the passion and love of her nature in the nurturing of her infant son, Arthur Valerian. That it had been the fate of such a woman to die in the throes of childbirth endeavouring to bring forth her second child into the world, was an act of God so capricious and so cruel that Baron Cloudsleigh closed his heart to that God and threw himself body and soul into his botanical studies.

Thereafter he had never known love. The son of this short but happy union was raised at Merryfield Manor by his grandparents and saw his father infrequently, at which times the Baron, naturally shy and immersed in his studies, found little to say to the lively young boy, who thought his father a poor specimen of a man when compared to his energetic and doting Uncle Ashford. Now in the gloom of his library, Baron Cloudsleigh felt a pang of sudden loss, more painful than the memories of his first wife, which were dimmed by time, as he realized that his son, Valerian, would never know the love that had once filled Cloudsleigh House.

He thought of the gentle presence of Euphemia Merrell and gently stroked the penwiper she had crocheted for him, and Caroline Wellton Cloudsleigh, Ashton's wife, who was a welcome refreshment after hours of study, with her rustling skirts and her sweet lavender perfume. Effie had fled back to Partridge Park for reasons which still perplexed Lord Cloudsleigh (perhaps she had really been in love with that penniless sailor who eloped with another girl) and Caroline was dead. He sighed and removed his spectacles to wipe the tears which had risen to his eyes; his book was now his only ambition and all such fragrant memories would only impede the progress of his remaining consolation in life.

His second wife, Lady Cloudsleigh, was notably missing from his list of women who had brightened his life. Even during their courtship he felt that in some inexplicable manner Nell was making a fool out of him, but her tantalizing beauty and her intriguing interest in a dried-up, old scholar had besotted him until after the marriage, when he understood what she really wanted. Not him, for she submitted to his eager embraces only a handful of times before she subtly let him know that he was not welcome in her bedroom. Not even his knowledge, for she changed the subject whenever he mentioned his book, and never entered the library. No, she was after his wealth and his house and his title, and he gladly gave her everything she requested, grateful that this lovely woman would grace his home and his name, if not his heart.

Nell was unperturbed by Caroline's death, though she quickly donned mourning and turned the occasion to her advantage by demanding new jewellery, gold and jet for the first six months, and amethysts for the subsequent period when she would wear only grey, lilac, and white. The Cloudsleighs congregated in her house were at times annoying, and they did prevent her from seeing much of Lanning Tombs, but this also could be turned to advantage for his picture of her changed from that of a benevolent patroness into a woman whom he desperately loved and needed but who was ever forbidden to him because of the anachronistic dictates of a morally antiquated Society.

Ashford, who removed to Cloudsleigh House, unwilling to reenter the house he and Caroline had occupied, and Valerian, who gave up his lodgings to be with his uncle, were perhaps the most affected by Caroline's tragic death. And yet their grief was laced more with remorse than sorrow, for neither had really liked the priggish, fretful, little woman who had tormented her husband and disapproved of his nephew.

Despite the constant visitors paying condolence calls at Cloudsleigh House, there was probably no one in London who had shed more tears or felt more genuine grief at Caroline's death than Kitty Merrell. Since the news of the railway accident, a message which had been brought to her house in the middle of the night, she had neither seen nor heard from her lover, and she knew that she might never see him again, for stricken with anguish about his neglect of Caroline—a factor which undoubtedly contributed to her death— he might wish to dissociate himself from all of those distractions which had led to her loneliness and perpetual invalidism. Little Alex and Clarissa were aware of their mother's depression and knew that their family was about to experience a time of great stress and upheaval.

Sibilla was forbidden, of course, to visit the bereaved family with a condolence call because the ban on communications with her sister Nell prohibited a visit to Cloudsleigh House. She sent instead a polite note and received, in turn, a polite and anonymous reply.

The first public appearance of any Cloudsleigh occurred almost a month after the funeral when Valerian was seen at the Great Exhibition. This day seemed an inauspicious one for a string of calamities took place.

Lucinda had ventured out of the house for the first time since Sophy's betrothal and expressed an interest in seeing the wonders which Sibilla had described in minute detail. Accordingly, they walked to the Crystal Palace, escorted by Baron Champford who immediately headed for the refreshment rooms and a particularly pretty and gentle girl named Jenny who had taken his fancy.

After viewing several of the British displays, Sibilla steered her still fragile cousin to the north side of the nave to look at the contents of a glass case which contained objects presented by the East India Company. The gorgeous coat of a Sikh chief caught the eye first, but after Lucinda had marvelled at this garment of gold, ornamented with pearls, rubies, and emeralds, Sibilla eagerly pointed out the Koh-i-noor, or Sea of Light, vases of rock crystal, and a necklace of ex-quisitely wrought gold. So rapt was Sibilla in her explanation that she failed to notice that Lucinda was no longer listening but had turned to watch a couple emerging from a transept, a sight so horrifying that she slipped to the ground in a faint.

During the subesquent frenzied minutes, Sibilla tried to revive Lucinda with the contents of a vinaigrette found in her pocket, and discourage the persistent efforts of an Italian gentleman who wished to assist her. The couple, whose presence had such a devastating effect upon Lucinda, passed by proceeding up the nave. But at the last moment, as Sibilla despaired of bringing any life into Lucinda's still form or of ridding herself of the offensive ministrations of the Italian gentleman who insisted that Lucinda's stays be loosened and volunteered to perform this duty personally, Dabney Griggs, for it had been the sight of him strolling with Sophy which had stricken Lucinda, turned and sprang to Sibilla's aid. Within a few seconds he had discouraged the Italian, awakened Lucinda, and carried her to a secluded alcove, advising Sibilla that she should take her sister, Sophy, on a short walk about the Crystal Palace while Lucinda recovered her strength.

The two sisters found little to say to each other as they perambulated the Crystal Palace, for Sophy could not bring herself to reveal her reservations about Mr. Griggs, reservations which had grown ten-fold at the sight of her intended's solicitous care for Lucinda, and Sibilla, believing that her sister's aloofness stemmed from her impending initiation into the ranks of married women, felt that they no longer had anything in common.

So it was that as they wandered aimlessly among the shifting throngs each was thrilled by the distracting sight of Valerian Cloudsleigh, sombre in black, and each characteristically responded differently. Sibilla, considering his recent bereavement and afraid to intrude upon either his melancholy thoughts or his absorption in a conversation with the Marquis of Dower and a pretty young woman in a coral-pink silk dress, hung back and might have passed by without acknowledging them, but her impetuous sister, delighted by this chance encounter with friends and never worried about whether or not her presence would be appreciated, ran quickly forward, exclaiming, "Oh, Valerian, Mr. Cloudsleigh, how wonderful it is to see you again. All of the parties have been so—well, so flat—since you have been gone."

Noting the marked difference in her appearance—the uncharacteristically bright flush upon her cheeks and the glitter in her eyes—Mr. Cloudsleigh bowed slightly and said,

"But I hear that you have found another to replace me in your affections, Lady Sophy. It is with great pleasure that I felicitate you upon your betrothal to my dearest friend, Mr. Griggs. He is certainly a lucky chap."

"Oh, that!" said Sophy with a little pout. "I had forgotten how long you have been out of Society. But let me assure you that you and your family, during your seclusion, have had my heartfelt sympathy and that all of us who knew Mrs. Cloudsleigh share in your—"

Valerian brushed aside this typical message of condolence, saying curtly, "And here is your lovely sister, Lady Sibilla!"

Sibilla, approaching sedately had heard the last of Sophy's speech and was nodding her head in agreement, but Valerian's brusque dismissal of the usual sentiments disconcerted her for a moment, and as she was trying to recover her poise, she noticed that the Marquis of Dower was hurrying away from Valerian's side, as if trying to whisk his female companion out of sight.

This action did not surprise Sibilla; it was by all means possible, and indeed even likely, that he had accompanied one of his lights-of-love to the Great Exhibition and would have been embarrassed to introduce her to two well-bred young gentlewomen. But it was the actions of the young woman which puzzled Sibilla, for she seemed displeased by her escort's efforts to hurry her away and kept turning to look over her shoulder at Valerian and the two girls.

There was something about the small, piquant face, framed by shining curls and topped by a frivolous hat of white lace that seemed heartbreakingly familiar to Sibilla.

TWENTY-FOUR

A Rendezvous at the Crystal Palace

"PEGGY!" SHE EXCLAIMED, recognizing her former maid and starting towards her at the same time, and Peggy, hearing her cry, broke free from the firm grasp of the Marquis and met her halfway.

After a few confused minutes of tears and embraces, the two stepped back and studied each other. While Sibilla had to admire the transformation of her long-time companion, her heart ached, for she realized that all of her fears about Peggy's ruin had come true. Peggy was garbed in the most expensive taste: a walking dress of coral-and-white pongee, trimmed with three full flounces, matching kid gloves, a tightly fitting basque with a rose tucked into the low corsage, and a similar rose peering out from the lace hat. Sibilla, while wincing at the seduction bespoken by these mute objects, had to confess that Peggy, who had been a shiningly pretty girl in her maid's uniform of plain black silk, was a stunning beauty in these elegant clothes. She could easily pass as a lady, and with this thought, Sibilla was overwhelmed by compassion for her friend who was trying so bravely to cross the insurmountable barriers of class.

"Oh, Peggy, how I've missed you and worried about you!" she said simply, and the two girls clung to each other again.

"Miss Sibil," pleaded Peggy, "you cannot know how sorry I am to have taken Slow away from you, but he cried so when I was leaving, and we were trying to make no noise at all so as not to rouse the household, and finally Ned begged me to take the dog along since it would surely break his heart to be parted from me."

"As if I would be more concerned about the loss of Slow, than your well-being," commented Sibilla.

Sophy now approached them cautiously, and though she greeted Peggy and hugged her gingerly, she was obviously horrified by the same evidence which touched Sibilla. The Marquis of Dower, who had shrugged his shoulders at the tempestuous reunion of his lady love with her former mistress, and who had been listening to their excited chatter with a doting amusement, now sensed the chill descending upon the company and stepped forward to claim Peggy. She went to his side obediently, but not before Sibilla implored her to keep in contact with her.

Feeling forlorn, Sibilla was comforted by the sudden reassuring touch of Valerian's hand upon her back.

"Imagine—" began Sophy indignantly, but Mr. Cloudsleigh cut her off and said instead, "I would be proud indeed to take his place, but where is your escort, ladies?"

"Oh, I came with Mr. Griggs—Dabney," answered Sophy quickly, "but Lucinda swooned when she saw—when she saw—well, she swooned as we were passing by, and he went to her aid and advised me—I mean—advised us to go for a short walk, whereupon—"

Sibilla interrupted her sister's tortured explanations to add, "Baron Champford came with Lucinda and me, but he has a lady friend who works at one of the refreshment rooms and so spends most of his time there."

"I will undertake to return you to Mr. Griggs's capable chaperonage," said Valerian, smoothly ignoring the information as to Sylvester's whereabouts, "and then we can inquire after the welfare of the invalid also." But they had only gone a short distance before they encountered Baron Champford, circulating blindly through the Crystal Palace, morose at being rejected by his Jenny for a boorish farmer who brought news from her village.

"Ah, the fairest blossoms of England's gardens!" he said gallantly, raising his monocle to his eye as he bowed deeply to the two Merrell sisters. "Really, Lady Sibilla, I think you have been most remiss in your duties, for you promised me a tour of the American exhibit, and only think, I have been searching for it this past hour and have not yet found it!"

With a laugh, Sibilla agreed to recompense her cousin for her oversight, and she and Sophy went off with him, while Valerian, following their instructions, sought out Mr. Griggs and Miss Pleet.

This was how he found them and uncovered the secret of Sophy's betrothal and her present nervous condition. Lucinda, the colour back in her cheeks and her eyes soft with unshed tears, was leaning back against Mr. Griggs's shoulders gazing fondly upon him and holding his one hand in hers, while he, if he was not really stooping to kiss her hair, was at least so close to performing this same action that it was fortunate for both that Valerian appeared when he did. Lucinda started and loosed her grip on Dabney's hand; he drew back and pretended to be asking her how she did.

Wisely, Valerian allowed them to believe that he had been taken in by this charade.

"Miss Pleet," he said warmly. "I am indeed delighted to find you recovered. Your cousins were both so anxious about your welfare that I volunteered to come along and make my own report to them. Dabney, old fellow, how have you been?"

"Well enough," mumbled Dabney, trying to appear at ease.

"It is good to see you again, Mr. Cloudsleigh," said Lucinda charmingly, rising from the protective shelter of Mr. Griggs's arms and addressing Valerian with a sweet dignity. "It is with great regret that we have heard of the sad occurrences in your family, and I hope you will accept my profoundest sympathy. And, of course, I speak on behalf of my mama also."

"I am grateful for your kind expressions of concern," Valerian replied in the elegant formula prescribed by the etiquette of mourning. "If you are feeling better, Miss Pleet, perhaps we should rejoin your cousins and—"

Lucinda blanched at this suggestion, and Valerian, responding to her sensitivity, quickly changed his proposal.

"Or perhaps I could seek out Sibilla and Sylvester and send them to you—"

"I appreciate your thoughtfulness," Mr. Griggs said stoutly, "but as I do not believe Lucinda—Miss Pleet—should remain in this stifling and crowded environment—now that she has fully recovered—I will volunteer to see her safely home—and the other young ladies may enjoy the Exhibition as they came to do."

With a whispered word to Lucinda, he strolled a bit away from her with Valerian, adding in a hoarse voice, "Give Sophy my humblest apologies for so deserting her—but I think she would prefer the gaiety of this panorama in the company of her sister. They have not been much together of late. Tell her I shall call upon her this evening for we are promised for a *déjeuner* at Lady Calverley's tonight."

Valerian, pretending not to notice the peculiarity of this message, memorized it dutifully and returned to the American exhibit, where he conveyed it accurately to Sophy, who did not seem at all perturbed and even appeared to brighten at the news.

It was a delightful afternoon. Baron Champford was at his most humourous, Sibilla provided a fascinating commentary upon many of the exhibits and asked intelligent questions about the industrial machines, whose workings she did not understand, while Sophy was blithe and insouciant.

It was with deep regret that Valerian watched the trio depart through the sun-dappled shade of the Hyde Park elms in the direction of Corrough House, and took himself off to perform an unpleasant task, one that had been nagging at his mind since the news of the railway accident.

Sibilla had noticed his ambivalence and unease about leaving them, and she watched him surreptitiously as he crossed the Park while Sophy and Lord Champford went on ahead.

A sudden shrill scream brought Sibilla's attention back to her sister, and she whirled about, frightened, to see Sophy frozen in what seemed to be horror, all of the colour drained from her face and her mouth still open. At the next moment, she had picked up her blue silk skirts in both hands and went racing across the grass towards a goal unseen by Baron Champford and Sibilla. This startling episode ended when Sophy reached her target and flung her arms about an anonymous young man, lounging against the trunk of a tree.

"Oh, it's only Leslie!" murmured Sibilla, relieved as she and the normally lethargic Sylvester scurried after Sophy.

"Leslie?" inquired Lord Champford in tones of amazement and disgust, as he took in the sight of the unfamiliar and rustic person who was kissing Sophy with gusto, despite the disapproval of the other Parkgoers.

"Yes, Leslie Whitefoot. His family's estate adjoins Partridge Park," explained Sibilla *sotto voce* before moving forward to break up the joyous reunion.

"Leslie, Mr. Whitefoot," she said coolly, whereupon he glanced up from his passionate study of Sophy's lips, "this is Sylvester, Baron Champford, our cousin. Sylvester, Leslie Whitefoot."

"Pleased to meet you, sir," said Leslie, not loosing his hold of Sophy, who smiled at Sibilla with an incredulous happiness.

Sibilla, sorely perplexed, pondered what action she should take. She could not permit her younger sister, engaged to Dabney Griggs, to make a fool of herself with her childhood sweetheart in the middle of Hyde Park, especially not before the eager eyes of Lady Muftow, whose carriage was just approaching along the road.

"Of course, Leslie," Sibilla said ruefully, "you have heard that Sophy is betrothed to Mr. Dabney Griggs, a very good friend. The marriage is planned for August."

She felt weak with relief when she saw that this underhanded tactic had achieved its purpose, and Leslie abruptly let go of Sophy, who turned a countenance full of anguish to her sister.

"Sibil, I wished to tell him myself," she pleaded.

"No need, Lady Sophy," Mr. Whitefoot said coldly. "Your mother informed me at the earliest opportunity. I wish you much joy," and he turned as if to leave.

"Oh Leslie, don't go!" begged Sophy, holding onto his arm. "Won't you come call upon us at Corrough House?"

"Certainly not," that young man responded stubbornly. "I am sure your aunt would not permit the intrusion of the humble son of a mere country gentleman."

"Oh Leslie!" moaned Sophy in agony. Her spirits brightened as her eye fell upon Lord Champford. "Sylvester will bring you and introduce you as a friend of his, won't you Sylvester?" she asked cajolingly.

Baron Champford, every bit as much of a snob as his mother, was offended by this suggestion, but could not bear to deny such a kindness to Sophy who stared at him with beseeching blue eyes filled with tears.

"Well, ah—" as he hummed and hawed, Leslie's next words ended the need for such a difficult decision.

"Sophy," he said with finality. "You don't think I would want to enter a household where I would be likely to encounter your fiancé. No, I came to London merely to visit the Great Exhibition, and I shall be leaving shortly, though I wish you the greatest of happiness in your new life as Mrs. Griggs."

His actions, however, contradicted his words, for he took Sophy's hands in his own and held them tightly while gazing deeply into her eyes. The tears long brimming there overflowed and spilled down her pale cheeks.

"Leslie, don't, please don't," she cried, but he had turned and was striding off across the Park. Sophy, now weeping hysterically sought shelter in Sibilla's arms.

"Come, come, now," said Baron Champford, ineptly pulling out a bilious yellow handkerchief which he pressed upon Sophy, who dabbed at her eyes with it ineffectually.

"Sophy, don't cry. Hush, darling," murmured Sibilla, stricken by her sister's sorrow.

"Oh, why did he come now? To torment me? Oh, I can't bear it!" wailed Sophy brokenly. "I should never have come to London. I should have eloped with him as you advised. Oh! I wish I were back at Partridge Park! Oh Sibilla!" and she clutched her sister more tightly and continued to sob as if her heart would shortly break.

"Hush now, Sophy. All will be well," promised Sibilla. "Everything will right itself. There is no need for tears. Please don't cry!" And though these reassurances would momentarily soothe her disconsolate sister, the memory of Leslie's cool dismissal would drive her into a fresh fit of weeping, all under the watchful gaze of

Lady Muftow, who had commanded her coachman to stop so she could observe this interesting scene.

In the end, it was Sibilla's mention of Lady Muftow's vigil and Baron Champford's exasperated comment, "I cannot think what she sees in the man. He's a rude fellow and was deliberately cruel," that roused Sophy, for her natural stubbornness asserted itself and she was determined not to be affected by what she now termed "Leslie's theatrics."

By the time they reached Corrough House, she had regained her composure and greeted with a sigh of relief the news that Dabney Griggs had already departed, making it possible for her to retire to her room with the excuse of a headache.

TWENTY-FIVE

A Thorn Among the Roses

VALERIAN STRODE PURPOSEFULLY through the crowded streets, unaware of the turmoil he left behind him, but painfully aware of the turmoil within his heart.

His first thought when informed of the railway accident in Chester had been of the lady he now intended to visit, a blasphemous thought when he should have been thinking of poor doll-like Caroline, but try as he might he could not remember her features clearly now, while the vision of the other woman, her irresistible smile, the way she tilted her head, her graceful gestures, filled his thoughts day and night.

But he was shocked to discover that she was a ghost of her former self, when the maid admitted him silently to the sitting room and he saw her seated at the rosewood pianoforte, her slender fingers picking out the notes of a melancholy song and murmuring the words to herself. She wore a gown of pale lilac, as if in mourning; her hair was clumsily tucked into a chignon, and for a moment, she looked enough like her younger sister that Valerian started and stumbled against an ottoman. As the woman at the piano turned towards him, a wild gleam of hope in her eyes that faded into sorrow, he saw that she was much paler and thinner than Sibilla. Her cheekbones were prominent in her blanched face and dark circles rimmed her eyes; she moved inside the mournful dress awkwardly as if she were a little girl parading in her mother's clothes. She remained seated and did not greet him, an act so contrary to her usual graciousness and hospitality that Valerian felt his cheerfulness to be artificial when he approached her and said, bending to kiss her hand, "Lady Kitty, how delighted I am to find you at home." Her hand remained in his, limp and lifeless and cold.

At last, as if it took her an eternity to remember the words, she said in a toneless voice, "I have been at home these past several weeks."

Valerian shuddered involuntarily and she withdrew her hand. It was as he feared, he thought studying her tragic face—she had been more affected by Caroline's death than any of the Cloudsleighs. Certainly Ashford was distraught. He had been the one who identified the bodies, and the memory of his wife's pathetic, still form haunted him, but a great burden had also been lifted from his shoulders, and he fought more against the joy he felt at his release from bondage than against the sorrow of his loss. Baron Cloudsleigh compensated for his grief by writing furiously at his book, and, for the first time in years, there was a lightness in his step and a confidence in his voice, for it now appeared that it would soon be finished. Lady Cloudsleigh was irritable; she and Caroline had been natural enemies and she abhorred the pretence of a sorrow she did not feel, though she was unhappy at the prospect of being incarcerated with her in-laws for weeks. Valerian, too, was impatient with the proscribed ritual of mourning; though he had pitied Caroline, he had never liked her. It was ironic that the only person who seemed shattered by Caroline's death was the woman for whose death Caroline would have prayed if she had known of her existence.

Kitty continued to stare at Valerian mutely and he suggested tentatively, "It seems a bit of sherry would do us both good. May I pour two glasses?"

Kitty only nodded and Valerian, feeling the ice of her mood creep into his bones, headed for the decanter on the sideboard and tried to shake himself free of his growing unease. He knew that Kitty was waiting to hear some news about Ashford, and he knew that Ashford had not mentioned her name since the tragedy in Chester. The only solution was to lie. "Damn it," he thought, and slammed the decanter down upon the sideboard. He had been infatuated with Kitty ever since her first Season, and she had only flirted with him lightly as she flirted with all of the men about town, until she met and fell in love with his uncle. Then he had been forced to play the role of a go-between and had done so willingly though it played havoc with his heart, for he loved these two people and wished for their happiness. And here he was again, playing Cupid, while Ashford sulked at Cloudsleigh House and Kitty was tragic.

"I am here on behalf of Ashford," he said, and Kitty brightened and took the glass he held out to her. "He regrets that he cannot come to see you, but he must honour the conventions." Kitty nodded; already a faint flush of pink had come to her cheeks. "But he sends his love and devotion." Valerian almost choked on these words, but continued, "You are always in his thoughts, and," he hesitated and concluded lamely, "he will come to visit as soon as he can."

Though he had interjected a heartiness he did not feel to this pretty speech, something in his words did not ring true. The roses which had bloomed in Kitty's cheeks faded and died. She stared at the sherry in her glass.

"He did not inquire after Alex and Clarissa?" she asked in a flat, strained voice.

Valerian winced, realizing too late his oversight. "Of course, he did," he replied hastily. "He particularly hoped that Clarissa was—"

"It's no use, Val," Kitty interrupted. "I know you're lying. It's very thoughtful of you, but—" She turned away, and he could see by the convulsive movements of her shoulders that she was sobbing silently. In a flash he had crossed the room and put his arms about her, but she remained stiff and cold as marble and refused to look at him.

"Kitty, don't cry, I beg of you," he pleaded. "I spoke the truth, though God knows, Ashford has been so tormented by all of this that he does not speak to anyone. I know that he thinks of you—"

At this, Kitty only wept with more intensity, although she still made no sound.

"Kitty, my love," pleaded Valerian. "Let me comfort you. You know that I adore you. I will marry you and care for Alex and Clarissa as if they were my own. Let me rescue you from this misery."

Kitty wrenched herself free from his grasp and ran to the window, pressing her face against the cool panes, saying, "Valerian. Stop this nonsense. If I did not already have troubles enough to last a lifetime, you try to comfort me by—" Her voice faltered. She did not see the wave of pain cross his face, for she continued to watch the traffic on Berkeley Street. "You know that I think of you as a brother, and in truth, I believe you delude yourself about your feelings for me. But all of that is nothing, for I love—" her voice broke for a moment "—I love your uncle with a love so—so immense that I have given—have given up my whole life to him and now—now it seems as if it were all for naught for he does not—does not—love me." She buried her face in her hands.

Valerian, afraid to touch her again, cried out, "No, Kitty! Don't think that! It's just that he's so affected by the—by the recent—occurrences that he does not—"

"Want to see me," Kitty concluded in a muffled voice. "You cannot suppose that I don't know exactly what he is thinking and feeling and suffering. That wretched woman kept us apart when she lived, and now that she is dead she has destroyed us. And yet, I cannot help feeling that I killed her. Yes—" She turned to face Valerian, her eyes reddened by weeping, one hand clutching the draperies grimly. "Yes, I killed her as surely as if I had murdered her. And I know Ashford feels the same, for if he did not, then," she moved her hands in a fluttering gesture of dismissal, "he would be here now." She paused and added bluntly, "Instead of you."

Valerian flinched but was quick to point out, "That's a ridiculous and completely unfounded assumption. Caroline died in a railway accident. An accident," he repeated stubbornly.

"But if Ashford had not neglected her," Kitty cried out in anguish, "because of me, she would never have been on that train!"

"Ashford neglected her long before he met you," Valerian explained patiently. "He married her, because he needed a wife to further his career, and she suited that purpose better than any other woman in London. Two years later he met you and fell in love." Valerian paused for emphasis. "Can you imagine what that must have been like for a man of his age not to have experienced love, not

188

to believe it existed except in novels, and then to discover it when he was thirty—"

"Twenty-nine," Kitty corrected bleakly.

"Nearly thirty," continued Valerian with fierceness, "and already married to a woman who made his every minute at home a torment; who went behind his back to jeopardize his career when she realized it was of more importance to him than she was; who never allowed him to enter her bedroom because she feared—"

"Valerian!" Kitty stopped him aghast. "We must not speak of the dead, God rest her soul, like this!"

"Damn it, Kitty!" snapped Valerian, exasperated. "I've never known you to be so priggish. You know I've said the same things when she was alive, did I not?"

"I suppose you did," Kitty responded listlessly. "But she is dead now. And I fear that her death was more important than her life. How can Ashford and I be together again with a ghost—with Death itself, between us?"

She shivered and stared at something invisible in front of her, as if she were staring at Caroline's spectre.

With a fresh shock of insight, Valerian saw her, not with the illusions of the past nor the pleasant memories of the gracious hostess, but as she would have appeared to a stranger. With her red-rimmed eyes, her trembling hands, pale, gaunt face, and vacant stare, she seemed to be in a trance. Nay, worse than that, she seemed a mad woman.

Afraid to touch her again and afraid to startle her, Valerian sought desperately for a new way to reach her.

"Lady Kitty," he said in a low, soothing voice. "I'd like to see little Alex and Clarissa, so I can tell—I would just like to see them. May I?"

Kitty glanced at him dimly. "Why not?" she asked with indifference and sank down upon an ottoman. Seeing that she would not rouse herself to call them, Valerian headed down the corridor and found the two children in the last room, sitting idly on the bed, jumping up with fear when Valerian entered.

"Oh, it's Mr. Cloudsleigh," said little Alex to his sister, who was trying to hide behind him. "Don't be such a baby, Rissa!" He stepped up to Valerian and held out his hand, saying, "How do you do, Mr. Cloudsleigh?"

About to reprimand the boy for his formality, Valerian realized that Alex was using this ritual he had seen performed by his mother's callers to assert his manliness.

"I am well, Alex," responded Mr. Cloudsleigh, shaking the proffered hand. "And you and Miss Clarissa?"

"We are upset about Mama," confessed Alex. "She is so terribly sad, and we cannot make her happy. What is wrong with her, Uncle Val?"

"I am not quite sure myself," Valerian replied sombrely, "but I know it is not right for her to be alone. You and Clarissa must come out and keep her company. And you must help to persuade her to go on an outing tomorrow. We shall all go—to the Derby—would you like that?"

Alex was transformed from a troubled young man to an excited little boy as he asked breathlessly, "To watch the horses race? Oh, I should love that! Wouldn't you, Rissa?"

Clarissa wrinkled her small nose in distaste. She thought horses were big, dangerous, smelly beasts, but Alex adored them, virtually lived at the stables behind the house, and never missed an opportunity to discuss them with his mother's gentlemen friends.

"Let's go out and ask her about it then, shall we?" said Valerian pleasantly, holding out his hand for Clarissa who accepted it after a few minutes of suspicious scrutiny. Alex raced ahead of them shouting, "Mama, Mama! Guess what? Uncle Val is going to take all of us to the Derby tomorrow to watch the horses race. Oh Mama, please say you'll go!"

Kitty had risen to her feet as Clarissa waddled into the room, escorted by Valerian.

"What's this?" she asked with a frown. "I can't go out. It's impossible!"

"Kitty," Valerian pleaded with her. "You cannot become a hermit. Look at the children! They need love and attention. I've never seen Clarissa look so shabby. Her dress is torn, her hair isn't brushed." Clarissa, hearing these criticisms, puckered her mouth into a mighty pout, wrenched her hand free from Valerian's, and flung herself at her mother sobbing. Kitty knelt and put a tentative arm about her daughter. "I found them cowering in the back bedroom—" went on Valerian remorselessly.

"We were not cowering!" said little Alex, hearing his mother attacked. "Mama said she wanted to be alone." Somehow he sensed this was not the right way to come to his mother's defense and stopped suddenly, looking at her with anxiety and fear in his eyes.

Kitty felt pierced to the heart by this gaze, and dropped her head upon her daughter's. "By the Good Lord," she murmured piteously, "leave me alone, Valerian!"

"That is precisely what I refuse to do!" shouted Valerian, panicked by the emotions he had stirred up. He thought of asking the children to leave the room, decided after one look at Clarissa, still sobbing, and Alex, standing stiffly alongside his mother, that they would not go, and said, "Kitty, there is almost no one in London who knows of your relationship with Ashford." She looked up blank with shock. "Not even that old gossip, Lady Muftow," Valerian continued without pity. "There may be a few who guess, but are all close friends, the Sylver brothers, Griggs perhaps. But how long will it remain a secret if you stay here immured in your mourning? If the pleasant myth of Mr. Meadows and your young widowhood is ever shattered and the real truth is exposed, then what chance do you and Ashford have for happiness? It is for his sake, for your children's sake, for your sake, and even for my sake, that I beg you, nay, I insist, that you be ready tomorrow morning when I call upon you, dressed in your brightest, prettiest dress, ready to go out and face the world again. God knows, you've played a part long enough. Play it just a little longer, and perhaps you will be able to leave the stage and find that happy role you play is yours in life." His voice became hoarse as he begged, "Do this one favour for me, Kitty, and if it does not work, I swear I will leave you alone!"

And without another word, he picked up his hat and cane and was gone, slamming the door behind him.

TWENTY-SIX

A Mother's Advice

Mrs. PLEET WAS HUMILIATED to hear of Lucinda's weakness at the Great Exhibition, horrified that Mr. Griggs had the effrontery to bring her home, and infuriated by the longing gazes Lucinda cast at him as he backed out of the door after seeing her safely to her mother's side. She missed the equally longing gazes which he returned to Lucinda, perhaps because she rarely saw anything she did not want to see. She allowed Lucinda to retire to her bedroom, and to absent herself from dinner, a dreary affair for Sophy had gone off with Dabney Griggs and Sibilla and her aunt dined alone, but Mrs. Pleet decided that it was time to have a *tête-à-tête* with her foolish daughter.

Usually overly protective where Lucinda was concerned, Lucy Pleet refused to listen to the excuses of illness that Lucinda sent down via Susan, and insisted that her daughter appear in the study. Lucinda did.

She was dressed in a hastily donned buff gown, with several buttons left undone, and she had not bothered to put on her crinoline so that the dress crumpled around her like a collapsed balloon. Her eyes were puffed from weeping and her face was covered with red blotches, for Lucinda was not attractive when she cried. But her mother, studying her as a gentleman would study a prize filly at Tattersalls, noted several points with approval.

The hectic pace of the Season and the recent bout of illness had caused Lucinda to lose almost all of what her mama had jokingly referred to as "baby fat." And her new slenderness, combined with the becoming coiffure which Sophy had recommended, made her a very pretty and desirable young woman.

Yes, she could possibly catch the eye of a man like the Marquis of Dower, or young Cloudsleigh, thought her mother with a sudden wild hope in her heart, but first, she had to be taught not to make a fool out of herself with a worthless scamp who also happened to be betrothed to her cousin.

"Sit down," said Mrs. Pleet.

Lucinda sat.

"Now, Lucinda," began her mother, helping herself to her third after-dinner sherry. "You have blossomed into quite a lovely young woman. Not that you weren't always a pretty child and a nice-looking girl, but of late you have been appearing to your best advantage." Lucinda who had frowned at her blotched face in the mirror before she came downstairs seemed perplexed by this, but her mother, not noticing, continued, "And it would not surprise me if you were married before the end of the Season to the catch of the Season!"

Lucinda, knowing the catch of the Season to be none other than the Marquis of Dower, who had never evinced the slightest interest in her, was surprised by this, but again Mrs. Pleet did not notice.

"However—" exploded her mother, whirling upon Lucinda, who had been expecting this and cringed in her chair, "no one will marry you if they learn that you have been carrying on with your cousin's husband!"

"But he is not her husband yet," said Lucinda, unaware of the significance of this statement, significant not because of what she said, but because she had said it at all. Lucinda, unable to recognize her own changes of character, did not realize that she had never interrupted one of her mother's orations previously, but Mrs. Pleet, noticing this unprecedented event, felt suddenly with an immense fear that she might not win this battle. A fear so irrational and preposterous that she quickly dismissed it, glared at her disobedient child and introduced a new element of pathos into her speech.

"Think of your father! Think of poor, dear, devoted Mr. Pleet!" she raised her eyes to heaven and fingered the brooch over her heart, one pudgy finger completely obliterating Mr. Pleet's dour countenance. "Think of how he slaved all of his life so that you could come to London for your Season, so that you could wear pretty dresses and stay out till four dancing, and all in the hopes that you would, as any dutiful daughter would, form an attachment for some quiet, well-bred gentleman of a good family who could provide you with an entree into the kind of Society that you could not enter otherwise, the only blessing which your father, may he rest in peace, was not able, despite all of his efforts, to provide for you!" She waited a moment to be certain that her captive audience had absorbed the full impact of this emotional argument, then expanded upon this foundation.

"Think what your loving father would say if he knew his daughter—who could have any gentleman in London at her feet — was instead throwing herself at a man who is engaged to her cousin, a man who is boorish, uncivilized, lacking any social grace, unattractive, in short, completely undesirable."

Lucinda wanted to protest, pointing out the contradictions for how could such an unattractive man be close friends with both Valerian Cloudsleigh and Lord Dower and have his suit for the hand of her cousin be so avidly accepted. But her mother's next words cleared up this perplexing puzzle.

"It is true that I am pleased he is marrying Sophy, and you may find that odd," Mrs. Pleet said like a teacher explaining Euclidean geometry to a very block-headed pupil. "But Sophy presents an entirely different problem. It's true she's of a good family, the Sylvers have ever been fashionable. Why, my father, your grandpapa, was part of the Carlton set, went about with Beau Brummel and the Prince of Wales, was an aide to the Duke of Wellington in the Peninsular campaign, and went to Almacks, and all the balls at Devonshire House. Unfortunately, he threw all of his money away on that Italian woman, and when she left him, he shut himself up in his country house and never came back to London again."

"Was that my grandmother?" asked Lucinda with interest, for she had heard often that she was a grandchild of the fourth Earl of Trendle, but never a word about his wife.

Mrs. Pleet annoyed by this second insolent interruption and aware in the dim recesses of her mind that the alcohol was causing her to say more than she should, replied with irritation, "Of course she was your grandmother. She was my mother, wasn't she?"

Lucinda, who had known nothing of the sort, nodded obediently, eyes shining.

"Not that she played the part of a mother at all," Mrs. Pleet said reflectively, her eyes glazing with the memories of those high-spirited days of the Regency. "She provided my father with four children—one son, the present Earl of Trendle—"

She stopped, a moment, lost in her childhood, and Lucinda eagerly encouraged her.

"And you, Mama!"

"Yes, I was the second," said Mrs. Pleet, still wandering through reminiscences, "and then Flora and Maria. And then," she awoke from her trance and finished harshly, "she left him!"

"But why, Mama?" questioned Lucinda softly.

"Why?" snapped Mrs. Pleet. "Because she had all of his money by then, in diamonds and rubies and emeralds, about her wrists and on her fingers and shining round her throat, and she ran away with the first young fool who appealed to her. I was only four at the time. Imagine, leaving your four-year-old daughter, and the others—Maria was an infant still."

"And so you were brought up without a mother," mused Lucinda. "He never married again?"

"No, he never married again. He was a broken man. He—" Mrs. Pleet was drifting again, a child of six watching a buxom maid emerge from her father's room giggling in the morning, a maid who had later become the housekeeper. Was it possible these horrible goings-on had occurred in her own family? She shook herself. "That was before our good Queen took the throne; immorality was rampant in the old days. But now things are better. We're the greatest nation on earth, and the family is the centre of our Empire."

Lucinda, not quite understanding the train of thought which led to this patriotic conclusion, tried to turn the conversation back.

"Was she very beautiful—my grandmother?" she asked quietly.

"How should I know?" cried Mrs. Pleet, enraged at her daughter's lust for such information. "Do you think a child, cruelly abandoned at four, remembers her mother?"

"No, I suppose not," said Lucinda crestfallen.

"Of course, there was a portrait," continued Mrs. Pleet, mollified somewhat. "By Lawrence. I saw it once. She was, well, Italian, dark hair, dark eyes. Maria favoured her the most, and I believe my father gave her the portrait when she was married. And Maria, though she never knew her, inherited her tendencies. My poor besotted father thought it amusing." Her voice shivered with rage as she thought of those days, for she had been the good and dutiful daughter who could never please her wayward hedonist of a father, while Maria, with a toss of her head or a cleverly spoken retort, would win his laughter and his love. "It was no wonder Maria was married so young. I am only surprised she did not disgrace her husband as her mother did. But she passed her flighty tendencies to her daughters, and that is why—" here, Mrs. Pleet gropingly returned to the topic of discussion, and her voice regained its full power "—I am pleased that Sophy will marry Mr. Griggs. In truth, the sooner that occurs, the better."

Lucinda lapsed into sullenness. It seemed the confidences were at an end and the mention of Dabney Griggs brought tears to her eyes.

"For those Merrell girls need a strong hand," Mrs. Pleet continued, pouring herself another glass of sherry. "Charlotte married a penniless rogue of a soldier, and Amy, a poor preacher, against their mother's wishes, and Eleanor, even if she did manage to make the marriage of the Season when she married Lord Cloudsleigh, is now known as one of the most abandoned and shameless women in London, contributing to the corruption of her own younger sister, Kitty, who has thankfully dropped out of the sight of decent Society, while I find Sibilla kissing strange men left and right—"

Lucinda brightened again for she had never heard of Sibilla's escapades, but Mrs. Pleet had finished with her summary of the Merrell family's faults and returned to her original point once more.

"So do you find it amazing that I am so pleased by Sophy's betrothal?" she asked indignantly. "No, I say the sooner, the better. I only wish that Sibilla was engaged also, though. I doubt that any sane man would offer for her," she said with a shudder. "When Sophy marries Dabney Griggs, she will be getting a good bargain, for he is quite wealthy, though totally unprepossessing."

Lucinda pouted.

"But you, miss," her mother said with enthusiasm, "are an heiress in your own right. To speak truth, I believe Mr. Griggs is marrying beneath his expectations, when he weds Sophia Merrell, but you would be lowering yourself if you wed him."

Lucinda wanted to respond to this statement, but nearing the climax of her oratory, her mother rose from her seat and placed her solid bulk directly in front of her timid daughter.

"And what do you suppose he thinks when you continue to cast sheep's eyes at him whenever he comes near you?" she asked in a dangerously calm voice.

"I don't," said Lucinda weakly.

"He thinks you are a foolish and stupid child," Mrs. Pleet shouted, bending over so that her pungent breath assaulted Lucinda with as much force as her voice.

"He doesn't!" Lucinda managed to gasp, before having to turn her head away.

"He does!" insisted her mother stubbornly. "He thinks that he should marry Sophia as soon as decency allows, so that he can be spared the embarrassment of your advances."

Lucinda had to admit that neither in words nor actions had Dabney ever given her the slightest reason to believe he did not love Sophy. She did not know that he had never done the same for Sophy, and began to cry bitterly:

"You are throwing yourself away on a man you cannot have, a man who does not want you, and a man who is beneath you anyway," said her mother triumphantly. "And that is why, when we go to the Derby tomorrow, you are not to show him the slightest interest, and you will not be sullen and sickly, as you have been of late."

"We are going to the Derby with—Mr. Griggs?" choked out Lucinda.

"Yes, we are," said her mother, bending closer to her cowering daugther. "You cannot avoid your cousin's fiancé forever. Lord Champford and Randall Sylver will accompany us. And you can't afford to miss the Derby. Everyone will be there. You will wear your new carriage costume. You will be alert and vivacious, and you will not plead illness as an excuse, young lady. Is that understood?"

After several minutes of trying to swallow back her sobs, Lucinda managed to squeeze out a tiny, "Yes, Mama."

"Very well then," said her mother, feeling benevolent. "You may retire to your room. I am certain we agree."

As Lucinda flung herself out of the chamber of inquisition, Mrs. Pleet sat back and poured herself a congratulatory glass of sherry.

TWENTY-SEVEN

A Scheme Is Set in Motion at Bob's Retreat

"SO YOU CAN SEE for yourself that Windsfall is the only horse to back for the Derby," concluded Major Garlinghouse enthusiastically, clapping Randall on the back.

That young man, his mind bleared by the alcohol he had consumed, his heart terrorized by the number of pounds he had just managed to drop in a game of hazard with the Major and the Captain, still managed to protest.

"B–b–but T–Teddington is the f–favourite," he stuttered.

"Ah, the Fancy likes to tout such a horse," interjected Captain Wheedle smoothly. "He's likely enough so that if he fails to place and the bookmakers collect their winnings, no one will suspect that they have been taken. They will think he ran poorly that day. But only a few of us in the know can tell you that Windsfall will win the Derby. How can you lose?"

Through the tunnel into which he had been trapped, Randall thought he could see a faint glimmer of hope.

"Ah, well," he said in what he trusted was a jovial voice, "I would be grateful for the tip, but, alas, I have no ready cash to place upon this venture. So you see that—"

"No need for cash," boomed out Major Garlinghouse.

Randall, cautiously sipping his fifth soda-and-brandy was so taken aback by this confident declamation that he choked and spluttered on his drink, which had somehow gotten confused and trickled into his lungs instead of entering his stomach. When he had, at length, ceased coughing and begun to wipe the tears from his eyes, he saw the ominous sight of both Major Garlinghouse and Captain Wheedle, watching him affably, both grinning like gargoyles. This horrible vision was multiplied for he saw two of each of them, and desperately he turned his head to try to clear his befuddled brain.

Dimly he heard Major Garlinghouse speaking to the bar maid who brought another round of drinks to their private room.

"Susan, my love," said the major in his honeyed tones and the girl squeaked with delight. "Send in Diggs Pullett. There, you're a fine girl, you are, and perhaps I shall take you to the Derby with me!"

"Oi!" Susan shrieked in her deep, mannish voice. "Lor' I should love that!"

"Then send the moneylender in," repeated the major placatingly. "If you do as you're told tonight—" and here he stopped for a brief foray beneath her petticoats, which ended in another squeal of pleasure from Susan "—you shall go to the Derby tomorrow!"

"In a fine carriage?" begged Susan, too dazzled to be aware that she was asking for more than Major Garlinghouse could promise.

"Yes, indeed, in a fine carriage," replied the Major with some irritation. "Now go and do as you were bid!" and he sent the girl from the room with a resounding slap upon her ample ass.

After a prolonged study of the crevice between the floor and wall had brought his eyes back into focus, Randall dared to turn his head around once more, to find a newcomer in the room. A small, grey, cadaverous-looking man, his bright beady eyes alight with something that might have been avarice and might have been impatience, his prim mouth pursed in disapproval, he was the moneylender of whom Major Garlinghouse had spoken, one Diggs Pullett, well-known to many impecunious sons of aristocrats who required the services of his discounting firm. Mr. Pullett was ill-at-ease in this sordid gaming hell to which he had been summoned by Major Garlinghouse. He did not like the Major, who was constantly borrowing money, but he had to admit, with unconcealed amazement, that all of the Major's debts were paid promptly. He had no way of knowing that his client was always able to cover his bills with the money he fleeced from the sorry young man who sat hunched at the end of the table and whom Major Garlinghouse now introduced to the moneylender.

"Mr. Pullett, you see before you Randall Sylver, beloved son of the Countess of Trendle, that is she who is married to Lord Trendle, the fifth Earl. Randall, this good man is Diggs Pullett, who has come to relieve you of all your monetary troubles."

"No! I cannot borrow," said Randall hoarsely. "I am in a hole — no end of a hole already."

As many young gentlemen, he lived constantly in a world beyond his means, belonging to clubs where "pounds and fives" were the lowest points, and surrounded by those who took odds on most events in the thousands. A few fortunate ones among his companions derived from families who could live on their inherited wealth for centuries, a wealth augmented by allowing certain sons to enter the more gentlemanly of the trades; others, like Randall and his brother, fought to maintain a facade of insouciance and even world-weariness, while living with the knowledge that all of the Trendle property was heavily mortgaged and that any moment the duns could be at the front door as they fled through the back towards exile on the Continent. The lucky remainder were men such as Dabney Griggs whose fathers had fought their way up from poverty to positions of immense wealth and power in industries and businesses which the aristocrats shunned as degrading.

Although Randall made his way through these perilous straits daily, he had contrived to avoid the more obvious pitfalls; he had never borrowed from anyone, neither moneylender nor friend, with the sole exception of Major Garlinghouse who had exploited early the inherent weakness for gaming that he recognized in the younger man.

Now he stared at the moneylender with an unfeigned horror which almost caused Mr. Pullet to depart in disgust. But Major Garlinghouse, witnessing the disintegration of his boldest scheme, assigned Captain Wheedle the delicate task of reassuring Mr. Pullett, while he took up a seat beside Randall, passing one arm over his shoulders, and uttering these soothing words,

"Come, come, my good fellow. We'll soon set you on your feet so that you need never concern yourself over the lack of the ready. I daresay you've forgotten that you can easily pay off the money-lender after the Derby with what you'll gain backing Windsfall. Odds are against him now, seven to one, though I have no doubts they'll improve as the word gets around town. You can borrow enough money to pay back what you owe me, then borrow an additional five hundred, and have yourself a cool three thousand by tomorrow. Take what you borrowed to Mr. Pullet and pocket the rest. You'll be set for life."

Here he vigourously thumped Randall on the back, but this jolt did not obscure a certain flaw Randall had spotted in the preceding speech.

"No need to borrow money to pay you back," he muttered. "I'll p–pay you after the Derby. With the money I win."

The Major clenched his teeth grimly, but widened this grimace into a grin.

"Now, now, Randall, you're already becoming tightfisted at the prospect of your new fortune. Would you ask your oldest and dearest friends, the men who have always been willing to lend you a few ponies when the luck is coming to you but you're short of the blunt, would you ask them to forego the pleasure of backing the very horse which is going to make you the richest young man in town tomorrow?"

"You just t–took all of my pocket money during that g–game of hazard," pointed out Randall suspiciously.

"Pocket money, old man, pocket money," rejoined the major cheerfully. "You said it yourself. You would come out with thousands, and we with hundreds. Not the way to treat your closest companions, now is it?"

"I c–cannot borrow," mumbled Randall. "My g–governor would disinherit me. It can't be done."

"He need never know," the Major was quick to say. "Tomorrow you'll be wealthy, pay back the moneylender, pocket your thousands, and that's the end of it. As a matter of fact, we'll have Mr. Pullett draw up the bill with the stipulation that you repay immediately after the Derby."

And with this comforting comment, he rose and approached the moneylender, who now sat at the table with his papers spread before him. Randall remained where he was, gloomily consuming his sixth soda-and-brandy, while the Major and the Captain directed the writing of the bill, and the Captain indorsed it before it was passed to Randall, who scribbled his name without even glancing at the contents, nor did he look at the money which was advanced as part of the transaction but crammed it thoughtlessly into a pocket.

Mr. Pullett, as he was ceremoniously ushered to the door by Major Garlinghouse, studied his unwitting victim with distrust, for he perceived that some scheme was afoot and that the unfortunate young man was the dupe. But the bill was certainly valid, though peculiar in that the due date was almost immediate, and the endorsement of the bill by Dabney Griggs (for this was how Captain Wheedle, a stranger to the moneylender, had written his signature) was more than satisfactory for Mr. Pullett knew well the reputation of Dabney Griggs. With a blink of his beady eyes, he scurried out of the gaming hell and back to his place of business, where he carefully filed away the document which would swiftly accrue tremendous importance in the lives of several people.

Once he had departed, Major Garlinghouse and Captain Wheedle celebrated their victory by ordering yet another round of drinks, and then brought in the final touch to their carefully wrought scheme, in the form of "Patches" Bagshaw, a clever Leg, who was known to go halves with a jockey who consented to rope the favourite. His nickname derived from the costume he always wore, a sporting cutaway coat, much too small for his massive frame, and held together by patches of assorted materials which covered the holes always created by the strain of his ample flesh against the ancient fabric. Considering this motley garment his lucky piece, he never replaced it with a new one, but he did have an extremely new, extremely flashy, and extremely large yellow neckerchief, which contrasted markedly with his extremely florid skin. He was as accustomed to lying (he preferred to call it "amplifying") as he was to gaming, considering both occupations more important than eating, drinking, sleeping, and wenching, and now, as he entered the private room and spotted his gull, he sauntered over to the bleary-eyed young man and said in his heartiest voice,

"So you are the lucky scoundrel who 'as been tipped by my wery good friends to that most 'andsome specimen of 'ossflesh ever to run in the Derby, that excellent and swift and noble crittur, yclept Windsfall."

Randall stared at him.

"Ah, you 'aven't told our young friend about me," shouted Patches, turning around to address the Major and the Captain. His rough voice made the flimsy walls of the chamber quiver. "I'm Patches Bagshaw, the luckiest member o' the Fancy, the King o' the Turf!"

Randall's unfocused but cynical glance at the man's dingy and patched coat revealed his disbelief of this glorious encomium.

"Ah, my good chap," continued Patches, intercepting this glance. "You scoff at this coat as an hexample of poverty, but, Mr. Sylver, I believe, if it is not presumptous so to hassume an hacquaintance not yet granted by hintroduction, so to speak, but I wander from my subject, this here coat o' many colours is my lucky piece. I hown more than a dozen new coats, but they 'angs in my closet onworn for I always sport this particler garment. Yes, I do, and the Major and the Captain can werify that, if they will."

He bowed to the two men who, with smug smiles, acknowledged the veracity of this fact.

"Now, look 'ere, Mr. Sylver," said Patches, seating himself with a flourish and helping himself to Randall's untouched drink. "Let's get down to business, right and proper like. I 'ear yer willin' to lay a bundle on Windsfall. And a wise choice that is, wery wise. Aye, for a young 'un you can pick 'em, you can." He wiped his mouth with his yellow neckerchief, and continued, "What I needs to know is 'ow much yer hintending to place on Windsfall." He leaned over confidentially as he spoke these words.

Still suspicious, Randall looked up wearily at the Major and the Captain and said indistinctly, "Ash musch as them."

With broadening grins, the pair of conspirators placed on the table the money which had become theirs, in repayment of previous debts, once the bill with the moneylender had been transacted, augmented by the earlier amounts won from Randall at hazard.

Patches took out his book from an interior pocket and solemnly entered the amounts, whereupon he counted the money carefully and deposited it in another cavernous pocket.

"And the gentleman?" Patches pursued his prey relentlessly.

Without even glancing at it, Randall pulled out a fistful of notes and thrust them at the Leg. When they were added, they totalled a sum of many hundreds, but Patches, after entering the sum and carefully placing it in yet another pocket, was heard to mumble,

"A pitiful hamount when you consider that yer fortune could be made on this 'oss."

A subtle signal from Major Garlinghouse warned him not to apply further pressure, and, shaking his head and muttering to himself, he finished off the soda-and-brandy.

Randall, experiencing an urgent need to relieve himself, stumbled to his feet, and Major Garlinghouse quickly offered his support. As they stumbled out through the main room of the gaming hell, Randall leaning heavily on the Major, he heard the excited speculations of the crowd upon the morrow's race.

"Take the field bar one."

"Two to one on Teddington."

"Too much riding; Secret Hope will not stand up."

"The Count comes from a good line, champions back to his grandsire, the fastest 'oss that ever ran."

"They say thirty-two horses will start—the largest field ever known."

But there was not a word. spoken in reference to Windsfall.

Beginning to believe that he had indeed been duped, Randall whirled about, increasing his dizziness, and cried desperately,

"What of Windsfall?"

This query was met by a round of guffaws and one old veteran summed up their disgust by spitting vehemently on the floor and saying, "That poor-spirited crittur! Never place; lucky to finish!"

Randall looked at the Major with eyes as stricken as a fox at bay.

"Never mind that," Major Garlinghouse whispered soothingly, swiftly ushering him into the coolness of the street. "If the world knew about Windsfall, the odds would be worse, and you would not stand to amass the fortune you will win on the morrow."

Giving his victim an amiable slap on the back, a slap which sent Randall reeling into the gutter, the Major stalked back through the inn to witness the last scenes of the charade.

As he expected the Captain had retrieved the notes he and the Major had given to Patches who sombrely ruled out those entries in his betting book. Sauntering into the private room, after buying a drink for every man in the tap room, Major Garlinghouse snatched up half of the money and flung it at Patches, commanding him, "On Teddington!"

"Aye, sir," replied the Leg, as he went through his ritual of pocketing the cash and making the entries. Having finished, he looked longingly at the mug of ale from which the Major was taking long gulps.

"I say, is that a hale, sir?" he asked. He ran one bright pink tongue over his lips thoughtfully.

"It is indeed," replied the Major, leaning back in his chair, putting his feet on the table, and lighting an enormous cheroot.

"I do so enjoy a pint o' hale with convivial friends about me," suggested Patches expansively.

"No more do I!" rejoined the Major, blowing the smoke from his cheroot at the dejected bookmaker. He took another long drag from his ale, smacking his lips expressively.

"Might you see me to a pint, guv'nor?" requested Patches abjectly.

"Might," was the monosyllabic return. There was a long silence as Patches stared mournfully at the mug, the Major studied the smoke rings about his head, and Captain Wheedle, his tight mouth curved in an ominous smile of triumph, glanced from one to the other furtively.

Suddenly Major Garlinghouse threw his cigar to the ground and stamped it out.

"What are the chances of Windsfall winning?" he snapped at the bookmaker.

"Nearly himpossible," replied Patches quickly, his face beaming again as he displayed his knowledge of the Turf. "Too heavy, hasn't won a major race yet, shows bad times in training. He likes to lead the field at the start but falls behind well before the Corner and never regains ground."

"But he could win—" speculated Captain Wheedle in chilling tones.

"'Ud be a miracle if he did," said the bookmaker warily.

"Can we make an arrangement that would insure that such a miracle did not take place?" asked Major Garlinghouse in a voice that assumed this was as good as done.

Patches, who was so accustomed to the shady in matters of the Turf that he assumed no horse that lost a race ever did so of its own accord, brightened at this recommendation.

"That could be easily harranged," he replied with enthusiasm. "I know the jockey, George Brock, personally. He's roped many a 'oss for me, and be willin' to do it again, if the price is right."

"What's the price?" inquired the major in bored tones.

Quickly calculating how much the Major and the Captain had to give, how much George would ask, and throwing in a commission for himself, Patches named a figure which to his surprise was willingly accepted by the other two men, and within minutes, the money was in his trembling fingers along with a generous portion of ale.

TWENTY-EIGHT

On the Road to Epsom

AN EARLY MORNING RAIN settled the dust on the roads and heightened the freshness of grass and flowers so that the occupants of the many carriages forging their slow passage towards Epsom Downs spent much of their travel time admiring the countryside. The thoroughfare was clogged with vehicles of every description, ranging from lumbering carts stuffed with apprentices on holiday to enormous carriages bearing noble coats of arms emblazoned on their doors. Occasionally a landaulet full of racegoers would draw up even with a chariot occupied by friends and they would carry on a prolonged conversation driving abreast of each other, slowing the traffic behind them for miles. At length, the mutterings and oaths thrown at them from the thwarted travellers would spur one of the vehicles onward, and somewhere up the road they would encounter another carriage of acquaintances and the scene would be re-enacted.

The malicious, sharp-tongued Lady Muftow surveyed the social panorama with delight from her seat in the swift phaeton driven by a nephew. Totally disinterested in the Derby, she nevertheless could not stomach the thought of another eagle-eyed old lady running to her on the morrow with a choice bit of fresh gossip. So she periodically jabbed her nephew in the back with the umbrella she brought in the event of rain, commanding him to drive even faster. She was a preposterous vision in her heavily tasselled royal purple foulard gown, a ridiculous bonnet covered with feathers and stuffed birds bobbing in the breeze, but whenever she came in sight, the Londoners quickly dropped their gaiety and flirtations and became sober, respectable, and quiet, praying that Lady Muftow's keen perception would not discern the skeletons in their family closets.

Spotting an exquisite and brand-new victoria down the road, Lady Muftow poked her unfortunate nephew in the back once more, signalling the vehicle which had caught her eye. As they approached, she saw with a surge of disappointment and resentment that the couple in the victoria were being chaperoned by the occupants of the Trendle barouche directly behind them.

Recalling Sibilla's transgression at the Trendle ball, Ludy Muftow stabbed her nephew again, this time an indication that he slow the phaeton, and studied Sibilla carefully, but the girl, in a becoming red-and-white striped carriage dress, was sitting silently beside her cousin, Lord Champford, who was eagerly regaling Lucinda on his other side with a story. Humph! thought Lady Muftow, she cannot fool me, the sly minx. It's outrageous, that's what it is. Her own sister is now engaged to that scoundrel who was making love to her at the ball.

She turned her attention instead to Lucinda, for a friend had come running with the news that Miss Pleet had been seen in Dabney Griggs's arms at the Great Exhibition. But Lucinda, dressed in a white muslin flounced underskirt with an overskirt of rich rose-coloured silk (white and red being the colours which the Marquis of Dower's horse carried) was flushed and pretty, listening to her cousin with animated interest.

Lady Muftow gave up on Lucinda too soon, for if she had continued to scrutinize her she would doubtlessly have seen that Lucinda was suffering under a tremendous strain, smiling with clenched teeth, and thanking God under her breath for His mercy in having placed her facing the back of the barouche, so that she need not be tormented by the sight of Dabney and Sophy seated together in the victoria in front of them.

Lady Muftow flicked her glance casually over Randall Sylver, seated beside Aunt Lucy, dismissing him contemptuously as a young man who had never and would never do anything of interest. Here again she missed a potential scandal, for Randall was unnaturally pale and could not utter a phrase without stuttering profusely this particular morning.

But Lady Muftow had focused instead on the couple in the victoria, an absolutely brand-new vehicle she noted with pleasure. It was a minor point, but at least she could report that Mr. Griggs had purchased a new blue-and-gold carriage in order to take his intended to the Derby. Sophy was dressed in an enchanting flounced gown of blue trimmed with gold braiding and, with a smile of triumph, Lady Muftow recalled that Mr. Griggs also had a colt entered in the Derby and that his colours were blue and gold. What was the name of that horse, Winter something?

"What's the name of Mr. Griggs's colt?" she shouted, sticking her nephew in the back once more.

Wincing, he replied, "Windsfall."

"Ah, Windsfall," repeated Lady Muftow sagely to herself. "Any chance he'll place?" she wanted to know next, again using her umbrella as a prod to alert her victim.

"None," muttered the bruised nephew.

"Humph, now," Lady Muftow cackled with glee. Still it was refreshing to see that Lady Sophia would ally herself with her fiancé's ventures. She would make a dutiful and becoming wife, but Lady Muftow remembered the day she had seen Sophy weeping in the Park, the same day her friend had reported the rendezvous between Miss Pleet and Mr. Griggs. Regretfully, she could discern no estrangement between the betrothed couple. Sophy was clinging to Dabney, one hand curled in the crook of his elbow, and chattering away excitedly, even having the impertinence to raise the other gloved hand and wave to Lady Muftow.

Satisfied that there was not one single item of interest to be gleaned from this cavalcade, Lady Muftow frowned and signalled her suffering relative to move on.

If only she had remained abreast of the shining blue victoria for another few minutes, she would have noted a man mounted on a massive chestnut pass the carriage. The rider nodded contemptuously in Sophy's direction before spurring his mount forward, and she blanched, withdrew her hand from Mr. Griggs's arm, and spoke only in monosyllables for the remainder of the journey, for the lone equestrian had been Mr. Leslie Whitefoot.

Missing this little drama, Lady Muftow nonetheless found much to interest her on the road ahead for they soon came upon a scene which was not only interesting but rewarding as it confirmed a rumour Lady Muftow had started earlier, that the beautiful widow, Mrs. Meadows, was, in actuality, the mistress of Valerian Cloudsleigh.

Here they were, like a pleasant family, bowling along towards the Downs in Mrs. Meadows's rose-coloured phaeton, for Valerian's had not yet been repaired. Mrs. Meadows, wearing an exquisite silk dress of the same rose tint as the phaeton, was holding an extraordinarily beautiful little girl with dark curls and dark eyes, while a small sturdy boy with the same Cloudsleigh colouring sat beside Valerian on the driver's seat, solemnly taking in instructions on how to manage the fine, matched pair which drew the carriage.

Seeing the notorious gossip, Kitty quickly unfurled her dainty, lace-trimmed parasol so that it shielded her face, but everyone knew that it was too late. Lady Muftow chuckled to herself as she poked her nephew and he obediently pulled ahead of the phaeton. This would show that meddling old biddy, Lady Calverley, who agreed with Lady Muftow that Mrs. Meadows must be a kept woman, but insisted that Valerian Cloudsleigh was not her paramour.

Those are Cloudsleigh children, Lady Calverley, mark my words, Cloudsleigh children, repeated Lady Muftow with grim triumph.

TWENTY-NINE

The Derby

LADY MUFTOW AND HER long-suffering nephew were among the first to arrive at the race track and find a spot for the carriage along the fence, from which vantage point Lady Muftow eagerly awaited the arrival of Lady Calverley.

The rose-coloured phaeton drew up shortly, but took up its position quite a distance away, and Kitty was careful to use her parasol as a barrier between herself and Lady Muftow's shameless gaze.

"Too late, young hussy, too late," muttered Lady Muftow, noting this flimsy deception.

"What is wrong, Lady Kitty?" asked Valerian softly, realizing as he spread out the contents of the luncheon hamper they had brought that she was upset.

"Oh, there are too many people here," replied Kitty, glancing fretfully in the direction of Lady Muftow and then at the carriages pulling up on either side of the phaeton.

"Come now," was Valerian's response. "I've escorted you to the Opera and riding in the Park. Why should anyone take it amiss that you came with me to the Derby?"

"She saw the children," whispered Kitty. "Lady Muftow."

"That old cat!" Valerian scoffed at her anxiety. "No one listens to a word she says."

Kitty shrugged her shoulders, looking at Alex and Clarissa with concern.

"There is a resemblance," she offered.

Valerian, studying the children in turn, remarked slowly, "Aye, they're Cloudsleighs, no doubt."

"Valerian, she thinks you are their father," Kitty confessed, her voice trembling.

Various reactions passed over the countenance of that young man, first astonishment, then envy, sorrow, and finally amusement.

"All the better!" he remarked with a brusque laugh. "All the better."

"A sad dog, a good dog, a bad dog," chanted Clarissa in her baby voice.

"Oh hush, angel," said her mother. "Where did you ever learn such a thing?"

"Most likely she heard someone say it of me," mused Valerian, with a curious expression in his eyes. "I have been a sad dog, running from one skirt to another, ignoring the…Why even Ned has his Peggy," and he turned to shout out a halloa to his friend, strolling by with his lady, who was becomingly attired in a cherry-red dress edged with Valenciennes lace.

"Peggy," repeated Kitty softly. "Peggy?" she said once more, following the direction of Valerian's glance, and then, "Peggy!" burst from her lips in an exclamation so wild and joyous that Peggy, some distance away, heard her and, hitching up her skirts in either hand, came running pell-mell towards the phaeton.

Thus it was that Peggy was the first member of the Partridge Park household to be restored to the prodigal daughter, and their reunion was tempestuous and happy. The two men were dismissed casually and told to go take Alex to inspect the horses, which duty they obligingly set off to perform, while the two women exchanged confidences, uncovering the details of their similar situations and commiserating with each other.

"Ah, if I were not merely a poor serving girl," Peggy lamented, "that would be the man I would marry, and Lord bless me, he would be begging to make me his wife. As it is—"

"But you are not a mere serving girl," commented Kitty provocatively.

Peggy looked at her startled.

"Surely you are my uncle's—the late Earl of Corrough's—only child," Kitty continued with enthusiasm, her usual *joie de vivre* beginning to emerge from under the shrouds of depression.

"Why how do you know?" inquired Peggy. "I harrudly know myself."

Kitty laughed, a pretty, lilting laugh. "Why even to a young girl, as I was at the time, it's fairly obvious. My papa goes to Ireland to settle his brother's estate and comes back with a child who looks just like a Merrell."

"Ah, but Ned doesn't know," Peggy said mournfully, lowering her head and drawing Clarissa up on her lap.

"Oh, he does not?" asked Kitty wryly.

"No," Peggy murmured softly. "I am just another—" she lapsed into decorum. "He has had many before me and will have many again. I should not have done what I did, but I confess to you, Miss Kitty, that God help me, I could not resist him." She turned a stricken face to Kitty, who drew her into a comforting embrace.

"Hush now, Peggy," she crooned. "You know, I believe you are wrong, and he does know after all."

"But then why?" were Peggy's muffled words.

"There are some men who desire an act of devotion rather than the mere promise of it," Kitty explained confidently, though the idea was as new to her as it was to her distraught audience.

"Then I did doubly wrong," moaned poor Peggy, "for I thought if I were to live my life always as a maid, to be ordered about and sent hither and thither without reason, I should accept Ned's—offer, and enjoy all of the things others have, for a brief time. But if I had been the acknowledged daughter of the Earl of Corrough, such a course would be shameful, would ruin me forever."

"Are things so much different for the daughter of the present Earl of Corrough?" questioned Kitty softly, and Peggy, realizing the blunder she had committed while pursuing her own self-indulgent grief, drew back quickly, ready to apologize.

"Oh Miss Kitty, I did not mean," she began, but Kitty silenced her with a wave of her hand, gazing fondly at Clarissa who had scrambled back into her mother's lap.

"I have my own rewards," murmured Kitty. Peggy studied the child briefly.

"Ashford Cloudsleigh," she stated simply.

Kitty tilted her head and looked at her companion with the bright, alert gaze so familiar to her friends. "You've heard a rumour?"

"Och, no," Peggy was quick to reply. "It's fairly well evident."

"Lady Muftow believes them to be Valerian's children," Kitty tried to interject a note of levity into her voice, faltered, and broke down.

"He has not come to see you since his wife's death?" was Peggy's second shrewd guess.

When Kitty, not trusting to words, merely nodded her head, Peggy continued, "In faith, Miss Kitty, surely you see that he cannot. The only way in which he can set himself free from his own remorse and self-accusations is to honour her memory in isolation, and the longer he does so, the more he will be entirely yours when he is ready to come to you again."

Kitty's sad eyes grew wistful as Peggy delivered these sentiments. "It's odd," she said after a short hesitation, brushing away the few tears which sparkled on her lashes, "but I am not even sure that I want to be married. Though I did not intend to be—to be his mistress, when it came about I thought how marvelous our love was, so noble and so pure and so strong without any of the ties that bind others together. But now it's become so sordid and so ugly, I wonder if—"

"You surely don't mean to tell me, Miss Kitty," interrupted Peggy with indignation, "that you would turn him down if he came to you now with an offer of marriage?"

"I—I do not know," Kitty stammered apologetically.

"Stuff and nonsense," was Peggy's blistering remark. "Marriage may have its pitfalls, though I am not especially qualified to speak of them, but, the Good Lord willing, it has its blessings also. Think of what you could do for Mr. Ashford as his wife. You could further his career—parties, friends, the support you would lend when he was uncertain if he was following the right course. And then for you and the children, he would offer stability, a settled home life, aye, especially the love of a father—"

Carried away by the grandeur of her oratory, Peggy was brought down from the clouds by Kitty's irreverent comment, accompanied by giggles.

"Can you imagine what Lady Muftow would say if I married Ashford? Why she must have told half the world that I am Valerian's mistress."

"So much the better," Peggy thought, and said so defiantly. "Let the world think what it wants. Why, in later years when they write the history of our time, they will mention the Great Society Scandal of 1851, when the mistress of Valerian Cloudsleigh married his uncle, and her jilted lover took to wife her younger sister, all the time unconscious of—how do they phrase it in books?—the dark currents beneath the surface."

"Which sister?" asked Kitty with a little frown.

"Oh Miss Sibilla, though I'm certain neither of them knows it yet. They quarrel and think that makes them natural enemies, not realizing that there is no surer sign of attraction."

"Are Sibilla and Sophy attending today?" Kitty wanted to know.

"Aye, I should think so," Peggy replied, scanning the carriages now lining the track on either side. "There! The Trendle barouche, you see Sibilla and Lucinda, Mrs. Pleet, Baron Champford, and his brother. And in the victoria, where the gentleman is just getting down, you see Sophy, and the gentleman, probably going to look at his horse before the race begins, is Mr. Dabney Griggs."

Peggy's guess was accurate for Mr. Griggs was going to inspect Windsfall and talk to his jockey before the signal to start, and he was slightly annoyed when Baron Champford refused to accompany him, declaring that nothing was so important at the Derby as the savouring of the viands which they brought in a hamper from Fortnum and Mason, and that the horsey odour which would cling to his clothing in the stable area would certainly curb his appetite. Randall also refused, with a look of terror, which derived perhaps from his fear that he would be recognized in the Ring by some low character, such as Patches.

So Dabney, with a kiss for Sophy, set off alone, and indeed, the first sight which met his eyes when he entered the Ring was a scoundrel in a patched coat expostulating with his jockey, George

Brock. He hastily broke off their heated discussion by moving towards George, who ordered his friend away with a glance of fear at the approaching owner of Windsfall.

"I believe you should be in the dressing shed; the saddling bell will ring shortly," was his gentle reproof.

"Aye, sir," mumbled the jockey disapprovingly.

"How is the colt looking today?" asked Dabney awkwardly as they moved towards the dressing shed.

George shook his head, keeping his bright eyes fixed on the ground, amazed that a man so ignorant in the ways of the Turf could have the ownership of so many fine animals, though Windsfall was not among this number, even in the jockey's mind.

"He'll do as well as 'e can be expected to do, which isn't well," was the jockey's circuitous reply. Windsfall was the least promising of a lot of horses sold at the auction of Lord Kramp's estate the year before. Mr. Griggs, while buying the group of thoroughbreds, also hired their trainer and the jockey, and the trainer, with a sort of stubborn martyrdom, insisted that because Windsfall's grandsire was a great racing champion, Windsfall would be so also, and despite every indication to the contrary, Windsfall had been entered in the Derby.

While his jockey was being helped into his blue-and-gold racing silks, Dabney Griggs stood outside the enclosure studying the grey colt, Windsfall, carefully, trying to discern the points which would alert men more learned in horseflesh to his chances on the flat.

"Your jockey rides him wrong," was the quiet comment of a handsome, young man, dressed in a plain brown suit, who stood next to Mr. Griggs. "He allows him too much head at the start, and the colt runs himself out early. Though he might never run well, for his action is a trifle faulty."

As Mr. Griggs nodded thoughtfully at this, seeming unperturbed by the criticism, the stranger dared to go further.

"You know I believe that your jockey has been paid to rope him in, for I saw an exchange of money between him and the bookmaker they call Patches. It seems preposterous for the colt will certainly do poorly anyway, and I can't imagine that anyone has much to lose on him. You, sir?"

"Ah, no, I have a token shilling on him," confessed Dabney Griggs cheerfully.

"The rest on Teddington?"

Mr. Griggs nodded. "The rest on Teddington, and some on Secret Hope, owned by a friend of mine. Ah, here he is now! Ned, come over and let me ask you a question. This is Lord Dower, the owner of Secret Hope, and Mr. Valerian Cloudsleigh and young Alex Meadows. This is—"

"Mr. Leslie Whitefoot," mumbled the stranger.

"Yes, precisely so," said Dabney, as if he had known that all along. "Gentlemen, Mr. Whitefoot brings a serious charge against my jockey. He believes that he has been paid to rope in Windsfall."

At this solemn statement, the Marquis of Dower broke into great whoops of laughter, while Valerian and Alex grinned broadly.

"Hah!" the Marquis managed to gasp at last. "That's a good one, it is. No need to rope in Windsfall, the colt does it himself. Though I have no doubt your jockey is capable of taking a bribe; he's a shady sort. You should dismiss him, Dabney."

"Then you think I should ignore this accusation?" Dabney pursued his subject stubbornly.

"It's not a question of ignoring it," said Valerian, looking apologetically at the stranger and shrugging his shoulders. "But how to prove it? Who can truly say whether the horse would or could have run better? And if we question the two principals, they are certain to deny it, probably fixing the blame on the poor stable boy whom you would have to dismiss. At least, we can watch the race. If Windsfall wins, our fears will be groundless."

But at this optimistic remark, the Marquis of Dower began to double over with laughter once more, so that Valerian, nodding stiffly to Mr. Griggs and Mr. Whitefoot, led him off, trailed by Alex, calling out, "Best to take your seats for the race!"

Mr. Griggs obligingly offered the young stranger a seat in his drag, but Mr. Whitefoot insisted that he had left his horse tethered to the rail at a fine vantage point for the finish, so they parted amiably, Mr. Griggs admiring the young man for the restrained and confident manner in which he presented himself, though he was clearly, from his speech and dress, a mere country gentleman, while

Mr. Whitefoot, returning to his mount, thought sadly that Sophy had found herself a very good husband.

The horses were being led from the saddling enclosure, the roar of the Ring swelled to a great crescendo as last minute bets were placed, the onlookers in the carriages circling the field rose to their feet to watch as the jockeys, in silks every colour of the rainbow, mounted and tried to restrain the restless animals.

Peggy, standing beside the Marquis of Dower, alongside Kitty's phaeton clutched his arm tightly while Alex jumped up and down screaming, "'Ray for Secret Hope! Hooray! Hooray!" his childish voice suddenly poignantly clear in the hush before the fatal word "Start!"

The flag was dropped and the horses went sweeping out across the field, Windsfall taking an early lead as usual, and Sophy looked at her escort with pride and excitement, knowing his low expectations for the colt, while Randall behind them, stared at the grey with saucer eyes, his whole being focused on that one animal, his muscles moving convulsively as if he were running in the Derby himself.

The race was now almost half-run and Windsfall began to fall inexorably back. Major Garlinghouse and Captain Wheedle, on top of a hackney coach with Susan, shook hands with great satisfaction, while Patches, at another place along the railing, patted his pocket and shouted "Attaboy, Brock!"

Teddington was far in the lead when Secret Hope, with a burst of controlled energy, drew abreast.

Peggy threw her arms around the neck of the Marquis of Dower, kissing him wildly, under the observant eye of Lady Muftow. Sibilla and Lucinda, both standing in the Trendle barouche, began to cheer and insisted that the champagne be opened immediately, an action which Mrs. Pleet was quick to carry out, helping herself to a generous portion first.

But Secret Hope's valiant effort came too late, for Teddington, hearing the sound of the hooves running alongside and feeling the breath of the brave filly on his neck, pulled away from this close competitor and crossed the finish line alone, the winner of the Derby by many lengths—Teddington!

THIRTY

A Moneylender
Tries to Collect

AT FIRST IT WAS a mere whisper, but as the friends of the victim did not deny it, the rumour swept like wildfire through the drawing rooms and clubs of London.

"Young Sylver shot himself!"

There were some who insisted that he was dead, a suicide. Others, who listened with closer attention to the conflicting re ports, were able to piece together a more accurate story.

It seemed that Sylver had gone to a low lodginghouse near the river, where, after consuming an entire bottle of gin to give himself courage for the fatal deed, he picked up the gun and pointed it at his head, but partially because the spirits had befogged his senses and partially because he was trembling so much, the gun went off early and the bullet pierced his shoulder. The report of the pistol went unnoticed in the usual pandemonium of the particular neighbourhood, and it was not until the next morning that he was found, unconscious from the pain and nearly dead from loss of blood. Taken to the charity ward of a nearby hospital, he went unrecognized for another day, and when at last his grim parent was brought to see him, the Earl insisted that he remain there, under the care of the surgeons, rather than return to the ancestral mansion to be nursed.

Lady Trendle, torn between her love for her favourite child and her shame that the heretofore spotless escutcheon of the Trendies had been sullied, dressed in mourning and sat hour after hour in a dark room, refusing to see anyone. Her irate husband declared that the worthless scamp could not ever darken the doorway of Trendle House again, and that he would be packed off to the Continent, or better yet, America, or even more appropriate, Van Diemen's Land, as soon as he was ready to be moved. Baron Champford, an amazing sight in his sorrow, for he did not know how to express it, having learned the role of disinterested observer so well, stormed about from friend to friend, demanding to know why his brother had done this. None could offer any suggestion, and Randall lay in his hospital bed, alternating between delirium and merciful unconsciousness, as yet not quite aware that he was not dead.

The moneylender, Mr. Pullett, who held the bill which was now past due, frowned when he heard of the attempted suicide, but the head of the firm, known to others in the jobbing and discounting trades as "Heartless" Hogg—considered more appropriate than his Christian name Henry—insisted that if the young fool was so stupid as to attempt to blow out his brains, the cosigner should gladly pay it.

Fearful that Mr. Griggs would scorn his impudence in trying to collect, Mr. Pullett thought hopefully of his long-time client, Major Garlinghouse, who might be able to advise him how to proceed. After many hours of trudging about asking for information (for Major Garlinghouse had always come to the dusty offices of Hogg and Company), he at last found out the direction of the Major's lodgings.

At his impatient knock, the door was opened by a tall, gaunt woman with tear-rimmed eyes and prematurely greying hair. A plump boy, sitting in the middle of the shabby carpet, was turning purple and his sister, a thin, leggy child, her pale face framed by dark braids, was trying to pick him up and shake him, but her fragility prevented her from accomplishing this mission.

Luckily, the sight of the unexpected visitor forced the issue of the peppermint candy which his mother refused to purchase for him out of Horace's mind and he expelled his breath in a mighty gasp, which quickly turned to chortles of joy as he rolled about on the ground pointing at man at the door.

Charlotte, recognizing Mr. Pullett as a dun, found nothing amusing about his presence on her threshold and began to shut the door in his face, saying coldly, "My husband is not at home and any questions you may have must be directed at him."

"My dear madam," said the moneylender offended, "I have no bill against you. Rather it is to aid a friend of yours that I have come."

"Captain Wheedle is no friend of mine," retorted Charlotte sharply, preparing to slam the door again.

"I know of no Wheedle," the moneylender snapped with pursed lips. "It is," he lowered his voice delicately, "on behalf of Mr. Randall Sylver."

The woman before him turned as white as snow, her hand dropped limply to her side, and she stared through the moneylender as if he were a pane of glass.

"Oh my God, no!" the words were forced from her lips as if by some deep internal pressure, her eyes shut and her teeth clenched as if she were in great pain.

"Madam!" Mr. Pullett said quickly, trying to rouse her from her trance.

Horace, spotting the weakening of his mother, took advantage of the opportunity to start a new campaign for candy and began wailing, "Peppermints!" at the top of his lungs, punctuating each expression of this magical word with a tremendous roar of frustration.

"Goddamnit, stop it!" screamed Charlotte, startled out of her usual benevolence towards her only son, and slapping him across his round, red face, an act so unprecedented that rather than being offended, Horace stopped crying and stared at her with open-mouthed astonishment.

"I suppose you had better come in, Mr. ..." Charlotte said wearily, returning to the door.

"Mr. Pullett," enunciated the suspicious man, stepping briskly inside and drawing up short at the dinginess of the parlour, furnished with one monstrous grey horsehair sofa and a dirty armchair. He refused to take the seat Charlotte offered, but insisted on standing near the door, as if at any moment he might have to bolt through it.

"What is it you want?" asked Charlotte crisply, settling herself primly on the sofa and sending the children into the back bedroom. "How is it that my cousin—" The moneylender frowned and Charlotte said with a sigh, "Yes, Randall Sylver is my cousin. How is it that he is involved with you and my husband?"

Mr. Pullet studied her with his bright, beady eyes, finally declaring in tones of disapproval, "He—your cousin, madam, transacted a bill with me, at the request of your husband who was there when the bill was signed."

Charlotte thought about this for some time. "But my husband did not sign the bill, am I correct?"

"Quite correct, madam," replied the moneylender. "A man by the name of Dabney Griggs signed the bill."

"Then," said Charlotte wearily, "I do not understand why you are here."

"I thought perhaps," was the curt reply, "that rather than trouble Mr. Griggs, who would surely think it offensive, Major Garlinghouse would be willing to cover the bill himself."

Charlotte laughed, an unpleasant, derisive laugh.

"Surely, if you know my husband at all, Mr. Pullets, you know that he never has any money to pay any bill. If he were here it would be interesting to see what he has to say to you, for I deeply fear that he is involved in some scheme. The truth of it is that he disappeared shortly after we heard the news about my cousin, and I have not seen or heard from him since. Don't misunderstand me. I find his absence quite pleasant, with the sole exception being that he left us without any money, so that we have existed for the past several days on the mercy of Mrs. Pritchard, our landlady. And now I do believe our interview is at an end. I would advise you to contact Mr. Griggs, for he was here once with Randall and seemed a good friend to him, though I am surprised he would encourage him to enter the clutches of a moneylender."

With these harsh but not unkindly spoken words, she ushered him out the door, and Mr. Pullett, realizing with irritation that there was more trouble ahead than he anticipated, sought out Mr. Griggs at his offices in the City.

Having passed the inspection and interrogation of countless junior clerks, Mr. Pullett was finally shown into a spacious room containing an enormous mahogany desk, behind which sat a red-haired man who looked up impatiently from some papers, and said briskly,

"Can I be of assistance?"

Mr. Pullett spoke up sharply.

"I am looking for Mr. Dabney Griggs. Be so good as to inform him, my good man, that I am waiting for him."

"It is as good as done, for you have found him," indicated the gentleman at the desk, pointing to himself. "Now, can I be of assistance?"

"Why, enough, sir, of wasting my time!" said the moneylender indignantly. "You are not Mr. Griggs."

With an expression halfway between amusement and annoyance, Mr. Griggs said with great forbearance, "I can be trusted to know the name I have borne since birth, I should think. As far as I know there is not another person with my name in any corner of the Empire, for the Griggses are a small family, and the name Dabney, a romantic notion on the part of my mother."

"I certainly am sorry to disagree with you, sir," replied the stubborn Mr. Pullett, in a voice which implied that he was not sorry in the slightest. "But there is another Mr. Dabney Griggs. He is a trifle under medium height, has dark hair, much slighter of build than you, sir, with a small dark moustache so," he held his finger straight across his upper lips, "and dark eyes, with skin of an olive tint, like one from Italy."

The Mr. Griggs before him threw down his pen and furrowed his brow. "Where and in whose company did you last see this impost—this other Mr. Griggs?"

Mr. Pullet considered this question for some time before replying brusquely, "In a gaming tavern, known as Bob's Retreat, in the company of Randall Sylver and Major Garlinghouse."

"Captain Wheedle!" exploded Dabney Griggs, lunging out from behind the desk in such a startling manner that Mr. Pullett retreated several paces.

"And what were you doing there?" he demanded, looming over the frightened little man.

"Sir!" retorted the moneylender, "I honestly cannot reveal my business. It is a private matter between the other Mr. Griggs and myself."

"There is no other Mr. Griggs," thundered Dabney, then abashed by his own ferocity, he turned to compose himself and came back with an embarrassed smile, proffering Mr. Pullet his hand as a measure of good faith.

"I must apologize for my outburst," he went on more calmly, "but you must understand my deep concern for my friend, Mr. Sylver, who—encountered an accident to his health, and I begin to fear some scheme is afoot."

"Exactly Mrs. Garlinghouse's words," burst out the startled moneylender, and he explained reluctantly under Dabney's probing questioning the nature of his interview with that woman.

"So, the two rogues have gone into hiding," mumbled Mr. Griggs, sinking back again into his chair, adding more distinctly, "Was it a bill that was drawn up at Bob's Retreat?"

"Yes, sir," was the unwilling reply.

"May I see this document?" asked Mr. Griggs, and after a great deal of hesitation and mumbling to himself, Mr. Pullett brought the paper over to him and pointed out the signature of "Dabney Griggs" under the glare of the gas lamp on the desk. "This is definitely not my signature," Mr. Griggs said with repressed anger, "and if the person you described placed this signature here, why then it's a matter of blatant forgery." His eye roved up to take in the amount of the bill, and Mr. Pullett saw his hands on the arms of the desk chair become so white that he feared the wood might snap.

"No wonder poor Randall—" gasped Mr. Griggs, under extreme duress. He dove into a desk drawer and coming up with a chequebook wrote out a cheque for the entire amount, holding it out to Mr. Pullett with the words, "If you will be so good, I will retain the document in exchange for this cheque."

The moneylender snatched at the cheque quickly, but was gracious enough to add suspiciously, "If the signature is a forgery, there is no need for you to—"

Dabney Griggs cut him off with the hasty words, "There is great need. I trust that the manner in which this bill has been settled will remain confidential. I doubt your employer cares little how he collects his money as long as it is collected, and I must thank you for bringing it so promptly to my attention. Now, good day, sir."

Dismissed for the second time in the short space of the afternoon, Mr. Pullet marched briskly out of the office of "Griggs and Griggs" and out of the plot.

THIRTY-ONE

The Two Foxes Are Tracked to Their Lair

MR. GRIGGS, CONFUSED BY the shifting aspects of the principals in the scheme of which he had become an unwilling partner, sought enlightenment from the victim, but Randall, tossing with fever, was incoherent.

"He carries on like this for hours at a time," was a surgeon's indifferent answer to Dabney's worried question. "Never says anything intelligible, then lapses into a sort of swoon."

Bending closer to the restless patient, Mr. Griggs was able to distinguish various jumbled words among them "the Major," "Captain Wheedle," "moneylender," "Patches," and "Windsfall."

He started back at this last and left the hospital thoughtfully. Was it possible someone had convinced the poor fool to bet heavily on Windsfall, and did this explain why the bill had come due almost immediately after it was drawn up? He had kept his secret mighty deep if this was his hope, thought Dabney Griggs, for not a word about the horse had he mentioned, though he had been unnaturally silent at the race. And yet the shooting accident (Mr. Griggs refused to label it "attempted suicide" and scoffed at those who did) had taken place quite shortly after the Derby.

Determined to know the truth, Mr. Griggs endeavoured to run those two wily foxes, Major Garlinghouse and Captain Wheedle, to the light, but they were hidden deep and had not been seen for a week at any of their usual lairs.

Charlotte protested that she knew nothing of any scheme or where Major Garlinghouse was at the present, accepting with gratitude Dabney's gift of money with which to buy food and his offer to pay the back month's rent. But she refused to allow him to pay for a month in advance, declaring stoutly that if her husband did not return by month's end, she and her children would return to Partridge Park to live.

In the grimy confines of Bob's Retreat, Dabney Griggs uncovered his first clue. At first the battered and grotesque habitués of the gaming hell refused to speak to the toff in their midst, but a few shillings dispensed for three pennyworth of rum to one sorry specimen, who seemed to be the official spokesman for the tap room, alleviated the silence somewhat.

"Do you know two men who are called Major Garlinghouse and Captain Wheedle, a tall fair-haired man and a small dark one?" brought the laconic reply, "Might."

"Do you ever recall seeing them with a young gentleman, Randall Sylver, a short, frail youth with plain brown hair?"

"Might."

Several unsuccessful forays trying to ascertain the activities of this trio at Bob's Retreat were answered with stout ignorance until Mr. Griggs hit on the happy notion of asking, "Was there ever a moneylender with them, a small, bristly man by the name of Pullet?"

"Aye, there was," the sorry specimen responded. Seeing that no more information was forthcoming, Mr. Griggs bought another three pennyworth of rum which elicited a further comment, "'Twas the last time they was here."

"Do you remember anything at all peculiar about that time?" probed Mr. Griggs.

"Aye, sure do," replied the spokesman, nudging his closest neighbour with a sharp elbow. "'Twas the time the young swell arsked us wot we thought of Windsfall." At this memory, he began to laugh uproariously, a laugh which spread infectiously around the tap room.

Dabney winced, realizing his colt was somehow the key to the entire scheme.

"Was there a bookmaker here that night also?" he bent once more to the interrogation.

"Aye, Patches, he's one o' us," said the specimen, jerking his head towards a figure in a motley coat at the bar.

Throwing a few shillings upon the table, Dabney rose hastily and, collaring the unsuspecting bookmaker, hurried him into the street where he flung him against the stone wall of the building and asked brusquely what dealings the bookmaker had carried out before the Derby with the Major, the Captain, and Randall Sylver.

"That young fellow, very frail, misr'ble 'un?" Patches wanted to know, looking about wildly for an escape or an alert constable.

"Yes, that one, Randall Sylver," answered Dabney harshly, taking the man by the frayed lapels of his shabby coat and shaking him against the wall.

"Why, the swell wanted to lay some money on Windsfall for the Derby," was the good-natured reply.

"How much?"

"Near a thousand, guv'nor."

"And you allowed him to do so when you knew the colt had no more chance of winning than I have of getting to the moon?"

"It's nothin' to me, guv'nor, how men choose to cast away their money." Patches, squinting in the growing darkness, eyed him suspiciously. "Say, ain't you the guv'nor that owns Windsfall?"

"I am," was the stern reply. "Now tell me, did Major Garlinghouse and Captain Wheedle bet on Windsfall?"

A look on Patches' face of avarice chased by obstinacy alerted Dabney that a special encouragement was required. Taking out a guinea he let it fall into the gutter, from which Patches eagerly rescued it.

"Now tell!" Mr. Griggs ordered, acting as if he would begin the shaking process again.

"They bet in front o' the young 'un, guv'nor," said Patches quickly, "but when he left, they wanted it back and put 'alf of it on Teddington."

"And the remainder—Did they give you the remainder to bribe the jockey to rope Windsfall?"

A closed look warned Dabney that neither renewed shaking nor a waterfall of guineas would evoke a response.

As he turned to walk away, thrusting his hands deep within his pockets, he heard the mumbled advice.

"'Tis yer jock, guv'nor. Ask 'im!"

This Dabney could not do until the following morning and though he made his way homeward with all of the pieces to the puzzle in his hand, the persistent question which nagged at him was, "What did the two scoundrels hope to gain from this?"

The identical question was being asked at the same time by one of the scoundrels to the other, as both were holed up in a waterfront dive, near the locale where the "shooting accident" had occurred.

"Damn it all, Wheedle. What was the purpose of this whole rig-amarole?" Major Garlinghouse demanded.

"Never suspected the young idiot would try to kill himself. Most provoking. Made sure he'd run to us with his problem," was the smooth reply. "We'd reassure him that Griggs would cover the debt and volunteer to represent him to his friend, then present the bill to Griggs, pointing mournfully that his friend, Sylver, must have forged his signature out of desperation. We'd get the money—"

"Which would go to Pullett," commented Major Garlinghouse with sarcasm.

"Wrong again, my friend Dudley," the Captain continued in his pleasant voice. "We'd give Mr. Pullett only part of the sum, and draw up an additional bill for the remainder which we would play out in the same manner as the first. And if anything went awry, we'd still have an excellent subject for blackmail."

"Faugh!" the Major snorted contemptuously. "So we're stuck here like rats, instead!"

"Never thought he'd—"

"Enough, man, enough!" shrieked the Major, close to madness from being closeted with his boon companion.

A double knock at the door was the signal which admitted Susan, bearing a basket of provisions, including a bottle of brandy, which the two men fell upon first. Every evening as soon as her work at Bob's Retreat was done, she hurried through the darkening streets, bringing smuggled liquor and leftover victuals to the un-lovely pair. Tonight, as she unpacked several half-eaten ham and veal pies, and one whole pasty, which Major Garlinghouse spotted and wolfed down before the Captain could protest, she said reprovingly, "A swell were at the place tonight inquirin' after the two o' ye."

Though exchanging swift glances, the two men feigned unconcern. "Probably a friend wanting a game of whist," was Wheedle's airy comment.

"No, he were askin' after the young genelmun the two o' yer allays took there to fleece, he were," replied Susan tartly.

"And what did this 'swell' look like, Susan, my dear?" the Major asked softly.

"Oh, a tall 'un, with red hair, very awkward lookin' as if his clothes didn't fit him right, whiskers like so," and Susan quickly sketched his form before their wary eyes.

"Griggs!" breathed Major Garlinghouse. "Who did he talk to?" he barked out, clutching the girl by her elbow.

"Not me, Lawd, let go!" she wailed. Seeing that her pleas had no effect whatsoever, she tried another tactic, stumbling over her words in her effort to get them out. "He spoke to Old Toby, somethin' about Patches, and then, shortly after he left, Patches came in with a brand-new guinea burnin' a hole in his pocket, though he said he didna even talk to him, the swell."

This information produced the desired effect, for the Major abruptly set her free and faced his friend with an accusing glare.

"Patches will never tell," was Wheedle's cool reply, helping himself to another swig of brandy. "It's his own neck, if he does."

Feeling an imaginary noose tightening about his own fair neck, Major Garlinghouse rose, tore at his collar as if it was strangling him, and burst out of the room, exclaiming in a strained voice, "I'll be back shortly."

Wheedle, accustomed to the Major's odd whims, only shrugged his shoulders and eyed Susan speculatively.

Running through the dark and dirty streets like the fugitive he imagined himself to be, darting into taverns where he was well-known to order a pint of ale oncredit, Major Garlinghouse eventually reached his lodgings at a far-advanced hour of the night in an advanced state of inebriation.

Charlotte, timidly opening the door to his thundering knocks, promptly harangued him with all her worries and fears throughout the past days while her husband devoured the pitiful supplies of food she had recently purchased.

Having delivered all of her charges and having received all of the usual evasive replies, Charlotte attempted one more blow.

"I should hope you've been reporting to duty, for God knows, you cannot expect to receive wages for nothing!" she shrieked, clutching a sleepy Horace to her bosom.

The Major, made bold by his situation, eyed her maliciously while cutting another slice from a cottage loaf.

"Good God, woman," he said calmly. "You don't mean to tell me that you still believe that paltry story. Why, every time I report for duty, I do so at Bob's Retreat. Wheedle and I were both cashiered from our regiments several years past, my love," this with a quick, scornful look, "for swindling a youngster at cards."

Charlotte, trying to voice all of the endless questions this startling disclosure brought to mind, worked her mouth like a fish gulping for air for several minutes. Then having answered internally all of her unspoken queries, she burst into tears and ran, still clutching Horace, for the bedroom, throwing the bolts behind her and sub-siding into hysterics on her bed, thinking dimly that since Major Garlinghouse had consumed all of the edibles in the house, there was nothing more he could take.

She was wrong, of course. For when she ventured out in the morning, the back bedroom was empty and both the Major and Lottie were gone.

While Charlotte wept and raged at the constable who told her that she could not bring charges against her husband for taking his own child, Dabney Griggs, at the end of a tedious journey, was discovering that George Brock had "up and run" after the Derby. A series of painstaking interviews with the trainer, the grooms, and the stable boys revealed nothing more startling than the news that Brock had departed with a tidy sum of money though he had been on his heels at the time of the Derby.

Hurrying back to London, Dabney wished that he had paid more attention to the stranger who had accosted him with the news of a purported swindle, for this eyewitness report, if not enough evidence for the Metropolitan Police, might be used to force a confession from the Major and the Captain, and thus clear Randall's name.

However, Mr. Griggs had to admit with despair that the odds against encountering that gentleman again in a London teeming with foreigners and visitors to the Great Exhibition were enormous. He recalled that this afternoon the ladies of Corrough House were "at home" and resolved to visit his fiancée, whom he had neglected of late in his self-imposed detective mission.

Once ushered into the ornate drawing room and provided with a cup of tea poured by a shrinking Lucinda, he discovered to his amazement that a new topic had completely obliterated the Randall Sylver scandal from the mind of the public. The three young ladies and their guests could not refrain from mentioning it in every second sentence despite the fierce looks of Aunt Lucy. For Nell, Lady Cloudsleigh, had issued invitations to a *bal masque*, which promised to be the social event of the Season, and she had impertinently sent one to Corrough House.

Much of London was profoundly shocked, for all knew that Cloudsleigh House had been the official centre of mourning for the bereaved Cloudsleigh family. Yet even those arbiters of fashion, Lady Muftow and Lady Calverley, could not bear to miss the spectacular goings-on which were part and parcel of the licentiousness and frivolity of a costume ball, and much though they would have liked to decline, they grudgingly sent acceptances. Corrough House was the only household in the city where attendance at the ball had been rigidly forbidden, for Aunt Lucy declared that as Nell was not admitted at their house nor they at hers, there was absolutely no reason to beg and plead and cajole in order to receive permission to attend this orgiastic affair.

Unwilling to believe that this harsh denial was final, the three girls delighted in teasing her by discussing their costumes and the expected guests with all of their visitors.

"I shall be a Spanish lady with a black lace mantilla over my face," declared Sibilla laughingly to Dabney Griggs, "and my hair piled up high, like so, with a comb. Or perhaps a dryad with trailing green filmy garments. Or even the Sibil herself, wrapped in long linen robes with my hair loose about my shoulders. What think you that Sophy should wear?"

Aunt Lucy having cast a stern look upon her niece as a result of this lighthearted speech, Dabney Griggs cleared his throat several times and stared at his betrothed.

"She looks quite nice as she is," he ventured hesitantly, but Sophy, resplendent in a crisp, new, spotted muslin tea gown, seemed perturbed by this compliment.

"You goose!" Sibilla cried, "she must look different than she normally does. Perhaps—" she studied her sister with mock seriousness "—a nun?" At this, Sophy threw the pillow she was embroidering at her sister, who slid off the piano bench swiftly, and, using it as a barricade, returned the missile with accuracy.

Aunt Lucy was visibly infuriated, but restrained herself remarkably, limiting herself to the harsh observance, "If Miss Sibilla wished to appear as she normally does not, I would suggest she adopt the role of a lady."

Lady Sibilla, unmoved by her aunt's sarcasm, re-emerged from behind her fort and asked Dabney brightly, "And what should Lucinda be? We are at a loss."

Dabney looked up in time to see Lucinda's pleading glance before she lowered her eyes to the tea service, which she had the appearance of guarding with her life. The gentleman's already florid complexion became a bright brick-red while Miss Lucinda paled to the colour of her white linen gown. Sibilla, noting his discomfort, attempted to smooth over the awkward pause, "We thought maybe a violet, all purple with green tendrils, or a bright canary with a yellow dress and feathers."

But her merry tones fell flat, for Lucinda refused to respond, Sophy grew sulky, and Dabney Griggs, made uncomfortable beyond belief by the combination of girlish chatter and Mrs. Pleet's stern disapprobation, rose early and excused himself neatly.

Just as he was about to step into his waiting carriage, he spotted the young stranger who had been in his thoughts so recently, lounging idly against a street lamp across the street. Heedless of his own personal safety, Mr. Griggs plunged across the crowded thoroughfare and confronted the mysterious individual so abruptly that Mr. Whitefoot was caught while forming the resolution to run for it.

To his immense relief, Mr. Whitefoot learned that he was not going to be whipped out of town by an irate rival, but that the considerate and enthusiastic gentleman before him, merely wished to corroborate the story of the events which had transpired at the Derby. While inwardly cursing the fortune which had betrothed this singularly admirable being to his true love, Mr. Whitefoot was moved by the tale of Randall Sylver's woes and eagerly volunteered his aid.

The two men withdrew to Mr. Whitefoot's hotel, where Leslie quickly wrote out an account of his observations at the Derby, and when Mr. Griggs set forth with this document under his arm he was in a high state of elation, convinced that he could now confront the rogues, if only he could run them to earth. He embarked on another round of visits to gaming hells and taverns, with little luck, until, just as he was about to leave Bob's Retreat, he caught a glimpse of the frightened face of the bar maid who was scrambling back into the kitchen. She looked familiar for an instant, and then he realized he had seen her, sitting with Major Garlinghouse and Captain Wheedle, on top of a hackney coach on the day of the race.

Following her into the kitchen, he began to question her gently about the two men, and, to his surprise, Susan, overcome with guilt at her complicity in the scheme which had driven a young gentleman to attempt suicide, quickly described their hideaway.

Thus it was that Dabney Griggs confronted the unsavoury pair in their den, and forced them to write out and sign a long confession. Triumphant, proud of his detective skill, and certain that the two would not consider a rash action—for he saw Lottie, the Major's child, sitting patiently on a chair throughout the proceedings—Mr. Griggs went off to fetch the local magistrate. But he was wrong, for when he had finally convinced the magistrate to send two policemen to apprehend the criminals, they returned to the lodginghouse to find a completely barren room. Neither Major Garlinghouse nor Captain Wheedle nor young Lottie Garlinghouse was ever seen in England again.

THIRTY-TWO

A Mask Hides
a Friendly Face

THE THREE YOUNG PRISONERS of Corrough House had never taken seriously the ban against Lady Cloudsleigh's *bal masque*. In fact, Sibilla had penned an eager acceptance on the very day they received the invitation, though Lucinda also dutifully printed out a polite refusal under her mother's watchful eye. They spent the better part of a week imagining and constructing their various disguises, and the only obstacle to their participation, Mrs. Pleet, thoughtfully solved the problem by taking to her bed early on the fatal evening with an attack of indigestion (which could have been more aptly described as "inebriation").

Once the way was open to them, both Sophy and Lucinda developed what Sibilla mockingly referred to as "chicken feet." In the end she had to assume command, ordering the carriage round, and seeing her two frightened co-conspirators into their costumes. Despite all of their wild fancies, economy and Aunt Lucy's prohibittions had put a damper on their exorbitant and extravagant plans. Sibilla wore a short, flounced skirt, a simple muslin bodice, an extravagant shawl, gold hoop earrings, and her dark hair loose about her shoulders in her depiction of a gypsy. Sophy was a pretty, but unconvincing, shepherdess in a plain blue dress, trimmed with artificial flowers, wearing her hair in plaits and carrying a crook, which was in actuality an old cane lengthened with bunched-up newspapers.

While Lucinda, in the puffed white gown she had worn at the quadrille ball, portrayed a bride, with roses and orange blossoms in her hair and Sophy's tulle veil obscuring her features. Sibilla and Sophy in order to avoid recognition, had surreptitiously purchased two masks, one black and one blue, which they donned in the confines of the carriage as they waited in a long line of vehicles to be discharged at the steps of Cloudsleigh House.

Again Sibilla had to fire her colleagues with courage, for the sight of the imposing mansion and the throngs of sophisticated and elegant guests parading through the open door, reduced both to fits of nerves during which they declared they would rather die than face such an ordeal.

But Sibilla, by promising that all three would stay together to offer each other aid in the event of need, shoved them out of the carriage and into the shifting throngs of brightly coloured masqueraders.

There is a peculiar air of exhilaration and carte blanche about a costume ball. Unable to distinguish old friends from old enemies, men from women, and staid dowagers from courtesans, one could assume any role or behaviour one wished. Surprisingly, Sophy withdrew into herself, becoming stiff and passive, unnerved by the ambiguity around her, while Lucinda, as a bride, blossomed into blushing radiance, assuming a dignity and poise that allowed her to pass unmolested through the profligate crowds. Sibilla adapted to her own notion of a gypsy, swinging her skirts freely with a sensuous, prowling stride, and indulging in the sensation of her hair loose down her back by tossing her head with hauteur from side to side. For the gentlemen who reached out to pinch her or tried to stay her with a hand on her arm, she had a wild, harsh laugh, and then, with a serpentlike wriggle, she would ease away with a taunting smile. In her wake, she left admiring suitors and a string of whispered guesses as to her identity.

"But for the hair-colour she might be Mrs. Meadows," suggested a bewildered Arab to his companion dressed in a country parson's garb.

Mrs. Meadows, standing nearby in a clinging white Grecian robe crossed over her breasts with a gold band, laughed aloud at overhearing this guess, and the familiar sound of her rich, lilting laughter further perplexed the Arab, one Mr. Crampton-Manners.

Several of the guests were immediately recognizable. Lady Muftow, in the dress of a seventeenth-century gentlewoman, with brocaded, panniered skirts, powdered hair, and a sequined mask, was still identified as she sat on a chair in the salon by her eager malevolent smile and the greed with which her bright eyes followed the revellers. But the stiff old woman by her side, dressed in Elizabethan court garb, with an enormous ruff encircling the neck, an elaborately dressed white wig, and sporting several prominent beauty patches, confused many who did not realize that this was Baron Champford, collaborating with his arch rival in the field of gossip for the first time as they vied with each other and placed extravagant bets on the identities of the other guests.

Baron Champford was especially exuberant for Dabney Griggs had approached him several days earlier with the signed confession, and after multiple interviews with his strait-laced parents, Sylvester had convinced them to welcome Randall back into the bosom of the family. The same joyous news was imparted to Randall, recently delivered from the crisis and on the road to recovery, and he was moved with all pomp and ceremony back to Trendle House where his mother acted the part of nurse, unable to leave her poor darling for an instant.

"Ah, definitely Sylvie Duchamps," cried Baron Champford in the mincing high voice he had adopted with his costume, pointing at the gypsy and naming a well-known *fille-de-joie.*

"No, no," corrected Lady Muftow, "that is a much younger woman, perhaps Lavinia Holly?"

"Ah, there I have you," chortled Baron Champford joyously, "for Lavinia Holly is the ballet dancer," and he indicated the irrepressible young lady in a very short ruffled dress revealing a generous expanse of legs in coloured tights.

"Shocking!" breathed Lady Muftow, holding up a lorgnon to inspect the shameless girl more closely. "How did her mother permit such a display?"

"I hear she's rather strong-willed," chuckled Baron Champford. "Her mother has little control, and it probably is of little consequence for she's past marriageable age. How old is she—thirty?"

"Thirty-three," snapped Lady Muftow, turning in another direction. "Where is our hostess? Is that Lady Cloudsleigh, in medieval clothes, looking like an awkward pre-Raphaelite woman?"

Baron Champford inspected the lady in question most carefully through his monocle. "I believe," he said at last thoughtfully, "that is the Contessa Juliana Guerini. She must be up to something new, for she's always dressed as an Italian Contessa heretofore." He squinted at her trailing velvet gown, clasped by a golden girdle. "And I think that is the pre-Raphaelite painter, Mr. Rossetti, with her." He gestured at the plump, dark, intense man in a scarlet domino beside the regal lady. "I hear that Lawrence Lanston is also invited. I wonder what will happen if they should meet?"

"What's the story there?" inquired Lady Muftow bright-eyed.

"Why they were lovers for ever such a long time," revealed her accomplice. "He had cut all ties with his family and they were living together. She even called herself Mrs. Lanston. Then one day he abruptly left and married a rich Cit's daughter. She disappeared for a time, re-emerged as Ashanti Davies, supposedly the daughter of an Indian princess and an English colonel, always dressing in filmy gauze and entertaining those turbanned monkeys and listening to that discordant music and talking of strange gods. Then she married the Duke of Lorimont—"

"That senile old fool," interposed Lady Muftow.

"They say she was good to him in his last illness," Baron Champford continued, "and she never used the title after his death. She became the Contessa Guerini instead. I wonder what her game is now?"

"Look, there's Lanning Tombs, Lady Cloudsleigh's pet!" exclaimed Lady Muftow, pointing at a pale, slender young man all in black, approaching the spurious Contessa and her Italian painter.

"But I thought that was him," complained Baron Champford, pointing out an identical figure at the other end of the room. "I will wager two ponies that is him."

"Ponies!" expostulated Lady Muftow. "Don't speak slang, young man. Speak the Queen's English!"

"Fifty pounds," mumbled a flustered Sylvester, which offer was eagerly accepted by his crony. Unfortunately for Lady Muftow, the slender, young gentleman before them chose that moment to remove the black velvet beret covering his head and a flood of thick, dark hair tumbled down his back.

"Why, it's Lady Cloudsleigh!" shrieked Lady Muftow in disappointment.

"So it is," was Baron Champford's jovial comment. "You now owe me two hundred."

"How dare she, the hussy!" Lady Muftow was provoked. "Where is her husband?"

"I believe he's the academician, over there," commented Baron Champford, pointing out a stooped older man in university robes who was being hurried along from guest to guest by the real Mr. Lanning Tombs.

"Outrageous!" muttered Lady Muftow, lapsing into sullenness. "Why she is smoking a cigar!"

Lady Cloudsleigh pushing her heavy tresses back under the velvet cap, after stunning her friends who had been totally deluded into thinking that she was Mr. Lanning Tombs, was exultant. This was her triumph, this gala masquerade, which she suspected would shortly degenerate into a romp. Moving away from the Contessa, who was now calling herself Lady Guenevere, Nell looked around admiringly at the salon, packed with the strangest assortment of people ever to congregate under any roof, at the thousands of wax tapers burning in the crystal sconces, listening to the sweet, rapturous strains of a waltz performed by the band stationed under a silk pavilion in the garden, and smelling the cloying, pervasive scent of the incense she had commanded to be burnt.

She took another draw from her cigar, savouring the heavy, yet fragrant taste of the Havanna tobacco, before grinding it out on the marble floor beneath one tiny booted foot, and watched her lover dragging her husband, Arthur, along relentlessly. For Lanning Tombs had finally become her lover, a rash move occasioned by her deprivation of his company during the weeks of mourning and the sweetness of their hurried, clandestine meetings, and Nell was now in the throes of passion, experiencing all of the tumultuous upheavals of a young woman of a fiery and intense nature who had heretofore known only the hesitant and apologetic gropings of an anxious-to-please husband. Lanning Tombs' ruthlessness, his eagerness, his insatiable appetite for her, awoke the same needs in her, and now, in a symbolic act, she repudiated all of the trappings of her position as Lady Cloudsleigh, spurning the elaborate gowns, the glittering rings, the heavy earrings, and even her femininity, to identify with her lover, who though a trifle shocked and humbled by her infatuation, yet turned every now and then to intercept her gaze with an immoderate regard which promised that they would not be separated for long.

Lady Cloudsleigh moved through the crowd unrecognized, studying her guests with a scientific curiosity, wondering if any of them were motivated by the fire burning within her. And the first couple on which she chanced to set her eyes was the Marquis of Dower and Peggy, both clinging to each other as if they were alone in a bower despite the buffeting of the partygoers who scurried here and there. Both were dressed as Irish peasants; the elegant Ned seemed at ease in his corduroy waistcoat, cloth jacket, cable-cord trousers, and a wool cap while Peggy was as saucy as an Irish lass in a cotton gown, voluminous shawl, and bonnet.

"Oh Nell!" squealed Peggy, identifying her hostess immediately, and stepping into her path. "Only think, you will be the first person who knows," and here she blushed furiously and dived into the arms of her Ned. The Marquis of Dower kissed her forehead, and imparted her news candidly, "We were married today, in the Roman Catholic chapel."

Taken aback, Nell managed to stammer out the appropriate congratulatory responses.

"We're leaving for Ireland tomorrow," the Marquis added, "but we came tonight to take leave of our friends."

"And you are certainly the first of them," Peggy rejoined, "for it was at your house that we met," and she dove back into her husband's embrace, as if still not quite certain of her great fortune.

"Of course, you know," said the Marquis of Dower sternly, "that Peggy is the sole heiress of the late Earl of Corrough, and we intend to apply to the Dowager Countess for some legal recognition of that fact, so that when I return to London with my wife—" Peggy giggled "—for the Season next year, I will introduce her to Society as such."

Nell was stunned again. "Why—quite—I should have known, yes, indeed, an excellent prospect," she ventured.

"You mean you never guessed?" was Peggy's eager question, slightly muffled by her husband's waistcoat. She poked up her ruffled head again, "Kitty knew. She stood as witness for us, with Ashford."

"Those scamps," cursed Lady Cloudsleigh. "And they never breathed a word to me. Where are they? I have a good mind to tell them what I think."

"Why, there's Kitty, the Grecian lady," offered Peggy, but as she pointed to her and as Nell followed the direction of her finger with her eyes, a singular event occurred. The gypsy, leading a procession of a bride and a shepherdess back from the refreshment table in the dining room with full glasses of champagne, had been pushed against the lady in question by the importunate grasp of the Arab, and the contents of her glass had drenched the white Grecian robes. Whirling about to apologize, Sibilla came face to face with her sister, Kitty, for the first time in eight years.

THIRTY-THREE

The Prodigal Lamb Rejoins the Fold

THE TWO WOMEN STOOD transfixed for a matter of seconds. Sibilla stared, her mouth open, as if drinking in every detail of her lost sister's appearance. Kitty, meanwhile, gazed at her with melting tenderness, and yet with timidity and hesitancy, as if she feared an immediate renunciation.

Then Sibilla with a hoarse cry of "Kitty!" flung herself at the Grecian lady who gathered her into her arms, as tears began to fall on the dark head nestled beneath hers.

Nell, aghast at the sight of this sentimentality in her drawing room, came scurrying through the crowd and swiftly ushered the group into her husband's library, which had remained closed, while Lady Muftow rapped her companion over the hand with her fan.

"Why did the gypsy and Mrs. Meadows jump at each other like that?" she demanded.

Baron Champford, unwilling to divulge the one secret he had managed to keep for several years, muttered that he did not know, "Perhaps they were childhood friends," and tried to divert his companion's attention.

Nell, nonplussed by the degree of sentiment expressed by the parties, withdrew from the library immediately and the reunion was effected.

"Can this be little Sophy, the baby?" asked Kitty in tones of wonder, indicating the reserved shepherdess, and Sophy, tearing off her mask, dissolved into the same fit of tears that afflicted Sibilla and Kitty. Lucinda, waiting only for an introduction and explanation of her presence, slipped discreetly out the open door, and the three sisters were left alone.

"Whatever have you been doing with yourselves, *mes petites*?" inquired Kitty, who had recovered her composure first and indeed glowed with an unusual self-assurance.

"The Season, you know," interjected Sibilla, waving her hand as if to dismiss it. "Aunt Lucy is trying to marry us off."

"Yes, the Season," agreed Sophy breathlessly. "But you, Kitty, where have you been?"

"Ah, it little matters where I have been, or who I have been," commented Kitty mysteriously. "But you must know, my dearest sisters, that I shall be leaving shortly for the Continent, and when I return I shall be married to Ashford Cloudsleigh. Peggy and Ned, who have just been wed, shall stand for us as we stood witness for them today."

This announcement had two different effects on the two sisters.

"You say that Peggy has married the Marquis of Dower?" exclaimed Sibilla.

While Sophy was astonished, "Ashford Cloudsleigh! But his wife just—"

"Yes, and yes again!" cried Kitty, with an irrepressible smile, tilting her head to one side as had been her wont of old.

"Peggy and Ned—the Marquis of Dower—were married today and are leaving for Ireland tomorrow. I know Peggy wants to see you before she leaves, Sibilla. She and her husband are dressed as Irish peasants, you cannot miss them. And yes, though it's much too soon, Ashford wants to marry me by this time next year, and after so many years of waiting, I have agreed. Oh my darlings," she said, drawing them to her, "you cannot imagine how happy I am!"

Sibilla looked distressed, and Kitty continued with more decorum, "You're worried about a scandal, are you not, Sibil? We are not so foolhardy as I have made it seem, though I don't doubt that Ashford may do something rash if we remain in town long. But he is going to stay at Merryfield Manor for several months, while I leave for

France in a fortnight with a good lady I have hired to be my companion and nursemaid for the children. Ashford will come to Paris in winter, and the story will be that he found me there, penniless and starving after the death of my no-good rogue of a husband, Mr. Meadows, with whom I eloped when I was only seventeen. He will escort me back to England, and we will be married at the village chapel in Merryfield. Thus, my children will have a father, I will be reconciled with my family, and there shall be a reasonable explanation for our hasty union! An ingenious solution!"

"But—" Sophy objected with a frown, "I do not quite understand. What children and where is Mr. Meadows now?"

Sibilla, who guessed the truth, turned pale, but Kitty unabashed answered tenderly, "There is no Mr. Meadows, or, at best, he is a very useful and old friend, the imaginary father of my two children."

Sophy looked more puzzled and upset. Kitty flushed and turned apologetically to Sibilla. "It is not a pretty story," she began grimly, then abruptly changed her direction, her streak of stubbornness and defiance asserting itself. "No, it is a beautiful story. You see, I knew the moment I first saw Ashford Cloudsleigh that I loved him, and he me. But that was during my first Season, he was married, and there was little we could do. I turned down every offer I received, thinking of him, and yet knowing that my hopes were pointless. But then I went visiting with Nell, and he showed up repeatedly, and soon the inevitable happened." She paused and studied the shelves of books across from her as if viewing the past. She shivered, then smiled, and went on, "He installed me in the Dower House of Merryfield Manor while I was waiting for my first child to be born—" Sophy gasped and retreated from her sister a little "—and his parents, the Marquis and Marchioness treated me as if I were their daughter. I cannot praise their kindness and compassion too highly. Of course, this was the time when you heard that I had vanished. Only a few people knew where I was, not even Nell was in on the secret. Valerian raced back and forth between London and the Dower House, taking messages for us." This time it was Sibilla's turn to wince, thinking of the construction she had put upon Valerian's familiarity with her sister, and Kitty, noting this reaction, studied her curiously for a minute.

"In all," she concluded, "I stayed in Cambridgeshire for nearly six years. I came to London last year, supposedly the widow of a Mr. Meadows, a common enough family name in the villages around Merryfield Manor. I saw little of Ashford while I was in town, out of respect to his wife, but I missed the Opera and the theatres and all of my friends. And now that Caroline is no longer with us, and may God be my witness that I never even hoped for such a future, the realization of our own happiness becomes our responsibility, and Ashford and I have agreed to search for it together, always mindful of the dangers in our path. And now," she said in a bantering but desperate tone, "am I forgiven?"

"Why, there is nothing to forgive," was Sibilla's soft, earnest reply, "but with all my heart, I am glad that you have found your happiness," and a fervent embrace sealed this declaration, while Sophy was quick to repeat Sibilla's words and also hugged her prodigal sister.

All three were again on the edge of tears, but Kitty forestalled another lachrymose indulgence by saying lightly, "You must understand how much better I feel, knowing that my little sisters have freely listened and accepted me. Yet, you both have other commitments. Sibil, you ought to find Peggy and Ned, and Sophy, I hear there is a young man who must be going wild trying to discover you."

"A young man?" parroted Sophy dully.

"Your fiancé," prompted Kitty.

"Oh, Mr. Dabney Griggs," Sophy said, with a touch of relief. "Is he here?"

"I assume so," Kitty confided, "for I heard a gentleman dressed as a Barbary pirate inquire after Sophy Merrell, and I trust that was Mr. Griggs, though he was some distance off and cleverly disguised."

Hesitantly, Sophy readjusted her mask and peered out the door of the library. Kitty, who had risen and followed her, cried, "Why, there he is! Just leaving the exotic drawing room," and indicated a dashing character who did indeed seem to be searching for something or someone, for he looked about restlessly. Because Sophy remained frozen on the threshold, Kitty laughingly gave her a little push, precipitating her into the arms of the quester.

Shutting the door discreetly, Kitty asked perceptively, "Why is Sophy so shy about Mr. Griggs? Does she want to marry him?"

Sibilla considered this thoughtfully. "I do not know. She seemed quite high-strung at first, but lately, she has settled down, and is always talking about her trousseau and how she will decorate her house. I suppose it was the shock of the sudden engagement."

Kitty ran one hand carelessly through her curls. "How did that come to pass?"

"They were alone together for a long time one day, and when they returned to the house, Mr. Griggs asked our aunt for Sophy's hand, and she was brought to the study and accepted his offer, so they must have spoken of it to each other previously." This was the only version of the story Sibilla knew for Sophy had never confided in any person, nor had Mr. Griggs, a man of honour, ever explained the circumstances of his betrothal to any of his friends.

Kitty was not entirely convinced by this tale. She wrinkled her nose for a minute, then dismissed the problem with a smile and urged Sibilla to find Peggy once more.

"B–but, Kitty," stammered Sibilla eagerly, as she donned her mask again, "may I come to visit you and see your children before you leave London?"

"Oh, *ma chere*," Kitty exclaimed, swooping down on her with an exuberant kiss. "What an excellent thought! You cannot imagine how lonely and dejected I felt the day I saw you walking down Berkeley Street and stopping to look up at me. Yes, by all means, come. Valerian can bring you. I shall be there for another fortnight."

Arm in arm, they left the sanctuary of the library and re-entered the riotous atmosphere of the *bal masque*. During the hour that had passed, the guests had become increasingly abandoned, the talk was louder, the shrieks of laughter more piercing, the postures of the women more provocative, and the advances of the men more bold.

No sooner had Kitty emerged from the library, than a tall gentleman, dressed in monk's robes, drew her into a fond embrace. Seeing Sibilla behind her, he whispered into the auburn curls of his companion and then with one arm about her waist, he came forward and clasped Sibilla's hand firmly.

"You cannot know how distressed I was when you confided in me at the reception at Corrough House," he said in the warm, rich voice, which identified him immediately as Ashford Cloudsleigh. "I vowed then to reunite you to your sister, for I knew you would accept her no matter what the circumstances, but before I could draw up a plan, the—the tragic event which took Caroline's—my wife's— life occurred," he stumbled through this part of his speech, "and now you have found each other without me. I can only express my great joy at being able to name such an intelligent and charming woman as my 'little sister.' When Kitty and I return to London and set up house here, we shall be delighted to welcome you as a member of our household."

He sealed this pact with an affectionate kiss upon her cheek and Sibilla, overwhelmed by the grandeur of the situation being offered to her (she need no longer return in exile to Partridge Park, nor marry some inferior being, such as Mr. Treswick, in order to remain in London), was unable to express her thanks.

Kitty rescued her sister by nudging her and pointing out the two Irish peasants, wandering hand in hand.

"Sibil must talk to Peggy and Ned," she told her lover quickly, and with a flurried curtsey, Sibilla was gone.

Peggy recognized her as she approached them and, after a few quick politenesses, the Marquis of Dower was dispatched to bring them refreshments, while the former maid, now the Marchioness of Dower, settled down on a sofa for a comfortable chat with her former mistress.

"Peggy," began Sibilla painfully. "I have wanted to apologize for my inconsiderate remarks on that awful night, but then you disappeared. And now it seems so silly to even recall that conversation, for all my fears have been proved groundless, and, what's worse, unforgivably cruel."

"Nay," Peggy responded quickly. "You were absolutely, completely, undeniably right, my dear Miss Sibil. I had one card, an ace, which you knew nothing of, and which, if I played it correctly, would bring me the thing most dear to me in the whole world." She smiled, a tender, rueful smile. "Before I could hit upon a scheme, Ned put it on the table for me."

"What was that?" inquired Sibilla avidly.

"I'm the only child, though unacknowledged, of the late Earl of Corrough," Peggy announced with a little shrug of her shoulders.

Sibilla's eyes grew wide as saucers and Peggy said pleasantly, "So you never knew. Miss Kitty guessed it at once. I must confess, it seems entirely superfluous at the present. But the knowledge of that secret sustained me when I was being ordered about here and there, carrying pails of hot water up and down steep stairs, dusting, scrubbing, airing the beds, oh, you know, I was used to all that, but then Mrs. Pleet's infernal smugness and cruelty on top of that. I could not picture myself as a maid forever, nor could I marry someone like farmer Hamm or Roscoe. I would have felt like an imposter. And then, my world was turned around when I met Ned. He understood my longing for Ireland, we talked about it often, and he loved my traits which others disliked, my stubbornness—"

"Her impertinence, her independent, arrogant nature," added that gentleman, handing both of the ladies a glass of champagne. Peggy smiled up at him affectionately.

"The conclusion is simple," she said to Sibilla, "I became his mistress, and we grew so close that he asked me to marry him before I ever played my card. Later he told me that he had often heard of the beautiful widow whom the late Earl of Corrough loved (the Dowers have a home in the same county), and he guessed that I was their child. Now he wants to approach the Dowager Countess and ask her to recognize me. Foolish man!"

"Nay," Ned replied earnestly. "This dream that you have been clinging to for nourishment all of your life must be validated. The Dowager Countess—I know her very well—longed for children most desperately, and I think it will give her great joy in her old age to find a daughter. Not that she won't snap and bite off my head at first; she's a very autocratic and determined woman, but she loved her husband dearly, knew of his foibles, I might add, and would probably cherish his daughter for his sake. He was a lucky man, being loved so well by two women."

"Poor Ned will have to content himself with one," remarked Peggy tartly, following this audacious sally with a lazy yawn.

"I fear we must leave," the Marquis of Dower said, with an elegant bow for Sibilla. "We depart early in the morning. The Marchioness of Dower—" Peggy giggled "—and I shall be in London next spring, and if you would be so good as to honour us with your presence, we would be glad to have you stay with us."

"I am equally honoured by your kind invitation," Sibilla replied, a little less astonished, since the equally dazzling offer from Ashford Cloudsleigh. "But we shall correspond in the meanwhile, Peggy. You can address your letters to me at Partridge Park. I will be there most of the winter, I trust."

"You mean that young scamp has not yet offered for you!" exclaimed the Marquis of Dower. "I shall send him a missive berating him for his stupidity while Peggy writes to you."

And without explaining to whom he referred, he led his bride away, after a series of sentimental embraces, kisses, and best wishes.

Sibilla sat down abruptly, feeling worse than abandoned. Was everyone in London succumbing to matrimonial fever? Would she linger on as the perennial old maid, staying with friends and relatives, while everyone around her paired off into cooing couples? She tried to calm herself, recalling that lovers in the first throes of romance always seemed to possess a supernatural happiness, but that this glow quickly faded. Witness Charlotte, witness Nell, witness her mother. However, this reflection only encouraged her melancholy for she was still an alien among her friends and would be for some time.

Resolved to ignore this gloomy train of thought, Sibilla rose, a trifle unsteadily for she had gulped the last glass of champagne, and went to look for Sophy and Lucinda. She was continually accosted, buffeted, and annoyed by the male revellers as she fought her way through the few inches of clear space existing in the crowded rooms. A few gentlemen plied her with champagne, which she accepted, and one, dressed as a Pierrot, whom she suspected to be Valerian Cloudsleigh, conducted a delightful flirt with her, but always she pressed onward, seeking her lost companions.

Having done the tour of the house twice, she ventured out onto the balcony and was glad of the chance to cool her fevered thoughts in the fresh night air. The garden was a kaleidoscope composed of coloured lanterns and the bright garments of the partygoers. Couples danced on the wooden dais constructed before the orchestra, which played under a silk tent, while others wandered in and out of the groves.

Try as she might, Sibilla could not discern either a shepherdess or a bride, and perhaps it was as well she could not, not if she had been able to pierce the shadows, she would have found both in the arms of a gentleman to whom they were protesting eternal devotion, and her despondency would have increased, though she might have been amused if she had learned the identity of their suitors.

THIRTY-FOUR

A Confused Mating

SOPHY, THRUST INTO THE arms of the pirate, had said apologetically, "Excuse me, Mr. Griggs, I hear you have been inquiring after me."

Imagine her surprise when he replied in low, intense tones, "I am not your Mr. Griggs, yet I have been inquiring after you, my darling!" for she recognized the voice of Leslie Whitefoot and almost swooned in consequence.

Her first sentence, however, after being ushered into the fresh air by her escort, was one of petulance.

"How came you to be here?" she asked sulkily.

"Your Mr. Griggs was good enough to invite me," he said with an engaging grin, and when Sophy was taken aback by this remark, he added soothingly, "It was as a result of some business we transacted together, having nothing to do with you, my love, and in truth, I hesitated to accept, knowing that it would be unsporting of me to take such an advantage of him. But the thought of your presence here so intoxicated me that I came, despite the urgings of my better nature, to see you, my angel."

"You were very presumptuous and I should not speak to you," was Sophy's agreeable comment, but she did not suit her action to her words, for she took his arm and allowed herself to be drawn towards the gardens.

"A dance, oh mistress of my heart?" asked the irrepressible Mr. Whitefoot as they approached the orchestra, and grudgingly Sophy granted him this right. By the end of several waltzes and a lively polka, she was more disposed to listen to his suit and took up a seat on a marble bench in a secluded spot with him.

"I cannot live without you, my heart," said the impetuous and romantic Mr. Whitefoot, going down on one knee before her.

"Get up, Leslie! Don't be silly!" Sophy replied disturbed. "I am engaged to someone else."

"Oh heartless goddess, how can you spurn me so coldly?" cried her lover, kissing her hand passionately.

"Leslie!" exclaimed Sophy, looking about hastily to make certain no one was witnessing this embarrassing scene. "You know that it is hopeless. My parents will not accept you. Besides, I am engaged."

"I asked you first, and you gave me every reason to believe you would be proud to be Mrs. Whitefoot, darling," he declared passionately.

"Yes, but when my parents refused to give their blessing, I withdrew my acceptance," Sophy pointed out crossly. "Really, Leslie, you are making a spectacle of yourself."

"It matters not," said her swain, burying his face in his hands. "I shall never be happy without you. Tell me, just to let me know that life might be worth living, tell me that you cared for me then, that it was not all a pretence, a game you played!"

"Leslie!" Sophy was horrified. "You cannot suppose I would have toyed with you so. Oh never, my darling," the endearment slipped out unbidden, and she bit her lip but did not recall it. "I truly cared for you."

"Cared!" said Leslie bitterly. "And when did you cease caring, since you refer to it in the past tense?"

Sophy withdrew from him, turned her head, and said in strained tones, "When my parents forbade it."

"Ah, then you do not mean it, my little one," was Mr. Whitefoot's cheerful conclusion, "for who can stop loving because of a parental dictate?"

"I can," said Sophy in a small voice.

"Not you, my adorable, compassionate love," Mr. Whitefoot declared, trying to draw her into his arms.

"Leslie, please, do not, I beg of you," cried Sophy, trying to stave off his advances, but when he managed to touch her lips with his, her struggles stopped, and she more than repaid his efforts with the warmth of her response.

"There!" said her lover triumphantly, tasting the salt of her tears as well as the sweetness of her kiss. "You have been lying to me. You still care!"

"Oh Leslie, I do!" wailed Sophy, throwing herself at him. Mr. Griggs had kissed her once, a swift, dry peck on the lips, and the comparison between the two men was driving her towards confession. "I have always loved you."

"Then why are you engaged to Mr. Griggs?" questioned Mr. Whitefoot, remorseless in the face of this new evidence.

Sophy was speechless for several minutes while her lover attempted to kiss away her tears, but then the story came spilling out, how they had been compromised, how Aunt Lucy had predicted her ruin, how Mr. Griggs was so nice and so eligible but so cold and so formal.

Mr. Whitefoot grew more serious as he listened to this pathetic recitation, for he sensed from Sophy's description of her fiancé's behaviour that he was no more in love with Sophy than she with him, yet it was a tremendous task to suggest an alternative.

"You must break off the engagement," he said at last.

"Oh no! I cannot!" pleaded Sophy. "The scandal it would create. He has been so considerate in every way, it would hurt him so—"

And while she and her suitor argued about the other possibilities, they might have been completely relieved of all the difficulties which presented themselves to their attention if they could have looked beyond the shrubbery which enshrouded them and seen the couple that occupied the arbour next to their's, for it was no other than Dabney Griggs and Lucinda Pleet, undergoing the same torments of joy and sorrow.

No sooner had Lucinda left the library to the three Merrell sisters, than she had encountered Mr. Griggs, who was unable to keep his eyes from her glowing countenance beneath the tulle veil.

Inquiring after her health and treating her as delicately as a piece of Dresden china, Mr. Griggs had encouraged her to partake of the refreshments and guided her out onto the terrace to gaze upon the stars in the heavens while he whiled away the time admiring the same celestial fires in her eyes.

Lucinda, rendered shy by his attentions, and yet undeniably exultant, inquired why they had seen so little of him lately, and when he humbly sketched out his part in clearing Randall Sylver's name, she thought him more of a hero than before. Swept away by the fragrance of the night, the high spirits imparted by the champagne, and the sweet music of the orchestra, they danced together and left the floor only a few minutes before Sophy and Leslie appeared there to promenade through the gardens. Lucinda would never have permitted herself to be drawn into the shadows with Mr. Griggs, except that they ventured off the path to study a statue among the greenery, and then agreed amiably that they should enjoy a brief intermission before resuming their stroll.

"Where is your estimable mother, Mrs. Pleet?" inquired Mr. Griggs, after an awkward interlude as they sat on opposite ends of the marble bench.

"Oh, she's not here!" offered Lucinda quickly. "I came with Sibilla and Sophy."

"Alone, unchaperoned?" questioned Mr. Griggs with a frown. When Lucinda nodded, he said, "Why, it will never do. You three alone at such a gathering. You must return home at once."

"We are costumed; no one will recognize us," suggested Lucinda helpfully. "I myself have seen no one of my acquaintance here, except for you, and that does not count."

Ignoring this last declaimer, Mr. Griggs begged to differ and explained without mincing words exactly the nature of this social occasion and the dangers inherent in it.

Lucinda listened with growing unease, and it would be difficult for anyone who did not know this remarkable young woman well to discover whether she was perturbed by Mr. Griggs's disclosures, or the fact that if she acted according to his wishes, she would be divested of his pleasant company.

Regardless of her emotions, she agreed to leave and, when she stumbled upon arising and fell into his arms, it would have been equally hard to tell whether she had actually twisted her ankle or whether she had chosen this method of remaining with him.

Mr. Griggs, while immeasurably affected by the sudden proximity of this lovely girl, dressed as he would have wished to see her before the altar, swearing to be Mrs. Dabney Griggs through eternity, maintained his usual reserve and laid her down upon the marble bench, asking what was wrong with the decorum of an older brother.

"I fear it is my ankle. I believe I stepped upon a rock and turned it," breathed Lucinda softly, closing her eyes as if in pain. Still, though yearning for her as she lay stretched out under the stars with the vibrant strains of a waltz underscoring his tumultuous emotions, Mr. Griggs retained his formality.

"What shall I do, Miss Pleet? Ask somebody from the house to fetch a doctor?"

"I believe," Lucinda replied softly, "that you could tell as well as a doctor whether it is broken or merely bruised. If there is nothing seriously wrong, I am sure you can help me to a carriage, and then inform Sibilla or Sophia that I have left."

Mr. Griggs nodded brusquely at this statement and, after asking which ankle had been affected, applied himself gingerly to the task described. Neither of them could have guessed the effect this endeavour would have upon him.

Unlike the other men of his crowd, he had remained aloof from women, not indulging in the usual pursuit of opera dancers and actresses, believing that the woman he married should receive the whole measure of his attention and devotion. While Lucinda, overwhelmed and overprotected by her formidable mother, only blossoming now into the beauty that had always been promised and always been denied, had never been touched by a man before.

The consequences of the present circumstances would have been obvious to any one but these two innocents. They were both shocked and yet helpless. For as soon as Mr. Griggs gingerly drew aside Lucinda's filmy white tulle dress and probed at her ankle, she felt a tremor of pleasure that coursed through her whole body, while he was overcome with the scent of her perfume, the intimate act of drawing aside her gown, and aware that the soft, cool flesh which lay so vibrant beneath his fingers belonged to the woman he admired more than any other.

With a hoarse cry, he took her into his arms for a prolonged kiss, which only bewildered the pair of them more.

Lucinda was the first to recover. Though aware of the extreme impropriety of her position, pinioned under the greedy arms of Mr. Griggs, and the dangerous intoxication that permeated the lovely night, she nevertheless said softly,

"Oh, I do love you, Mr. Griggs."

This occasioned another harsh cry and another equally draining kiss. Then appalled by his behaviour, Mr. Griggs covered his eyes with one hand and begged her forgiveness for his deplorable lack of courtesy.

Lucinda, aghast and infuriated by his refusal to admit what his kisses revealed, swung herself upright.

"Sir," she cried, "you are a coward and a fool!" And so saying, she swung back her hand and slapped him hard across the cheek.

For a moment, the two stared at each other, there under the stars and in the darkness, tears streaming down Lucinda's cheeks for she had injured her beloved, and Dabney, struggling with his conscience and his heart. Then he surrendered to his feelings, and drawing her into his arms with continuous declarations of undying devotion, they undertook another voyage into the mysterious realm of a kiss.

This left both Lucinda and Mr. Griggs trembling, and destroyed the barriers which had inhibited honesty of expression for so long. Mr. Griggs revealed the circumstances of his betrothal for the first time, at almost the exact moment Sophy was confessing the same to Mr. Whitefoot, but he left no hope that he could withdraw from it, while Lucinda, her veil thrown back and her eyes clearly intoxicated by the sight of him, declared her admiration with looks rather than words. They reached the same impasse in their negotiations reached by Sophy and Leslie, and yet they continued to belabour the point, for an admittance of their limitations would have meant the end of their *tête-à-tête*.

It was at about this point in time that Sibilla was languishing on the terrace, trying to distinguish her lost companions. The stars, the fragrance of the gardens, the blissful strains of the orchestra did not have the same effect upon her as upon the lovers, for they only heightened her experience of loneliness. Sipping a fifth glass of champagne, on the verge of tears, she was irritated by the approach of an individual dressed as a seventeenth-century gentleman in satin breeches, tights, powdered wig, velvet cloak, and a brocaded waistcoat, and resolutely showed him her back.

"Lady Sibilla?" asked the unknown personage tentatively.

"What business is it of yours?" snapped Sibilla.

"Just that I thought you resembled her," replied the mysterious stranger in a vaguely familiar voice which Sibilla could not place.

"Well, you are mistaken. I am not the lady you seek," stated Sibilla flatly, trusting that would discourage him.

Instead he shrugged his shoulders and remained where he was.

"How provoking," her admirer said pleasantly. "I know how much she enjoys dancing and was looking for a partner myself. Perhaps you also like to indulge?"

"I detest dancing," Sibilla lied, continuing to gaze out over the balcony.

"Ah, I see," her companion responded amiably, "you are a nature lover and you long to be strolling about the vistas which present themselves to your view."

"Indeed, I do not!" replied Sibilla coldly.

"No, you prefer to sulk," observed the gentleman, in same honeyed tones.

"I am not sulking," Sibilla answered distantly.

"Then address yourself to one who has the thoughtfulness to attempt to befriend you," commanded her companion, grasping her by the elbow and turning her remorselessly until she faced him, whereupon he swept her into an impetuous embrace. Sibilla had not been kissed before or after the one encounter with Valerian Cloudsleigh, and she was amazed to find that she responded identically to this stranger. Excusing her weakness upon the champagne, she fought free of him and begged him to leave her alone.

"How can I leave the woman I have been searching for all evening?" inquired the unknown, though his voice was not as lighthearted as previously but rough with a sort of desperation.

"Easily. You walk away. That way!" and Sibilla indicated the french doors leading back into the house.

"Minx!" swore the gentleman under his breath.

After a few moment's reflexion, he drew off his mask and revealed his identity.

"Oh Valerian!" said Sibilla weakly. "You frightened me."

"You did not seem frightened, sweetheart, when we were like so," he replied, taking advantage of her moment's hesitation and enfolding her in his arms once more.

This time Sibilla did not try to escape but laid her head meekly against his shoulder. "You cannot imagine what a fatiguing evening this has been," she murmured, close to collapse. "First, my sister, Kitty, then Peggy, and now I can't find Sophy or Lucinda, and we must leave before Aunt Lucy notices our absence."

"Not to worry, sweetheart," replied Mr. Cloudsleigh, stroking her tumbled curls. Something in this gesture seemed to excite him for he began to plant kisses upon her loose tresses and then upon the fair neck showing beneath them, until Sibilla begged him incoherently, "Please, Mr. Cloudsleigh. I cannot bear it. I'm too—too confused."

Whereupon he took her hand and drew her into the most secluded thicket of the garden, a rustic space uncivilized by any piece of statuary or marble bench, so that Valerian spread his velvet cloak upon the ground and handed Sibilla to a seat upon it. A rosebush in full bloom was next to them and its rich, unbearably sweet scent filled the air, while the sounds of the orchestra and the laughter of other partygoers, seemed infinitely far away.

"Oh!" exclaimed Sibilla, abandoning herself to the sensual splendour of the velvet cloak, the rose perfume, and the dark star-studded night. Valerian was not slow to take advantage of this tempting weakness and flung himself beside her to continue the pleasant process they had begun on the terrace.

Perhaps of all the couples in the garden, they were the most passionate, for there was no danger of interruption, while Sibilla fatalistically surrendered to the intoxication of the champagne and the setting, and Valerian, well used to the seduction of young women, plied her with every incitement in his repertoire, made more bold by her eager responses.

First, he explored her mouth, till certain that he had savoured every bit of sweetness it promised, he ventured farther, covering with kisses her curls, her eyelids, her soft earlobes, her neck, and when his expedition took him farther afield, Sibilla, who knew that she must resist him now or never, found herself even less willing to discourage him. Occasionally she thought that this was the process by which Peggy and Kitty had been ruined (but with what success!). Occasionally, she opened her eyes to watch the constellations overhead, thinking that another lovely pattern such as the one they mirrored in the heavens, was unfolding in her life. But most of the time, she revelled in the sensations of pleasure Valerian was evoking from her body and the reassuring feeling of his lean, hard body above hers.

"What disgusting debauchery is this? I demand my daughter!" a harsh familiar mannish voice brought Sibilla to a horrified consciousness. She struggled upright and Valerian, seeing her rumpled loveliness, the disordered curls, the flush in her cheeks, the muslin bodice slipping off to reveal one creamy shoulder, pressed himself against her with a desperate urgency.

"No, Valerian," wailed Sibilla. "It's Aunt Lucy. She must have come here. Oh, let me up, I beg of you, Valerian."

Again the voice shattered the tenderness of the night. "Where is she? What is she suffering here? She is ruined, I tell you, ruined!"

The word seemed to echo in Sibilla's head, and she shuddered for the first time under Valerian's thoughtless attentions. He withdrew, confused and shaking with frustration.

Afraid to even look at him, Sibilla abjectly begged for his aid in repairing the damage he had done to her costume. With trembling fingers, that he prevented with great self-control from lingering too long at their task, he did up the buttons that had come undone, smoothed the flounces of the skirt, and prompted her curls into seeming order.

"There she is! My darling! My baby!" shrieked the voice, which created a rift through the party noises every time it spoke.

The mask could not be found. After vainly searching for it, Sibilla turned to Valerian and said, "It's of no consequence. I must go now."

"Sibilla," said Valerian, holding her by the shoulders under the starlight. She turned wary eyes, as tender as a doe's, towards him. "Sibilla," he said urgently, "I must have you. Will you come to me?"

Sibilla studied him without flinching or betraying her fear and disappointment because he did not mention the redeeming word "marriage."

"Tonight?" he begged.

"Lord, no! Not tonight!" Sibilla exploded. "You must be mad!"

"Then another night?"

His hands clasping hers burned as if they were ice and her whole body swayed with desire.

"If I can," she promised solemnly with one more haunted gaze, and then, with a rustle of silk skirts, she was gone.

THIRTY-FIVE

Pilgrimage from Partridge Park

"DISGUSTING! INFAMOUS! UNBELIEVABLE! Revolting! Abominable! Odious!" These and strings of other disagreeable adjectives were the only words that Mrs. Pleet spoke to the three culprits throughout a week.

She had been awakened by an unpleasant nightmare after retiring early on the night of the *bal masque*, and had gone downstairs to help herself to a few more glasses of sherry to soothe her into an untroubled sleep. On her unsteady way back to her room, she had seen a light under Lucinda's door, a lamp left burning by Sophy after helping to do Lucinda's coiffure for the party, and, thinking that her daughter was still awake, Aunt Lucy stumbled into the room to wish her a pleasant night. But the chamber was empty and its disorder indicated that Lucinda had dressed hastily before going out. Swearing volubly and blundering against objects, such as footstools and doorjambs that leaped into her path, Aunt Lucy flung open the doors to Sibilla's and Sophy's rooms and uncovered the same telltale signs of primping and a hurried departure. Too late, she recalled that this was the night of Lady Cloudsleigh's costume ball, and groped her way back down to her study, ringing for the servants who finally confessed that the young ladies had ordered the carriage and gone to Cloudsleigh House hours ago.

Unwilling to essay the stairs again, Aunt Lucy demanded that her maid, Esther (who replaced Jane, who had suddenly eloped with the butler), dress her in the study. This process was a source of some amusement to the other servants who watched through the crack of the door, but only a fount of mutual vexation to the two involved.

"I shall give my notice tomorrow, I shall!" declared Esther to the other servants after Mrs. Pleet was gone, having polished off the remainder of the bottle of sherry while waiting for a hackney coach. "Imagine, the nerve, expecting me to dress a fat old woman in a high state of inebriation in a study of all places. I've never heard of such a ridiculous request. No self-respecting lady's maid would put up with it, and nor shall I. I'll be gone, just wait and see!" And she was true to her word.

By the time Mrs. Pleet gained entrance to Cloudsleigh House, the party had degenerated into a bacchanal and many of the guests tried to guess the nature of her disguise as she stormed through the house, yelling with all the formidable power of her lungs, "You sinners, you shall all fall. Just as Rome fell, you shall fall. Where is my innocent lamb? You devils, return her to me!"

The Pierrot hazarded a guess. "She's one of the Furies!" he announced with pride. "Erinyes! Furies! You know, damn it. Read about them at the University."

His listener, a somewhat unsteady Arab, refused to accept this interpretation. "Shfairly obvioush," he pointed out. "Shesh's a Lollard, y'know those preashing fellows. Notish the allushions to lambs and devils. Religioush, my good chap, not, no deshidedly not, Greek or Roman or whatever your Furiesh are!"

Most of the guests thought her quite amusing, whether or not they had a conjecture about her role, and their laughter only infuriated Aunt Lucy more. She found her way to the champagne before she found her way to the terrace, whereupon her strident voice startled the three girls in their various bowers. They came creeping out, one by one, as timid as mice, only to find that she was near stupefaction from the prodigious quantities of alcohol she had consumed. Rather than being swept through the crowd by an angry guardian, they had to guide and support her through the glittering rooms to the carriage drive.

"Ah, the three Graces," commented the Pierrot as they passed; he was very fond of classical allusions.

Sibilla dismissed the hackney coach and the three young women panted and puffed as they attempted to squeeze the limp enormous form of Mrs. Pleet into the waiting carriage. Without the aid of a footman, they assuredly would never have succeeded.

Once within the vehicle, which set off rapidly for Corrough House, Mrs. Pleet became maudlin. The vision of her daughter in a bridal gown confused her into thinking that she had just attended Lucinda's wedding and between great, noisy sobs, she made broken comments about what a beautiful bride she made, and how many people had attended, and how proud Mr. Pleet would be if he could see this moment.

It was all rather pathetic, and neither Sibilla nor Sophy would have been capable of disliking their aunt again were it not for her behaviour on the subsequent day. She kept to her bedroom throughout the morning and afternoon, suffering the pangs of overindulgence, but she appeared in the dining room for supper and spent the meal castigating the two Merrell sisters, who she denounced as "vipers which she had nourished in her bosom" (Sibilla choked on her soup as she pictured this metaphor) and repudiated her daughter for being so weak and spineless as to follow the urgings of evil companions.

Surprisingly, Lucinda did not attempt to avoid the scolding by assigning all of the blame to others as she would have done in the past, but listened politely and yet without remorse.

The tirade was interrupted by the arrival of the new under-parlour maid, Alice, who brought a note for Lady Merrell.

Both Sophy and Sibilla jumped, the first thinking it came from Leslie Whitefoot, the latter assuming it was a message from Valerian Cloudsleigh. Their guilty reactions did not escape Mrs. Pleet, who asked the maid casually to place it on the sideboard and serve the next course.

An interminable succession of underdone roasts, overdone entrees, and stringy game birds followed, accompanied by an endless chain of arguments proving that Sibilla and Sophia had both ruined themselves and had probably destroyed Lucinda's reputation by their example and proximity to her.

The table was cleared for dessert and the note remained mute on the salver while the girls nibbled on fruit and Aunt Lucy waxed more and more eloquent about their disgraces. At last the plates were removed, and Aunt Lucy called for the butler.

"Bring me the note that lies yonder," she commanded.

Sophy paled and Sibilla arose, indignant. "That is a note to one of us!" she cried. "How dare you open personal correspondence."

The butler, with a hasty bow, handed Mrs. Pleet the note and withdrew quickly.

"A gentleman's hand," commented Aunt Lucy with glee, as she slipped one stubby finger beneath the flap and broke the seal.

Sibilla pushed back her chair as if to take the note by force, and Mrs. Pleet halted her with a deadly look and the icy statement, "You are in my household, under my care and command, though you choose to ignore both. As your guardian, I have the right to know about everything that concerns you."

She drew out the crackling piece of paper which had a few bold lines penned upon it. Sibilla flushed a fiery red while Sophy seemed about to faint.

"God damn my soul!" exploded Aunt Lucy; it was a favourite oath of the late Mr. Pleet, and in this moment of extremity it rose unbidden to her lips. "I declare, I wash my hands of the whole lot of you. Your sister has eloped!"

She flung the note to one side as if it were a dirty thing, and Sibilla, not quite certain which sister was meant, sprang to retrieve it. Sophy scurried around the table to read it over her shoulder. It was short and to the point and yet imbued with typical drama.

> *When you receive this, I shall be on my way to Italy with Lanning Tombs. Arthur deserved a better wife than I have been, and I deserve Italy, poetry, and Lanning!*
>
> *Your affectionate sister who could have signed herself Lady Cloudsleigh but for love,* NELL

Lucinda snatched up this missive as Sibilla let it fall in amazement and read it quickly.

"You have a very brave and noble sister," she commented wistfully.

"A fool! An idiot!" snorted Aunt Lucy. "She had everything and gave it all up. For what? For nothing! A miserable existence trudging from one flea-infested inn to another, traipsing behind a man young enough to be her son. Oh, I can see her scheme now, that audacious harlot! She summoned all of London to her house for an extravagant party, knowing that in the morning she would be gone, and that no one would be able to talk of anything but her outrageous, insolent behaviour for weeks to come."

Despite the hostility which directed this statement, Mrs. Pleet was not far wrong. Nell could never simply disappear, and the *bal masque* had been doubly delightful because it was her last and grandest party, and because no one knew that she would leave with Lanning Tombs forever. Very discreetly, she had already packed, and the trunks were stowed in Mr. Tombs' hired carriage: Nell was not so foolish that she neglected to pack all of the jewels Baron Cloudsleigh had bestowed upon her since their marriage, though she decided, in all justice, to leave the pieces which belonged to his family. And all of London was indeed buzzing with the news, admiring as well as deploring the audacity of Lady Cloudsleigh and pitying her poor, deserted husband.

Baron Cloudsleigh, however, was experiencing an immense relief since the moment he found his wife's perfumed note upon his pillow. He had retired early and knew that she was still in the house with her paramour, but he chose merely to undress and go quietly to sleep. Nell always had her way and, heaven knew, he did not go in for scenes. In the morning, he found his new circumstances immeasurably more agreeable. People flocked to the house all day long. Nell's creatures he told the butler to dismiss; his friends were ushered into the library where they found that he cheered them more than they cheered him.

"She was too good for me," he chuckled, amazed by his own folly. "She had everything, wit, youth, beauty, ambition. What could she do with an old scholar?"

When a few of his anxious male guests discreetly pointed out that it was most unpleasant to be cuckolded, he laughed even more uproariously. "Why, I don't go gadding about in the world. If the world chooses to come to me, well enough. They shall hardly call me a cuckold to my face, and there is nobody to whisper behind my back." He turned to face the shelves of books behind him and laughed even harder at his own joke.

The inhabitants of Corrough House, though quite capable of imagining the tempest of gossip engulfing London, did not experience any of it, for all callers were refused at the door and the three girls wandered the house aimlessly. They did not confide in each other, though all recognized that the others had changed in some indefinable way since the night of the *bal masque*. Sophy could not reveal her resumed love affair with Leslie Whitefoot; Lucinda did not dare to mention Dabney Griggs, the fiancé of her cousin; and Sibilla, while cherishing the memory of her moments with Valerian Cloudsleigh, would have been mortified to confess that he certainly had none but dishonourable intentions towards her person.

And so they roved through the house, amiable ghosts, exchanging pleasantries, and longing for the end of their imposed confinement.

The end came sooner than expected for the Earl and the Countess of Corrough arrived unexpectedly with a retinue of servants and their spinster daughter, Effie, from Partridge Park.

Charlotte Garlinghouse had recently descended upon them, clutching Horace, full of tales of woe and mistreatment at the hands of her husband, who had vanished. The already tense atmosphere was ignited further by the receipt of a note from Nell, similar to the one received at Corrough House. Despite the scores of maladies and ailments which afflicted her, the Countess insisted that she could never sleep again, and would doubtless pine away altogether if she could not reassure herself of the safety of her two babies, still in that wicked town.

Knowing that this onslaught of maternal devotion would be brief, the Earl resigned himself to his fate and ordered up the carriages. Charlotte was left behind in the country, declaring that she never wished to see the city again, and the long procession set off for Upper Grosvenor Street.

Effie, with all of the patience and practicality of one who had long played the part of nurse, travelled with her mother, who was always on the verge of a relapse or fit throughout the jolting ride, while the Earl preferred to occupy the box of the luggage carriage, where he could conduct short and mutually satisfactory conversations with the coachman, Jem. They reached London near twilight, and Jem was relieved to see the number of windows lit in the house, but they were denied admittance with the mumbled words, "Nobody is at home." An avalanche of heavy and threatening knocks at the door, supplemented by kicks, encouraged the butler to appear once more, whereupon Jem asked him the name of the house.

"C–C–Corrough House," stammered the frightened butler.

"Aye, indeed it is," said Jem sternly. "And I have the Earl of Corrough and his Countess waiting in those carriages yonder while ye try to stave me off wi' nonsense about nobody home. Do ye think I should advise the Earl to apply to a hotel because no one will admit him at his own house, do ye, man? Don't stand there like a country idiot gawkin' at me! And when the Countess's two lovely daughters, Lady Sibilla and Lady Sophia, are under this roof, and the Countess pinin' away for a sight of them two sweet things. An' ye still insist no one's home."

"Oh! They're home right and proper. Only they asked me to say nobody was at home," cried the butler, swinging the door open.

"There, my good man," proclaimed Jem, extending one large, grimy hand to be shaken. "Jem's the name," he said with good nature, "And your'n?"

"C–C–Charles," spluttered the butler. "Charles Whitley. Can I help you in some way?"

"If ye could assist wi' the Countess. She's a mighty fragile woman, that she is," pronounced Jem solemnly. The butler, eager to be of service, ran to the carriage and helped to support the invalid into the drawing room where she cried immediately for a roaring fire and more shawls.

The butler ran to fetch the parlourtuaid to see to the fire, and Effie ran to get more shawls. Sibilla, who had been reading quietly in the back sitting room, heard the commotion and ventured forth, only to find her father in the hall.

"Papa!" she cried, running into his arms.

"My little Sibil," he said fondly, holding her at arm's length. "My, you have turned into a fine woman, since you've been in London."

"Oh Papa," she murmured. "What are you doing here?"

"Your mother insisted," he replied genially. "She's in the drawing room. But I believe no one has announced our presence yet, or else it's a monstrously unfriendly house."

"You're right on both accounts, dear Papa," exclaimed Sibilla. "But I shall make up for the deficit on my part." And she went off to announce the guests.

Thus it was Sophy, routed out of her bedroom, who first presented herself to her ailing mother.

"Dearest Mama!" she cried, throwing herself at her parent, who submitted with forbearance to this filial affection.

"My baby, Sophy," the invalid said at last. "And so you are to be married to Mr. Dabney Griggs. Tell me about him."

"Oh, he is a very good man," Sophy said hesitantly. "A gentleman, most considerate and kind."

"And very rich and refined and cultured," added her mama with great satisfaction. "Exactly the sort of man I knew you deserved while you were holding hands with that young Whitefoot puppy."

Sophy looked down at the carpet and then with courage said firmly, "Leslie Whitefoot is in town, Mama!"

"Think of that!" her mother commented vaguely, as Effie applied several shawls to her shoulders.

"I have seen him, Mama," Sophy was unwilling to drop the subject.

"And I'm sure you were glad that you had rejected him," the Countess said sweetly, "for if you were the impoverished wife of a country gentleman's son, you could never have come to London and never met your wonderful Mr. Griggs."

"Of course," Sophy murmured dispirited.

"In fact, dear heart," her mother continued, "it is my fondest hope, and I am certain it will be yours once I relate it, that your marriage to Mr. Griggs, which is planned for August, should be moved up a month, so that I will not have to come to London twice to witness it. I fear my poor, broken body will not survive that horrible journey again."

Sophy, though she ought to have offered sympathy for her mother's afflictions, was too taken aback by her suggestion to even notice the plea for sympathy.

"But, Mama!" she declared. "Why then the wedding would take place within a week!"

"And a very good distraction that would be from this rumpus Nell has created by running away," the Countess said with the air of having settled it all.

Sophy attempted another objection.

"I'm sure the church would not be available earlier, and we could not send the invitations or finish all of the preparations."

"Ah, then we shall have to change some of our plans," was her mother's sphinxlike reply.

Sibilla's precipitate entrance into the room stopped further discussion, and Sophy, in a state of shock, retired to a corner.

"Sibilla! You have failed!" declared the demanding invalid.

"I, Mama?" asked Sibilla, kneeling to kiss her cheeks and helping adjust the pillows in the chair.

"Yes, indeed—a little more to the right, please, my dear," said her mother. "For Sophy is engaged to a very estimable young man, and we hear nothing of your conquests. And I was so certain you would take."

Sibilla thought of Valerian Cloudsleigh and bright spots of colour came to her cheeks, but she replied dully, "I guess I have not taken, Mama, for I have neither conquests nor estimable young men."

"True enough!" came a gruff confirmation, and Aunt Lucy waddled across the room to greet her youngest sister for the first time in nearly a quarter of a century. She had been in her wrapper when Sibilla brought the news of the guests, and the new maid, Sarah, who had replaced Esther, had found it difficult to dress her quickly. "Glad to see you, Maria!"

Maria, who thought of herself alternately as Mama or Her Ladyship according to who was addressing her, started.

"Lucia?" she asked hesitantly.

Aunt Lucy merely nodded and inserted her ponderous bulk into an armchair near the fire.

"What a prodigious waste of wood!" Mrs. Pleet remarked with a frown. "Who commanded such a fire?"

"I did, sister," replied the Countess, falling prey to a fit of coughing, which Effie hurried to alleviate with a spoonful of ipecac. "It's frightfully cold in here," added Her Ladyship petulantly. "How have you been Lucia?" Her eyes wandered over the other's bloated form.

"Well enough," replied her sister, aware of the gaze and its scorn. "I am in very good health! Not sick a day in my life!"

"So!" breathed the Countess. She struggled to raise herself in her chair, and Effie sprang forward again. "I can manage for myself," the Countess declared irritated, and Effie retreated.

The Earl of Corrough entered at this moment. "Dear, don't overexert yourself," he said cordially to his wife. "Mrs. Pleet, I assume, pleased to meet you. Where shall I tell my servant to put the trunks?"

"Trunks?" exclaimed Aunt Lucy. "You cannot be planning to stay here. Why there is no room—none—whatsoever—absolutely none!"

"Oh, they have done all the work in vain," commented the Earl amiably. "Jem!" he shouted out the door. "Have the baggage put back in the carriage!"

A few minutes of silence, during which Sibilla imagined Jem struggling between his indignation and his sense of obedience, were broken by a mumbled oath and the sound of trunks being scraped along the floor.

"Where do you propose we shall go?" asked the Earl of Corrough with good nature.

Sibilla was horrified by her aunt's lack of hospitality, though she knew the house was small and no rooms were ready. "It would not be impossible for the servants to air and furnish the extra rooms," she offered quickly.

"Nonsense, daughter," her father replied with determination. "If Mrs. Pleet says it cannot be done, then it cannot be done. I merely wondered where we should apply for lodgings."

"It might seem unusual under the circumstances," began Aunt Lucy primly, "and yet it could be viewed as an act of charity also—"

"Well?" prompted the Earl of Corrough.

"I propose that you visit your former son-in-law, Lord Cloudsleigh," Aunt Lucy concluded crisply. "He must be feeling lost, alone in that great house."

The Earl pondered this proposal for a moment; he had enjoyed the company and conversation of Nell's husband on the few occasions they had spent much time together.

"A capital notion," he concurred stoutly. "What do you think, my dear — why, what is this?"

Thoroughly accustomed to remaining unobtrusively in the background, Effie had slid from her chair and lay crumpled on the carpet in a swoon, without having uttered a cry.

THIRTY-SIX

Lady Sophia Does Something Rash

UPON BEING BROUGHT TO her senses with the aid of the smelling salts which she carried in a vinaigrette around her waist for the benefit of her mother, Effie insisted that she was too ill to be moved and must remain at Corrough House overnight.

Her father, touched by this rare fit of weakness in his abnormally healthy and stolid daughter, tried to encourage such a plan, but his wife, unaccustomed to being upstaged in her role as martyr, refused to hear of it.

"There's nothing wrong with the silly child," she declared crossly. "Why, Effie is as strong as a horse! If I must go traipsing across town, I cannot possibly do without her!"

"Please, Mama?" begged Effie, in an abject voice, distinct from her usual hearty tones. Sophy viewed with compassion the sight of her older sister, always private and stubborn, content tramping about the countryside for hours, now pleading for a concession to frailty. Sibilla, of a more intellectual frame of mind, repressed her feelings of sympathy, and cast back in her memory of the conversation for the topic which might have caused the incident.

She was given a clue by her father, who said with distress, "She fainted last week too, my dear, when you read the note from Nell."

"And well she might!" the Countess responded, pressing one hand against her forehead. "Anyone would have been distressed at such a shocking, incredibly inconsiderate piece of insolence." The bitterness which underlined these words arose from a sense of mortification that she had not considered swooning first. "You are much better now, are you not, Effie?"

"Yes, I am, Mama," Effie answered dutifully, her voice regaining a measure of its usual strength.

"Then help me back into the coach!" demanded the invalid, and so the unexpected guests were swallowed up by the night, after repeated promises to call in the morning.

Cloudsleigh House appeared less inviting than Corrough House, and Jem, aggravated by the treatment his employer had suffered, battered upon the door like a hailstorm.

Baron Cloudsleigh, enjoying a comfortable chat in his library with Ashford and Valerian, heard the commotion at his door before the servants did, and went out to open it himself.

"Aha!" he thought to himself as he flung open the door, "Nell would never have permitted me to do this!"

"Be this here Cloudsleigh House?" asked Jem suspiciously, knowing this was not the butler, but uncertain how to address this alert, older man in a brocade smoking jacket.

"Yes it is, and I am Baron Cloudsleigh," said Arthur pleasantly. "May I be of service?"

"Aye, sir," Jem removed his cap and crushed it between his gnarled fingers. "The Earl of Corrough and the Countess have come on a visit!"

"Humph. I thought they were in the country," replied the Baron. "Well, show them in," and he led the way back to his library. Nell had always despaired of her husband because he would invite Dukes as well as stable boys to share the clutter of his library, rather than making use of the elegant formal salon she had created, and he was as like as not to forget to offer refreshments.

The Earl was the first to enter the library, bouncing in and greeting all three of the Cloudsleigh men with obvious delight. The Baron made perfunctory introductions and began on another round when the frail form of the Countess appeared in the doorway.

"Lady Corrough, my brother, Ashford Cloudsleigh, and my son, Valerian—"

He broke off to peer in bewilderment at the person who supported the Countess.

"Why, it's Euphemia!" he said, donning his spectacles to study her more carefully. With one bright look, Effie averted her eyes to the ground.

"Oh yes, I had quite forgotten that Effie spent a Season—or part of it—with you," remarked the Countess, swaying into the room, all lavender perfume and fluttering ribbons. Her usually afflicted eyes had quickly spotted Valerian Cloudsleigh as an eligible husband for Sibilla, and she was determined to appear at her best.

Effie, suddenly bereft of her role in life, stood awkwardly on the threshold, looking as lonely as an orphan.

Annoyed that her daughter appeared before such a sophisticated company like a rustic lass, the Countess added maliciously, "Perhaps you can explain why she bolted for the country like a rabbit. She will not tell us."

"I'm sure it's as much a mystery to me as to you," said the Baron, putting down his eyeglasses sadly, for Effie would not look at him. "We were most distressed by her sudden departure."

Valerian stared at the discomfited girl without thinking of his rudeness; the incredible spectrum of qualities exhibited by the Merrell females fascinated him—flighty, greedy Nell; laughing, loving Kitty; the bewitching yet stubbornly elusive Sibilla; the soft, warm pliancy of Sophy, and now this ungainly, reticent spinster.

"Allow me, miss," he said gracefully, rising and proffering his seat, which she fled towards as if searching for shelter.

More puzzled than before, Valerian lounged against the mantelpiece and was surprised to have his meditations interrupted by the Countess, who asked abruptly,

"Have you met my daughter, Sibilla?"

"Yes, Your Ladyship," he replied promptly. "I am acquainted with both Lady Sibilla and Lady Sophia."

"Sibilla is a very well-educated, and I might add, with a mother's prerogative, intelligent young woman," pointed out the Countess.

Valerian, beginning to see the drift of this conversation, shifted uncomfortably and tried to ignore his uncle's grin, for he had spent the afternoon regaling Ashford with stories of Sibilla's desirability, while Ashford vainly tried to point out that this had always been his opinion but Valerian had been too fatuous to see it.

"She plays the piano reasonably well and sketches and writes," continued the Countess ingenuously.

"Indeed, Lady Cloudsleigh," interrupted Valerian, determined to end the subject for all time. "She would make some lucky young dog an excellent wife. I only regret that I am not yet ready to settle down, but I have a host of friends who should wish to espouse her in a minute."

The Countess, aghast at this forward speech, opened her mouth and then shut it again, musing upon the acquaintances of Mr. Cloudsleigh.

Ashford, feeling constrained by the presence of his mistress's parents, excused himself and departed, with Valerian following shortly. The Earl of Corrough attempted to apologize for Nell's unaccountable lack of good taste and good sense, a theme which made everyone ill at ease, so that they were all glad of the excuse to retire.

Always the first to arise at Partridge Park, Effie woke long before the rest of the household, donned her most feminine lavender muslin gown, read her Bible, and strolled briefly through the gardens, finding many mementoes of the previous week's party, among them a black mask dangling from a rosebush. The exercise brought a pretty flush to her cheeks and loosened a few tendrils from her severe braids.

When Baron Cloudsleigh and the Earl, her father, entered the dining room, she was quite a lovely sight, enthroned like a queen behind the large silver tea service. She made a fuss over the two men, fixing the tea exactly to their liking, serving them herself, and making gentle conversation about the weather and how distinguished they both looked. Her father, who adored this amiable side of his ugly-duckling daughter's character, smiled so much he found it difficult to eat, and Baron Cloudsleigh, after a few startled looks, settled down to this ceremony as if it were an old familiar pattern.

This last observation provoked a sharp pang of jealousy in her father, who thought he could now understand why she had left London. Probably Nell had interrupted such a pleasant and innocent *tête-à-tête,* and had lost her volatile temper, accusing Effie of all sorts of sly designs which never could have entered Effie's head. Deciding that he had just solved the mystery, the Earl patted his daughter's hand fondly and she thanked him with a beatific smile.

"Well, I must be off to work on my book," said Baron Cloudsleigh, pushing back his chair. "It's nearly finished," this last was directed with an enthusiastic smile for Effie. "I trust Lady Corrough will excuse my unsociable behaviour?"

"Oh yes," murmured the Earl, "we have many engagements and are ever in your debt for your great generosity in allowing us to stay here."

"Was the indexing ever completed?" asked Effie wistfully.

"The indexing?" Baron Cloudsleigh turned about in his progress towards the door. "Why, no, it remains as it was. Unfortunate, since the text is nearly ready to be submitted, and a good index, such as the one you began, would be an invaluable aid."

"I could take it up again!" offered Effie eagerly.

"Oh no, my dear," the Baron said vaguely, reaching in his confusion for his glasses which were not yet on top of his head. "You have just arrived in London, and must have a multitude of visits and pleasant outings planned."

"But you know that I detest—dislike such things," Effie pleaded. "I would be ever so much more happy working for you. I would feel as if I were doing something useful, instead of frittering away my time."

The Earl of Corrough watched this interchange with amazement, but when he was appealed to for his opinion, he said agreeably that Effie was old enough to know her own mind and she should do whatever pleased her.

"Oh thank you, Papa!" she cried, running to him to plant a kiss on the top of his balding head, before eagerly flying out of the room to catch up with Lord Cloudsleigh.

It was left to the Earl to explain this state of affairs to his fretful wife, who did not approve and made it clear in no uncertain terms.

Her husband carefully pointed out to her that Effie was normally the most docile and dutiful of daughters, but that when she was adamant, she was extremely adamant, and that there could be no success in an attempt to alter the situation.

With ill grace, the Countess agreed, and leaning upon her maid, she entered the carriage to call upon Sibilla and Sophia.

This was the start of a delightful week for Sibilla, for Aunt Lucy could not refuse other callers when the Earl and Countess of Corrough were there all day long. The house was always filled with visitors and the evenings were crowded with dinner parties and receptions.

Sophy was not so pleased, for the Countess' first action upon arriving at Corrough House had been to consult Aunt Lucy as to the advisability of advancing the date of the wedding. Mrs. Pleet agreed and the appropriate arrangements were quickly made. The church was not available at the earlier date, and so the wedding was scheduled to occur in the garden. Sibilla jokingly suggested that Muffin and Oscar could be bridal attendants, a suggestion which met with sour frowns from Aunt Lucy and an irritated pout from her mother. Because there would be little room for guests, invitations were limited to the immediate family. Sophy asked that a larger reception introducing the newly married couple to all of London Society occur after the honeymoon, and the Countess decided to approach Lady Trendle with the idea that this reception be held at Trendle House.

These plans did not suit Lucinda any more than they suited Sophy, but she had learned a measure of self-possession and was unfailingly gracious. In fact, during this period of time, she received her first proposal, from the same Mr. Treswick who had earlier offered for Sibilla. Aunt Lucy rejected his suit out of hand, but Lucinda acquired another degree of confidence when informed of the overture.

The Countess of Corrough was at first taken aback by the appearance of her prospective son-in-law. She was not prepared for this lanky, awkward, red-haired man with the rough voice. But she was quickly reconciled by his unfailing politeness, and especially, the prospect of his fortune, and adopted him as a sort of pet, who should always be seated next to her. This allowed Sophy a certain amount of freedom, and she was usually found whispering in corners with Valerian Cloudsleigh, who did not drop his attentions towards Sibilla. He presented her with a pair of canaries on one visit, but he seemed to prefer the company and conversation of her younger sister.

The Countess had still not given up her scheme to reunite her family with the Cloudsleighs, despite Valerian's harsh words, and tried to throw Sibilla at him on every opportunity. Usually this occasioned humiliation for Sibilla and amusement for Mr. Cloudsleigh, but upon one afternoon it proved to their mutual benefit. Her Ladyship insisted that the two children take the carriage and go for a drive, and Valerian, once they were alone, suggested they call upon her sister, Kitty. Sibilla eagerly agreed.

Kitty was in the sitting room with her children and Ashford Cloudsleigh, who spent most of his time with her, trying to avoid meeting her parents at Cloudsleigh House. The home he had shared with Caroline had never been reopened since her death and was now in the process of being leased.

Sibilla was enthusiastic over the decorations of the house, and even more over Alex and Clarissa, who both warmed to her and insisted that she help them build a fort under the piano. She spent the greater part of her time, crawling about with them under the counterpane which served as a tent, shooting at imaginary bandits, while Valerian, Ashford, and Kitty talked politics. Valerian was planning to run for the borough Ashford would vacate in order to travel on the Continent, and they discussed the needs of the district, a topic which Kitty knew well, though Valerian's gaze strayed every now and then to. watch Sibilla's spontaneous enactments of terror and grim satisfaction (when the bandits attacked and were successfully driven off) and her unfeigned joy at the unbridled imaginations of the two children. Kitty and Ashford smiled fondly at each other over Valerian's head at these moments.

"A Member of Parliament needs a good wife," said Ashford smugly.

"You didn't have one," was Valerian's reply, without averting his eyes from an enchanting view of Sibilla's backside as she crawled under the piano and gathered Clarissa into her arms.

"Ah, but I had Kitty," remarked Ashford, his fond glance as tangible as a touch. "And when we return, we shall roust you from your seat if you have succeeded in winning it, which I doubt, knowing your distractions, and you shall be shunted aside, a debauched, exhausted bachelor."

Regretfully, Valerian plunged back into the political conference, suavely outlining how he would manage to be the best Member ever to stand up for the borough.

"Why, he has your voice already, Ashford!" crowed Kitty, clapping her hands together.

"There might be nothing left for us, my love, but to settle down and become a respectable married couple," mourned Ashford.

"A fate worse than death!" agreed Kitty, pretending to wipe tears from her eyes. "We shall have to mount an impressive campaign against this young scoundrel."

"Oh Kitty!" cried Sibilla, brushing the dust from her skirts, as she emerged from the tent. "You have the most intelligent and delightful children."

"Why does everyone praise the mother, when the father is as much to blame?" asked Ashford, of no one in particular, and no one in particular noticed his query.

"Shall you want a couple of your own?" inquired Kitty softly.

Sibilla blushed prettily. "I never thought of it, till now," she confessed. "I've known only Charlotte's children, and though Lottie is a little angel, Horace is—" she shuddered expressively. "And then Amy's children. They're most well-behaved, but there are so many of them."

"Oh, you've visited Amy!" cried Kitty. "Pray tell me her address. I should dearly love to visit her before I leave."

The two sisters exchanged addresses, and Kitty said sorrowfully, "You know we shall depart in several days, Sibil. I doubt I will see you again for a year."

"You will not visit our parents, now that they are in town?" Sibilla requested, "and let them know you are well?"

"No," Kitty answered flatly. "I am certain they never mention me," Sibilla did not hasten to correct this impression since no one had spoken of Kitty, "and I shall visit them first when I return from abroad as Mrs. Ashford Cloudsleigh."

She added softly, "You know that Val has agreed to give up his lodgings and stay here till we reappear, so that I will not have to store all of my belongings. I only pray that he will not have opened business as a menagerie keeper and when we come back, we will find all of London flocking to our door to see wombats or marmosets or some other strange beast."

Sibilla glanced at the person thus mentioned, and Valerian, well aware of her delight in the appointments of Kitty's home and her love for animals, grinned like a gargoyle.

"Now, Val, do not bring her here and compromise her," Kitty rebuked him as she did her children.

"Oh no, I have already accomplished that once," said Valerian, with a widening smile, "Or perhaps twice."

Sibilla flung a contemptuous glance at him, and after embracing the children, crying over Kitty, and being kissed by Ashford, allowed Valerian to lead her to the waiting carriage.

As the vehicle undertook the short journey from Berkeley Street to Upper Grosvenor Street, Valerian said with unusual awkwardness, "Lady Sibilla, I must apologize for the manner in which I conducted myself on the night of the *bal masque*. I can make no excuses, except perhaps for the loveliness of the night and my companion."

"Enough," responded Sibilla crossly. "I myself should ask your pardon for my deplorable lack of decorum and, in addition, for the unforgivable attitude of my mother towards you."

"Oh that!" said Valerian, dismissing it with an airy wave of his hand, and then, without warning, drawing her into his arms for an embrace which lasted until the carriage came to a halt before Corrough House.

"Damn it all!" exclaimed Valerian, raising his head. "Shall I command the man to drive around the Park?" and then, without waiting for Sibilla to concur, he lifted the trap and gave those directions.

Would any reader be surprised to learn that Sibilla at last succumbed to Valerian's advances during this fateful interlude? But, being a well-brought-up young Victorian woman, she did not, though Valerian was perhaps much closer to his goal than he imagined when the carriage stopped again before the house on Upper Grosvenor Street.

He begged for a few more minutes, but Sibilla, horrified by her own weaknesses, tried to repair the damages he had done, remarking tartly, "You treat me poorly, Mr. Cloudsleigh!"

"Ah, but I love you madly," confessed that young man, and though Sibilla was not loath to hear this confession, she did not hear the word "marriage" and hopped out of the carriage, saying cheerfully, "Good day, Mr. Cloudsleigh."

She regretted her hasty action as soon as she re-entered the house, for she was subjected to another interminable afternoon chatting with her mother, sister, cousin, and aunt, along with Lavinia Holly, Lady Holly, Mary Crank (recently recovered from her illness), Mr. Treswick, Baron Champford, and Dabney Griggs. Her mother had revealed on the first day of her visit that Charlotte had fled to Partridge Park, and Sibilla finally learned on this occasion from Baron Champford the dastardly role Major Garlinghouse had played in the deception of Randall Sylver, and his probable flight from the country in order to avoid prosecution.

So the afternoon was not wasted, and though Sibilla had hoped Valerian would join them, he did not reappear.

In truth, he did not present himself at Corrough House for nearly two days, and this was the eve of Sophy's marriage to Dabney Griggs. He confided to Sibilla in an aside that Kitty and the children had left for the Continent the previous day and that he had been busy moving his belongings and settling his accounts. Sibilla was already privy to this information, for Amy and her seven children had called on an earlier day (the Countess declaring herself incapable of venturing into the filthy rookery where Amy resided), and Amy had confessed to Sibilla her pleasure at seeing Kitty. The little Brittles who accompanied their mother behaved with the utmost decorum, but they were a most amazing sight, scattered all over the sitting room, and several less-than-serious suitors abruptly disappeared at the sight of such fecundity and domestic bliss.

After his brief words to Sibilla, Valerian addressed himself to Sophia and remained seated by her side throughout the afternoon, occasionally arguing with her as could be seen by his wild gestures and contorted expressions, and more often soothing her by taking her hands in his own.

There was a dinner party at Corrough House that night in honour of the morning's ceremonies, and while the Earl led in Mrs. Pleet, the Countess willingly gave up the escort of Mr. Dabney Griggs to his soon-to-be wife, while she accepted the arm of Admiral Crank. Sophy and her fiancé were followed by Lucinda and Valerian Clouds-leigh (Mrs. Pleet had often remarked on the absence of the Marquis of Dower until she was informed that he had left for Ireland) and Sibilla and Mary Crank brought up the rear with Baron Champford and Mr. Treswick.

Throughout the course of the long dinner Sibilla attempted to escape the boxing recollections of Mr. Treswick by turning to Valerian Cloudsleigh on her other side, but he was more often occupied in a lively discussion with Sophy on his right. Mr. Treswick meanwhile had diverted his attention across the table to Baron Champford. Left entirely on her own throughout this festive meal, Sibilla was not in good humour when the gentlemen left for a bachelor party being hosted by Valerian Cloudsleigh, and retired to her room early.

Upon the morrow she would be the only one of the Merrell sisters, excepting Effie who was always the exception, not married, though she had to admit that Charlotte had been deserted by her husband and Nell had left hers. She tried to console herself with thoughts of the upcoming Season which she could spend with Ned and Peggy or Ashford and Kitty, yet Valerian Cloudsleigh kept menacing her dreams. He was certainly ardent when alone with her but worse than neglectful in the presence of others.

At this inauspicious moment, Sophy burst into her troubled train of thoughts, entering the room like a bride, cheeks flushed and eyes fevered.

"Oh Sibil!" she cried. "I have to tell you."

"What?" asked her sister crossly, pretending to be busy rearranging the brushes, combs, and bottles of toilet water on the bureau.

"I have been seeing Leslie Whitefoot," exclaimed Sophy, seating herself on the bed.

"Well, what of that?" was Sibilla's unfeeling response. "You will be married tomorrow."

"Valerian has been counseling me to elope," Sophy confessed softly.

"Valerian?" Sibilla said quietly, frozen for a moment at her task. She regained her sense and continued harshly, "But Mama loves Mr. Griggs."

"True enough," Sophy agreed heartlessly. "But then Mama should marry him, for I love him not."

"Mama is already married," was Sibilla's abrupt reply.

"Well, I just came to bid you farewell, Sibil," said Sophy tearfully.

Aghast at her rudeness and selfishness, Sibilla wordlessly embraced her sister, who trundled off to her bedroom in the same high spirits with which she had entered Sibilla's.

Perturbed by her sister's confessions, Sibilla could not sleep and went down to take the two dogs, Oscar and Muffin, for a walk. Though it was strictly forbidden, she savoured the experience of rambling about Mayfair at night with the two animals. It was a hot, stuffy night, the avenues were crowded with vehicles, and the gas lamps flickered fitfully.

Returning to the house shortly before midnight, Sibilla was amazed at the sight of a hackney coach drawn up in the stableyard. But as there was no activity in the lower floors of the house, she dismissed it as unimportant and went to her room to fall into a turbulent sleep.

284

THIRTY-SEVEN

Unexpected Proposals

A SCREAM PENETRATED SIBILLA'S fitful dreams, and she roused herself and donned a wrapper to find her mother in the passageway, wearing her wedding attire and scanning with disbelief a note she seemed to have found in Sophy's room, for the door to that chamber was open.

"Oh my God, she's eloped!" shrieked the Countess of Corrough, flinging herself at Sibilla, who laid her down in her own bed and plied her with smelling salts before extracting the crumpled note from her fist.

Sophy seemed to have taken a lesson from Nell, for her letter was equally short and to the point.

> *I have eloped with Mr. Leslie Whitefoot who I dearly love. Please give my apologies to Mr. Dabney Griggs, a very good man who I earnestly hope may find a more sympathetic wife than I would have been.*
>
> SOPHY

Sibilla, almost more affected than her mother, burst into tears. So that had been the reason for Sophy's confidences on the previous night and she had, with characteristic selfishness, refused to listen, just as she had berated Peggy on the eve of Peggy's disappearance. She did not deserve to be anyone's friend, she wailed, as Lucinda and Aunt Lucy reached the scene of the disturbance.

Lucinda was already attired in her bridesmaid's dress, but she was delighted by the note, reading it with an open mouth which quickly resolved into a foolish grin. Her mother, however, was for once at a total loss.

"What shall we do? The minister? The groom?"

Sibilla assumed the command which her mother, prostrate on the bed, would not assume. She sent a message to Mr. Dabney Griggs, which reached him just as he arose, slightly the worse for wear as a result of the previous night's debauch.

"How could she do this, to me?" the Countess asked fretfully over and over again, while Aunt Lucy repeated grimly, "Another shameless flirt, like her sisters."

No one thought to pursue the fleeing couple, except perhaps for Sibilla, who never issued the instructions which would have initiated this task.

Within the space of an hour, the main principals in the wedding, minus the bride, were seated in the Corrough House drawing room.

Dabney Griggs, in his wedding attire, black walking coat, white piqué waistcoat, and grey trousers, top hat in his hand, sat alongside his best man, Valerian Cloudsleigh, in a similar costume. Baron Champford in a black frock coat, grey trousers, and black waistcoat, the proper garb for an usher, occupied an armchair. Sibilla had decided to put on her bridesmaid's outfit, and she and Lucinda came down in soft blue silk gowns, trimmed with white roses. Effie, for she had agreed to leave off her task as editor for the happy event, led her mother into the room, and Aunt Lucy, in perpetual mourning, preceded the Earl of Corrough.

"The problem is," said the Earl uncomfortably, feeling that it behooved him to take command of the situation, "the problem is—"

"That Sophy has eloped," finished Effie tartly. "Somebody," and she nodded at Sibilla, "might have been able to recall her in time, but no one did, and now we must deal with the consequences."

"The question is," resumed the Earl, "what to do?"

"I, for my part, do not hold your daughter accountable," said the supposedly brokenhearted groom resolutely. "It appears to me now that this entire rigamarole was forced upon us as the result of a situation in which we found ourselves," he directed his speech to

Aunt Lucy, who retreated farther towards the windows. "And though I might add that I deeply esteem and honour your daughter as a thoroughly delightful young lady, she is not the woman I would have chosen for my wife," and here he looked directly at Lucinda, "had the circumstances been different. Therefore you need not spare my feelings."

"Indeed!" declared the Earl. "Well spoken, young man. I have always like Leslie Whitefoot, a childhood beau of Sophy's," he explained to Dabney Griggs, who seemed astonished by the name, "and I am sure they will deal admirably together."

"The horror! The disgrace!" breathed the Countess on the apparent verge of swooning. "The guests will be here in an hour."

"Quite," concurred the Earl, the unofficial chairman of the gathering. "How shall we prevent this from assuming the proportions of a full-fledged scandal?"

"Perhaps," said Lucinda quietly, but with conviction, "we should substitute brides."

"I'm not quite certain I understand, my dear child," the Earl responded, wiping his brow with a handkerchief. "If we substituted brides, then we'd have to produce another groom from somewhere. And they decidedly do not grow upon trees.

"I doubt that we shall have to do so," replied Lucinda, who had been regarding Mr. Griggs steadfastly since the moment of her startling proposal. "Dabney," her voice swelled to a passionate intensity, "do I have to propose, also?"

This brought the jilted groom out of his chair and down upon one knee in front of her, quicker than the description can be read.

"No, my darling," he replied in a low voice, and then turning to the assembled company, declared, "There is no woman in the world whom I hold more dear or whom I would cherish so deeply as this woman, if she will consent to do me the great honour of becoming Mrs. Dabney Griggs!"

"Oh, I will, I will," cried Lucinda with tears in her eyes.

A harsh voice spoke from the shadows.

"Since no one has asked my permission, you are both making unnecessary fools of yourselves."

"I do not need your permission, Mama," answered Lucinda defiantly, standing to face her mother. "I shall marry Mr. Griggs in any manner possible, with or without your consent."

"Well, that's all very fine, my dear," interposed the Earl of Corrough rapidly, "but I don't see how it solves our quandary. Surely everyone would realize you are not Sophy?"

"We need not fool anyone at the actual wedding," pointed out Lucinda earnestly. "Who will be present except those now in this room?"

"And Amy and Reverend Brittle, and Lord and Lady Trendle," volunteered Sibilla.

"They will understand," Lucinda said desperately.

"The invitations!" wailed the Countess indistinctly through the cologne-drenched lawn handkerchief she held to her lips.

"Have not been sent as yet," Lucinda declared. "Not the invitations for the reception at Trendle House."

"But so many people saw Sophy going about with Mr. Griggs after the betrothal was announced," Sibilla stated tentatively.

"It will all have changed," Lucinda said fiercely. Like a tigress brought to bay, she was fighting with all of her instincts for her life.

"It could be done, I think," Effie entered the fray. "We announce to the guests today that Sophy was previously engaged, and that the wedding is going forward because Mr. Griggs, freed from his obligation, has announced his interests in Lucinda. They go away on a honeymoon as planned, and when they return for the grand reception, all of Society will be so thunderstruck that they will not have the effrontery to question the newlyweds directly."

"Oh yes, it's so audacious, it has to work!" announced Sibilla. "Lucinda, run upstairs and put on Sophy's dress. We have only a few minutes and the wedding will be ready to begin on time!"

And so the marriage took place after all, only a trifle behind schedule. The Earl of Corrough gave away the bride, and Dabney Griggs gratefully accepted her, while Sibilla and Valerian stood as witnesses. Muffin and Oscar broke out of their temporary confinement in the woodshed just as Dabney was bending to kiss his radiant bride, and frolicked around the couple like a pair of benevolent cherubs. The reception immediately afterward was brief but merry, for Lucinda inspired all with her high spirits and radiance. She and her husband left early to catch a train to Brighton where they would spend two weeks, and after they had departed the strain of the day's events took its toll on the participants.

Aunt Lucy, who had borne up magnificently, witnessing the ceremony without a murmur of dissent, somewhat mollified by the Earl's promise that he would bear all the cost of the wedding as planned, and that all the gifts should be Lucinda's, waddled off to bed forgetting her usual nightcap. The Countess of Trendle, having promised in the shock of the moment that she would be just as pleased to host a reception for Miss Pleet and Mr. Griggs as she would have for Lady Sophy and Mr. Griggs, was borne home by her husband and son, both trying to convince her that she had made a magnanimous gesture. Sibilla, near nervous collapse, declared she could not spend the night under the roof of Corrough House since she had been abandoned by her sister and her cousin simultaneously. Her mother, too weary to protest, permitted her to accompany them to Cloudsleigh House, with an entourage consisting of Oscar, Muffin, the guinea pigs, and the canaries.

The following days were disillusioning ones for Sibilla. Effie and Baron Cloudsleigh applied themselves daily to the arduous tasks involved in readying "The Book" for publication. The Countess, after receiving a letter from Sophy saying that she was married and would greet them as Mrs. Whitefoot when they returned to Partridge Park, gave in to her nerves and spent all of her time in bed. The Earl wanted to see the Great Exhibition before he left London, and Sibilla spent her afternoons as a tour guide. It had been decided that she would accompany her parents back to Partridge Park, and since she knew only one person who interested her in London, she agreed passively. Oddly enough, she was always "not at home" when that one interesting person, Mr. Valerian Cloudsleigh, came to call, and he, not knowing of her imminent departure and concluding that she was suffering through a period of depression, ended his visits.

His conclusion was correct, though his method of handling it was not, and Sibilla who had experienced a perverse delight at refusing to see him, fell into a deeper fit of melancholy. Not any of the delights of Astley's nor dining at Alexis Soyer's Gastronomic Symposium of All Nations with her father, could bring a smile to her lips.

Lucinda and Dabney returned from Brighton and took up residence at Corrough House. Sibilla visited them twice, but the radiance of Lucinda, the smugness of Mrs. Pleet (who had decided that this was what she had wanted all along), and the unfailing good humour of Dabney Griggs, only exacerbated her condition.

The Earl, hoping that a change of scenery, would cheer his unhappy daughter, broke the news at dinner one night.

"I have consulted my good wife," he said uncomfortably, "and we both agree that we must cut short this most agreeable visit. We propose to leave tomorrow on the morning train, for Her Ladyship feels it will be more agreeable than the carriages. So you should pack tonight, Effie, my dear."

"Yes, I should, Papa," said Effie brightly. "But I am not going."

"Not—going," repeated her father dully.

"No," Effie explained patiently. "Arthur," and she joined hands with the Baron who sat to her right, "has promised to hire me as his assistant—until the book is done, of course."

"Of course, you will come to Partridge Park then," said her father with relief.

"No," replied Effie good-naturedly. "Then I shall take on the position here as housekeeper. Arthur needs a woman looking over all of the little things for him."

"Effie—a housekeeper?" her father questioned with a frown.

"Not very different from my duties at home, Papa," Effie replied quickly, "except that I shall be paid. And then…" Her voice trailed off, and she looked to Baron Cloudsleigh for reassurance. He nodded, and she continued. "…When the divorce is granted, I shall marry Arthur."

"Marry!" exploded the Earl. He held his head in his hands for a few moments, then murmured brokenly, "There have been so many marriages of late—it requires a little adjusting." Having accomplished the adjusting, he looked up and asked heartily, "How long have you two known of this?"

"Oh, I have known forever," whispered Effie, blushing and clinging tightly to Baron Cloudsleigh's hand. "That is, since my Season in

London. That is why I left so suddenly—when I discovered it—how I felt—I knew I should go. But Arthur—"

"But Arthur," Baron Cloudsleigh spoke up firmly, "is a slow learner. I should have known why I appreciated Euphemia so much. I thought it was her cheerful presence, her unflagging energy, her attention to the prosaic little details that make life run smoothly, her helpfulness and sympathy, but like the old hermit I am—" Effie made a little face at him "—I never realized that I loved her until she reappeared in my life. Now I shall never let her go!"

Though it was awkward, Effie buried herself in his arms, and he fondly kissed the top of her head.

"We have been holding hands in the library like two school-children!" announced Effie from her retreat.

"I was infatuated with Nell, sir," said the Baron solemnly. "I should never have married her."

"Ah, I have no doubt that was more Nell's doing than yours," commented the Earl wryly. "Well, my children, I see no objections. I'm sure you're most suited to each other, and indeed, I think Effie is making the wisest choice of any of my daughters."

Inexplicably Sibilla, who had been a silent but avid spectator until this point, burst into tears and fled from the room.

Upon the morning she was enough recovered to wish Effie and Baron Cloudsleigh much joy and happiness, adding slyly, "and many children." Baron Cloudsleigh coughed at this, but Effie remarked easily that she would embark on this pleasant task as soon as decently possible. The Countess swept downstairs, determined to ignore her willful daughter. The expedition to London had been disastrous as far as she was concerned: one daughter eloped with a mere country squire's son, one would act as housekeeper to her sister's husband, and the third, Sibilla, whom she had now elevated to the position of favourite, unthinkingly, had been passed over by all of the eligible young men of London.

As her mother stepped uncertainly onto the threshold, groping for Sibilla's waiting support, Effie called out in anguish, "Mama!" and the Countess turned, stricken, and embraced her heretofore favourite.

"I shall miss you, Effie!" was all she could bring herself to admit as they clung together.

"Mama always sees things from her point of view," commented Effie ruefully as she and Baron Cloudsleigh re-entered the library after waving farewell to the departing carriages.

They had just settled down to their usual task, Baron Cloudsleigh, behind the desk, scribbling away at his manuscript, and Effie, turning over the completed pages and making entries into a ledger for the index, when the butler announced, "Valerian Cloudsleigh to see Lady Sibilla."

"Oh, I suppose I should tell him she's gone," said Effie with irritation, putting aside her ink-spotted apron and smoothing her dress.

"Don't be long, dear," called out the Baron as she passed through the door.

Valerian, waiting impatiently in the hallway, was surprised to see Effie approaching him.

"I know," he said bitterly, turning as if to go, "she is not at home."

"No, indeed, she is not," replied Effie, disconcerted by his distress. "They left today for Partridge Park."

"Left!" Valerian halted in his path, frozen like a statue.

"Yes, they're taking the morning train," Effie continued, but before she could finish he was running down the steps and flinging himself into his phaeton.

She closed the door after him thoughtfully and retraced her steps to the library.

"Your son is a strange young man," she said, resuming her seat.

"Willful! Impetuous!" commented the Baron without looking up or staying his pen.

As there was no luggage to be stowed away, for it would all travel by carriage to Partridge Park, along with the servants and pets, and as the tickets had already been purchased, the small party of Merrells arrived at the station only minutes before the train was due to depart and found their seats.

Sibilla, in more of a brown study than ever, hunched up sulkily by a window, and her father, leaving his wife to the ministrations of her maid, took up the neighbouring seat companionably.

"You have never been on a train before, have you, Sibil?" he asked cheerfully.

"No, Papa," was her disinterested reply.

"Sibilla!" The cry echoed through the station. Valerian, having just arrived and seeing the train about to pull away, chose this direct method as the only way of locating the object of his search.

"Sibilla!" he cried again in anguish, and was rewarded by the sight of a small face pressed up against a window.

Running towards that car, he called her name again and threw out his arms in supplication.

Sibilla appeared on the platform of the car as the train began to slowly draw away.

"Valerian?" she called softly, so softly he did not hear her.

"Sibilla!" he shouted over the noise of the train. "Sibilla! I cannot live without you. I want to marry you!" He was running along with the train.

Without a second's thought, without a glance at her parents who were watching in amazement, she leaped from the platform and fell into his arms. The following car of third-class passengers on holiday cheered lustily as she disappeared into his ardent embrace.

About the Author

WAVERLY FITZGERALD learned to write at about the same time she learned to type—at the age of eight. One saga, composed when she was twelve, grew to three hundred pages before she lost interest.

She wrote her first novel, *St. John's Wood*, while working at the Los Angeles Museum of Art, researching the book as she rode the bus, back and forth to work. She began teaching novel writing through the UCLA Writers Program, with her friend and colleague, Ellen Pall, shortly after her novel was published by Doubleday.

In 1980, she moved to Seattle with her young daughter, changed her name to Waverly and continued to teach writing, for the University of Washington and Seattle Central Community College.

After publishing three novels with Doubleday and one with Jove, she took a long break from novel writing, focusing instead on non-fiction writing about seasonal holidays and natural time. Her book, *Slow Time: Recovering the Natural Rhythm of Life*, was published in 2009.

When she began writing novels again, she took up the mystery novel. Waverly wrote one series featuring a female Seattle PI and then co-wrote a series of humorous mystery novels, featuring a talking Chihuahua, with her friend and colleague, Curt Colbert, under the name Waverly Curtis. The first book in that series is *Dial C for Chihuahua* and was published by Kensington in 2012.

She currently teaches online for *Creative Nonfiction* magazine and Hugo House, the literary arts center in Seattle. Her most recent novel is a Victorian historical mystery.

Learn more at http://www.waverlyfitzgerald.com.

www.ingramcontent.com/pod-product-compliance
Lightning Source LLC
Chambersburg PA
CBHW030027180626
46810CB00001B/256